Praise for Wild Heather

"The quintessential love story with a fresh plot that contains plenty of twists and turns."
Romantic Times BOOKreviews magazine

"*Wild Heather* is a romance with heart AND soul, one that readers will remember for a long time."
The Romance Reader's Connection

Praise for Catherine Palmer's Books

THE BACHELOR'S BARGAIN

"Captivating, with genial, witty characters . . . Readers will not be able to turn pages quickly enough to learn the fate of more than just the hero and heroine."
Romantic Times BOOKreviews magazine

A DANGEROUS SILENCE

"Palmer's contemporary thriller reads plausibly and sweeps readers into the story, pairing deep emotions with numerous suspenseful scenes. . . ."
Publishers Weekly

TREASURES OF THE HEART SERIES

"Each of the Treasures of the Heart books is a delightful read. The energy, adventure, and romance kept me intrigued to the end. . . ."
Francine Rivers

FINDERS KEEPERS

"A romance that tackles deeper issues."
Library Journal

Wild
Heather

Wild Heather

CATHERINE PALMER

Tyndale House Publishers, Inc., Carol Stream, Illinois

Visit Tyndale's exciting Web site at www.tyndale.com

Check out the latest about Catherine Palmer at www.catherinepalmer.com

Cover designed by Jessie McGrath

Interior designed by Zandrah Maguigad

Edited by Kathryn S. Olson

Library of Congress Cataloging-in-Publication Data

Palmer, Catherine, date.
Wild heather / Catherine Palmer.
p. cm. — (HeartQuest)
ISBN 0-8423-1928-X
1. Yorkshire (England)—Fiction. 2. Vendetta—Fiction. I. Title. II. Series.
PS3566.A495 W55 2004
813'.54—dc21 2003015854

ISBN-13: 978-1-4143-1351-1
ISBN-10: 1-4143-1351-9
Printed in the United States of America

13 12 11 10 09 08 07
7 6 5 4 3 2 1

To Betty Louise Noe Cummins.

Thank you for being such a wonderful mother to me.

I love you!

Live in complete harmony with each other—
each with the attitude of Christ Jesus
toward the other.
Then all of you can join together with one voice,
giving praise and glory to God,
the Father of our Lord Jesus Christ.

Romans 15:5-6

Acknowledgments

Heartfelt thanks to Raoul and Joanna Guise of Otley, England, who have helped me so much in bringing the setting of *Wild Heather* to life. My appreciation to Karen Solem for listening to me babble with such animation about the hedgerow. Deep gratitude also to Tim Palmer, Kathy Olson, and Anne Goldsmith for their careful reading and editing of the manuscript. May God bless you all with His richest gifts!

The Legend of the Hedgerow

LONG AGO IN ENGLAND, two knights—Hewes and Sherbourne by name—defended the king with such valor that he elevated each of them to the rank of baron. Furthermore, he endowed the men with adjoining expanses of Yorkshire moorland.

Hewes—Lord Chatham by title—built a stately home of gray stone and named it Chatham Hall. Sherbourne, who became Lord Thorne, erected a home of similar size and grandeur and called it Thorne Lodge. Best of friends, the two men purchased flocks of sheep, hired shepherds from the nearby village of Otley, and married beautiful young ladies who soon saw to it that Chatham Hall and Thorne Lodge rang with the laughter of children.

Many generations came and went, and someone—no one remembers who—planted a hawthorn hedge near a stream in order to protect the sheep and to divide the Chatham and Thorne properties. On observing the new border, the then Lord Chatham declared that the hedgerow had lopped off a substantial corridor of his property. Lord Thorne countered that it actually encroached on *his* land. Both men applied at once for a royal survey. Sadly, all records of the original transaction had been destroyed in 1666 during the Great Fire of London.

Chatham then took matters into his own hands. He and his men marched upon the offending hedgerow by dark of night and chopped it down. Thorne, on seeing this foul trespass, attacked Chatham's group and pushed them back to what he deemed to be the true property line. A violent sortie occurred, in which two men and six sheep were slain. Chatham and Thorne now swore enmity and posted guards along their supposed borders in order to prevent further encroachments.

In the ensuing hundred years and more, the row of hawthorn stumps sent roots deep into the Yorkshire soil and branches high toward the Yorkshire sky. Hedgehogs toddled across the pastures and set up housekeeping in the hedge. Toads and frogs hopped by and decided to stay. Blackbirds, robins, and wrens found the hedge a quiet haven in which to raise nestlings, while butterflies and bumblebees flitted over the blackberry vines that threaded among the branches.

As the hedgerow went on nurturing life, the Chathams and Thornes occupied themselves with despising one another. Yet, no one dared touch the hedgerow, which grew and thrived until at last it became a haven for all living creatures.

Chatham Hall and Thorne Lodge, meanwhile, housed the most resentful, bitter, and distrustful souls in Yorkshire. Though they purchased goods in the same shops, shared many of the same friends, and worshiped God in the same church, they neither looked at one another nor spoke a single word.

It was at church, in fact, that one day the unthinkable happened. . . .

One

The village of Otley
Yorkshire, England; 1813

" 'LET THE PEACE of God rule in your hearts.' " The young minister lifted a hand and held it over his congregation in benediction. " 'And the peace of God, which passeth all understanding, shall keep your hearts and minds through Christ Jesus.' "

Olivia Hewes, heiress to the Chatham family fortune, blew out a breath that sent the dark curls on her forehead dancing. Thank heaven, the service was over at last. She reached for the beaded bag in which she had placed a lemon sweet to freshen herself before greeting friends.

But as she drew apart the gathers of the reticule, the Reverend Berridge cleared his throat. " 'Finally, brethren,' " he spoke again, his voice resonating from the high oak beams of the stone chapel, " 'whatsoever things are true, whatsoever things are honest, whatsoever things are just, whatsoever things are pure, whatsoever things are lovely—' "

Oh, get on with it, Olivia fretted. To her dismay, she had discovered that Otley's new minister enjoyed sermonizing for what seemed like hours. On and on he went—and who could attend to such lengthy discourse? Weighted by her many pressing responsibilities, Olivia tugged on the fringe of her pink cashmere shawl. How could she manage to slip away from church without undue delay? And would she arrive home before disaster once again befell the family?

As was customary in the morning, her mother had not been at all well, and her brother, Clive, had stayed behind to look after her. In Olivia's opinion, this was a most unsatisfactory arrangement. Yet nothing she said could sway Lady Chatham from her decree that one of the family must make an appearance at church every Sunday morning.

" 'Whatsoever things are of good report,' " the minister droned on, " 'if there be any virtue, and if there be any praise, think on these things.' "

There is not. Olivia threaded her gloved fingers together and squeezed them so tightly that her blood stopped flowing. *There is neither praise nor virtue to be found in Otley,* she thought. And certainly there was nothing of good report in her own life. Her father's death when she was barely nineteen had forced her to take on the management of Chatham manor. With no preparation for such a task—and with her mother ill and her brother requiring much attention—she had thus far failed to turn any profit. Indeed, the financial situation had grown dire.

Though Lady Chatham believed the answer to their problems lay in a good marriage for both her children, Olivia had no desire to repeat the misery of the union she had witnessed at Chatham Hall. She loved to read tales of grand adventure and romance. As a young girl, she had often prayed that a handsome young hero might sweep her off her feet and carry her away to everlasting happiness. But over the years, she had seen enough of reality to dampen that dream. Besides, God rarely answered her prayers—so rarely that she often wondered why she bothered.

No indeed. Now that she was responsible for the manor, Olivia planned never to marry but to focus all her attention on bringing the estate back to solvency. To that end, she was planning to urge old Mr. Tupper, the family steward, into retirement, and she was searching for a new steward who could assist her in all her goals.

Olivia thought of herself as something like a tuft of the wild heather that grew on her beloved moor. She had set her roots into the stony soil of her homeland, and she would not be budged. The winds of change, the hail of misfortune, the storms of sorrow—none of these could dislodge her. Though she grew dry and old, she would not surrender. The land belonged to her—to every Chatham who had come before her and to every one who might follow—and she would cling tenaciously to it with a determination that had been bred into her through the centuries.

" 'Those things, which ye have both learned, and received, and heard, and seen in Me, do.' " Reverend Berridge closed his Bible. " 'And the God of peace shall be with you.' "

As the young man turned away from the pulpit, the congregation began to rise. At last. Olivia drew her shawl over her shoulders, popped the lemon sweet into her mouth, and slipped out of the pew. She would have no choice but to greet the Bowdens of Brooking House and the Baines of Nasmyth Manor. Though beneath her in society, they were respected families and must be acknowledged. And she really ought to invite Mrs. Berridge to tea. Being new to town, the young woman must be in want of female solace.

"Mrs. Baine, good morning!" Olivia dipped an elegant curtsy before her elderly neighbor. "How delightful to see you. And how well you look."

Moving on quickly, Olivia escaped the Billingsworths by tilting her bonnet just so. She evaded the Kibbles and the Seawards, who evidently were greeting the Thorne family. The Thornes occupied pews in the western side of the church—and Olivia, whose family took residence on the eastern side, would never deign to glance in *that* direction.

The owner of the Otley worsted mill, John Quince, who could not be avoided, touched her elbow. "Dear Miss Hewes," he said, bowing smartly. "You are looking bright today. Very lovely indeed."

An elegant man of great wealth, Quince employed many of Otley's citizens, whose wooden shoes could be heard clattering along the cobblestone streets as they hurried toward the mill at seven every morning and home again at eight each night of the week. Quince sent wool to individual families to be combed clean, while in his factory, men and women earned five shillings a week for their labors at the sixty-horsepower engine that ran the spinning machines. Children who pieced the worsted fabric earned two shillings a week. Olivia had heard rumors that the harsh labor often caused crippling injuries. Though she had no sure evidence of this, she knew the mill's overseers severely beat the children, for she had seen these little ones in the streets and had observed for herself the dreadful evidence of their cruel mistreatment.

Olivia did not admire John Quince, but his influence in the community must not be underestimated, and so she gave him a warm greeting. "How pleasant to see you, Mr. Quince. And how do you get on, sir?"

"Very well, indeed, thank you. But where is your dear mother?"

"She is unwell, I fear. She lies abed."

"Shocking news. Do convey my deepest sympathies. I shall call at my earliest opportunity."

She tipped her head and forced a smile. "You are always welcome at Chatham Hall, Mr. Quince."

And, finally, only the Bowden family blocked her path to the church door. "Mrs. Bowden, charmed," she greeted the stout lady whose husband was fond of quoting Scripture and poetry. "Ah, Mr. Bowden, was that not a fine sermon?"

"Capital, Miss Hewes," he replied with a bow. "None finer, nor more appropriate to the current deplorable contention in our town."

For an instant, Olivia was stricken mute. As landlord of more than a score of tenant families, she made it her business to be informed on every issue of import to Otley and its surrounds. In the midst of the difficulties that plagued her own family, had she failed to learn of some discord among the townsfolk?

She laid her hand on Mr. Bowden's arm. "Of which contention do you speak, sir?"

"Why, the doctrinal matter plaguing our village, of course. Reverend Berridge could not have chosen a better sermon topic than that of peace. As King Solomon so eloquently reminds us, 'Wisdom is a tree of life to them that lay hold upon her. Her ways are ways of pleasantness, and all her paths are peace.' "

"You have it backward, Father," his eldest daughter, Ivy, said gently. The lovely young woman smiled at Olivia. "The verses in Proverbs—they go the other way round."

"My dear girl, their meaning is the same," her father replied. "It is most unwise for the town's leaders to perpetuate this divisive, injurious, and most disputatious of issues!"

Olivia clenched her jaw. "And the issue is . . . ?"

"Was the earth created in six days, or was it not? By extension, one must ask if the Bible should be taken literally in its every word—or might it be allowed some small flaw of translation or be open to personal interpretation? I tell you, this topic is of great doctrinal import. Conversation in our drawing rooms cannot escape it. Indeed, the matter colors even the discourse between husband and wife, father and daughter."

"In *our* house it does," Ivy said with a twinkle in her eye.

"Miss Hewes," Ivy's father continued, "I must be frank. I believe it behooves your esteemed mother to make every attempt to resolve this issue and quell the discord."

Olivia longed for her fan. She felt hot and annoyed and terribly anxious, yet she had no choice but to stand and engage Mr. Bowden in this meaningless chatter. Was the earth created in six days? How silly! How utterly trivial in comparison with the issue of the moment—the chaos Olivia's brother might be wreaking even now at Chatham Hall.

She willed herself to concentrate. Her mother, who ought to tend to duties in matters that beset the townspeople, was all but unable. No one knew the extent to which the mantle of responsibility had fallen on Olivia's shoulders. And she intended to keep Lady Chatham's condition a secret for as long as possible. Indeed, Olivia would do everything in her power to protect her family's reputation.

"To be sure, Mr. Bowden," she said. "The Chatham family are committed to the good of everyone in Otley."

"But what of this lecture to be given by William Buckland on the fifteenth of the month?" he asked. "You know what that man believes, and his speech can only foment hostilities. Miss Hewes, can you be persuaded to speak to Lady Chatham about the situation?"

"Of course. Yes, certainly—oh, can this be Miss Clementine?" Olivia spotted the golden-haired child peeking out from behind a pew. Gratefully turning away from Mr. Bowden, she knelt on the stone floor to greet the little girl. "What a lovely young lady you are, my dear. And how tall you have grown! I declare, you must be eight years old by now."

"No indeed, madam, for I am barely six." Flushing with pleasure, Clementine Bowden made a curtsy. "Miss Hewes, you must come to Brooking House and see our polliwogs. We have ever so many in our stream."

"Polliwogs." A genuine smile came to Olivia's lips for the first time that morning. "I liked polliwogs once . . . and I believe I should like them still. But I fear I must hurry home at once to my own dear mama."

With that, Olivia attempted to stand. But for some reason, her gown refused to budge. Disconcerted, she straightened, and the fabric suddenly gave way with a loud ripping sound.

"Upon my word!" She looked over her shoulder to discover

her hem trapped beneath the heel of a man's large leather boot. "I declare, sir—you are treading upon my gown!"

The man turned, and their eyes met. His were blue . . . the bright and glorious blue of a Yorkshire lake in midsummer. Olivia stared, her lips parting and her breath unmoving as every rational thought in her head, every worry in her heart vanished. She looked into a face that might have been chiseled by a Greek artisan—a noble nose, a jutting chin, a square jaw, and the plane of a cheek so fine and smooth it could have been hewn from marble. Yet the color that suffused the flesh of this face gave it life and beauty and bearing.

Such a man! Such breadth of shoulder, such imposing stature, and such a head of hair . . . warm chestnut curls that tumbled over his ears and brushed his collar as he removed a top hat of the finest beaver.

"Dear madam," he said, and his voice was deep and rich. "I sincerely beg your pardon."

His blue gaze tore from her eyes and fell to her gown. Olivia glanced down, too, and saw the astonishing rent. Great ghosts! The embroidered white lawn fabric of her skirt had ripped cleanly away from the back of her bodice! A button hung by a single thread, and the gathers in her skirt were even now unfolding like accordion pleats.

"Lord Thorne has torn Miss Hewes's gown!" Clementine Bowden exclaimed. "I can see her petticoat!"

The announcement brought cries of dismay from those around her as Olivia snatched her pink shawl and attempted to cover the gap with the length of cashmere. The man reached to assist, but someone stayed his hand.

"This is Miss Hewes!" John Quince said quickly. "Do come away, Lord Thorne."

Thorne! As that most hated of names registered in her brain, Olivia dropped the corner of her shawl. She sucked in a shocked gasp, and the lemon drop flew to the back of her throat. Lord Thorne? Could it be? She began to choke. Had she actually looked at a Thorne? Had he looked at her?

"Miss Hewes, I fear you are unwell." Thorne took another step toward her, his hand held out solicitously. "May I assist—"

"No, no!" She backed up, coughing the lemon drop into her palm as she stumbled into the group of stunned onlookers behind her.

"Indeed, I can see I have caused you great distress." He was surrounded by Thornes—relations, friends, associates . . . oh, dear!

"Miss Hewes is the daughter of Lady Sophia Chatham," Quince sputtered in warning. "I insist, sir, that you—"

"But she is . . . I have torn her—"

"I am well, my lord," Olivia blurted out. "Do not trouble yourself, I beg you."

"Come, brother!" A man in the Thorne party spoke up. He was nearly as tall as Lord Thorne but younger. "Miss Hewes has pardoned you. Leave it at that. We have had enough trouble from her family to last a lifetime."

The bitter tone slid through Olivia's bones. "Trouble from *my* family?" she retorted. "What is your meaning in this accusation, sir?"

Not deigning to answer, the younger man took his brother's elbow and turned away. "Randolph, the ladies await us in the carriage."

Lord Thorne detached himself and gave Olivia a bow. "I assure you, madam, I meant you no affront."

"Good morning, sir," Olivia managed while executing a self-conscious curtsy.

His blue eyes fell upon her once again. She clutched the sticky lemon drop in her glove and hung suspended in his gaze. For a moment, she felt certain he would speak again. Instead, he returned his top hat to his head and followed his brother through the church door.

"Dear Miss Hewes!" Ivy Bowden appeared at Olivia's side. "Please allow me to offer you my own shawl, for it is prodigiously large. Folded into a triangle, it will—"

"Lord Thorne trod upon Miss Hewes's gown!" Clementine cried, jumping up and down on tiptoes. "He tore it!"

"My shawl is finer than yours, Ivy," Caroline Bowden, another of the sisters, said. "Put two together, for no one will think twice—"

"Two together?" Old Mrs. Baine stared in horror. "Two shawls on one lady?"

"I have a needle and thread," Mrs. Berridge spoke up. The minister's young wife stepped through the crowd clustered around Olivia. "I keep them in my reticule in the event my husband tears his robes while climbing the steps to the pulpit. Miss Hewes, will you allow me to—"

"No, please!" Olivia held up her hands. "Thank you all, but I must go home. Truly, I must."

"But your gown," Clementine blurted. "I can see your petticoat!"

"Hush, child!" Ivy Bowden clapped a hand over her sister's mouth.

"Good morning to you all." Olivia draped her own pink shawl over the widening gap in her skirt and hurried out the door. Her carriage awaited, and the footman was ready to assist her. As she slid onto the smooth leather seat, she tore off her bonnet and buried her face in her hands.

Olivia fought back the tears that stung her eyes as the carriage pulled away from the church and began the journey to Chatham Hall. How could she bear this new mortification? How much more must she be asked to endure? Her mother hovered at the edge of a deadly affliction. Her brother—labeled a lunatic by physicians who had examined him—became more volatile and unsteady with each passing day. The burdens of managing tenants, overseeing flocks and land, tending to her family weighed heavily upon her.

And now . . . now Randolph Sherbourne, Lord Thorne, head of the dynasty that had brought such suffering upon her own dear family, had dared to trespass on her person. He had trod on her gown! He had torn it!

Olivia opened her hand and stared at the small lemon sweet stuck to her white glove. But he had not meant to step on her hem. She knew that, just as she knew that she had not meant to look into his blue eyes and suck her lemon drop into the back of her throat.

For countless generations, Chathams had avoided every contact with Thornes. Thornes had done the same. They averted their eyes when standing near. They crossed to the other side of the street when their paths might meet. And no Chatham ever spoke to a Thorne.

Now it was done. For one instant, Olivia Hewes had forgotten she was heir to the Chatham fortune. Randolph

Sherbourne had neglected the duties of his role as Lord Thorne. And for that brief and very public moment, they had bridged the chasm between their two families.

"Did you see her face?" William Sherbourne chuckled as he addressed his brother. "I do believe she considered herself horribly violated by you!"

"As indeed she was." Randolph gazed thoughtfully at the young woman now fleeing the church to the shelter of her carriage. "Bad enough that any man should trespass upon a lady in such a way. But I am a Thorne and she a Chatham. Can you not see how my error will be perceived in the town?"

"Come, man, your gravity is mistaken." William grinned at the pair of elegant ladies who occupied their carriage. "Do you not agree, Miss Bryse? Miss Caroline?"

"I view the occurrence as a subtle and brilliant revenge for the tragic loss of your father," Beatrice Bryse responded. "And cleverly executed."

As the carriage rolled forward, Randolph leaned back in the seat. The death of the late Lord Thorne just a month earlier had wounded him deeply. Though Randolph had spent many years away at Eton and then Cambridge, he cherished fond memories of his father. As a boy, he had followed the tall, dignified gentleman everywhere. They hunted and fished together, took long rides across the moorland, and sat by the fire discussing the affairs of the manor. The elder Lord Thorne was devoted to his three sons, but Randolph always received the special attention due the primary heir. The untimely death and its cryptic circumstances had been a bitter blow, and Randolph could not dwell upon his loss without considerable pain.

The funeral had brought the younger of his two brothers home to Yorkshire. The other—a missionary in India—could not break free of his work there. But William Sherbourne had arrived from the Royal Naval Academy in Portsmouth with a close friend, Captain Charles Bryse, and his two sisters, Beatrice and Caroline. The entire party had stayed at Thorne Lodge nearly a full month now, and Randolph had long been eager to send them all on their way.

"Clearly my misstep in church today was accidental, Miss Bryse," he said to the older of the ladies. "How can you term it revenge?"

"Unless you can prove the culprit, the law prevents you from taking retaliation for your father's death," Miss Bryse explained, "yet we feel certain the Chathams were the cause of it. How could it be otherwise?"

"Exactly," William concurred. "Our father was known as an excellent hunter and would not have been careless with his weapon. Clearly someone shot him, and the marksman must have been hired by the Chathams."

"We have no proof of this," Randolph said. "None whatever. Though Father's death is suspicious, you know I have taken great pains to investigate it, William. The constable questioned countless people, including those in Chatham employ, and we have studied the scene at length. The only conclusion we can draw is that Father accidentally dropped his gun, and it discharged."

"Impossible! We may have no evidence of it, but I am

certain the Chathams are at fault. Who else but that family desired his death?"

"True," Beatrice Bryse concurred. "Sadly, your suspicions against them cannot be substantiated, Lord Thorne. But you have taken some revenge upon them today, for in the most innocent of places . . . and with the most sincere regrets . . . you tore that vile creature's gown."

"A master stroke!" Captain Bryse said with a laugh. "It was a direct affront upon her person—and a perfect stab at her family. You cannot be accused of anything, Thorne."

"Best of all," William continued, "in some measure, you avenged our father. Well done, my good man!"

"Enough, brother," Randolph said, annoyed at their light-hearted air. "The matter is ended."

"Come now." Miss Bryse reached across and laid a gloved hand on his arm. "You must not be so glum, my lord. I wager that one day you will recall this event with great amusement. We shall all laugh about it. Indeed, I wish Caroline and I had not been waiting in the carriage. I should like to have seen the look on Miss Hewes's face when her gown began to unfold."

"And her petticoat!" Miss Caroline spoke up. "Did you actually see it beneath the—"

"What I saw," Randolph cut in, "was a most elegant and . . . I daresay lovely . . . young woman who—by my clumsiness and inattention—was publicly humiliated. She was shocked to the point of choking."

"Choking! Oh, that is rich!" Miss Bryse laughed.

"Indeed, her face went as red as a tomato," William chimed in. "I thought she must swoon. But she was too busy attempting to cover the gap in her gown as her skirt unraveled."

"How diverting! My lord, truly you must see the humor in this." Miss Bryse leaned against Randolph. "You have honored your family name by this 'accident,' and you must learn to laugh at the sport you made of the girl."

"I do not take pleasure in making sport of anyone, madam, let alone an elegant and beautiful young lady."

"Beautiful?" William chortled. "Come, brother, she is a Chatham! Do you forget yourself?"

"Chatham or not, Miss Hewes is lovely."

"What—brown eyes and brown hair? I thought her plain."

"Did you not note the curve of her brow? the pink of her cheeks?"

"Pink cheeks, aye, for she was choking to death!" William's grin faded as he glanced at Miss Bryse. "She was very plain, I tell you. A mousy creature."

"Were she not a Chatham," Randolph said, "I should not hesitate to call her a great beauty."

"But that is the material point, is it not, brother? She *is* a Chatham. Neither of us should have deigned to look at her. Nor should you have spoken. She is beneath us."

"Her family has caused ours undue suffering—that is true. But Miss Hewes herself cannot be held responsible for evil done by every Chatham in history."

"As a Christian and a gentleman," Miss Bryse said, "you feel the weight of this morning's incident, my lord. But do not let this discomfort blind you to the truth. Your dear brother has told us of the many atrocities committed by that family through the centuries. And now you labor under the grief of your father's recent death. The Chatham family—and this lady is one of them—have caused every woe that has befallen the great Thorne dynasty. And you must not forget it."

Randolph stared out the window at a large flock of sheep grazing on the fell. This land, these animals, and the people who tend them must be his primary concern. Yet his brother and Beatrice Bryse were correct in stating that his sadness over his father's untimely death colored everything in his life.

"Not only have Chathams caused us pain for centuries," William said, "but this particular family is said to be reaping the harvest of malevolence their own ancestors have sown. Lord Chatham died three years ago of an illness that must go unmentioned in the company of ladies. Lady Chatham—after the birth of their daughter, Olivia—bore countless hideously deformed babies who survived no more than a day or two. Indeed, their family cemetery is littered with tiny gravestones. And at last the poor lunatic was born—what do they call him?"

"Clive," Randolph said.

"Yes, Clive. An imbecile. Unable to attend university. Unable to go out into society. Unable even to ride a horse. Can you imagine? And now the mother lies abed day after day, rarely making an appearance even among friends. Some say she is afflicted with the disease that killed her husband. Others believe she is a besotted old—"

"William!" Randolph barked. "Enough of this recitation of rumors and gossip. We truly know nothing of that family save the litany of sins they have committed against us. And lest we pride ourselves too highly, we must recall that for every one of their trespasses, we have responded with a revenge equal or worse. All of that culminating today in my effrontery upon the person of Miss Olivia Hewes."

The carriage rolled to a stop in front of Thorne Lodge, and Randolph threw open the door without waiting for the footman. He had started up the steps into the house when his brother called after him.

"Randolph, your behavior frightens Miss Bryse! And you have reduced Miss Caroline to tears. You are altogether too serious."

Randolph paused. "Life is serious, William, and you would do well to begin to see it as such. For my part, I have had quite enough of your whist games, enough of charades, and more than enough of the pianoforte."

"Good heavens, Randolph!"

"Lest you forget, I am now Lord Thorne, and my greatest aim is to live up to the expectations of my father. I have a manor to oversee. I have sheep to be washed and shorn. Wool to be sold at the worsted mill. Meadows to be mown. Fields to be plowed. Carts to be greased and repaired. I have a town to look after—a town that seems determined to tear apart its own church in an argument over the infallibility of Scripture. Moreover, I am charged with the responsibility of continuing the Thorne name by marrying and siring sons. Each of these, dear brother, is a serious matter. I take them all seriously, just as I take seriously the fact that this morning, I publicly affronted not only the heir to the Chatham legacy, but a very lovely young woman."

He gazed at the astonished faces of William and the three Bryses. His brother shifted uncomfortably, looking more like a confused child than a dashing navy captain.

"Well, what do you intend to do about it? Miss Hewes, I mean."

Randolph thought for a moment. "I shall do what any gentleman ought. I shall write her a letter of apology."

As he stepped into the house, he heard his brother give a cry of exasperation. "But she is a Chatham, Randolph! We do not converse with them or acknowledge them in any way! And we certainly cannot write them letters of apology."

Randolph strode past the butler and began the long climb up the staircase to his rooms. *Yes,* he thought, *we can.*

Two

"WHERE IS OUR LYE, Mr. Tupper?" Olivia leaned back in the worn leather chair and rubbed her temples. "You can see that I ordered it last month. Here is my record in the ledger, plainly written."

The Chathams' steward looked glum. "Miss Hewes, I am certain I dispatched your chit directly to Leeds on the coach. The lye ought to have come—yet it has not."

Olivia studied the ledger once again, unable to believe that her order had gone astray. In the library of Chatham Hall on this Monday—as had become her custom each afternoon for the three years since her father's death—she reviewed the business of the manor. The care of sheep, the planting and harvest of crops, and the welfare of tenants all fell to her.

James Tupper, the family steward, had been employed by Olivia's father many years before, and she trusted the man implicitly. But his advancing age worried her. More and more often, he was fuzzy on details such as the lye order. Yet she could not manage the manor without a faithful steward.

All winter, she had been making inquiries in the hope of finding a younger, more competent replacement. She needed a steward who understood far more than finances. Like Mr. Tupper, he must know practically everything about sheep and farming. He must be familiar with the customs and the temperament of the Yorkshiremen. And he must possess the willingness to serve under a young but determined woman. No one she had interviewed thus far met those expectations. In a way, this was a relief, for the thought of turning out the faithful old man was more than she could bear.

"It is said," Mr. Tupper intoned, "that the Thorne family maintains close ties with Yorkshire's coachmen. I would not put it past them to intercept our post, madam. Without the lye, our sheep cannot be washed. And if our wool is sandy, we shall get a lower price for it from Mr. Quince—a great boon for the Thornes."

"Aye, Mr. Tupper, and yet I see no value in blaming the Thornes when we have no evidence of their guilt." Olivia struggled to prevent the memory of Baron Sherbourne of Thorne from invading her thoughts. She could see him as he had been yesterday in church—his blue eyes and dark hair, his deep voice as he made his apology, the sincerity and kindness in his manner. Truly, he had acted the gentleman in every way. The incident was best forgotten, therefore, and she must set it aside.

She focused on her steward. "The material issue now is to find enough lye to let us wash our sheep. Where shall we apply?"

"Not in Otley certainly. No one here will possess such an amount." He scratched his bald head. "Harrogate or Bradford, perhaps. But I think it best to dispatch a man to Leeds and investigate the missing shipment. Our supplier may have the washing lye awaiting transport even now."

"Can you go, Mr. Tupper? I cannot trust a task of such import to any other in my employ." The tinkle of a bell brought welcome relief. Olivia closed the ledger. "I am called to tea, sir. Please consider my request. We will speak of the matter tomorrow."

"Miss Hewes, I shall prepare for a journey to Leeds at first light." He bowed. "You may be assured that I shall not return without an answer and, I should hope, the lye."

"You are good, sir." She swallowed back the emotion that rose inside her and made him a curtsy. "I cannot think what I should do without you, Mr. Tupper."

He bowed as she left the room and started down the corridor toward the drawing room. At this rate, the washing would be late, and the shepherds would be forced to delay their shearing. Would Mr. Quince wait to view the Chatham fleece before setting out an offer to the Thornes?

For the three years since the death of Olivia's father, Chatham wool had failed to bring a premium price at the local worsted mill. This shearing season, if Quince did not make a healthy offer, she would have no choice but to seek other markets. Olivia blamed herself in all this, yet she had hardly expected her father to perish in the prime of his life. She had planned to be wed, settled, and the mother of sons before that should happen, and she had trusted that her husband would take over management of the Chatham manor.

Olivia's mother insisted that at two-and-twenty, her daughter's priority must be marriage. Yet the thought of a union with any man of her acquaintance repulsed her. The very idea of spending an entire life locked in battle, as her parents had been, made her ill. But financial circumstances grew more dire by the day. If she could not find a competent steward and force Chatham land to turn a profit, she would have no choice but to marry soon—and to marry profitably indeed.

As she approached the drawing room, Olivia turned her attention from the manor to her family. To her surprise, God had elected to answer her fervent prayers from the previous morning's church service. Her brother had behaved himself admirably, and their mother had recovered enough to enjoy a peaceful afternoon. Now Olivia must create a reasonable excuse to refuse all callers until life at Chatham Hall had resumed normalcy—if ever it would.

"Mama, how well you look," she said as she entered the large comfortable room. Clad in her white mobcap and a gray satin gown, the woman leaned heavily on her cane as she turned from the fire to greet her daughter.

"I am not at all well, my dear," Lady Chatham said, "for I endure the most dreadful headache, and for a second day. Indeed, all morning it has plagued me and now half into the afternoon. I am fairly blinded by the pain."

"Poor Mama." Olivia hurried across the carpet and took her mother's hand. "Do sit down, I beg you. Look, the tea has come. Let me pour you out a cup."

Lady Chatham spread her gown and took her place in the large chair near the fire. "Where is your brother? That boy gives me nothing but trouble. I thought he would torment me to death yesterday. And you stayed so long at church—

no doubt chattering away with your friends while I endured the most fearful poundings inside my head—and no one to comfort me. Oh, the sufferings that beset me!"

"Reverend Berridge is given to lengthy sermons, Mama," Olivia explained. "I left the church as soon as possible."

"I want to go riding!" Clive burst into the drawing room, his thin frame clad in an oversized green wool greatcoat, jodhpurs, and tall leather boots. His father's clothes. "I am going directly when tea is finished. Livie has promised to take me!"

"I promised you nothing of the sort." Olivia set the teapot on the tray and handed a cup to her mother. "The last time you were allowed to go riding, Clive, you took the horse into Otley—and I vowed I should never permit you out again."

"That is a lie! I never went to Otley. I never go to Otley. I never go anywhere. I stay here at home all the time, and I am bored." He jerked off his top hat and sent it sailing across the room. "You promised to take me riding today, Livie! You said you would, and I mean to go. I shall have my tea, and then we shall go riding. I want to ride on the black horse."

Olivia tried to pour out her brother's tea without trembling. At sixteen, Clive looked much younger than his age and was troubled with regular bouts of illness. Years ago, Olivia's father had taken the boy to London, where a doctor had fitted him with spectacles, pronounced him "sickly," and labeled him a lunatic. Though he enjoyed his sister reading to him, Clive had never been able to learn under a tutor, and he knew little of literature, mathematics, or science. Indeed, he could neither tell the time nor comprehend a calendar. Information slipped in and out of his head at random, which perplexed his sister no end.

"Sit down, Clive," Olivia ordered. She had learned to give instruction in single sentences, for her brother could never obey more than one command at a time.

He marched across the room, nestled against Olivia on the settee, and gave her a kiss on the cheek. "Riding," he said, "is my favorite thing."

"Oh, speak sense to the boy, Olivia," Lady Chatham moaned. "He cannot go riding. He will fall off the horse and kill himself. Then there will be no one to take the manor upon my death, and those horrid Thornes will chop down the hedgerow and steal our sheep and claim all our land! Oh, dear! Oh, heaven! My head throbs with such violence!"

"Mama, do calm yourself—"

"Fetch my sherry, Olivia! Bring it to me before my head breaks into a hundred pieces."

"Mama, it is too early in the day for sherry. Take your tea instead. Truly, you must not—"

"I shall fetch Mama's sherry," Clive said. "I am a good boy, and I do whatever she says, and I never tell lies like Livie."

"Sit down, Clive!" Olivia stood and grabbed his arm. "Mama must not have sherry now, for it is barely four o'clock!"

"Who cares about four o'clock?" he said, twisting away and racing for the liquor cart. "We must fetch the sherry, so we can go riding!"

Determined to prevent her mother from taking a drink before dinner, Olivia set off after her brother. "Stop it, Clive! Stop it now!"

"My head is breaking!" Lady Chatham wailed. "I am coming all to bits!"

"Fetch the sherry, fetch the sherry," Clive chanted as he

reached the cart and laid hold of the crystal decanter. "I have got the sherry, Livie—so ha, ha, ha!"

"Lady Chatham, the post has come." The announcement at the door brought Olivia to a halt in her headlong dash across the drawing room.

Breathing hard, she crossed the room to the footman and swept the stack of letters from the tray. As the servant left, she gritted her teeth against the screams of frustration that swelled up inside her. The family must not appear so chaotic in front of the staff! No one must guess at the havoc tearing the Chathams apart.

Though Clive's condition could not be disguised and their mother's illness was apparent to all, Olivia knew that she herself must make every effort to remain calm. If the town learned of their instability, the family would lose respect. People might begin to suspect the delicate state of their financial affairs and refuse to take their trade.

Olivia shuddered to think of it. What if the Chatham family were extended no more credit? What if Mr. Quince turned away their wool? What if they were cut off and isolated from all society? Worst of all—what if they were forced to sell their land in order to survive?

Behind Olivia, the clink of glass gave evidence that Lady Chatham's demand for sherry had been met. Olivia closed her eyes and pressed the letters against her breast. How could she put a stop to this abomination? For many years, she had prayed that her mother would give up the sherry. But God had disappointed her. Sophia Chatham drank more now than ever. Indeed, Olivia could not remember a time when the decanter was not ever present at her mother's beck and call.

Resolving to put everything into order as soon as possible, she turned toward the fire and took her place at the tea table again. "We have had a letter from the Bowdens. Shall I open it, Mama?"

"Oh, the prolific Bowdens! All those daughters!" Lady Chatham took a sip from her glass and let out a breath. "They will want to call on me, no doubt. Invite them to tea on Friday afternoon. Perhaps I shall be better by then."

"No, Mama. I think it would be most unwise." Olivia glanced at her brother, who was busy dunking a scone into his teacup. "I believe your delicate condition begs for careful consideration of our visitors. For the present, I shall turn away all callers."

"Indeed not, Olivia! The whole town will believe me to be lying on my deathbed, and then what will become of us? With Clive unmarried and no heir . . . what have you done to arrange a meeting with the Wilsons in London? They are such amiable people, and their eldest daughter is said to be quite a beauty."

"Mama, you cannot possibly think Clive is ready to marry."

"I want to go riding," he said around a large mouthful of scone. "I want to ride on the black horse."

"Well, never mind!" Lady Chatham waved her lace handkerchief at her daughter. "Who else has written? We shall sort them all out and make a schedule. Surely the Berridges have sent a note. They must come to dinner one evening, for they can testify to the trouble I have from my poor head. And they may assure everyone in town that I am not dead."

"The Kibbles have written," Olivia said, studying the letters one by one. "As have the Berridges."

"You see! I knew they would write to offer me their condolences. We shall invite our dear minister and his wife for dinner as soon as may be."

"Mama, please see reason. You are not well enough to take callers." Olivia glanced down at the firm black ink strokes on the next letter and caught her breath. *Lord Thorne!*

"Why do you gasp, daughter?" Lady Chatham trilled. "Who has written?"

Olivia could not bring herself to answer. This was impossible! Thornes did not write to Chathams. There must be no connection between them. She should not even lower herself to touch the paper on which—

"Who has written to me, Olivia? Get on with it, for my head pounds so!" Her mother picked up her glass and sipped the sherry as her teacup sat untouched.

Olivia slipped Lord Thorne's letter behind the others and quickly read the next. "The Baines. Shall I open it and see what they—"

"No, but you have missed one! Go back, go back, girl. Read the letter you put away there, or pass them all to me. You cannot take this so lightly, Olivia, for social engagements are of the utmost importance."

"Mama, the letter is of no concern to you."

"No concern? How can you say such a thing? Oh, I feared I could not trust you with matters of consequence. Without Mr. Tupper, where should I be? Why did your father have to die? Why was I left with no help, no succor? Why has God visited upon me such woes, such travails, such—"

"The letter is from Baron Sherbourne of Thorne," Olivia cut in. At her mother's incessant wailing, the slender thread that held Olivia in control snapped. She ripped open the seal. "Yesterday in church, Lord Thorne stepped on the hem of my gown and tore it. This is a written apology, nothing more. You see?

"Dear Madam,

I beg you to forgive me for the unfortunate incident that occurred this morning in church. I assure you, I had no ill intent toward you. Indeed, my action was purely accidental. I am tormented to think that you suffered not only injury to your gown but humiliation before your friends and family. If you will be so good as to receive my apology, I shall be most grateful.

Please also accept my offer to repair your gown. Better yet, allow me to replace the garment entirely. Select any fabric you like, and direct your seamstress to forward the charges directly to me.

I may not rest until I am assured of your acceptance of my offer. I remain most sincerely,

Your humble servant,
Thorne"

Olivia folded the letter, wedged it back in among the others, and whipped out the missive from the Baines. "There, you see? It is nothing. And what do the Baines have to say? Ah, they invite us to—"

"Stop!" Lady Chatham screeched. "Stop at once!" Trembling so fiercely that the sherry sloshed out of her glass, she leaned forward and glared at her daughter. "A *Thorne* has written to us?"

"Mother, it is merely a formal apology—nothing more than a gentleman ought to do under the circumstances."

"A gentleman? Dare you call any Thorne a gentleman?"

"Indeed I do, for you heard his words yourself. He sincerely regrets what occurred, and he means to make reparation by any means necessary."

"You should write to him, Livie." Clive peered over her shoulder at the message. "He sounds nice."

"He is not *nice!"* their mother exclaimed. "He is a Thorne. Why has he written to us? What evil scheme lies behind this letter?"

"There is no scheme, Mama."

"So you say, but you are young. You know too little of that family and their wiles. Oh, your dear father suffered abominably at their hand. They stole our sheep and tore down our stone walls. They poisoned our ponds one year, Olivia. Did you know that? And a thousand other things, all of them culminating in the death of my poor husband."

"Mama, my father died of the smallpox."

"And where did he fall ill? In Portsmouth—the very place where those wicked Thornes send all their sons to university."

"To the Naval Academy, and it is only the youngest who studies there. The other is in trade in India, I have heard. Or Africa perhaps. It was merely a coincidence that Father—"

"Nothing is a coincidence, Olivia. Those Thornes infected him with that dreadful disease and left me here all alone—a poor suffering widow with no one to look after me." She dabbed her eyes with her handkerchief. "Oh, dear Clive, pour me some more sherry, for I feel my headache coming on again."

"Mama, truly you must not take more sherry."

"I shall give her the sherry, Livie," Clive said, "and you answer the letter. We have to go riding."

"Honestly, Clive!" Standing, Olivia tossed the letters onto the tea table. "Come, I shall take you fishing. We must leave Mama here to her sherry."

"Fishing! I adore fishing!" He leaped up from the settee and threw his arms around his sister. "I love you, Livie. I love you!"

"And I love you, Clive."

As Lady Chatham reached for the letters, Olivia took her brother by the hand and led him from the drawing room. By dinnertime, their mother would be well into her cups. Clive would chatter on and on about nothing. Olivia would sit and worry about the missing lye. Everything would go on as it always had—prayers unanswered, dreams unmet, and hopes utterly futile.

Randolph's horse leaped gracefully over a fallen tree and cantered across the moor toward the western border of the Thorne manor. Eager to escape William and his three friends, Randolph had chosen to forgo tea and make a last survey of his flocks before sunset.

Before his father's death, the two had enjoyed such pastimes together. Even now, Randolph longed for the accompanying thunder of another horse's hooves, and he missed the booming cheer of his father's voice as he pointed out tenants building a stone wall, shepherds moving their flocks, or the increased flow of a brook after a rain.

An ancient hedgerow ran along the disputed border between the Thorne and Chatham properties. A stream coursed down its length toward the River Wharfe, its natural curves snaking back and forth from one side of the hedgerow to the other. The water was used heavily by the livestock of both families. As was their custom each June, the Thorne shepherds had dammed the channel just below an outcrop of gray stone and were bringing in the sheep for washing.

Early summer was Randolph's favorite season of the year, and since boyhood he had ridden out with his father to watch the washing of the sheep. First, foul and loose wool around the udder was removed. Then each animal was driven into the water where it would float about, easily turned by the shepherds who parted the fleece and scrubbed it with lye.

"Ho, Bartholomew!" As he guided his horse up the fell toward the man-made pond, Randolph called out to his headman. "How goes the washing?"

"Splendid, milord!" The elderly fellow—missing all his teeth, but cheery just the same—tipped his cap. He supervised from the bank while several of his men stood inside barrels in the water. "We're nearly done with this lot."

"How much longer before you begin the shearing?" Randolph dismounted and led his horse toward the stream. Nearby, the lambs—separated from their mothers for the first time—cried continuously, a din that made it difficult to speak without shouting. As the ewes climbed out of the water on the other side of the stream, the pair would be parted forever. Though the piteous *baa*s of the lambs saddened Randolph, he knew the weaning was for the best.

"A week at least, milord," Bartholomew said. "We'll keep

an eye on 'em till t' wool is dry and t' yolk seeps back in. Once t' skin is taut again, they'll be ready."

Randolph grinned at the sight of the men standing in their barrels while struggling to wash the sheep. It was a pleasant scene—the late-afternoon sun casting a soft golden glow on the sheep, glinting in the stream, dancing on the green leaves. Randolph's heart swelled with gratitude to God, and he offered up a silent prayer of thanksgiving. Though both his parents had died too young, Randolph was well prepared to take over management of the Thorne manor. He often joined in the manual labor, which earned him the respect and affection of his workers.

His primary order of business now was to get himself a wife, and by her a son and heir to the noble family Thorne. Though William had not spoken of it openly, Randolph knew the Bryse sisters had come to Thorne Lodge on approval. Beatrice Bryse seemed particularly determined to catch Randolph's eye, but he could not bring himself to like the young woman. She took things far too lightly—absorbed in herself and her own small thoughts and quite oblivious to the greater world around her.

Randolph wanted a wife who could match him in intellect and wit. And he hoped to find someone who might share in the spiritual discourse that so occupied his heart. While at Cambridge, Randolph and his brother Edmund had been thrown into a period of deep mourning by the news of their mother's death in a carriage accident. Seeking counsel, they came under the influence of a minister who had served many years as a missionary in China. This man had taught both Randolph and Edmund the importance of constant communion with the Savior, vigilant repentance of sin, and diligence in the reading and study of Scripture.

William, who had not yet begun his studies at the Naval Academy, remained at home during this time of grief and took solace in the licentious behaviors of the world. But Edmund had grown so fervent in his desire to share the message of salvation through Jesus Christ that he had joined a missionary society and sailed away to India. Randolph might have gone too, but his own destiny lay with Thorne Lodge and the many souls who served upon that vast manor. Though his purpose now was to marry, he had ruled out Beatrice Bryse as a potential wife on the day they met.

For one thing, he did not approve of her appearance. Beatrice was a prickly creature. Pointed nose, sharp lips, and slashed eyebrows complemented a figure pinched and prodded in far too many unnatural directions. Add her favorite accessory—a turban adorned with a crisp quail feather—and Randolph could hardly make himself go near her for fear of a violent jab.

He much preferred a softer sort of woman, one with gentle curves and full lips and large liquid eyes. The memory of Olivia Hewes instantly came to his thoughts. How startled he had been to find such an attractive creature standing inside his own church. It was odd to think that he had never met her—yet they had grown up on neighboring estates, enjoying many of the same friends and diversions.

For some reason, Randolph had imagined the Chathams to be as hideous in their form as they were said to be in their hearts. He had heard tales of the countless grotesque infants born to Lady Chatham, and he pictured the two who had survived as equally repulsive. But Olivia Hewes's sweet beauty had quite taken Randolph's breath away. Her deep brown eyes had gazed into his and set his heart to racing in his chest. Her long neck was white and lovely, and her hair—such a cloud of glossy brown curls!

Having long heard of an imbecile brother, Randolph had expected Miss Hewes herself to be dull and witless. But she had blushed and curtsied and spoken with such gentility that he could not doubt she was an educated and accomplished lady of the very highest order. How shocking. Indeed, he had been so stunned by their meeting that he had been able to think of little else since. The wiles of the two Miss Bryses could do no more than draw him into the most mundane of conversations since that moment.

Though Beatrice was fixed on Randolph, her sister had her heart set on William, who knew it. Though William was her superior in intelligence and temperament, he admired the young lady's polished beauty, and she adored his ten thousand pounds per annum. A sad and empty attraction, but Randolph could do nothing about it.

No, he would far rather sort sheep than future brides. Indeed, the town of Otley provided little hope of meeting his requirements, for none of the families were his equal in society. He knew he would have to apply to acquaintances in Leeds or London, and the thought of such an effort made him cringe. Had his father not died—or been murdered, as Randolph and his brothers suspected—the baron would have introduced an array of possible wives from which his heir might select. But now the matter was left to Randolph himself.

"I'm told there's some merchants in t' north buyin' wool by

weight," Bartholomew spoke up as his men began to round up the weaned lambs. "That bein' true, we wouldn't need to wash 'em at all, would we? Ye could 'ave yourself a fine flock of sandy yellow sheep, and make a pretty penny off 'em!"

Randolph laughed. "I should very much like to be paid for dirt."

"Aye, milord!" The shepherd cackled as he slapped his thigh. "Paid for dirt! There ye 'ave it, sir!"

They were both chuckling when a large ewe in the stream suddenly decided she'd had quite enough of her lye bath. She reared up and thrust her two front hooves at the shepherd's chest. Before the man could steady himself, the old ewe shoved him over backward, and he landed with a mighty splash.

"She's done it now!" Bartholomew cried, slogging toward the water in his heavy boots. "Sent 'im under!"

Randolph sloshed into the stream beside Bartholomew and assisted the other men in righting the shepherd. He had floated out of his barrel and was soaked head to toe. The ewe, meanwhile, trotted straight up the bank to the other side and snatched herself a mouthful of green grass.

"Look, Livie!" a shrill voice called out above the hubbub. "Come, you must see! A sheep has thrown a man into the water!"

Surprised at the high-pitched cries, Randolph glanced across the hedgerow to see a young man standing on a stone outcrop that rose above it. The youth gave an excited wave, his fishing pole swaying from side to side. Randolph lifted a hand in return.

Thinking no more of it, he assisted the poor wet shepherd to the bank. Thankfully, the fellow took great amusement in his sudden bath and declared that he had been in need of a wash himself.

Bartholomew hurried forward with a mug of rich, dark tea he had poured from the kettle they kept over their nearby fire. "That'll warm ye, right enough," he said to the dripping shepherd. "Would ye care for a cup yourself, milord? 'Tis good and 'ot."

"No, thank you, I—" Randolph paused—"indeed, Bartholomew, I should like that very much."

"Good on, then." He hobbled toward the fire. "Follow me, sir."

"It was him, Livie! That one! The wet one!" The high voice drew Randolph's attention again. Now the boy was joined by a young woman from whose own pole swung a small fish. She lifted a hand to shield her eyes as she stood on the stony ledge.

"He fell into the water!" the boy cried. "That wet one! The sheep pushed him in. It was ever so amusing, Livie!"

For a moment, Randolph thought they must be Chatham tenants on an afternoon outing. But the silken sheen of the lady's pale gown and her brightly ribboned bonnet prompted him to take a closer look.

No tenant, she. That was Olivia Hewes.

Three

HIS THIRST FOR TEA FORGOTTEN, Randolph gazed at the young woman, who stood poised like a startled fawn on a tumble of gray gritstone. The rock ledge jutted above an expanse of heathered moorland stretching out behind her, a frame of pale misty greens surrounding this creature in a gown of soft, glowing white.

She saw Randolph, too, and as recognition dawned, her dark brows lifted, and she clapped a hand over her mouth and dropped her fishing pole. Grabbing for the boy, she clearly intended to hurry them out of view.

Randolph raised his hand. "Miss Hewes!" he called to her. It came out as more of a croak, but it covered the thirty paces that separated them.

She halted and glanced his way again. "Lord Thorne." She managed a curtsy, a bit wobbly on the tilted stone. As the boy shoved her pole into her hand, the still-flopping fish swung forward. It would have slapped her in the stomach had she not made an agile side step, an event which sent her companion into gales of laughter. At that, she lifted her skirt and made to depart.

"I say, Miss Hewes, have you caught a trout?" Randolph asked.

"It is a tench, I think." Her voice was tentative but melodious.

"We are going to eat it!" The boy—her brother, Randolph assumed—fairly danced about on the ledge. "We shall take it to Cook, and she will bake it for us! We shall eat it with lemon-and-butter sauce. I love to catch fish! I adore it! It is my favorite thing to do."

Randolph smiled. So this was Clive Hewes, Baron Chatham, the one they called the imbecile. He did not seem so very dull witted. At least he could speak with some sense.

"I am fond of fishing myself," Randolph called back.

"Livie likes it, too! We fish often in our streams and lakes. We love to fish. It is our favorite thing to do."

"Excuse us, my lord," Miss Hewes said. "I can see you are much occupied with your shepherds."

"Aye, but . . . but how is your gown? Did you receive my letter?"

"Livie cannot answer the letter," Clive shouted. "Mama says it is an abomination because it is from a Thorne, and we hate Thornes. They stole our sheep and poisoned our ponds and killed my father!"

"Clive, please!" Miss Hewes tugged on her brother's arm.

"Stole their sheep?" Bartholomew had come to Randolph's side, bearing a mug of hot tea. "We never did no such thing, sir. Them Chathams brought t' fly to our flocks one year. And as for poisonin' t' ponds, well—"

"Bartholomew, do forgive me, but I must speak to Miss Hewes about this in private."

"But you're Lord Thorne!"

"Indeed, I am." Randolph took the mug. "And who better to address the matter?"

He walked to the dam his shepherds had built in the stream and crossed it easily, not wanting to provide Clive additional amusement. Though he could see that Miss Hewes was eager to be gone, she could not budge her brother, who was about to leap straight out of the enormous riding boots he wore.

"I saw the shepherd fall into the water!" he shouted. "The sheep pushed him! I saw it. He is the wet one."

"It was a ewe," Randolph called. "A ewe pushed him in."

"Me? I did not do it! Tell him, Livie. Tell him I did nothing of the sort."

"He is not accusing you, Clive." She took her brother by the shoulders and clutched him close against her. "Settle yourself, now. Breathe deeply, dearest."

"But he said I pushed the man into the water!"

"No, no. It is all right, Clive." She deftly turned her brother away just as Randolph approached the hedgerow. "Look, did I see a fish leap? Just there in the pool where we were standing before? Go and see if you can catch it, Clive. Cook will be ever so grateful."

Drawn to the tenderness in her voice, Randolph climbed to the top of a large jutting slab of gritstone. And there she stood, now ten paces away, separated from him only by the hedgerow. The hawthorn shrubbery stood at least eight feet in height. It grew nearly as wide and was as impassable as a medieval fortress.

"Good afternoon, Miss Hewes," he said, removing his hat. "It is indeed a tench."

"Oh?" She glanced down at her fish. "Oh, yes. So it is."

"And you *did* receive my letter?"

When she lifted her chin, he could see that bright pink spots had blossomed on her cheeks. "Indeed, sir. Thank you. I do accept your apology. You need not make restitution. The incident is entirely forgotten."

"Forgotten by you perhaps. But I cannot escape the memory of that moment. I believe it is etched in my mind forever."

She glanced at him, then looked away quickly. "Do not think of it again, sir."

"Impossible."

When she did not speak, he realized how uncomfortable he made her. As a gentleman, he ought to let her go. She knew too well the strictures against such a conversation between them, and no doubt the shepherds would spread news of their meeting the length of the dales. Thorne and Chatham—speaking! How scandalous!

Randolph was aware that all his friends and relations held the Chatham family responsible for his father's tragic and untimely death. He, too, believed it must be so. But how could such a delicate young woman—with an ill mother and a disordered brother—plot and carry out such an evil mission? Did Miss Hewes have an advisor? Was she under the influence of an accomplice who wove schemes and villainies through her head? Randolph was determined to learn more.

"You fish with your brother, do you? He is quite young still."

"Clive is sixteen."

"I thought much younger."

"He is not well. Quite often, he suffers ailments of the lung and heart. Clive is very thin, you see, and small."

"And he adores fishing."

Her sudden smile lit up the gathering dusk. "Yes, he does. As he reminds me regularly, it is his favorite thing to do."

He chuckled. "But I take note that *you* are the one with the fish this day, Miss Hewes."

"Aye, by chance, for I am not a great fisher."

"I do not believe in chance, madam. Chance implies random coincidence. Fate, if you will. But all things are known to God."

"Even fishes and hooks?" Her brown eyes sparkled. "Do you mean to say that Providence directed this particular tench to my particular hook, sir?"

"I mean to say that God knows you are fishing today. Just as he knew I intended to look in on the washing of my flock. And so we have met again."

"By design? I hardly think God would bother." As if to change the subject, she turned to study his men at work in the pond. "Your sheep are looking very white."

Randolph glanced over his shoulder. "My shepherds do good work. As do yours, for we battle it out each year at John Quince's worsted mill, do we not?"

"Indeed we do, sir." At this reminder of the rift between them, the light faded from her eyes. "I must go. I beg your leave."

"But you have not answered the question in my letter. Will you allow me to replace your gown?"

"No, please, I—"

"I insist upon it, Miss Hewes. The fabric was torn beyond repair, and I must make restitution."

"That is wholly unnecessary, I assure you." She stood in silence for a moment, her focus moving from him to the shepherds in the distance. Finally, she spoke. "May I be so bold as to ask, Lord Thorne . . . do you have a great supply of washing lye?"

"Washing lye? Yes, of course."

"My order has not arrived from Leeds. I cannot begin the washing until I have it."

And the shearing, of course. Randolph immediately understood her predicament. Though he had never considered it before, he now saw that with her mother ill and her brother unfit for such duty, Miss Hewes must have been obliged to take management of the Chatham manor upon her father's death—and at a very young age. She could not be much beyond twenty. This was a heavy burden indeed.

For some reason, she did not have lye. And without lye, the Chatham sheep could not be washed or sheared—and their wool could not go to the worsted mill. For Randolph, this was an obvious boon. His fleece would get there first, Quince would have little with which to compare it, and thus he must offer a good price for the wool.

"Did you send a chit to Leeds for the lye?" Randolph asked.

"Aye, last month." She knotted her fingers together. "My steward travels there tomorrow to see what has become of my order."

Though the town of Leeds lay but ten miles south of Otley, it was an arduous journey on a poor road built of nothing more stable than crushed sandstone—a surface that turned to gullies in the rain. Often travelers were required to leave their carriages and walk a good distance. A wagon laden with washing lye might easily become mired in the sand. In foul weather, the journey to Leeds could take two days—and more to return.

Randolph sensed an agonizing twist of the muscle in his chest, as though his very frame were at war with itself. If he gave Olivia Hewes his surplus lye, he would betray his family. Selling it to her would be just as loathsome. And he knew little of Miss Hewes save her alluring brown eyes and sweet smile. It was possible—as rumor had it—that she had plotted with her men to kill his father and make it look like a hunting accident. An economic victory over the Chathams would bring great admiration from his society. And he needed it.

Though Randolph had been educated at Eton and Cambridge, and though he had been trained by his late father to run the manor, he had not proven himself as a capable lord and master. He was young—not yet thirty—and untried. Now his first test lay before him. An opportunity to sell his wool at a good price and, at the same time, a chance to humiliate the Chatham family.

He studied Miss Hewes for a moment as he prayed for direction. How would the Holy Spirit lead him to treat a woman who appeared so innocent and so much in need—and yet who was his nemesis?

Breathing hard, she worried her bottom lip as she glanced from her brother to the shepherds and then to Randolph. Finally, she squared her shoulders. "Sir, if you wish to make recompense for your injury to my gown, you may sell me enough lye that I may wash my sheep."

Taken aback, Randolph appraised her expression. So this was her scheme! It was devious indeed, and now he began to doubt his early good opinion of her. Did her innocent mien disguise the dark heart for which the Chatham family were known?

"You exact a harsh penalty."

Her brown eyes met his. "I need the lye."

"You must know I cannot provide it. Such a transaction would go against every belief, every tenet—"

"Yes, against everything our families have stood for these long years." She tightened the bow on her bonnet. "I beg your pardon, sir. For a moment, I forgot to whom I was speaking." Turning away from him, she lifted her skirt and picked her path down the stony ledge until she had joined her brother.

Randolph turned on his heel and started toward his shepherds. What an impudent creature, this Olivia Hewes! He had offered to replace her gown—and she had asked for lye instead. He had extended an olive branch, and she had grasped for the whole grove. How could she think he would give up his own lye—and to the Chatham family? How could she believe he would in effect sabotage his prospects for success?

Deeply disturbed, he downed his tea and returned the mug to Bartholomew. The old shepherd had helped round up the last of the freshly washed flock and had lit a lantern against the growing darkness.

"Will ye take a light, milord?"

"My horse is surefooted, Bartholomew," Randolph said. "And I shall be home before the sun is fully set."

"Right then." The man nodded in the direction of the hedgerow. "Pretty lass, that Miss Hewes, ain't she?"

"She's a Chatham." He made no attempt to disguise the hardness in his voice. "I had thought to make a sort of peace between us. But it was not to be."

"Peace? With them people? Nay, milord. Badness be bred into 'em—'tis in their very blood. Some folks can never change—and Chathams be t' worst of 'em."

The Thornes were not much good at change either, Randolph thought as he mounted his horse. Returning injury for injury. Greed for greed. Hatred for hatred.

It had always been so. And who was he to think of altering it?

Olivia stood at the library window and watched through the thick glass as rain shrouded the moorland. The heather, which would not set its beautiful purple flowers for another two months, appeared hunched and gray in the downpour. The bracken had hardly begun to show its summer green, and it huddled low in the grass as if shivering in the chilly mists. No birds ventured out across the sodden sky, and not a sound could be heard save the sound of droplets on the pane.

Four days had passed since Olivia's conversation with Lord Thorne across the hedgerow. In that time, Mr. Tupper had journeyed to Leeds and had returned with the washing lye. Her order had indeed gone astray. The lye maker, however, had anticipated her need for it. After more than twenty years of providing washing lye for Chatham sheep, he had trusted the need would be the same again this season.

Concocting such a large amount of lye involved long, hard labor, as Olivia knew from observing the process as a child.

Many wagonloads of hardwood ash must be gathered and placed on cloth inside a twig-filled lye dropper—a wooden trough with holes in its base. After water had dripped through the ash into a tub, the caustic liquid must be boiled down until it was concentrated enough to float an egg. The lye maker's effort—with no order to back it—had been a great risk, and he charged heavily for it.

Olivia trailed a fingertip along the frigid windowsill. Why did God so seldom answer her prayers? And why, when He did, must He make everything still so difficult for her? Yes, she had the lye. But the cost! Her ledgers showed the gradual seepage of Chatham money, and all at her hand. Oh, why had she not paid better attention to her father's discussions with friends and tradesmen? Why had he never thought to teach his daughter how to manage a manor?

How hard she had prayed for the lye to come! But now she wondered why she had agonized with such humility. Everything God gave her came with a steep price. Where was God, and why did He not love her more? What had she done wrong? All her life she had tried to be good and kind and loving. How had she displeased Him so?

Though the washing finally had begun, the sheep could not be sheared for many days. At this very moment, the shepherds were standing out in the rain and scrubbing away the sand and grit from their unhappy flock. Standing inside barrels would do the men little good, for they surely must be soaked to the skin in this downpour. And how soon would the sheep dry and their lanolin return?

Olivia's shipment of fleece was certain to arrive at John Quince's worsted mill many days after that of the Thornes.

Lord Thorne would sell all his wool and receive a good price. Chatham wool—once again—would fare the poorer. And if Mr. Quince could not purchase all of it, Olivia must seek out other tradesmen willing to take it. The struggle never ended, and the profits never ceased to decline.

Would life always be so difficult? Did she worship a God who enjoyed making His creation miserable? Perhaps she did not know Him so well as she had thought. Perhaps she knew Him all too well—and was beginning to admire Him less and less. Or perhaps, as she had begun to suspect lately, God did not care for her in the least. The world, it seemed, bored its Creator, and He had abandoned it. Like the wild heather, gorse, and bracken that fought for life on the inhospitable moorland, each human must eke out his own existence without assistance from the Almighty. He had turned His back on His handiwork, and certainly He paid no heed to the woes of a young Yorkshire lass.

Turning away from the window, Olivia stepped to her desk. It was almost time for tea, and now she must face the ever-present battle to bar her mother from the sherry, to calm her brother, and to keep their family from making a spectacle before the servants.

Feeling as though she wore the yoke of an ox across her neck, Olivia recalled the way Randolph Sherbourne—Lord Thorne—had called out to her so jovially. How light his step had been as he crossed the stream and climbed the stone outcrop to speak to her. How happy his demeanor. But he had been taught well. He knew how to balance ledgers and order lye and find tradesmen to buy his wool. Now he had only to chat with his shepherds and take amusement in his neighbor's troubles.

No doubt Thorne considered himself triumphant after their meeting at the hedgerow. He surely regaled his brother and their friends with the tale of the way Olivia Hewes had fairly begged on her knees for his lye. And how they must have roared with laughter when he told them that he had turned her away with nothing but a brusque retort.

Olivia closed her ledgers and set her pen on its stand. Why had she asked Lord Thorne to help her? Why had she admitted her need? How he must be reveling in her misery!

The tea bell rang, and she swallowed back the lump of regret in her throat. She should not have asked for the lye when he had offered only to repair her gown. Her impetuous request had placed him in a bind. Indeed, in this light, could she be viewed as the crass one?

Lord Thorne had been kind and generous to her until that moment, in every way a true gentleman. How noble he had looked as he stood upon the stone that evening. The setting sun had lit his blue eyes and bathed his face in a golden glow. He had spoken to Clive with genuine friendliness, and he had addressed Olivia with great gentility. They had chatted almost as friends. And then she had tried to coerce him into helping her against the welfare of his own family.

How thoughtless of her! How rude.

Unwilling to consider the consequences of yet another rash action, Olivia took up her pen again. Seated at the desk, she wrote out a hasty note.

Dear Sir,

I beg you to forgive my request of you on Monday last. You intended kindness, and I disregarded your generous offer in an attempt to address my own needs. Now it is my turn to apologize and to plead that my hasty words soon may be forgotten.

Sincerely,
Olivia Hewes

Determined not to waver in making this apology, she blotted the letter, folded it, and set her seal upon it. There. Now the issue was closed. He had trod on her gown, and she had forgiven him. She had spoken hastily, and certainly he would forgive her in turn.

Gathering her shawl close about her shoulders, she picked up the letter and left the library. On her way down the corridor, she passed the footman bearing his customary tray of letters. After taking them, she set her own upon the tray and instructed him to see it delivered at once.

"There you are, my dear!" Lady Chatham, already sipping sherry, waved a handkerchief at her daughter. "We thought you would not come to tea today. We thought you had abandoned us, did we not, Clive?"

"Where were you, Livie?" Clive munched on a strawberry tart. "The tea bell rang ever so long ago."

"I had to finish some business."

"Oh, do let Mr. Tupper take it on, dearest," her mother said. "He can manage the manor every bit as well as your father could. I always said what a good man Tupper was, and how thankful we are to God for him. If all falls down around us, at least we shall have Tupper."

"If all falls down around us, Mama, we shall need more help than Mr. Tupper can give." Olivia poured her tea and began to stir in milk and sugar. Now that her communication with Lord Thorne was at an end, she felt much better. Quite relieved, as a matter of fact. She would not think of him again.

"Papa always used to say that the world is changing at a rapid pace," she told her mother. "One must do everything possible to keep up with it. He went to agricultural lectures in London and held conferences with colleagues and read all the newspapers. I should very much like to do that."

"You?"

"And why not? The management of the manor falls to me."

"But Mr. Tupper—"

"Mr. Tupper deplores lectures and rarely talks to anyone but me. He never looks at the newspapers, and I wish he would. Just yesterday I read that some merchants in the north are now buying wool by the pound. Heavier is better. Fleece filled with sand and grit, therefore, is more valuable than clean."

"Dirty fleece? Who would want to buy such rubbish?"

"Lord Thorne was talking about that," Clive said. "They were talking about washing sheep."

"Lord Thorne?" Lady Chatham stared goggle-eyed at her son. "What are you saying, boy?"

"I had that information from the newspapers," Olivia declared. To this moment, her brother seemed to have forgotten the meeting by the hedgerow. Olivia rushed on in hope of burying his comment. "Mr. Quince will not have dirty wool, of course. Our miller will pay for only the whitest of fleeces. For myself, I am inclined to continue our practice as we always have—though certainly it would be simpler to shear the sheep without the laborious process of washing them. Did

I tell you my order failed to arrive at the lye maker in Leeds, Mama? But he made enough for us anyway, and Mr. Tupper fetched it."

Quickly, Olivia dipped her head and took a long sip of tea. Her mother had fallen silent, and for once, Olivia was grateful for the sherry. Perhaps it already had muddled Lady Chatham's brain enough this afternoon that she would forget Clive's outburst.

"Do pass the tarts, please," Olivia told her brother.

Clive was swinging his feet against the floor—*bang, bang, bang.* He could never be still. Grabbing a tart with his sticky fingers, he thrust it at Olivia.

"Pass the *plate,* Clive," she admonished him. "Honestly, can you remember none of the manners you were taught?"

"You said to pass the tarts, so I did. I did what you said. You told me to pass the tarts. Did she not, Mama? She said that. To pass the tarts, not the plate! The tarts!"

"Enough, Clive!" Olivia cried.

"Stop it!" Lady Chatham covered her ears. "Stop shouting, both of you! My head has been breaking all morning, and now I come to tea, and you both shriek!"

Olivia reached for the post. "Shall I read your letters, Mama? I see we have heard from the Berridges again."

Her mother leaned her head back on the chair and closed her eyes. "Oh, it is good to have a minister who cares for his flock! Yes, indeed, read me their letter, Olivia, for I am in dire need of spiritual sustenance."

"What about this packet?" Clive cut in. "Will you not open this packet, Livie? Here it is! Open it at once!"

Olivia barely caught the paper-wrapped package as he

tossed it at her. Tied in brown string, the packet was directed to her—though it bore no return address. She had hardly begun to untie the string when Clive ripped away the brown paper and jerked out a great billowing length of soft white sarcenet embroidered entirely in pale blue roses. A second packet within the first contained yards of narrow blue silk ribbon and an equal quantity of white lace.

Olivia gasped, knowing at once who had sent the fabric. Lord Thorne—and the hue of the lovely ribbon exactly matched his blue eyes! Her heart swelled even as her mind raced for a way to explain to her mother this unexpected gift.

Then Clive snatched up the ribbon and began to race around the room, holding it high as it fluttered and looped behind him. "It is mine; it is mine!" he cried.

"Stop, Clive!" Olivia sprang to her feet. "Bring that back! It is not yours—it is mine!"

"I like it! It is my favorite thing. Oh, please, Livie, give it to me!"

"No, you cannot have it!" She leapt for it and caught the end. "The fabric was given to me for a new gown, and I mean to trim it with the blue ribbon!"

Clive burst into tears as Olivia began winding the ribbon around her hand. Wailing loudly, he fell onto the floor and threw himself about, banging into table legs and toppling a chair.

Frightened, Olivia cast the ribbon onto the settee and dropped to her knees at her brother's side. "Calm yourself, Clive!" she cried. "Good heavens, you may have the ribbon. You may have it!"

"I want the ribbon!" he screamed, turning red and shaking with rage. "I want a packet! I want blue ribbon!"

"You may have the blue ribbon, Clive." Olivia ran her hand over his hot forehead. "There, now. Calm yourself. There is no need for such shouting."

"But I wah-wah-want blue ribbon," he sobbed.

"Oh, my head!" Lady Chatham got to her feet, swaying as she held her temples. "My head is breaking!"

"Mama, I beg you to sit down." Olivia left her weeping brother and hurried to the elderly woman who tottered toward the door. "Mama, come back. Let us have tea together. We shall all sip quietly and speak of the weather."

"My dear girl. How tormented I am! Do you see it? Day upon day, hour upon hour." Lady Chatham allowed Olivia to lead her back to the settee. "Oh, how I longed for a son. Instead, God has visited this monster upon me. This imp from the bowels of perdition!"

"Mama, do not speak so of Clive. Your son is weak-minded, that is all. He is not evil, and I beg you never to say such a thing again."

"Weak-minded? No, indeed, for you see how he behaves."

"He behaves badly, but that does not make him a monster." Olivia seated her mother and returned to her brother, who had curled up on the floor with the blue ribbon wound around himself from head to toe. He seemed to be asleep. She patted his head, let out a breath, and sat down again. "Such a rainy day," she commented, reaching for her teacup.

"Very bleak." Lady Chatham sipped her sherry, then leaned her head back and closed her eyes.

"Blue ribbon," Clive murmured. "It is mine."

For more than a minute, they sat in silence. Olivia's tea had gone cold, but she hardly cared. At least for this moment, they had peace. At a knock on the door, she stood and walked on tiptoe to discover Mr. Tupper in the corridor outside the drawing room. The steward made a deep bow and then beckoned to speak with her in private.

"Mr. Tupper, I thought you were gone into Otley already," she whispered as she stepped into the hall. "Were you not to speak to Mr. Quince this afternoon about the delay with our washing?"

"Yes, madam, but I felt I must impart some news to you first." He rubbed the back of his neck. "The lye. It has come."

"I know, Mr. Tupper." Concerned for his declining mental prowess, she laid a hand on his arm. "You brought the lye from Leeds yesterday, sir. The shepherds are washing the sheep even now."

"But there is lye at the gate, madam. More lye." He shifted uncomfortably. "I wonder, Miss Hewes, if perhaps you misdirected the original order."

"Misdirected it?"

"You sent an order to Leeds, but our lye maker did not receive it. Now, a quantity of lye has come, yet it is not from our lye maker."

"Who sent it?" Even as she spoke the words, Olivia felt the answer wash over. "Oh, dear!"

"I thought so. You must have sent the order to another lye maker, madam. But not to worry. We shall store this for next year's washing."

"How long has it been at the gate?"

"For more than two hours, madam, and I have spent that

much time trying to trace its source. It appeared there, and no one saw the man or the wagon that brought it. It does not even have a note to say it is intended for us. I thought it might have been meant for someone else, you see. I wondered if perhaps it was the Bowdens' lye. Or . . . or the Thornes'."

Olivia tried to prevent herself from flushing at the look in her steward's gray eyes. "It is certainly . . . certainly a good thing to have spare lye." She forced a smile to her lips. "We shall not have to worry at all next year."

"But how are we to pay for two orders of lye, madam?" He stared at her. "We shall have to pay for this one when asked."

"Was there no charge sent with the lye?"

"None at all. It appears almost as though it were a gift. I cannot determine its source. Unless you would have any knowledge of the matter?"

Olivia swallowed. "I am sure without a note of charge, we cannot know at present who sent it. Can we, Mr. Tupper?"

"No, indeed. Certainly not. Though it would not be wise to find ourselves in any sort of debt . . . to anyone."

"Of course not. I shall see if I can locate the source of this lye and see that it gets to the proper owner."

"That would be wise, madam." He nodded. "Chatham connections have always been reliable and trustworthy. Breaking tradition, stepping into unknown quarters . . . one might find oneself among the enemy, Miss Hewes."

"Yes, sir."

"One can never be too careful."

"Of course not." She curtsied. "Do greet Mr. Quince on my behalf. Tell him our flocks are very fine this year."

As the steward made his way down the corridor to the

foyer, Olivia leaned against the wall and let out a deep breath. Mr. Tupper had no doubt of the lye's source. And who else knew? Her conversation with Lord Thorne at the hedgerow must be common knowledge, and it would not be long before her mother became aware of it.

At the same time as her stomach churned with fear and worry, Olivia's heart soared. He had not even received her letter, and he had sent the lye! And such a glorious fabric for her gown! How could any man—especially one as ill used by her as Lord Thorne had been—behave so gallantly? She had insulted his offer to pay for her gown by insisting that he supply her with lye instead. Now he had done both. It was too much!

Tears clouded her eyes as she pressed her hand against her heart. She had prayed for lye, and God had given it to her—twice! She had prayed for hope and help and joy, and they came to her in the form of a man she must never see again.

And oh, such a man! How could she forget the stance he had taken on the rock ledge—his shoulders so broad, his boots so firm upon the stone, and his greatcoat drifting at his ankles? He had spoken to Clive with friendly words—words of genuine interest rather than revulsion. But his manner with Olivia had been the gentlest of all.

How could she bear never to see him again? Yet she must bear it. Any knowledge of a connection between them would destroy her business relationships. Mr. Tupper could not have spoken more plainly on that account.

Worse, the very thought of her daughter in conversation with a Thorne would surely put Lady Chatham on her deathbed. And what would become of Clive if Olivia were to send

Chatham manor into further turmoil? The young man must be cared for, and Olivia would have that responsibility all her life. She must think clearly and not allow the smallest hope of happiness to misdirect her thoughts.

"Olivia, dearest!" Lady Chatham's voice from the drawing room was filled with despair. "Do come back and see to your brother. He is chewing on the ribbon, and he has got blue dye all over his face!"

Olivia's shoulders sank. "Yes, Mama."

~ Four ~

"YOU HAVE GONE TOO FAR, Randolph!" William Sherbourne laid down his cards and pushed back from the table. "You sent the Chathams our lye?"

"I have just told you that, brother. There is no need to repeat it." Randolph stood and walked to the hearth. "Miss Hewes mentioned to me that her order had not arrived, and as we had plenty, I sent our surplus to her. It is no crime. As it is, our wool will arrive at Quince's worsted mill well before theirs."

"But Miss Hewes is a Chatham!"

"William, I am well aware of her lineage."

"Does anyone mean to play at whist?" Beatrice Bryse spoke up. "Or is our game at a sudden end?"

"I beg your pardon, Miss Bryse," Randolph said. "I have little patience for cards tonight."

"No, I see your thoughts are elsewhere." The young woman gathered up the cards. She and her sister excused themselves from the table and joined their brother by the fire. "Miss Hewes, I believe, has captured all your attention."

"You mistake me, madam."

"Oh?"

Randolph cleared his throat. "In fact, I am much occupied with the lecture to be given by William Buckland in a week's time. Reverend Berridge called on me this morning to discuss the situation. The members of the Otley Gentlemen's Club invited Buckland to speak at the Assembly Hall, and our minister is most concerned. With the current tensions in the church, we agree it can do no good for anyone to hear the lecture. And yet, I am certain the meeting will be well attended."

"Does Mr. Buckland not speak merely of fossils?" Beatrice asked. "I have heard he rides about on a poor black mare heavily loaded with bags of rocks. I should think anyone who listens to his lecture must find it amusing rather than scandalous."

"Buckland does not hold to a literal interpretation of the book of Genesis," Randolph explained. "He calls himself a Christian and is most eager to defend the Creation. And yet, to some his views are considered heresy. I should like to find a way to prevent his coming."

"You are influential enough for that, I should think," William said. "Unless your flirtations with Miss Hewes have caused you to lose all sense of propriety."

Randolph glared at his younger brother. "Upon my word, William, I am hardly flirting with the woman. You observed my offense against her yourself. I tore her gown."

"Yes, and hardly had it happened before you sprinted away to Otley to comb the shops in search of the most costly fabric you could find to replace it."

"It *was* a lovely cloth," Beatrice said. "I should have been very happy to have it myself. Miss Hewes must be greatly in your debt now."

"In my debt?" Randolph turned on the woman. "How can you say such a thing? I was in her debt, and now I have discharged my duty."

"And how do you reconcile the gift of our lye?" William grumbled. "I am most eager to hear this."

"I have no need to defend my action to you, brother. I am Baron Sherbourne of Thorne, and I do what I think is right."

"Your action will be taken very poorly by your associates, I assure you," William predicted. "And do not suppose you can keep it quiet. Nothing in these parts is a secret for long."

"If I intended to make it a secret, would I have mentioned it just now at cards?" Randolph let out a hot breath. "As I see it, this endless enmity with the Chatham family has done us no good whatsoever."

"To say the least! We lost our dear father at their hand."

"We do not know this for certain, William. We *suppose* it—just as we *suppose* everything about them. Are you aware that the so-called idiot brother can speak as clearly as you and I? He and his sister were fishing last week near the hedgerow—"

"You spoke to him? to young Lord Chatham?"

"Honestly, William, open your eyes. The Chathams are humans and not so different from us."

"Indeed?" William stalked across the room toward his brother. "Is this how you mean to manage our father's manor? Do you intend to toss out every relationship, every value, every belief that our family has held dear for generation upon generation? Aye, the Chathams are human, but they are given to the vilest evils known to man. We have countless records of our dealings with them—endless accounts of poisoned sheep and fields sown with weeds and cutthroat dealings at the worsted mill. Not to mention the list of unexplained deaths, including the shooting of our dear father!"

"Do you know that Clive Hewes related just such a litany of crimes supposedly committed by Thornes?"

"He is an imbecile!"

"Whatever he is, it is clear they think as ill of us as we do of them. When will it end, William?"

"Never!" The young man balled his fists and appeared eager to punch his brother on the nose. "What good could it do us to make peace? We have our business partnerships, and they have theirs. If suddenly we became friendly neighbors, what do you suppose would happen? All the tradesmen who have relied upon our commerce and fixed their prices accordingly would rush to the Chathams to see if they could get more money for their goods. Chatham allies would resent us even more than they already do, and ours would be at our gates howling in protest at the insupportable situation. It would create havoc, Randolph."

"It is havoc now. The whole town has been forced to choose sides. Families must invite either us or the Chathams to balls and dinners—but certainly not both at the same time. A tradesman with a desirable product must sell either to us or to them. Under normal circumstances, he could do business with both of our families and thereby expand his trade. But our relations with the Chathams are anything but normal. And we are the poorer for it. Upon my word, William, we hardly dare even look at that family! Heaven forbid we should speak to them. Even the church is divided down the middle by this conflict. Our friends sit on the west, theirs on the east. Can you imagine what God thinks of this buffoonery?"

"Indeed I can. God has ordained the Thorne family to leadership both in business and in personal transactions in Otley."

"Really, William? And on which Scripture do you base this belief?"

"It is common knowledge that the Thorne family is to set an example of right living and fair trade. This is a holy endowment, Randolph, and as eldest brother, you have been given stewardship over it. If you wish to bring Scripture into the Thornes versus the Chathams, recall the words of St. Paul to the Corinthians: 'Be ye not unequally yoked together with unbelievers: for what fellowship hath righteousness with unrighteousness? and what communion hath light with darkness?' We are to come out from among them and be separate. Only then will God receive us."

"Well said, Mr. Sherbourne!" The younger Miss Bryse clapped her hands. "Brilliantly put."

"I agree, of course," her brother said. Captain Bryse had been reading beside the fire, but now he put down his book. "Thorne, you cannot reasonably flaunt years of tradition. These traditions evolved because they were found to work best—and they always will. The neighboring family clearly has nothing but ill intent toward yours. You would do well to set aside your interest in Miss Hewes and turn your attention to other matters. Why not go to town? We could all stay in London together, in fact, for you would find our society there most diverting."

"Oh, brother, what a lovely idea!" Beatrice Bryse exclaimed. "I should so love to return to town. Come, Lord

Thorne, surely you find the country a bit dull. Caroline, is this not a marvelous idea? And Mr. Sherbourne, you must come, too. Certainly, the navy can spare you another month at least. You will see to it, brother, will you not?"

"Of course." Captain Bryse nodded at Randolph. "Your father's death warrants as much time as necessary for mourning and recovery. Thorne, do say you will join your brother in town. You must both stay at our house, and my sisters and I would be pleased to introduce you to our friends. I assure you, the change of setting will do you great good."

Randolph could hardly believe the naivete of the Bryses. But his brother would understand perfectly. "I thank you, Captain Bryse," Randolph said, "but I am much needed here. The shearing has begun already, and soon it will be time to take the fleece to the worsted mill. And of course, my crops have just been planted."

"Oh, dear!" Beatrice took out her handkerchief, and her sister hurried to her side. "I cannot bear to think of you here, sir, suffering so. And all alone."

"I mourn my father's death, Miss Bryse," he said, "but I am quite content to continue my solitary sojourn at Thorne Lodge. I belong on the moorland with the heather to line my pathways and the staff and livestock to keep me company. Here is where I am likeliest to find solace for my grief. Though I enjoyed the society in London while studying at Cambridge, I could not have been happier to return to the country. I thank you for your invitation, Captain Bryse, but I must decline."

"Randolph, honestly," William said. "Why do you delight in making everyone as miserable as you? Look at the ladies—both of them weeping over your rebuff. How I wish Edmund were here to talk some sense into you. You always listened to him."

"Were Edmund here," Randolph said, "our brother would urge me toward duty."

"I disagree. Edmund himself cares nothing for duty. As second eldest, he should be here at Thorne Lodge, preparing to take control of the manor if you are unable. Instead, he has taken himself off to India and rarely bothers to write to tell us if he is even alive."

"Our brother has placed duty to God far above duty to man, William. I forgive his failure to write more often, and were Edmund to come to harm, I am certain we should hear of it at once."

"How should we hear of it?" William demanded. "He lives in a village in the middle of nowhere. He has no wife or family, no friends, no one to write us but himself. He could be eaten by a tiger or poisoned by a snake or stricken with cholera, and we might never hear of it for years!"

"Or murdered by the Chathams," Randolph added. "Perhaps their long arm of villainy reaches all the way to India."

William planted his hands on his hips. "To be sure, Randolph, now you make light even of our father's death!"

"Absolutely not. You know very well I have done all in my power to investigate the incident. As difficult as it is to accept, William, we must try. Father died by accident."

"Impossible! He was an excellent huntsman. He always took prodigious care with his weapons, and he taught us to do the same. I cannot believe his gun discharged accidentally as the coroner ruled. Someone killed him—and I have little doubt the assassin was hired by the Chatham family!"

"Do be reasonable, William. How would Father's death benefit them? They knew I was prepared and of age to take his place. Beyond our own grief, we have suffered nothing. Our finances, our manor, our business alliances all remain as they were. No indeed, the Chathams can have no motive for murder."

"Can they not?" Captain Bryse spoke up. "If the tales I have heard on my sojourn here are true, I believe the Chatham family is bent on malicious destruction. They appear to act with random violence. But even if this were not such an indiscriminate event, your father's death certainly could be chalked up to revenge. The years of enmity between your families would provide reason enough for them to wish the death of any man who bears the title Baron Thorne. Indeed, if I were you, sir, I should watch my back."

Randolph turned to the fire, dismayed that a man he had known for a month should be so intimate with the hatred that had plagued his family for centuries. Was this the reputation of the Thornes? Were they known not for the quality of their wool, the care of their tenants, or the bounty of their harvests, but for generations of malevolence?

Was he duty bound, as head of this family, to continue to promote animosity with his neighbor? to suspect that every mishap to befall him occurred at the hand of the Chathams? to fear that at any moment he might fall victim to their treachery? Was this the only legacy of his ancestors' lives?

"As a Christian," Randolph said, turning to his brother and speaking evenly, "I am determined to follow Christ's teaching to love my neighbor as I love myself. As greatly as it pains me, I shall accept that our father's death was a tragic accident and that no one is to blame for it. I shall beware the Chathams, of course, but I shall not instigate ill will between our two families. I refuse to believe that a young woman with a sick mother, an immature brother, and an entire manor to oversee would take the time and trouble to murder my father. And until I am proven wrong, I shall give no credit to such accusations. Moreover, I shall not tolerate rumormongering in this household. Have I made myself clear?"

William lifted his chin. "Indeed you have, brother. It is clear you are so addled that I cannot trust you alone here for one day. I shall stay on at Thorne Lodge until your infatuation with Miss Hewes is at an end and I am convinced that you have regained your sanity."

"Miss Hewes is nothing to me, William! I have seen her as she is and not as I believed her to be. She is not a monster, not an ill-formed and evil demon birthed from the bowels of perdition. She is merely a young woman—a lady who is kind to her brother, who speaks with the greatest of gentility, and who bears a burden heavier than either you or I have ever known."

"You are besotted!" William cried.

"It is too true," Beatrice chimed in. "Smitten! One glance at the lovely creature, and his heart was lost forever. I see it as a hopeless matter, Mr. Sherbourne. Your brother is in love with Miss Hewes, and there is nothing to be done about it."

Randolph could scarcely believe his houseguest's gall. In love? What utter nonsense. Pure tripe.

"Miss Bryse," he said, "until you know me better, I beg you to refrain from making judgments about the condition of my heart."

"Is that a challenge, my lord?" She rose, her pale blue eyes sliding to meet his. "Do you dare me to know you better? For I confess, I am most eager to learn the condition of your heart."

At this, the others in the room began to chuckle. Randolph felt the tension ease, and he made her a genteel bow. "As you wish, Miss Bryse, though you may find my heart rather full at the moment. And the one who occupies it is not Miss Hewes."

"Ah," she murmured. "Might one inquire the name of the lady who rules your heart, sir?"

"It is not a lady at all, madam. As William can tell you, my heart for quite some time has been filled to capacity with the presence of God."

"God?" Her sculpted eyebrows lifted.

"He teases you, Miss Bryse," William said. "Randolph and Edmund fancy themselves modern-day monks, if you will. They are wholly devoted to Scripture reading and prayer and tedious discussions of doctrine. Edmund has gone off to be a missionary, while Randolph has converted Thorne Lodge into his own personal hermitage. I am surprised he does not shave his head and wear a brown robe."

"Enough, William," Randolph said, grinning at the caricature. "I am not so holy as that."

"No indeed, for I recall there was a time when you greatly enjoyed the pleasures of this world—including the company of lovely ladies. I have confidence that the right woman, with the right sort of persuasion, will soon set you to rights."

"That is welcome news," Beatrice said. "We must resolve to make a search for this perfect woman."

"I wish you all the best," Randolph said. "For now, duty calls. I must send the servants home and see the house locked up. And thence to my humble cell to read my Bible."

"Oh!" Beatrice turned to William with a laugh. "A monk indeed!"

"Off with you, then, brother. Meditate on your Scriptures and pray over the wisdom of making peace with the Chathams. The Bryses and I, meanwhile, shall plot the restoration of your right mind."

Randolph gave them a departing bow and made his way across the room to the hall. Though he wished William and his guests would leave at once for London or Portsmouth or any other city in the realm, he would endure them as best he could. He loved his brother and could tolerate the Bryses with little difficulty. It would not be long before he convinced them of his disinterest in their scheming, gossiping, and attempts at merrymaking. And he had no doubt they soon must concede his complete indifference toward Miss Hewes.

As Randolph climbed the stairs, he wondered if that young woman might attend church again this Sunday. Would she be wearing the fabric he had sent? Might she thank him for the lye? Perhaps he should make it a point to ask if she had received it.

He did not like to make her uncomfortable, but he wanted to speak to her just the same, for it would do well to reveal his intentions of peace before the whole town. And Miss Hewes would see that he bore her no ill will. They might talk as acquaintances. Friends. Nothing more or less. He would doff his hat, and she would smile and look into his face. And her cheeks might flush that pretty shade of pink . . . and her hand might flutter to her throat . . . and her brown eyes might meet his and set his heart to pounding, just as it pounded now, even at the thought of her.

"Upon my word, Mother, it cannot be wise for you to go out this evening." Olivia gripped her reticule as Lady Chatham descended the stairs to the foyer. "You are not well, and I am perfectly capable of attending the lecture—"

"Silence, girl!" The woman held her closed fan outstretched like a sword and regarded her daughter with rheumy brown eyes. "Reverend Porridge called on me yesterday . . . and . . . and . . ."

"His name is Reverend Berridge!" Olivia hurried forward as the dowager staggered down the last few steps and swayed out onto the marble floor. "Oh, Mama, please, you are not fit to go out!"

"Not fit? Not fit?"

"Unwell is what I mean. You are too ill. Please return to your room, I beg you!"

"No, I shall not be moved." Lady Chatham set her jaw. Leaning heavily on her daughter's arm, she made her way to the front door. "I shall hear that heretic and have my say in the matter. I was asked by the mister . . . the mister . . ."

"The minister."

"Partridge—"

"Berridge!"

Olivia blinked back tears of desperation as her mother tottered toward the door. Lady Chatham had been at the sherry all afternoon and did not appear at dinner. Believing her mother had forgotten about the lecture by William Buckland on this night, Olivia had ordered a carriage and then bathed and dressed herself.

She was eager to escape the house, for Clive had been out of sorts all day. At teatime, he had thrown such a tantrum that Olivia had been forced to lock him in his room to prevent his coming to harm. Looking forward to an evening in the company of friends, she had dressed in the new gown stitched from the fabric Lord Thorne had sent her. With her brother asleep and her mother resting quietly, she had felt lovely and calm and eager for a change of pace. Now she saw this was not to be.

"Berries?" her mother said. "What an odd name."

"Berridge—oh, please, Mama, can I not persuade you to stay at home? I shall come to your room directly from the lecture and report all that has been said."

"No, indeed, for the important thing is to make an appearance. To be seen. We are Chathams, and we must be sheen!"

"Oh, dear heaven!" Olivia stood back in dismay as the footman assisted Lady Chatham into the carriage. There was no hope for it. They would go out in public, and all would be revealed. Olivia's efforts to protect the family reputation must come to naught. Everyone would see! Everyone would know!

Feeling as though she were suffocating, Olivia took her place in the carriage. She must come up with an excuse for her mother's behavior. She would have no choice but to lie. She would say that Lady Chatham was ill and that the apothecary had given her a strong new medicine this very morning. She would say that although her mother felt terribly unwell, her call to duty ruled supreme, as always.

"What is his name?" Lady Chatham asked. "The man giving the lecture?"

"William Buckland," Olivia replied. "He speaks on fossils."

"On what?"

"Fossils. Bones of animals."

"Nasty thing to talk on! Why should anyone want to listen to that?"

"I believe he has made several noteworthy discoveries. He is reputed to be a great man of science."

The carriage had begun its journey to Otley, and Olivia knew any thought of preventing her mother from attending the lecture must be put away. She abhorred the idea that her friends and acquaintances would see Lady Chatham in this state. No doubt Mr. Bowden would admonish the gathering with Scriptures reviling drunkenness. The Baines would gawk in disbelief. Oh, it would be too horrid! Panic clutched at Olivia's chest, twisting and choking her.

Perhaps when they arrived at the Assembly Hall, she could simply step out of the carriage and run away. Run all the way home to Chatham Hall and hide in her room. Or maybe she should put out her foot and trip her mother. A fall would explain away any nonsense Lady Chatham might talk, and everyone would be so solicitous that they would never mention the odor of sherry on her breath. But for Olivia to harm her own mother? Was that right?

"Reverend Parish says this man is a heretic," Lady Chatham spoke up.

"Berridge, Mama. Our minister's name is Berridge. And he does not say that William Buckland is a heretic, for he has never heard the man speak. Rather, he fears that Mr. Buckland may speak heresy—or that he may be perceived to speak heresy—or . . . oh, who can say! And how can it matter when . . . when all is so very abominable!"

"No, no, you mustn't worry, dearest." Her mother patted her hand. "I spoke with Mr. Quince, and all is well."

"Mr. Quince?"

"About the wool. Our wool. He is going to help us."

Olivia let out a breath of frustration. "We were talking of Reverend Berridge."

"No, but you said all is abob . . . abomid . . ."

"Abominable."

"Yes, and I am telling you that you have nothing to dread. I spoke to Mr. Quince about the wool. We have made an agreement."

"What sort of agreement? When did you speak to him?"

"Long ago. We worked it all out with Mr. Tupper!"

"Mama, what can you mean? Why was I not told of this meeting?"

"Calm yourself, dearest. Honestly, Olivia, you are too worried about everything."

"Indeed I am, and for good reason." Her breath came in shallow gasps. She hated to speak the truth. Somehow she hoped that keeping silent would make it all untrue. But now she knew she must say what was on her heart. "Mama, I am most dismayed that you have been drinking sherry!"

"Of course I have. Everyone drinks sherry after dinner."

"But you have been drinking all day."

"All day? Nonsense! I had only a sip or two to calm my nerves. My head is so painful these days, you know, my dear."

"Yes, Mama. I know."

"What a lovely night!" She straightened to peer out the window as the carriage rolled to a stop in front of the Assembly Hall. "It is too bad we must spend it listening to a heretic!"

Olivia gulped down her anguish as the dowager descended to the street. The Assembly Hall was well lit with candles, and several horses and carriages lined the entrance to the building. Many of the townspeople already had entered and taken seats, but more than enough stood outside to witness a calamity.

Scanning the crowd for friend and foe, Olivia stepped down and hurried to her mother's side. She must take Lady Chatham's arm. She must tell everyone about the apothecary and the new medicine. She must be calm and sensible and—

"Miss Hewes, good evening." The deep voice at her ear sent the blood to Olivia's knees. "You are looking lovely tonight."

She turned, and it was he. "Lord Thorne."

"I see that you received my packet."

"Sir?" She must find her mother. Lady Chatham could not be allowed to—

"Your gown. It is made from the fabric I sent."

"Oh yes. Thank you so much, sir. But I—"

"And the lye? Did you receive it?"

"Yes, indeed. My order arrived from Leeds, however, and I shall return yours."

"Certainly not. You must keep it against any unforeseen future shortages." He was smiling, his blue eyes bright in the moonlight. He had doffed his hat, and his hair moved against his ears in the slight breeze. "I looked for you in church last Sunday. Did you not see me?"

"No, sir. I was . . . much occupied with . . ." She let out a breath. "You sit in the west, sir."

"Do you never look west, Miss Hewes?"

"Not in church."

"It is rather much like the east, you would find. In fact, both halves of the church are quite identical—save several paintings. You view the holy Nativity, while we regard the Resurrection."

"Ah."

Now he laughed, and it was a round and happy sound. "I cannot think the builder had any idea of creating east and west to be any different. Indeed, it is not the least bit frightening to permit one's vision to stray across the center aisle. You must try it sometime, Miss Hewes."

"I shall," she said. "If Thorne and Chatham are speaking . . . how can it be wrong to look?"

"There! My thoughts exactly." He gave her a bow. "Enjoy the lecture, Miss Hewes. I am given to understand that we may be treated to quite a display of rocks."

As he walked away, she bit her lip to keep from giggling. The swelling in her heart was pinched shut, however, when she spied her mother attempting to climb the steps to the front door of the hall. Gracious! In half an instant, she could be lying on her back in the street.

Gathering up her skirts, Olivia rushed ahead, edging past Lord Thorne and the entire Bowden clan. Just in time to prevent disaster, she slipped an arm around her mother.

"There you are, Olivia!" Lady Chatham said. "I wondered where you had got to. But I was speaking to our new mister . . . minstrel . . ."

"Minister," Olivia whispered.

"Reverend Porridge," she muttered. "Such a nice man."

Five

RANDOLPH HAD EXPECTED to do no more than endure the lecture. After all, he had little interest in fossils, and he dreaded the potential controversy William Buckland might bring to Otley. His brother and the three Bryses, moreover, had insisted on accompanying him—and they had made it clear their purpose was to ridicule every word spoken and every person in attendance at the event. Yet despite these discomforts, Randolph discovered a great many things to occupy his interest during the evening.

William Buckland proved himself quite the showman, for he had brought with him a number of specimens, large-scale geological maps, and brightly colored diagrams. A young man at only twenty-nine, Buckland introduced himself by stating that he had graduated from Oxford in 1805. Now a professor of geology at that university, he had spent the years from 1808 to 1812 making frequent geological excursions on horseback to various parts of England, Scotland, Ireland, and Wales. He also had taken several journeys to the Continent for purpose of research and study.

This very year, Buckland informed his audience, he had been appointed Reader of Mineralogy and had taken residence on the ground floor of the Old Ashmolean Building on Broad Street in London. In addition, he became the unofficial curator of the museum on the upper floor of the Ashmolean, and he gave lectures and private instruction to everyone who traveled there to meet him.

Though Randolph could not help but respect the man's education and position, he found Buckland's outlandish attire more than a little amusing. Not only did the professor make a spectacle of himself in his way of dressing, but his behavior during the lecture grew flagrantly silly. He repeatedly grasped a specimen from his display and leapt toward his onlookers with shouted queries. "What do you see here, sir?" he would demand, or "Madam, upon what do you now gaze?"—and he would thrust a craggy fossil at an audience member in menacing fashion.

The listeners, who were seated on rows of chairs in the candlelit room, would fall back with shocked gasps. Without waiting for a response, the scientist answered his own question with a cry such as, "Why, it is a hyena's jaw, of course!" Then he would hold high the specimen for everyone to admire and applaud as though it were a crown jewel.

Randolph found the fellow amusing enough, as Buckland stalked around the assembly room in imitation of the gait of a giant bird he believed had left fossilized footprints across England and the Continent. He related an interesting account of his exploration of Kirkdale Cave, in which he said he had found a variety of vertebrates, including hyena, elephant, rhinoceros, hippopotamus, bear, and fox.

But it was not Buckland's posturing antics or entertaining anecdotes that concerned Randolph. It was his ideas.

Before beginning his tenure as a teacher, Buckland had studied theology and had taken holy orders. During his lecture, this vicar-cum-scientist took great pains to espouse his faith in Jesus Christ and his reliance on the Bible as the word of God. He gave the sloth, both living and extinct species, as a prominent example of divine design. He used descriptions based on a megatherium skeleton found near Buenos Aires in 1789 to further support his position. But the scientific ideas he set forth caused murmurs of protest to ripple through the room more than once.

These angry whispers were warranted, in Randolph's opinion. As the scientist pressed on with his theories, it became clear that Buckland did not hold to a literal interpretation of the Creation as described in the biblical book of Genesis, especially in terms of geologic time. Other topics he touched on held great potential for controversy also. While pointing out evidence of the flood that occurred in the time of Noah, Buckland stated that this deluge was actually the last in a series of catastrophes that had befallen the earth. Indeed, he believed he could prove that one such catastrophe occurred when a thick layer of ice crept over every inch of land and sea! This ice, according to the scientist, had killed many of the world's creatures, just as the flood had done.

The enthusiastic Buckland went so far as to promote the field of coprology—the study of fossilized animal waste! The mention of such a distasteful subject before the women in attendance brought a frown to Randolph's face.

One lady in particular had captured his eye, and her

response to Buckland's lecture riveted Randolph's attention. Miss Olivia Hewes had taken a seat only two rows in front of him and just five seats to the east. Again, Randolph knew a sense of wonderment as he realized that the lovely creature had attended lectures and exhibitions in this very hall her entire life—as had he—and yet he had never taken notice of her in all these years. The Thorne family customarily occupied the western portion of every gathering place in Otley, while the Chathams always took the east. Randolph's mother had taught him from infancy never to look over *there,* as though he might be stricken senseless if he did!

Stricken senseless, indeed. Randolph realized that his mother had been correct, though not in the way he once had feared. As though bound to Miss Hewes by an invisible cord, he found that he could hardly keep his attention from the young lady. In fact, her every move enchanted him.

The moment she entered the room with her mother, she removed her pale blue velvet pelisse and passed it to her footman, who carried it away for safekeeping. As William Buckland began to prance about with his beloved fossils, Randolph took note that Miss Hewes's seamstress had fashioned an exquisite gown from the white sarcenet fabric he had sent her. Its discreetly scooped neckline revealed enough of the lady's pale shoulder to allure but not enough to cause improper temptation. And yet he was tempted, Randolph admitted. Tempted to gaze on her and no one else. Tempted to stare in fascination at the gentle curls that caressed her cheeks. Tempted to dwell on the pillowed softness of her lips and the flutter of her long dark lashes.

Determined to concentrate on Buckland's speech, Randolph

repeatedly forced his attention to the front of the room. But no sooner did Miss Hewes lift a hand to touch one of the embroidered blue flowers on her puffed sleeve than Randolph found himself staring at her again. She kept her focus squarely on the lecturer, however, and no amount of wishful thinking on Randolph's part could force her to turn that pretty head in his direction. He willed her to glance over her shoulder at him. He even prayed that God would draw her to look his way. But her eyes remained steadily fixed on Buckland, and Randolph was left to fret over whether she even recalled his presence on the same flooded, iced, and fossilized planet as herself.

At Buckland's mention of his study of animal waste, Randolph made to stand and call for a dismissal of the lecture. Enough was enough. But at that moment, the scientist deemed it time for an intermission. After announcing a half-hour break, he invited his audience to approach the table on which he displayed his precious collection of fossils. He offered yet another collection for sale—each piece listed at what seemed to Randolph an exorbitant price.

As the crowd pushed to the front of the room, elbowing for a closer look and attempting to form themselves into a queue, Randolph rose. He hoped that he might edge his way toward Miss Hewes and even—if God willed it—address her mother. He would like to ask after Lady Chatham's health, for he believed such solicitousness would draw attention from Buckland's incendiary ideas and train it on the prospect of peace between the two leading families in the town. But Miss Hewes kept her arm firmly linked through her mother's as she turned her back on the Thorne party and stepped toward a group of acquaintances.

"I am for home," William spoke up, giving an indiscreet yawn as he stood to join his brother and the Bryses. "Mr. Buckland is entertaining, I grant you, but I have had more than my fill of his fossils."

"I find him low," Beatrice Bryse opined. "What does he mean by leaping about the room and shouting at us? By reputation, he is highly educated, yet he is no gentleman. Indeed, he behaves little better than a common showman."

"Like those horrid monsters we saw at the traveling museum, sister?" Caroline Bryse shuddered and reached for William's arm. "Oh, Mr. Sherbourne, you would have been greatly offended at that spectacle. There was a wolf woman on display, her face and arms covered in long dark fur. And the elephant man! Dear me, his skin was all bumpy and his head swollen like . . . like . . ."

"It was a mistake to go," Beatrice said, "for Caroline has never recovered from it. And I fear this is much the same sort of thing. The man will give us all nightmares. Hyenas roaming about in the caves of England? Appalling thought!"

"I am more concerned about Mr. Buckland's views on Holy Scripture," Randolph said. "And I cannot agree to depart this hall until we have heard him out to the bitter end."

"I cannot think that anyone here cares in the least about floods and ice ages." William frowned at his brother. "But, of course, you would give your whole attention to them."

"Lord Thorne does not give his whole attention to Mr. Buckland's lecture," Beatrice said coyly. "I noticed his eyes wandering rather often toward the visage of the lovely Miss Hewes."

"Then I fear you were failing to give the lecture your own

due concentration, Miss Bryse." Randolph nodded at her. "But you are correct. I am glad to see both Lady Chatham and her daughter in attendance, for their presence here may help to quell any discord in the town. Should trouble arise from Buckland's lecture, both our families must take responsibility to address it."

"And yet, I believe you were noting the fineness of Miss Hewes's new gown more than the presence of the dowager."

"Was I?"

"Indeed you were, sir, for attentive women such as I take note of all these small things. It is a beautiful gown. Extraordinary, in fact. She must have engaged a most accomplished seamstress. And the lace!"

"Lace, yes, but every gown must have lace." Irritated, he turned from her. "William, do you see our footman? I believe we must have some refreshment brought in from the carriage."

"Refreshment!" William Buckland exclaimed as he thrust himself upon their party. "May I offer you a moment of respite in my private chamber? But I forget myself! You are Baron Sherbourne of Thorne, and I am most humbly honored by your presence here tonight, sir." With that, he gave a grand bow.

Randolph responded, though not with equal theatrics. "You are most kind, sir. May I introduce my brother, William Sherbourne? And here is Captain Charles Bryse and his sisters, Miss Bryse and Miss Caroline."

"So pleased to meet you all!" Buckland bowed again.

Very ingratiating, Randolph thought. But to what purpose? He forced a smile. "I thank you for your offer of refreshment, sir, but we have brought with us a basket of tea."

"Tea? Come, something stronger is in order." He beckoned and started for a door near the display, where an assistant did a brisk business peddling fossil specimens. "Come, come! I must hear your thoughts concerning my lecture. Fossils are the thing, you know. Keys, they are! Keys to unlock the great mysteries of creation!"

Randolph briefly scanned the hall and failed to locate Miss Hewes. Lacking that diversion, he decided the opportunity to interview Buckland might prove worthwhile. He followed his brother and the Bryses into a small chamber outfitted with a settee, several chairs, a serviceable carpet, and enough lamps to light the room to satisfaction.

"Now, then, I have secured the finest Bombay gin in the realm," Buckland said, opening a small wooden chest and removing a bottle of clear liquid. "And for the ladies, a dry red wine."

"I do not take strong spirits, thank you," Randolph informed the man when offered a glass. "Tea is more to my liking."

"My brother is religious," William explained. "I fear you may find him tedious, sir."

At titters from the ladies, Buckland shook his head. "Tedious? No indeed, for I myself am a religious man. As you have heard, I am a scientist, and yet I take great pains to understand the earth's secrets in light of our heavenly Creator."

"Yet you do not believe the world to have been created in six days?" Randolph asked.

"Do I not?" Buckland handed Miss Bryse a glass. He lowered his voice only slightly. "You are not pregnant, I hope?"

"Of course not!" She gasped and then giggled. "I am not married, sir."

"In these licentious days, such holy traditions hardly matter to some. You have heard, no doubt, of the immoral behavior of our own Prince Regent. But enough on that. Should you become pregnant, madam, I adjure you never to take a sip of alcohol during the entire length of your confinement. I am recently returned from the Continent, and in France, I was blessed to meet with a brilliant physician. Dr. Lanceraux had read of the gin epidemic here in England in the last century, and he is studying the damaging effects of drink upon the life of the unborn child. As Christians, we should know of this already, for God spoke in the book of Judges, the thirteenth chapter and seventh verse, saying: 'Behold, thou shalt conceive, and bear a son; and now drink no wine nor strong drink.' Lanceraux is a brilliant man, brilliant, and I must tell you, he was most intrigued by my fossils!"

A bemused Randolph studied the scientist. As in his lecture, Buckland rushed from one topic to another, and yet he did appear—in essence—to be an honorable man.

"Well, I am not . . . bearing a child," Beatrice Bryse said, taking a sip of wine. "And I must say, Mr. Buckland, that I find your speech most indelicate. Accomplished ladies such as ourselves are not accustomed to public discussions of . . . of animal waste and . . . and childbearing—"

"I do beg your pardon, dear lady!" Buckland grasped her hand and kissed it firmly. "It is never my intent to insult or offend in any way. I merely aim to educate! To enlighten! To extol the power, wisdom, and goodness of God as manifested in the Creation. To bring the glory of His mighty works into the realm of understanding by the common man!"

"My friends and I are hardly common, sir," she replied, removing her hand.

"No, most certainly not. And may I say again, how very honored I am to find you here tonight."

"We would not consider missing this event," Randolph told him. "I make it a point to acquaint myself with every matter pertaining to Otley and her citizens. I should find it unconscionable to do any less."

"Of course, of course! And I was most fortunate to be introduced by your miller, Mr. Quince, to the Chatham family. Lady Chatham is a fine woman! How blessed is Otley to have two such grand—"

"We do not associate with that family, sir," William cut in. "Chathams and Thornes have no communion."

"Ah." Disappointment draped his animated face like a wet cloth. "I am sorry to hear this. I am well acquainted with controversy, as you may suppose, and I find it most unhappy. Most unhappy, indeed."

"Yet you persist in espousing such fictions as this age of ice," Randolph said. "Your beliefs, it appears, reject biblical literalism. Sir, I find you are tolerant of too much."

"Tolerant?" The man's brow knitted, and he stared at the floor for most of a minute. "I hate to think I am tolerant. I should not like to be tolerant of anything unbiblical. I prefer the word *inquisitive.* Sir, I am searching. Searching for truth—that is all."

"Truth is found in Holy Scripture."

"Oh, to be sure, it is. But must science and Scripture be

exclusive of one another? Because the Bible does not mention an ice catastrophe, can there not have been one?"

"I think not."

"But the Bible does not speak of Otley, either, and we do believe in this town's existence." Buckland grinned and gave a small shrug. "Everything in the Bible is true, sir. But not everything true is in the Bible."

Randolph tapped his fingers on the arm of his chair. "Sir, you tread dangerously close to heresy. There are those in Otley who will agree with you—and those who will not. Shall our town be divided by a man who makes his living by peddling rocks?"

Buckland's shoulders sagged. "It is neither I nor my fossils who would divide your town, sir. It is doctrine. Philosophy. Tradition. Fear makes men cling to what they know and shun the unknown."

"And yet it may be possible to know too much. In your digging and theorizing, you might evolve an idea that is contrary to all holy teaching. Then where will you stand, sir?"

"I do not believe it possible to know too much, my lord. I believe that all knowledge comes from God, and therefore any truth I may uncover will mesh wholly with the teachings of Scripture."

"But with your series of catastrophes, you appear to stretch Creation well beyond the biblical six days."

Buckland took another sip of gin and shuddered as it went down. "I confess—" he squinted at Randolph—"I am not entirely certain about the six days. Six literal days. Twenty-four-hour days, so to speak. In the book of Second Peter, third chapter and eighth verse, it is written, 'Beloved, be not ignorant of this one thing, that one day is with the Lord as a thousand years, and a thousand years as one day.' You see then, sir, that it is possible—"

"Possible, perhaps, but not probable." Randolph stood. "I find it best to take the Word of God as it was written and not ascribe possibilities to it. More important, however, is the necessity of peace among the people of God. And the people I am particularly concerned about are the townsfolk of Otley. My people. Mr. Buckland, I adjure you to refrain from speaking any word here tonight that might be interpreted as heretical. Do I make myself clear?"

Buckland rose and set down his glass. "You are clear, sir. And yet I find it impossible to keep my tongue silent. I delight in giving evidence of design by an all-wise Creator. I must relate my exciting discoveries in the field of geology."

"Geology, yes. Religion, no."

Buckland stared directly into Randolph's eyes for a long moment. "It is difficult to take seriously a man who claims a longing for peace and yet will have no communion with his neighbor."

"I have heard enough," William said. "Come, brother. This man knows nothing of our town or our history. He refuses to hear reason. He clings to his ideas despite their obvious lack of merit. Let us return to Thorne Lodge and take our rest."

"Absolutely not." Randolph squared his shoulders. "I shall stay for the remainder of Mr. Buckland's speech. And if he ventures into questionable waters again, I shall call for his immediate dismissal from the Assembly Hall."

Without addressing the man further, Randolph stood, threw open the door, and stalked from the chamber. His path led straight into the company of a group of ladies, who parted in surprise at his intrusion and left him face-to-face with none other than Miss Olivia Hewes.

"I beg your pardon," he said, feeling suddenly off balance—as though he had stepped to the edge of a cliff without knowing it was there. "I meant no offense."

"No, of course not, sir." She made him a curtsy. "None was taken."

"You are well?" he fumbled. "Enjoying the lecture? Mr. . . . uh . . . Buckland?"

She smiled, clearly amused at his discomfort. *"Enjoyment* may be too strong a word. I shall say I am *intrigued."*

"Randolph!" William barked from a distance. "The ladies await!"

Randolph nodded at his brother, then returned to Miss Hewes. "May I ask what you make of this business of an ice age, madam?"

"Ice and water are in essence the same substance, are they not?" she replied. "I cannot see how Mr. Buckland may declare that he views evidence of flood in one fossil and ice in another. How should he know that the water was frozen during one age and liquid during another? According to his own testimony, both catastrophes occurred long before he was born."

Impressed by her perception, Randolph nodded in approval.

Miss Hewes glanced at an acquaintance, and her cheeks flushed a rosy hue. "Perhaps I speak too boldly," she said. "Good evening to you, sir."

She made to turn away, but he caught her hand. "No, indeed, this is a legitimate observation. You must put the question to Mr. Buckland."

"Oh no, I—"

"I urge you, dear lady, for he is most determined to continue with his public distortion of the Scriptures. Just now, he confessed to me that he has no confidence in a literal understanding of the six days of creation. He believes these days may have been a thousand years each."

"A thousand years?" She stepped toward the door to which he pointed. "Each day?"

"Yes, madam," he said, escorting her into the chamber. "And though he cited Scripture as evidence, I believe that this clearly contradicts every—"

He halted, realizing suddenly that he had led Miss Hewes into an empty room. She drew down a deep breath as the door swung shut behind them.

"I beg your pardon," he said quickly. "I assumed that Mr. Buckland was still—"

"Oh my!" She clapped her hands on her cheeks. "But you and I are not to talk! Have we been seen?"

"Yes, clearly so." He watched her closely. It occurred to him that he had given no thought as to whether Miss Hewes had any interest whatsoever in a peace between their families. "Your friends observed us, and we now risk discovery."

"Dear heaven! My mother will swoon."

He reached a hand toward her. "Do not swoon yourself, I beg you."

"I never swoon." She lifted her chin and arched her fine eyebrows. "How little you know of me, sir."

"I know you better than you may suppose."

"You know nothing at all—save that my lye went astray."

He could not take his eyes from her face. "I know that you adore your brother."

"I took him to fish, that is all."

"You protect him and care for him, as you do your mother."

"She is unwell."

"Yes, and because of it, you are left alone to manage your family's manor. I understand this now, and my estimation of you has greatly grown. Such a task is most challenging even for a man trained to it from his earliest days. You have my highest regard, Miss Hewes."

She moistened her lips as she looked away from him. "Perhaps you do know a little of me."

"I should like to know more."

Her eyes darted to his. "Sir, it is unseemly to speak so. We are enemies by tradition."

"By tradition, yes, but not in fact."

"Indeed we are, for you and I must compete at the mill, at the market, and in every other—"

"Must competition make us despise each other?"

"It has these many centuries."

"Centuries? But I am not yet thirty years of age, and you are younger still. I find I cannot summon centuries of hatred for you, Miss Hewes. Indeed, I cannot summon even one day of it." He paused. "Nor one moment."

Her liquid gaze absorbed him. "Sir, I am duty bound in every aspect of my life."

"Duty bound to hate me?"

Her lip trembled. "Yes, sir."

"Why? Do I repulse you?"

"Your family—"

"Not my family! *Me*—do I repulse you?"

"No," she whispered. "You are good and charitable in every way."

"And you are beautiful, accomplished, kind—"

"Dear sir, I cannot allow you to—" She caught her breath as a knock fell on the door.

Randolph sprang to the small desk near the window and took a pen from its rack. He thrust the pen into the inkwell just as the knob turned. "Six days," he said loudly, drawing a line across the blotter. The door opened, and Mr. Quince entered, followed immediately by Lady Chatham. "Six days are outlined most clearly in the book of Genesis, Miss Hewes, and I believe there can be no argument whatsoever on that point. No argument in Otley, at any rate."

"I agree entirely," she burst out, as William and the three Bryses stepped into the chamber also. "I see no room at all for an ice age, for it is—"

"Indeed, there must be no—"

"Lord Thorne!" Quince exclaimed. "Miss Hewes!"

"Daughter, what is the meaning of this?" Lady Chatham pushed her way past the miller and grabbed her daughter's arm. "What are you thinking? You cannot speak to this demon! This pagan!"

"Lady Chatham," Randolph addressed the woman, giving her a perfunctory bow. "I assure you, I meant no harm in speaking to your daughter. We were merely discussing Mr. Buckland's—"

"Randolph, come away at once!" William interrupted his brother. "I insist upon it. We must go home."

"Allow me to explain—"

"There is no explaining to be done here!" Lady Chatham roughly jerked her daughter toward the door. "That family whose name shall never cross my lips killed your father, Olivia, and now its scion lures you into a secret chamber. Thank heaven I arrived in time!"

"Upon my word, Lady Chatham, I meant your daughter no—"

"Killed Lord Chatham!" William exploded. "Do you hear how she accuses us, Randolph?"

"You will be murdered, Olivia!" Lady Chatham went on admonishing her daughter as if no one else were in the room. "And then who will look out for us? My own child, tricked into—"

"Murdered?" Randolph said, stepping in front of the woman. "Tricked? I have no ill will toward your daughter, madam. In fact, just the opposite. I have every intent and hope of making peace between our families—and by that, peace in this town."

"Peace, do you say?" The dowager narrowed her eyes and turned her head away from him as she spoke. "You mean to make murder, as all Thornes have done since the planting of the hedgerow! The Thorne family have accomplished no good—nothing but evil all the days of their lives. And this is more evidence of it! Leading my daughter into an empty room! Feigning peace as you have feigned all reputable things through the centuries! You are a liar spawned by the father of lies! You are a murderer spawned by—"

"Mother!"

"Lady Chatham," Randolph declared, "I beg you will

control your tongue in this public place. It was neither I nor my excellent father who caused the death of your husband."

"It was caused by a foul disease!" William shouted. "A disease brought about by Lord Chatham's well-known licentious behavior!"

"And furthermore," Randolph continued, "it is *my* father whose death carries the taint of suspicion. It is my father—a superb hunter—who lies dead and buried even now, and his murderer is generally regarded to be under your employ!"

"My father died of the smallpox!" Miss Hewes exclaimed, her face ashen.

"A different pox, more likely," William hurled back.

"You accuse my family of murder?" At this, Lady Chatham faced Randolph for the first time. Holding tightly to her cane, she trembled as her tight lips formed the words. "You accuse my husband of infidelity and licentiousness? Shameful man! Abominable, wicked liar!"

Breathing hard, Randolph listened to the echo of her cries in the chamber. Her cries . . . mingled with his own. He looked at Miss Hewes, who was staring at him in shock and horror. Then at his brother, nostrils flaring and fists clenched. And again at Lady Chatham, chin tilted upward and eyes as hard and cold as lumps of coal.

He swallowed hard, seeing the damage. Understanding the complete truth for the first time. Knowing the utter impossibility of his dream of peace.

"I beg your pardon, Lady Chatham," he said, giving her yet another peremptory bow. "I intended neither you nor your daughter any malice. Come, William. Captain Bryse. Ladies."

Fearing a resumption of the old woman's invective, he

turned on his heel and left the room. There now could be no option of staying for the remainder of Buckland's lecture. The two families must part and return to their homes this evening lest the whole town take up sides and come to battle.

As he strode across the hall, Randolph caught sight of William Buckland, the scientist whose own reprimand rang in his head: *"It is difficult to take seriously a man who claims a longing for peace and yet will have no communion with his neighbor."*

And yet there could be no communion between the Chatham family and his own. Not now. Not ever.

Six

"DREADFUL MAN!" LADY CHATHAM rubbed her temples and winced at the afternoon sunlight streaming in through the long windows of the drawing room. "Oh, my poor, poor head!"

Olivia reached to halt her brother in his determination to drop a fourth sugar lump into his teacup. Nearly a week had passed since the travesty at the Assembly Hall, yet at every meal, at every tea, and at every time she passed her daughter in a corridor, Lady Chatham could do nothing but bewail the occasion. She moaned, she mourned, she wept mightily into her handkerchief. There was little anyone could do to console her. Instead, she turned to the ever-present decanter of sherry for solace.

Olivia sympathized with her mother's misery. The Thorne family had behaved in a truly abominable fashion, shouting accusations and ascribing terrible crimes to the Chathams. Olivia could hardly endure the memory of Lord Thorne's brother insisting that her father had died of an unspeakably foul illness. It had been smallpox—she was sure of it! To suggest that he had succumbed to any other sort of pox cast dreadful aspersions on the late Lord Chatham's reputation.

Olivia had loved her father dearly, and she believed him to be the very finest of men. On learning of his death, which occurred while he was away at a meeting in Portsmouth, she had been nearly inconsolable. How tragic that this adored man had borne such agony far from hearth and home, far from the daughter who cherished him. Even now, three years later, the memory of his suffering reduced Olivia to melancholy. What a despicable fiend was William Sherbourne to make such a malicious statement about her father. And in public! She could not help but abhor the man.

Almost as intolerable as Mr. Sherbourne were the two ladies who had accompanied him into the chamber that night. Olivia could hardly bear to think of them with their pinched noses and beady eyes. Oh, they were finely dressed . . . but the sneers upon their faces! The pride! The insufferable conceit!

Lord Thorne himself had said hurtful words. Did he truly believe that someone had murdered his father? Impossible. Every account Olivia had heard claimed the death was a hunting accident. To think that the Thornes blamed the Chathams . . . appalling!

A lump came to Olivia's throat when she recalled the change in the man she foolishly had permitted herself to admire. Until the encounter with Lady Chatham, he had acted the gentleman in every way. Upon discovering that he had led Olivia into an empty chamber at the Assembly Hall, he had been deeply dismayed. Rightfully concerned about the gossip their presence together would cause, he had been most solicitous toward her. How her heart lifted even now when she recalled his words to her in those few moments they were alone. He had professed his high estimation of her. He had called her beautiful and accomplished. She had reveled in the sincerity in his blue eyes as he spoke those words, and she had believed them with every fiber of her being.

But as Lord Thorne faced her mother, an alteration came over him. His face hardened and his eyes went icy. With every word Lady Chatham spoke, he grew more rigid. Disdain suffused his being. And then he unleashed his own accusation!

The memory of that onrush of angry words haunted Olivia. Harsh. Venomous. Dripping with innuendo. So different from the way he had spoken to her a moment before. Each time she thought of the words, they tumbled through her heart like sharp, cutting stones, and she could do nothing to block their course.

Though she willed him away, she discovered he had somehow possessed her. This man—this Randolph Sherbourne, Lord Thorne! Every waking moment he dominated her thoughts. At times she recalled him as he once had been. She saw his tall, handsome form, his broad shoulders, and darkly curled hair. She heard his message of peace—his desire for peace between the families and peace in their town. And then, suddenly, he had transformed into a monolith of contempt and bitterness. He accused the Chatham family of murdering his father!

Murder. There could be no doubt that Olivia's mother

had been correct in her estimation of him. If Lord Thorne harbored such beliefs, such suspicions, in his heart, he could not have spoken truthfully about a desire for peace. He must have had a malevolent purpose in mind when he tricked Olivia into entering the chamber. Only when confronted by the truth had his own dark heart and his wicked scheme been revealed.

Betrayal tasted bitter on Olivia's tongue each time the image of the man stalked through her mind. And he did trespass on her memory. Daily. Hourly. Oh, she must remove him!

"What of the brother?" Lady Chatham warbled, dabbing her nose with her handkerchief. "The brother!"

"The brother!" Clive repeated.

Olivia took a sip of tea to fortify herself. "The issue at hand is not the Thorne family—"

"Never speak that name in my presence, daughter!" She waved the lace-edged cloth before her face, as if she might erase the very sound of the word. "I hate that name! I despise it!"

"The more important name now is William Buckland," Olivia said. She had attempted this topic in the past, to no avail. "Mr. Tupper informs me that the town is in an uproar over the lecture."

"Over that? Over fossils? No, indeed, I assure you! They are in an uproar over the confrontation they witnessed between our family and the . . . the . . ."

"The Thornes," Clive supplied. "The Thornes were there, most abominable and horrible and terrible. The Thornes."

"Clive, I have told you again and again not to say that name!"

"Mother, it is not their name we must dread," Olivia

insisted. "It is the family themselves. If they actually believe we murdered their father, we must be on guard against them."

"Of course, but Mr. Tupper will not hire anyone to protect us, Olivia. No one at all, and I think it very wrong of him."

"We cannot afford to post guards about Chatham Hall. We have far too many doors. The house has twenty-two windows at ground level alone."

"Doors and windows!" Clive cried, swinging his legs and banging his heels on the floor. "Twenty-two windows. And I have eaten 'leven scones."

"Eleven," Olivia corrected him.

"Is it eleven or 'leven?"

"Eleven." She patted his knee. "And you have not eaten eleven. You have had five, dearest, which is far too many at one teatime."

"Did you say 'leven or eleven?"

"Eleven!"

" 'leven?"

"Oh, my head is breaking!" Lady Chatham wailed.

"It is eleven!" Olivia snapped. "Honestly, Clive, why will you not listen to me? Eleven, eleven, eleven!"

The boy's brown eyes flooded with tears. "It is hard to remember, Livie. My head is breaking."

Olivia let out a hot breath. "Goodness, come here, Clive." She drew her brother into her arms and rocked him back and forth on the settee. "I am sorry I shouted at you."

"It is those dreadful Thornes," he said.

"Yes, it is. They have put us all at sixes and sevens."

"And 'levens."

Olivia sighed in resignation as the footman entered the room with the day's post. "Please go and fetch our letters from Thomas, dear boy," she said. "For I must have a moment to think of a new excuse for turning away our callers."

Clive hopped up from the settee and took the messages from the tray. He glanced at his mother, who was staring morosely into her sherry glass; then he returned to Olivia and set the post in her lap.

"The Bowdens write to us again," she said, breaking the seal on the first of the two letters. She scanned the missive, which had been written by Ivy, the eldest of the four Bowden sisters. "I am asked to a luncheon at Brooking House tomorrow. Miss Clementine wishes to show me the polliwogs in the stream at the end of her garden. It seems they are growing legs."

"Legs?" Clive exclaimed. "I want to go and see the polliwogs, too."

"We cannot go anywhere until Mama is better."

"But I want to see the legs! I want to watch the polliwogs grow! I love polliwogs. They are my favorite things!"

"You were not invited, Clive, and I shall not be going either."

"But I want to—"

"Oh, good heavens!" She dropped the next letter as though it were poisoned. "He has written to us!"

"Who has?" Lady Chatham looked up. "Not *him?*"

"Him." Olivia stared at her. "What shall I do with it?"

"Give it to me."

"Mama, you are not well enough to see it." She realized she was shaking as she gazed down on the bold black ink strokes. She did not need to see the direction from whence this message had come, for she had recognized the writing at once.

"Read it aloud, daughter," Lady Chatham commanded. "We shall hear him out, and then we shall know how to take action against him."

Olivia pressed her thumb against the red-wax seal with its familiar curves and moldings. As the page fell open on her lap, she smoothed it with her hand.

" 'Dear Miss Hewes,' " she began. She focused on her mother. "He writes to me alone."

"Of course he does! It is you who have become his object. You are the key upon which his whole scheme turns. It is through you that he means to undo us. Read on, girl!"

Olivia drew in a breath. " 'Dear Miss Hewes, once more I must come to you in deepest apology for words spoken by me and by my brother at the Assembly Hall on the night of the lecture given by William Buckland. I regret every accusation made, and I most humbly apply to you and your esteemed mother for forgiveness. I assure you that I intended you no malice. As God is my witness, I give you my word that no such statements will ever be repeated by me or any of my family, friends, or acquaintances. I remain most humbly yours. Thorne.' "

Olivia eyed her mother in the silence of the drawing room. To be certain of what she had just read, she studied the letter again. Then she lifted her head. "I believe he means to make peace with us," she said.

"Peace? Is that what you think?" Lady Chatham rolled her head back on the chair. "Oh, daughter, when will you begin to see the world as it really is? When will you grow up?"

Olivia read the letter a third time. "But he apologizes, Mama. He begs forgiveness. He promises no renewal—"

"Promises? Do you place your trust in promises made by that family? Do you accept apologies given by a man who casts aspersions on the esteemed name of your dear father?"

"No, it was his brother who—"

"They are all the same! There is no difference between one and another of them. From their infancy, they are trained to villainy."

"But, Mama, I wonder if the eldest of the three brothers may be different somehow in his character. He may not be like the others you have known from that family."

"He certainly is! They are all alike; you mark my word. Oh, the things they have done to us. You hardly know the extent of it, Olivia, for we kept it from you."

"Kept what from me?" The pale expression on her mother's face sent alarm coursing through her. "You must tell me at once, Mama, for I am responsible to protect our manor from ruin."

"Mr. Tupper can care for it. You do not need to concern yourself on that matter."

Exasperated, Olivia picked up the letter and shook it at her mother. "If his family inflicts evil upon ours, the consequences will fall to me and to Clive. Mama, be reasonable! I am the one who holds our future."

"God holds our future."

"God has hardly bothered with us in years! It is I who keep the ledgers and order supplies for the sheep and buy seed and tools for the crops. It is I who see to the welfare of the tenants. It is I who run the household and make certain the servants are paid. It is I who plan the menus, insist that the silver is polished, and oversee every other small thing that keeps your life comfortable. Now tell me, Mama, what has this family done to us? If you do not speak plainly, they may very well do it again!"

Lady Chatham let out a low groan. Then she took a sip of sherry and held it in her mouth for a moment before swallowing it with a shudder. "Your father did not wish to alarm you," she said finally. "The years were hard on him. Very hard indeed. He suffered mightily at the hand of our neighbors, I assure you. We all suffered. I have endured such agonies. Oh, the pains . . ."

"What sort of suffering did they cause you?"

She covered her eyes and bowed her head as if she were ill. "They . . . they poisoned our sheep. And I—all unaware—ate the meat. Not once. Many times. The pains that tore through me were horrific! And then . . . then . . ."

"Mother, is this true?" Olivia stiffened in shock. "You suffered the loss of your babies from eating tainted mutton?"

"I am certain of it."

"But how could you not know the sheep were poisoned? The shepherds would have seen signs of any such malady. Surely you were not served meat from an ill animal."

"The sheep seemed well enough to one and all. They were slaughtered, and I ate." She shook her head, rocking back and forth at the memory. "And then began the terrible racking agonies! Each time I lost a baby, I lay in my bed praying to God for deliverance. Begging for death!"

"Mama, this is too horrible."

"And it is too true." Damp with perspiration, she took up

her sherry and drank down an entire glass. "Days of infamy," she muttered.

"But how can you be sure of the cause?"

"The sheep lay dead the next day. One of them. Sometimes two or more."

"Mama, sheep do die at random. There are so many things that can kill them. Perhaps it was not poison."

"Do you doubt me?" She pointed a finger at her daughter. "But you are young. You have never known the agonies of childbearing. When the poison swept through me, I knew. I felt it. I felt its murderous pangs."

"Awwwkkkk!" Clive's cry of horror chilled Olivia to the marrow, and she swung about to find her brother curled up on the settee and hitting himself in the head. *"Aaaaa! Aaaaa!"*

"Clive, what is wrong?" Frightened, she grasped his shoulders. "Stop it! Stop hurting yourself!"

"The pangs! The murderous pangs! The poisoned mutton!" He threw his arms around Olivia and burst into tears onto her neck. "I am frightened, Livie! Frightened! *Aaaaa!*"

"It is all right, Clive. It is over now."

"Murderous mutton!"

"Clive, do calm yourself, I beg you."

"Poison pangs!"

"Dear me!" Olivia looked up as the door swung open and the footman stepped into the drawing room once again.

"You have callers, madam." Averting his eyes from the weeping boy, he addressed Lady Chatham. "The vicar of Otley, Reverend Nigel Berridge, and his wife, Mrs. Harriet Berridge."

"Do not send them in!" Olivia cried as he vanished. "Oh, Mama, you must put away the sherry! Clive, please—"

"Good afternoon, Lady Chatham." The affable young minister appeared in the doorway, his pretty wife at his side. "Miss Hewes, how are you? And Mr. Hewes—" As his attention turned to Clive's tear-streaked face, his own broad smile disappeared. "I do hope we are not interrupting anything."

Olivia leapt to her feet and moved to block their view of her mother's half-empty sherry decanter on the table beside her chair. "Reverend Berridge. Mrs. Berridge, how good of you to call. But as you can see, we are—"

"No, no, let them sit down, Olivia." Lady Chatham motioned the young couple to take places on a settee near the fire. "We were just discussing the dreadful event of last week at the Assembly Hall. It has been most upsetting to all of us."

"But that is precisely why we have come!" The vicar leaned forward eagerly. "Lady Chatham, you heard Mr. Buckland's lecture yourself, and you cannot be unaware of the furor it has caused in the church. A good number of my parishioners were very impressed by the eloquence of Mr. Buckland's speech and his display of fossils. They believe he is absolutely correct in his understanding of the events of history, and they hold him in the highest regard. But an equal number deplore the information that was given out. They are certain that Mr. Buckland spoke heresy, and they have asked me to decry the message from the pulpit."

"It is a delicate situation," his wife put in, glancing at Olivia. "You can imagine how my poor husband agonizes over it, Miss Hewes."

"Yes, of course," Olivia replied. While the minister had been speaking, she had managed to back against the table and seize the sherry decanter. Keeping it behind her, she side-stepped toward a chair and sat down, the glass bottle pressing into her spine. "I am certain you have suffered terribly from the dispute."

"Indeed, we have," Mr. Berridge said. "And thus, I call upon you today, dear Lady Chatham, in order to make an ardent request for your assistance."

Seeming confused over the whole topic under discussion, Olivia's mother frowned at the minister without speaking.

He studied her for a moment, obviously awaiting a response. When he received none, he continued. "I implore you, madam, to invite the leaders of Otley here—to Chatham Hall—to listen to your words of reason on the matter."

"Perhaps you could give a tea," Mrs. Berridge suggested. "We dare not ask too much of you, Lady Chatham, and yet a tea might be just the thing to promote an atmosphere of congeniality."

"Aye, for as my dear Harriet so thoughtfully suggested to me this very morning," her husband went on, "you could address the entire gathering at once. You could tell them that God's purpose for His flock is not division but unity. You might propose that each man search his own heart to see if God does not require of him both peace and harmony with his brothers in Christ."

"Peace is what we have been discussing at home, Nigel and I," Mrs. Berridge added. "In any church there may be some division of mind as regards doctrinal matters. But this current dispute cannot be Christ's divine will for His people."

"No, indeed," the vicar agreed. "I have preached for peace from the pulpit, but you see how people choose to quarrel. And therefore, I see no hope for the matter unless it be addressed by one so esteemed in the town as you, Lady Chatham."

Olivia had been turning from the minister to his wife in astonishment as they spoke. It was not so much their topic as their manner that amazed her. Having witnessed scenes of hostility between her mother and father all her childhood, she was struck by the contrast these callers presented. Reverend Berridge spoke; then he gave way to his wife, and then he spoke again. They addressed each other tenderly and with respect. Despite his clear superiority of education, he obviously discussed all matters with her, and he valued her opinion. How unusual. How very stunning.

"Lady Chatham?" Reverend Berridge was saying. "Will you consider my request?"

The older woman blinked at him for a moment and then turned to her daughter. "What is he talking about, Olivia? Do you make anything of it?"

Mortified, Olivia quickly spoke up. "Dear sir, I thank you and your wife so very much for visiting us today. I am sorry to tell you that my mother continues unwell at this time and finds it most difficult to . . . to think about . . . to concentrate on . . ."

"Yes, yes, but what of the scandal?" Lady Chatham said. "What do you say to that, Porridge?"

The minister gulped. "The scandal of Mr. Buckland's lecture?"

"My mother refers to the events that occurred in a small chamber during the intermission of the lecture." Olivia wrung her hands. "Here at home, we can talk of little else. Indeed, we are somewhat unfamiliar with this issue you bring before us. And as you surely see, any thought of an assembly here at Chatham Hall—"

"Yes, at the Assembly Hall." Lady Chatham waved her handkerchief. "Their vile accusations rob me of sleep, deprive me of all peace, haunt me day and night!"

"The sheep were poisoned," Clive blurted out. "The pangs were murdered!"

"Oh my!" Harriet Berridge's blue eyes went wide. "We had not heard this news, Mr. Hewes."

"My brother speaks of events in the past," Olivia said. This was going from bad to worse, and she could think only of how to remove the Berridges from the drawing room as swiftly as possible. "You are new to our community, but certainly you have heard of the difficulties between this family and our neighbors."

"The vile and abominable Thornes," Clive said.

"Do not speak that name!" Lady Chatham wailed.

"And because of the event that occurred the night of Mr. Buckland's speech," Olivia went on as her brother began to bang his feet on the floor, "we find ourselves again at odds. That family has caused years—centuries, I daresay—of trouble for ours. Even now, you see, the very mention of the name causes anguish for us. So, dear Reverend and Mrs. Berridge, I regret to tell you that we are unable to assist in your very worthy and admirable cause."

Before either of them could speak again, she stood. "We thank you so much for coming to call. Please know that our family respects you greatly, and we admire your intention of bringing peace to Otley."

The vicar and his wife rose from the settee. "I had been

told of the unfortunate encounter between you and Lord Thorne," he said, "and I am sorry to say—"

"Do not speak that name!" Lady Chatham clapped her hands over her ears. "I cannot bear the sound of it. Oh, my head is breaking! Where is my—"

"Livie sat on it!" Clive jumped up and whisked the sherry decanter from behind the cushion on Olivia's chair. "She tried to hide it, but I have found it! Ha-ha, so there!"

Olivia stared in horror as her brother poured Lady Chatham's glass to the brim, and she tipped it up and drank down the entire contents. Turning to the vicar and his wife, Olivia saw that they were both gaping at the spectacle, their mouths parted from the shock of it.

In a panic, Olivia grabbed their arms and pivoted them toward the door. "I do thank you both for calling," she fumbled as she hurried them across the room. "And please do know how very much we . . . well, we thank you . . . yes, and we appreciate . . . your . . . your . . ."

"Miss Hewes." In the corridor outside the drawing room, the vicar stopped and laid his hand on Olivia's arm. "Do calm yourself, I beg you. Please take confidence in the knowledge that neither words spoken nor events observed by my wife or myself are ever discussed outside the boundary of our marital union."

Feeling as though she were suffocating, Olivia nodded. "Thank you."

"We shall pray for you," Harriet Berridge said. "And for your dear mother and brother."

"Indeed, we shall. And should you have any specific concerns to discuss with me as your vicar—"

"No," Olivia said. "No, indeed. My concerns are ordinary—they deal with managing the manor. Yet, as you can see, we are very comfortable here at Chatham Hall, and we get along quite well." She pasted a smile to her lips.

The Berridges nodded, bade their farewells, and hurried down the corridor to the door.

Olivia let out a breath, her shoulders sagging from the weight she bore. Pray for her, indeed, she thought. Let them pray. Pray away to a God who did not hear. Did not listen. Did not care.

Randolph scanned the horizon as his horse crested a rise near the border of the Thorne manor. The hedgerow. Above the long, undulating hawthorn barrier hung low gray clouds, the imminent threat of rain. He knew he should return to the lodge at once, but the idea of a good soaking was almost welcome. For nearly a week, he had watched for the post, hoping in vain for a return letter from Olivia Hewes. Now he could no longer deny the truth. She had refused his apology.

Dispirited, he led his horse toward the stream where he had once spoken to her. Each day, he had come this way, imagining that he might hear her laughter beyond the hedgerow. Perhaps she and her brother would come to fish here again. Perhaps Randolph might speak to them, might make atonement in the kindest and most sincere words. And perhaps, if God had softened her heart, she might accept them.

She had not come. Nor had he seen Miss Hewes or any of her family in church the previous Sunday. Word went out that they were ill, all of them. Was it true? Had the terrible row that occurred the night of William Buckland's lecture contributed to some physical malady?

As he thought of Miss Hewes lying sick, and all at his hand, Randolph heard a sound from the other side of the hedgerow. His heart leapt, and he directed his horse up the rocky scree to the limestone outcrop.

"Come, fishies . . ." The voice was filled with melancholy. "Come here. Please come, fishies."

Randolph dismounted and climbed to where he could see over the hedge. Seated on the bank at the edge of the stream, young Clive Hewes dipped his fishing line into a pool. He was alone.

"Come on, come on," he sang in a low tuneless song. "Come, dear little fishies."

Randolph debated turning away. The rain clouds boiled now, and in the distance, tongues of lightning licked the wild-heathered moorland. Lifting up a prayer for guidance, he stepped closer to the hedge. And then he noticed that tears traced paths down the boy's thin white face.

"I say," Randolph called out, "have you had any success today?"

Clive lifted his head and ran his arm beneath his drippy nose. "No. None at all."

"What bait do you use, my good fellow?"

The boy lifted his pole from the water, and Randolph noted that the hook was bare. Clive gave a cry of dismay and hurled the pole into the water. Then he buried his head in his arms and began to sob loudly.

Without stopping to think, Randolph scrambled down the stony height, drew his knife, and stepped into the stream.

Where water coursed beneath the hedgerow, the hawthorn held weak footing. Indeed, at that place, the barrier was little more than a tangle of wild honeysuckle vine interlaced with bramble, clematis, and guelder rose. In moments, he had cut a narrow breach.

"Now then," Randolph said as he slipped through the hedge, waded across the stream, and stepped out onto the bank to where the boy sat. "What seems to be the trouble today, Master Clive?"

"The bait!" Clive lifted his face, tears clinging to his long eyelashes. "I forgot it! I forgot!"

He knotted his hands into fists and hammered his thighs. Choking cries of frustration tore from his chest. "I hate it! I hate fishing, and Livie would not come to help me! I hate her!"

"Is your sister ill?" Randolph knelt beside the boy and laid a calming hand on his bony back. "Perhaps she did not feel well enough to come."

"It is her stomach. She says it hurts all the time, and she cannot ride with me or fish with me or anything else! She will only sit in the drawing room and sip peppermint tea and work at her ledgers. And when I try to help her, she tells me to go away, because I cannot . . . I cannot add the numbers."

Dropping his head, Clive burst into tears again, his thin shoulders shaking with his misery.

Randolph sat down beside him on the bank and lifted the pole from the stream. "One thing is certain," he said. "You must have bait if you wish to catch any fish at all." He paused for a moment. "Do you want to know a secret?"

Clive sniffled. "What kind of secret?"

"Why, a secret for catching fish, of course. Right there, in the hedge, sits a bait that cannot fail to catch fish."

"Where is it?"

"Come, I shall show you." He helped the boy to stand, and they waded through the water until they stood near the thick growth of hawthorn branches. Randolph studied the greenery for a moment until he spotted a perfect specimen. "Do you know your colors, Master Clive?" he asked.

"I know them all. Red, yellow, purple, blue—"

"Green and black is what you want to look for. A large green-and-black caterpillar. Search carefully now." He pointed in a general direction and stepped back.

"There!" Jumping up and down, the boy began to squeal. "There it is! There it is! Bait! I see the bait!"

"This is the caterpillar of an emperor moth," Randolph explained, gingerly lifting the insect from the leaf. "It is very fat, and it tastes delicious to all sorts of fish. And this hedge, my good man, is full of them. All the bait you could ever want is right here. Now, what do you say to my secret?"

Clive threw his arms around Randolph and hugged him tightly. "It is a wonderful secret! It is my favorite secret! Let us catch a fish."

"A fine idea, except that the rain has begun to fall. If you do not return quickly to your house, you will get wet indeed."

"But I want to catch a fish! I love to go fishing. It is my favorite thing!"

"Aye, but the fish will be here tomorrow, as will lots of green-and-black caterpillars just waiting to become your bait."

"No! I won't go! I want to catch a fish." Splashing back

across the brook, Clive threaded the caterpillar onto his hook and dipped it into the pool.

Randolph squinted up at the dark sky. Perhaps his attempt to calm the boy had been misguided. They could hardly escape the rain now. But this looked to be more than a gentle patter. In fact, the wind was picking up, and the thunder growled across the heath.

"One fish," Randolph said. "You shall catch one, and then you must go home."

"I want to catch 'leven. Is it 'leven or eleven?"

"Eleven."

Clive fell silent as the rain began in earnest now. "Livie says it is eleven. Livie is very smart. She can read. She reads books to me. Sometimes I know the words, but sometimes I cannot remember them. Livie knows all the words. She adds numbers in her ledgers. She can tell the time. When she looks at the clock, she says, 'It is half past three, dearest Clive, and almost time for tea.' "

"Does she now?"

"I am not clever like Livie is. I am an idiot. I am an imbecile spawned from the depths of perdition."

"Good heavens." Randolph had been fretting over the nearness of the lightning when the boy made this pronouncement. "Who says such things about you?"

"Mama says them. But only when she has been drinking her sherry. She drinks it all the time."

"I see." The avowal confirmed Randolph's worst suspicions. In fact, he had made inquiries about a curious matter that had nagged at him ever since the night at the Assembly Hall. "Clive, I fear I must disagree with your mother. I do not think you an idiot. It is very difficult to know how to like idiots, for they are silly. You are not silly, and I like you very much indeed."

A grin creased the boy's narrow face. "I like you, too. I love you!"

Moved beyond expectation by this impulsive yet sincere declaration, Randolph swallowed against the lump that formed in his throat. "Will you be a good boy, then, and go home?"

"I want to catch a fish."

"Do you see the lightning, Clive? It is very near."

"I want to catch a fish and eat it."

By now, they were both soaked to the skin. When a bolt of lightning struck the moor not more than a mile away, Randolph made a decision. "Do you like to ride?" he asked.

"I love to ride! It is my favorite thing, but Livie will not take me riding. She says I went away to Otley by myself, and she will never take me out again. But I did not go to Otley. The horse went to Otley. It went all the way, and what could I do, for I was sitting on its back?"

"I can see your problem. Would you like to take a ride on my horse? He is just there, through the hedgerow."

"To Otley? Livie will get very angry."

"To Chatham Hall. I shall take you home to your warm fire and your tea."

"I should like that very much. But what about my fish?"

"Leave your pole here, and tomorrow you may find that your caterpillar has caught you a tench."

Without a moment's hesitation, Clive tossed down his pole and leapt to his feet. Randolph traversed the breach in the hedge and, after quickly cutting a wider swath, led his horse back through it. As hail began to pelt the ground, he mounted and settled the young Chatham heir protectively against his chest. And then they were off, flying across the moor to the ring of boyish laughter and the boom of lightning.

Seven

"MAMA, I MUST GO OUT." Olivia threw her heavy wool cloak over her shoulders and lifted her bonnet from the table near the door. "I can see no other way."

"But you will catch your death! You will fall ill and die, and then where shall I be?"

"I am in good health, Mother—"

"No, you are not! You have been in pain all these days—"

"It is merely a stomachache. I must go after Clive. You cannot think to leave him out in this weather alone."

"I certainly can!"

"He will not know what to do in the rain. He did not take a hat or a jacket. Truth to tell, Mama, you should not have permitted him to go fishing while I was working on my ledgers."

"But you are always working on your ledgers."

"That is because they must be balanced daily, and Mr. Tupper, bless the dear man, cannot remember to do it."

"He is much occupied with the shearing."

"Aye, and yet the ledgers must be tended." Olivia tied her bonnet ribbon firmly beneath her chin. "Nelly has been saddled and is waiting, Mama. I must go at once."

"But, Olivia!"

Unwilling to hear more of her mother's protests, Olivia threw open the door. Pebbles of hail bounced on the steps as she lifted her skirts and hurried down to the drive. The horse strained at her bridle, unhappy at being out in inclement weather, but Olivia knew she had no other way to travel in search of Clive. She began untying the reins as a groom ran from the stables to help her mount.

"Livie! Livie!"

The shouts barely registered through the roar of rain and the staccato drumming of hail on her bonnet brim. Olivia peered through the downpour, straining—hoping—to see who had called her name.

"Livie, I know a secret! It is my secret, and not yours! So there, ha-ha!"

Prickles of relief rushed down her arms as Olivia left the horse to the groom and ran down the drive toward the faint image of an oncoming rider. But her gladness turned to shock as she recognized the tall man who sat straight in the saddle, his face obscured by the rain dripping from the brim of his dark hat.

"It is bait!" The high voice resonated as Clive's head emerged from beneath the greatcoat of Lord Thorne. "Black-and-green bait! It is in the hedgerow! It is our secret!"

"Clive, upon my word, Mama and I have been frantic with worry!" Olivia lifted her hands as Thorne drew back on the reins. "Do come down at once!"

"You are wet, Livie!"

"Of course I am. I was on my way to search for you."

"Is your stomachache gone?" He slid down from the horse into her embrace.

"Dearest Clive," she murmured, squeezing him tightly, "I feared you had drowned! Hurry into the house now. Mama will be relieved to see you."

Clive gazed at her for a moment, his grin broad. "He told me the secret! Him!" Turning, he pointed at Randolph Sherbourne, Lord Thorne. "It is our secret and not yours!"

Olivia forced herself to look at the unwelcome visitor. "I thank you for bringing my brother home, sir."

"Miss Hewes, may I be so bold as to ask if I might step inside for a moment?" Despite the hail, Thorne removed his hat. "I wish to speak to you."

"But I cannot . . . my mother would forbid it, sir."

He gazed at her, his blue eyes dark. She gave her brother a gentle push. "Go on, Clive! Go inside! Tell Mama to ring for tea."

As her brother started up the drive, Olivia squeezed her hands together. How could she turn away this Good Samaritan who had rescued her brother from the storm? Yet how could she admit him? At the sight of the man, her mother would collapse into a swoon—or worse.

"Miss Hewes, please allow me to say what must be said." He dismounted before she could reply. "I beg you to hear me."

She hovered, torn between obedience and desire. Finally, she gave an exasperated cry. "Oh, for heaven's sake, come inside. This weather can do neither of us any good."

She grabbed her sodden skirts and made for the stairs. What use was it to stand outside in such a downpour? If her mother perished of apoplexy at the sight of her nemesis, so be it.

Olivia reached for the door, but Lord Thorne's leather-gloved hand was already there, pulling it open for her. Stepping into the hall, she beckoned a footman. "Speak to the groom, Thomas. Tell him to see the horses stabled. There are two."

"I shall not be long, my good man," Thorne called after him.

As the footman hurried away, she moved to take off her cloak—but again, he anticipated her. He lifted the heavy garment from her shoulders and hung it on a hook near the door.

"You are chilled," he observed as she loosened her bonnet ribbon. "Has a fire been laid in the drawing room?"

"Aye, but—"

"May we speak there?"

"My mother and brother will be awaiting me there, sir." She took off her bonnet. "My mother is not . . . she is not well."

"Yes, I know."

Olivia found she could not respond. His words held a certainty, an understanding, that disconcerted her. Did he believe her mother ill of some common malady? Or did he know the true source of Lady Chatham's headaches, slurred speech, and unsteady gait?

"It is not your mother I wish to address," he said. "And yet, I believe we must find a fire."

"You mean to be brief, sir. Have your say now, and then please be gone from us."

"Is this all the consideration I am to receive from you, Miss Hewes?"

Olivia looked away. "You are not welcome at Chatham Hall. You know this. And the incident at the Assembly Hall merely confirmed it."

"But that is why I have come."

"I thought you came to return my brother to me." She narrowed her eyes at him. "You deceived me once—leading me into an empty chamber for what purpose I cannot tell. Is this another of your schemes, Lord Thorne?"

"Schemes?" His jaw tightened. "Upon my honor, I have no plot against you or your family. My purpose in speaking to you at the Assembly Hall was in the hope of forming a united position concerning Mr. Buckland's lecture. My purpose today was no less legitimate. I discovered your brother at the pool near the hedgerow where you and I once spoke, madam. He was most upset."

Olivia grew alarmed. "Why?"

"He had caught no fish. And when I pointed out that he had forgotten to bait his hook, he became even more distressed. At that time, I took it upon myself to cut a breach through the hedge in order to assist him. When the rain and hail began in earnest, I believed it prudent to transport him home. As I rode, I considered the sequence of events and came to understand that God had directed them for the purpose of putting me in your path once again. That is when I knew I could not depart without making my apology to you in person."

Olivia set her bonnet on the table. "You are very sure of God, sir."

"Scripture reminds us that His ways are not known to us. We can beseech God, but we cannot direct Him. And yet, Miss Hewes, you are correct when you say that I am sure of God. I have no doubt of Him whatsoever."

"How comfortable you must be in your assurance."

"That is faith, is it not? 'The substance of things hoped for, the evidence of things not seen.' "

"I am a creature of little faith and no hope—neither in God nor in man."

His dark brows lifted. "This I cannot accept. Everything I have observed about you leads me to believe you are a woman of great faith."

"Your skills of observation fail you, sir."

"I think not. But perhaps you do not know yourself as well as you might suppose, dear lady. In my eyes, you possess every great virtue. And this is the reason that I cannot allow another day to pass without making atonement for my behavior and attempting reconciliation with you and your family."

To her dismay, Olivia again realized how very noble this man appeared. He stood before her with every reason to disdain her and her mother. And yet he humbled himself to beg her forgiveness.

Lady Chatham would insist this was part of his plan to deceive her. That he meant her harm. That he would do them all ill. But how could Olivia believe that? His blue gaze traced the outline of her face, lingered on her lips, and then returned to meet her eyes.

"Miss Hewes," he said, "will you pardon the harsh words I spoke that night at the Assembly Hall? Can you excuse the accusations my brother made—aspersions based on rumor rather than fact? Can you permit yourself to forgive us one and all? Dear Miss Hewes, may we be at peace?"

"You astonish me, sir," Olivia said softly. "I hardly know what to make of you."

"I am as you see me. Nothing more or less."

"I have been taught to see you as my sworn enemy." She shook her head. "And yet you speak with humility. You act with kindness. Truly, sir, you mystify me."

"How so?"

"I am told you are a demon. Yet you believe God guides your every step. More than that, even, for you trust that He has directed your path, orchestrated a rainstorm, provided you with a poor boy who cannot catch a fish—all for the purpose of allowing you to apologize to me."

"I do believe it, most assuredly. And why not? Each morning at my prayers, I ask God to do that very thing—to guide me. I should hesitate to take even one step into the day before I had made time for communion with my Father. Do you not pray, Miss Hewes?"

Her stomach churned, as it always did when her troubles grew too great. "I pray," she murmured. "I pray ardently. But my petitions fly into the wind and are never heard again."

"Why bother then?"

"I hardly know. Habit, I suppose."

"Or faith."

"What faith I have is as thin as the soil on the Chevin," she said, thinking of the rocky mount that rose near the village of Otley. "What in my life would lead me to believe that God hears my prayers? I ask . . . and I receive nothing."

"Prayer is more than petition, madam. It is praise. Worship. Adoration."

"It is difficult to praise someone who never listens to you."

"I believe God always listens. Yet it is difficult to listen to someone who is always asking for things."

Chagrined, she could not hold back a laugh. "You do make a point, sir."

"What do you ask for that you have not received, Miss Hewes? You have a home, a family, servants, land, wealth. The casual observer would call you blessed indeed."

"The casual observer does not know me well enough." She shrugged. "I have asked God for many things. I begged Him not to let my father die. Yet he did. I asked for healing for my brother, and as you see, he is unwell. I have asked that my mother might . . . that she might . . . be better. But nothing changes. Nothing at all."

"I hate to think of myself as nothing," he said. Smiling, he touched her cheek with the curve of his forefinger. "I hope I may be a bit of an unexpected change in your life. As you have been in mine."

She turned away. "You are not in my life, Lord Thorne. Nor am I in yours. You should go home."

"But you have not yet agreed to—"

"Who is there, Olivia?" Lady Chatham's voice echoed down the foyer. "Clive tells me that . . . that . . . great ghosts, it is true!"

She paused, weaving as she reached for one of two chairs that flanked a large Chinese vase on a pedestal in the corridor. Grasping the gilt chair arm for support, she gaped at the man standing in the foyer. Her shawl slid from her shoulder.

"Lady Chatham, good afternoon." Lord Thorne bowed. "I assure you, I come in peace."

Unable to speak, the woman stood with her hand at her breast and her face growing more pale by the moment. Strangled gasps came from the back of her throat. She wobbled, gave a cry, and then sank onto the chair.

"Mother?" Olivia left Lord Thorne and raced down the hall, her gown sending droplets across the marble floor. "Calm yourself, Mama, I beg you. Lord Thorne means us no harm."

"Oh, daughter! Call for Tupper! Call the guards!"

Olivia sank to the floor at her mother's side. "He has brought Clive home, that is all. And now he wishes to apologize to us. It is nothing more."

"He will kill us all! He will run us through with his knife!"

"He does not have a knife." Olivia swung around. "You do not have a knife, do you, sir?"

"Yes, he does!" Clive had ambled out of the drawing room, a plate of sticky buns in his hand. "He has a very big knife. A long one! He cut through the hedgerow with it."

"Oh, heaven!" Lady Chatham wailed.

"He made a hole in the hedgerow, Mama," Clive said. "A big hole—big enough for his horse to go through. He cut it with his knife. Show it to them, sir, for it is ever so enormous!"

"No, indeed, Master Clive," Thorne said, moving toward them. "I have no intention of frightening your mother further. Lady Chatham, I beg you not to trouble yourself so. I mean you no harm."

"Call the servants, Olivia! Summon Tupper!" Lady Chatham's hands fluttered before her face. "Oh, I am perishing! I cannot breathe! Bring my smelling salts at once."

"I shall fetch the sherry!" Clive cried. "I shall pour your glass all the way to the top."

"No, Clive—" Olivia reached for her brother as he skipped away toward the drawing room. Her mother was gasping for air, sinking lower and lower into the chair. "Mama, please. Lord Thorne will do us no harm!"

"But he is here, Olivia! Here in the hallowed halls of . . . oh, my chest is aching. My heart is bursting open! I shall die! We shall all die!"

"My lord, I beg you," Olivia said, turning to Lord Thorne, "leave us at once."

"No!" Lady Chatham blurted. "Make him stay—and fetch Tupper, Olivia! Order Tupper to kill the villain!"

"Mama, we cannot—"

"He did it! He and his vile family. Every evil that has happened to us sprang from them. From their hands! Their schemes! Their wicked plots!"

"Lady Chatham," Thorne said, "pray consider your words before you speak them. I have come in peace. I mean to make amends with you."

"Amends!" At this, the enraged woman came up out of her chair, all sign of her bursting heart vanishing as she lunged for him. "You stole our land with your abominable hedgerow! You poisoned our sheep! You cheated us at the worsted mill! It was you who—"

"Madam, I have never done anything to—"

"You put arsenic in our water and sowed weeds in our corn! You killed our calves and set fire to our barns!"

"Upon my honor, Lady Chatham, I did nothing of the sort!"

"Liar! Liar!" She stalked him, finger outstretched. "You and all your family are liars! Thieves! Cheats!"

"We are honorable men!" he cried, squaring his shoulders and standing his ground. "My family has endured many hardships through the centuries, madam—"

"And you blame us! Always blaming us—and retaliating!"

"Mother, please!" Olivia tried to keep hold of her mother's hand, but the woman had surprising strength as she pressed toward Lord Thorne. "Do not speak so, Mama!"

"Vengeance! That is all you Thornes think of in your great hall," Lady Chatham shouted. "Revenge against your neighbor! Hated man! Wickedness runs through your veins. You should be ashamed of yourself and those you call your brothers!"

"I bear no shame whatsoever," Thorne retorted. "We are a reputable family, and I refuse to countenance—"

"Reputable—ha! Cavorting with wicked women and birthing the devil's spawn! And you dare to come into my hall, fiend? You, who have plotted the downfall of my family! You, who murdered my husband!"

"I have never laid a hand on your husband, madam, and if you will not stop—"

"Threats! Do you see how he threatens me, Olivia? He would take out his knife and slay us all, just as he killed your brothers and sisters! All of them, tiny babies dead before they took their first breath! Helpless creatures born with poison coursing through their veins—"

"I assure you," he cut in, his voice booming above hers, "neither I nor any of my family—"

"Killed them! Murdered them!"

"It was you who killed your own babies, Lady Chatham! You, with your drink! Gin babies, all of them." He stiffened, breathing hard. "You, madam, are the one who bears the fault in the illness and death of your children."

"What?" Olivia gasped. She stared at him in horror. "How dare you say such a thing? How dare you! Get out! Get out of our house!"

"As you wish, madam." Thorne set his hat on his head. "My attempts at peace are at an end, Miss Hewes. I shall never trouble you again."

Too angry to reply, Olivia turned to her mother as Thorne stalked out into the rain, slamming the door behind him. Lady Chatham's brief moment of strength had faded, and she sagged into her daughter's arms. Frail as a baby bird, she laid her head on Olivia's chest.

"Oh, daughter," she moaned. "Do you hear him? Do you hear what he has said?"

"Indeed, I have heard it all!" Still furious, Olivia helped her mother back to the chair. "He is gone away, thank heaven, and we must have help. Thomas, are you there? Come at once!"

The footman hurried down the corridor as Olivia fanned her mother. "Fetch the smelling salts, Thomas," she ordered. "On the table beside my mother's bed."

"Yes, Miss Hewes." He bowed. "Shall I send for a doctor?"

"Not yet. We shall see how she fares."

Thomas took the stairs two at a time in his haste to fetch the smelling salts.

"Here is your sherry, Mama," Clive said, holding out a glass.

Olivia blocked him. "No, Clive—"

"Yes, give it to me!" Lady Chatham sat up and took the wine. "Oh, thank you, dear boy. What a good child! What a thoughtful son!"

Olivia laid a hand on her mother's cheek as the woman drained the glass. "Mama, you are very warm. I fear you have a fever."

"Yes, oh yes, I am terribly ill. My head breaks, and my nerves are all aflutter. Did you hear what that demon said? Did you hear how he accused me?"

"Do not think of him again," Olivia said. "He meant only evil in his accusations."

"Indeed he did. Blaming me! I am far from perfect, and may God forgive my many sins. But that vile man accused me of harming those I love most!" She held out her empty glass to Clive. "Fill it again, dear boy, lest I swoon a second time. I am grateful for the elixir, and you know that sherry is nothing like gin, as he alleged. It is only wine and not at all harmful. It is a help to me, a great help now, as it has been these many years."

Olivia patted her mother's forehead with a handkerchief. "Calm yourself, Mama."

"It was wrong of him to come here!"

"Aye, very wrong."

"And wrong to say such things! He is just like your father always was—shouting at me!"

"Mama, please."

"You remember it. You heard your father shouting at me, defying me, humiliating me. He used to say the very same thing! 'It is your fault, Sophia, your fault. If you would not drink . . .' But it was the sheep, you know. The poisoned mutton that did it! I never took a drink before the first baby. I lost the first baby not even a year after you were born, and I never had any sherry at all before that. It was the mutton, you see. The poisoned mutton."

"Of course, Mama, I am sure of it." Olivia tried to make sense of her mother's rambling. "Sit quiet, I beg you."

"It was those Thornes! They poisoned me so that I might not bear a son. But I did, you see. There he is, my darling Clive." She took the boy's hand as he brought her a second glass of sherry. "I was so unhappy after I lost the first one, and that was when I discovered the calming effect of the sherry. And then the others were lost, you know, but your father blamed me!"

"No, Mama, I am sure you are mistaken."

"Yes, he did. He blamed me for the loss of them, when I was the one who wanted them most of all."

"Certainly you did."

"Mine were not like those gin babies, the ones your father used to shout at me about. 'Gin babies,' he would say, just as Lord Thorne did. And it was not gin. I never drink gin. It was the mutton."

"Poisoned mutton," Clive confirmed.

"Oh, here is Thomas! What a good man." Lady Chatham took the smelling salts. "I shall hold the bottle in my hand in the event I should start to swoon again. Now, Thomas, do help me back to the drawing room, for I am chilled. Dreadfully chilled! I shall catch cold and die, and then that horrid man will rejoice at killing yet another of us!"

As the footman bent to assist his mistress, Olivia stepped back. Her mind reeled with the words that had poured forth in the space of only a few minutes. Incrimination, blame, threats . . . she could almost hear Lord Thorne denouncing her mother: *"It was you who killed your own babies, Lady Chatham! You, with your drink! Gin babies, all of them."* Vile accusation! And yet Olivia now recalled those same words from her own father's mouth: *"You did it, Sophia. It was you, with your drink!"*

She had not understood. She did not understand now. Taking on her father's role, she had spent these three years since his death trying to hide the sherry, attempting to prevent her mother from sipping at her glass before dinner, quietly suffocating from the unbearable hopelessness of it all.

"Gin babies," she said aloud.

Lady Chatham looked over her shoulder as Thomas led her toward the drawing room. "What did you say?"

"Gin babies. I understood that William Buckland spoke of them."

"It was the mutton!" She beckoned Clive. "Come, dear boy. And, Olivia, do bring me down another shawl, for I am quite chilled. Indeed, I believe I can feel a heaviness in my head already. I am sure I shall die of a cold, and then what?"

Olivia stared after her mother, unable to make herself obey. Gin babies? What had her father meant? And what did Lord Thorne know about this matter? Why had he said such a terrible thing to a poor ill woman?

Was the Thorne family so evil? Had they brought about every tragedy that had befallen her own? Or were they innocent of wrongdoing, as the baron claimed? Could it be true that Lady Chatham's fondness for sherry had led to more than the headaches of which she daily complained?

If she were to lead this family back to health and security, Olivia must have the facts. She must uncover everything that had been kept from her in childhood. Secrets were destroying her. Hidden evils were creeping out of their caves, no matter how determined her parents had been to lock them away. They crept and they grew and they threatened to strangle her.

Unwilling to delay another moment, Olivia grabbed her damp cloak and pulled it over her shoulders. Her bonnet would do little good, but she stuffed it onto her head and pulled the ribbons into a hasty knot. She could not take the time to tell Thomas to summon a groom. Instead, she pulled open the door and hurried out into the rain.

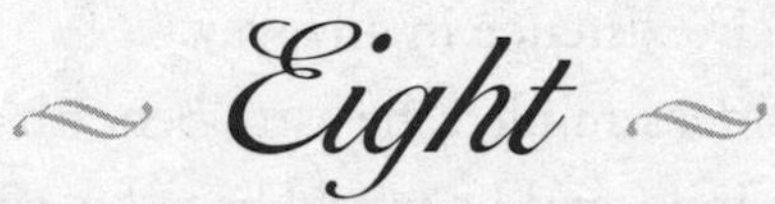

Eight

RANDOLPH HAD NEVER been more eager to set foot in his own hall, to stand before his own fire, to drink from his own cup. As he rode his horse through the pouring rain, he fumed over the calamity that had erupted only minutes before.

Wicked old woman. How Lady Chatham had spawned such a lovely daughter, he would never know. The dowager's tight lips had spat words of hatred. Her eyes had glittered like lumps of hard black coal. And that clawlike hand—the way she had pointed her bony finger at him! As though he himself were to blame for every mishap she had endured.

Bitter, hateful creature. He abhorred her. He despised her. Leave her to her liquor and her dank, dreary hall. Let her stew in her own cesspool of fetid gall. Everything he had heard of the Chatham family was true. They were a selfish, spiteful, vile people who deserved neither the bounty of their land nor the loyalty of their tenants.

Spurring his horse down the last of the long drive, Randolph gratefully passed through the Chatham gate and onto the open road. Never again would he venture into that poisoned land. He would resume the practice of his ancestors and refrain from speaking to any member of such a despicable family. Certainly he would never again look at them or acknowledge their existence in any way.

A peal of thunder rumbled the earth beneath his horse's hooves. Another mile, and he would be at his own gate. On the way to his rooms, he would send for tea. A change into dry clothes, a pair of warm socks, and he would be a new man.

Perhaps he would call for charades this evening after dinner. The two Miss Bryses and their brother were pleasant enough company, and certainly William would welcome a change in his elder sibling's humor. Randolph would entertain his guests at last. He would set aside his mourning for his father and be charming and witty. No longer would he brood over the mysterious Miss Hewes. No more would he ride to the hedgerow in the vain hope of an encounter with her. All thought of peace was forgotten. All hope of restoration was dashed.

Olivia Hewes could be little different from her mother, he reasoned. She was softer-spoken, perhaps, but her heart must be as calloused. She had told him she had no faith in God. What would be the point of Randolph attaching himself to such a woman? He wanted a companion who shared his love for God, who believed in the power of prayer, who read the Scriptures daily and tried to behave as the Lord commanded.

Miss Hewes could not possibly enjoy such a faith, for she had been brought up at the feet of the foulest witch in the kingdom. The mere thought of Lady Chatham set Randolph's blood boiling again. He was glad—very glad indeed—that he had shouted to her face the truth about her wickedness. Let her have no doubt that he knew. He knew her sin. He would announce it from the rooftops if—

"Be ye angry, and sin not."

The admonition of St. Paul to the Ephesians jolted through Randolph like a shaft of lightning. He shuddered with the power of the words. Where had they come from? Who had spoken them?

He took a deep breath. God, of course, had brought the verse to his mind. Randolph had immersed himself in the Bible for this very purpose, that its teachings would come to him during each experience of his life.

Truly, he was angry, he realized. Yet, had he sinned? Certainly, it had not been wrong to castigate such a fiend as Lady Chatham. She could hardly be called a Christian. Her tongue was a two-edged sword, and she wielded it without heed to consequences.

How dare she accuse Randolph of lying? He never lied. She herself was the liar. The father of lies himself had been her tutor. The memory of her accusations incensed Randolph. She insisted that he had plotted the downfall of her family. That he had murdered her husband. She alleged that he—Randolph Sherbourne—had somehow killed her babies! She deserved nothing better than to suffer in a bitter, drunken stupor.

"Be ye angry, and sin not: let not the sun go down upon your wrath: neither give place to the devil."

At the rumbling echo of the words through his chest, Randolph reined his horse. Breathing hard, he sat motionless upon the saddle. Rain pattered on the brim of his hat and seeped through his greatcoat onto his shoulders as the words of St. Paul continued to form in his heart.

"Let no corrupt communication proceed out of your mouth, but that which is good to the use of edifying, that it may minister grace unto the hearers."

Randolph closed his eyes. Corrupt communication? He had told the truth. Yet, had his words been edifying? Had they ministered grace? He thought of Olivia Hewes's stricken face as he had lashed out at her mother. She did not know the rumors about her family that circulated. She could not understand what he had meant by his accusations. To her, he had not been a minister of grace but a roaring offender full of rage and hatred.

"Let all bitterness, and wrath, and anger, and clamour, and evil speaking, be put away from you, with all malice: and be ye kind one to another, tenderhearted, forgiving one another, even as God for Christ's sake hath forgiven you."

Forgiving one another. . . . *Dear Lord, am I to go back there and beg forgiveness? How can I, when I am not the least bit sorry for what I said? What am I to do?* He clenched his fists on the strip of leather in his hands, fighting his rage and beseeching God for direction.

At this place in the road, he was less than half a mile from the vicarage. Randolph had no doubt that Reverend Berridge and his wife would welcome him out of the rain and give him solace beside their fire. The minister would listen to a recounting of all the grave events of the past weeks, and he would offer Randolph spiritual wisdom.

But what if Berridge advised yet another attempt at harmony between the two families? How could Randolph do such a thing? How could he humiliate himself one more time? Lady Chatham would never agree to see him. Indeed, she would likely send someone after him with a sword. Miss Hewes certainly thought him wholly bad. She could not—

"Lord Thorne!"

The voice drew Randolph from his confusion. He turned to see a horse galloping along the road toward him, its rider bent low with a long dark cloak flying out behind. Alarm coursed through Randolph as he realized that his concerns were well-founded. Lady Chatham had indeed sent a man to confront him!

Realizing he had only his knife for protection, Randolph assessed his options. He could stay and fight, but the very idea repulsed him. It would resolve nothing and would likely bring grave injury to his foe. If he continued on the road, the man might overtake him and insist upon a duel. Deciding to make straight for his house, Randolph turned his horse into the nearby pasture.

He knew the best course to take—every hillock and stream that must be crossed. Leaning against his horse's neck, he spurred the stallion into full gallop. Mud flew as the animal churned the soggy moorland. Randolph glanced over his shoulder and peered through the rain. The Chatham man had veered off the road as well and was now closing the gap between them.

Chagrined, Randolph formed another plan. He spurred his horse toward a stone wall that formed a barrier between this pasture and the next. Erected higher than most, the wall posed a challenge for the average rider, yet he had been accustomed to crossing it from his boyhood.

As he approached, Randolph crouched into the horse and urged it toward the wall. With a surge of coiled muscle, the stallion leapt over the barricade. Two hooves hit the dirt and then the other two—all surefooted—and they were across. He pushed the horse on a little farther before venturing a backward glance.

As he had hoped, the pursuing rider had balked at the unexpected wall. The gray horse circled, blowing steam, clearly ill at ease. Surely the man would now turn and go. Randolph peered through the rain as his own steed stamped in eagerness to be away.

But just as he had made up his mind to ride on, he saw that the man intended to try the barricade. At some distance, the gray horse faced the wall. The cloaked rider laid himself along the creature's neck. And they surged forward. Closer . . . ever closer.

Randolph's heart raced. He should be off, away to Thorne Lodge and the safety of his gates. But he could not resist watching as the horse increased speed, faster and faster, nearing the wall.

At the last moment, just as the horse should have made a leap, it planted all four hooves in the mud and slid to a dead stop. The rider catapulted from the saddle, tumbled through the air, and dropped from sight behind the wall.

Randolph straightened. Good. He had succeeded in his escape. Now he would return to his lodge and let his pursuer hobble home in the opposite direction.

Behind the wall, the gray horse ambled in circles, bending its head now and again. Surely the rider would stagger to his feet in a moment, Randolph thought. He would shout a few curses. Perhaps he would mount again. But the chase was finished.

And yet, there came neither sound nor movement from the other side of the wall. Curious. Randolph edged his horse forward. Concern prickled through him. Could this be a ruse? Perhaps the man had a pistol and would rise up momentarily to shoot his foe through the heart.

"I say, sir," he called out, "are you injured?"

No answer.

Randolph urged his horse toward the wall. "Good man, I mean you no harm. I come in peace. Are you well?"

Again, no sound.

Now Randolph was near enough to peer over the wall. He leaned from the saddle and studied the tangle of sodden cloak and mangled bonnet.

Bonnet?

"Great ghosts!" He quickly dismounted, clambered over the wall, and jumped down. "Miss Hewes? Is it you?"

Dismay suffused him as he dragged away the bonnet. Rain pelted the young woman's pale face—her lips ashen, her eyelids closed, her cheeks a deathly white. Kneeling at her side, he formed a protective tent above her with his greatcoat. He removed his gloves and gently touched her chilled skin.

"Miss Hewes? Dear lady, I beg you to open your eyes." He brushed the rain from her forehead and cheeks. "Please speak to me. Miss Hewes? Olivia?"

Her eyes fluttered open, dark lashes hung with droplets.

"Thank God!" He took her hand. "Can you move? Speak to me, please."

Her lips moved. A low groan. And then a shallow sigh.

"I must take you home at once," he said. "Can you tell me where you are hurt?"

"My head," she whispered.

"Yes, of course. Allow me to—"

"No!" She pushed at his arm.

"Please do not be alarmed. I mean you no harm, Miss Hewes."

"What . . . why am I here?"

"You fell from your horse. At the wall. You pursued me, but your mount balked. Dear lady, I believed you were someone else—a servant sent by your mother to do me harm. Had I known it was you, I should never have—"

"I cannot recall it . . ."

"Truly, I must carry you out of this rain. You look very ill." Without waiting for her consent, he lifted her into his arms. "Miss Hewes, I must take your horse."

"Nelly," she murmured.

A smile crossed his lips at the unexpected word. "Yes, we shall go on Nelly."

With little effort, he settled them onto the mare and prepared to ride. But the thought of returning to Chatham Hall filled him with dread. If he were to arrive bearing an injured Olivia Hewes, unpleasant scenes must certainly ensue.

If he took her to Thorne Lodge, she would be well cared for. A doctor would be summoned, and she could recover her health in optimum comfort. But to place Miss Hewes at Thorne Lodge meant he would be reviled. Distrusted. Lady Chatham would be outraged, and her friends and tenants must follow suit. Those tradesmen and laborers whose living depended upon the Thornes would revolt at this evidence of their master's good intent toward their competitors. His brother would view the act as utter lunacy.

Taking the reins of his own horse across the wall, Randolph goaded Nelly toward the road. Miss Hewes reclined unmoving against his chest, her head nestled in the curve of his neck. Remorse flooded through him as Randolph recalled the manner in which he had shouted at her mother. He could no better control his own tongue than Lady Chatham could hers. He was no less guilty than she of fomenting enmity between them. And because of their rage, this poor young lady had suffered a grave injury.

"Be ye kind one to another, tenderhearted, forgiving."

Finally the wall ended, and Randolph led the two horses out onto the road. Self-recrimination filled his thoughts. He should have made for Reverend Berridge's house the moment he had departed Chatham Hall. The minister would have helped him to—

But that was his answer! He would carry Miss Hewes to the vicarage. Under the care of her minister and his wife, she could rest in security and comfort. She would be close to the doctor, and her mother could have no objection to her tenure in such an amiable residence.

His heart lifting at this first ray of light in the miserable day, Randolph turned the horses toward Otley. Miss Hewes moaned slightly, and he tightened his arm about her. Such a slender waist. He laid his cheek against her damp hair. How soft was her skin and how delicate her form. Why had she come after him? Was it possible that she despised the gulf between them as much as he did? Could it be that she cared for him . . . as greatly as he was drawn to her?

"Lord Thorne?" A woman's surprised voice drew Olivia from her daze. "But why are you . . . ? Oh, my—come in, come in!"

"I bear Miss Olivia Hewes."

The man who carried her . . . Lord Thorne it was . . . stepped out of the rain and into the hall.

"I fear she is gravely injured," he said.

"Injured? Lay her here upon the settee." The young woman in a white mobcap and a green gown ushered him into a softly lit room. "I shall call my husband, for we must send for the doctor at once! Nigel! Nigel, do come quickly, my dear!"

Olivia sensed herself being removed from the enveloping warmth of the man's strong arms as he eased her against a large cushion. Swallowing, she tried to form words of gratitude. But her head . . . how it ached! Her legs trembled, her stomach rolled, and she feared she might be ill.

"Miss Hewes, may I take the liberty of removing your cloak? It is very wet." He knelt beside her, his handsome face so close. How blue his eyes were in the firelight, and how kind the expression on his mouth. "Your bonnet was left in the meadow, and I greatly fear you may suffer much from the effects of the rain."

"Aye," she said, sighing deeply. "I am cold."

"As I suspected." He unclasped the cloak at her neck and lifted her again to draw it away. Next he took a dry shawl from a hook near the door and wrapped it around her shoulders. "I shall stir the fire. And you must take tea momentarily. May I fetch you anything else? Another shawl perhaps?"

Olivia stared at him, knowing who he was but uncertain how she came to be in this strange room with him. "I cannot think clearly," she murmured. "My head is muddled, and I—"

"Lord Thorne! Good afternoon to you, sir." Reverend Berridge burst into the room, his coat only half pulled up onto his shoulders. "I was just studying my sermon and—Miss Hewes? Good heavens! You are . . . both of you . . . you are here. Together."

"Miss Hewes suffered a fall from her horse, sir," Thorne explained. "I witnessed the occurrence and took it upon myself to carry her here. I trust you will welcome the lady into your home until she is recovered."

"Indeed so! But of course."

Without his round hat and frock, the vicar appeared to Olivia strangely young and boyish. He had a head of sandy curls, and he wore a pair of bright red slippers on his feet. As he approached the settee, his wife hurried back into the room, a servant bearing a silver tea tray close behind her.

"Gracious, Miss Hewes," she cried, "you are wet through and through! Lord Thorne! Go and sit beside the fire; I insist upon it. I have sent for the doctor, but I believe we must help Miss Hewes into dry clothing at once. Tea, of course. Take some tea, sir!"

"Yes, take some tea." Reverend Berridge bent to pour the cups.

"I should not move her further, madam," Thorne cautioned as the minister's wife knelt at Olivia's side. "I believe she lay senseless for some minutes after her fall. Her head may be injured."

"But she is damp, and I always say to my dear husband that

dampness leads directly to a cold. Miss Hewes should not catch a cold, for that would make her injuries the worse."

"The damp will not cause the trouble, my dear Harriet," the minister intoned. He addressed Lord Thorne. "I have walked many miles in the rain, and I assure you that rain does not cause a cold. It is close proximity to a person who is ill that does it."

"Do you hear him?" Harriet Berridge's blue eyes were bright as she handed Olivia a cup of tea. "Such nonsense he talks, for everyone knows that rain and chill can cause a cold."

"My darling girl, you may believe as you like, and I shall do nothing to try to change your mind." Her husband patted her on the arm as he crossed the room to settle himself on a bench near the fire. "But it has been my observation while walking to visit the ill that rain or no rain, if someone has a bad cold, I shall return home with it myself."

"He is so silly," Harriet confided to Olivia in a low voice. "As though a cold were like a plate of scones that could be passed around from one person to the next. But drink your tea, Miss Hewes. Please take at least one sip, for truly you appear most peaked."

Olivia placed her lips on the warm porcelain and tipped the tea into her mouth. The hot, sweet, fragrant liquid slid across her tongue, down her throat, and into her fragile stomach like a heavenly balm. She closed her eyes and allowed herself to sink fully into the pillow. Though wet, muddy, and aching all over, she knew she was safe. He had rescued her. Saved her life, for she had no doubt that had she remained on the moor, she must have perished. How had she come to be there? Why had she been riding Nelly in the rain? Following Lord Thorne . . . and filled with fear . . .

"Gin babies," she said suddenly. "Oh, no!" Sitting up, she tipped her cup over in the saucer. Tea splashed down her gown and spilled onto the floor.

Mrs. Berridge leapt to her feet. "It is no trouble, my dear Miss Hewes, I assure you!" the woman said before Olivia could offer an apology. "You see, the cup is not even broken. Allow me to pour you another. But, oh dear, your gown is quite ruined—and such a lovely blue muslin. Nigel, I really must put her into something clean and dry—"

"Now then, Harriet darling, do calm yourself." The vicar took his wife's hand. "Look, Miss Hewes is quite recovered from the event already. Sit down, I beg you, for your own cup grows cold. The doctor will be here directly, and then—"

"But that is just it. Should he see her in such a way? Should Dr. Phillips see Miss Hewes of the Chathams sitting about in all these damp clothes? And here is Lord Thorne himself, as wet as anything. Gracious, we have not even asked to take your greatcoat, sir! Oh, this is too, too wrong!"

"Please, Mrs. Berridge." Thorne leaned back in his chair and gave a chuckle. "You trouble yourself too much. I assure you, I am perfectly well. Indeed, I feel that I may be dry already, for your fire heats my garments, your tea warms my throat, and the pleasure of your amiable company comforts my heart. I cannot thank you enough for your assistance at this difficult time."

Mrs. Berridge blushed a bright pink. "You are very welcome, sir. I confess, I am all aflutter, for my husband and I are not accustomed to entertaining such esteemed guests as

Miss Hewes and yourself. We are new to Otley, as you know, and in our previous parish, we did not have so much as a baronet, let alone a real *baron*. Nigel and I . . . we are mannered people, but . . . well, we were brought up among the common man."

"As is perfectly proper for a vicar and his wife." Thorne stretched out his long legs and crossed his boots at the ankle. "I believe a holy calling supersedes the peerage. After all, madam, I received my title merely from my father, while your husband was given the name *Reverend* by God Himself."

At this, the minister's wife appeared so pleased that Olivia thought she might burst from the pleasure of it. Truly, it was a most engaging scene—the young couple seated beside the fire, sipping tea and conversing so pleasantly with Lord Thorne. Olivia observed it all in a kind of rosy haze. She felt warm and comfortable. Her second cup of tea was going down very nicely. And she had forgotten that troubling thing . . . the reason she had insisted on setting out in the rain . . . following Lord Thorne . . . trying to get poor Nelly to leap the wall. . . .

"Gin babies!" She sat up straight and gripped the back of the settee. "Oh, that is it! I must . . . I have to . . ."

"Dear lady, are you ill?" Thorne reached for her just as a knock sounded at the door.

"It was what you said to my mother," Olivia murmured, grasping his arm. "What did you mean? Why did you say it? What is the—"

"Please, Miss Hewes, you must not distress yourself so." He took her hands and tried to urge her down onto the pillow again as the Berridges hurried to answer their door.

"I was wrong—very wrong—to speak to your mother in such a way. I realized it nearly the moment I left Chatham Hall. Indeed, I had almost settled upon coming to this very home to speak to Reverend Berridge about the matter—to confess all and to seek his advice. But then I saw you following—"

"Yes, I had to go after you. I must know the truth. You must tell me everything."

"Miss Hewes, Dr. Phillips wishes to speak to you." Reverend Berridge led the elderly physician into the drawing room. "He would like to make an examination of your injuries. Mrs. Berridge will stay with you. Lord Thorne, we have a comfortable sitting room just down the hall—"

"No, you cannot go, sir." Olivia gripped Thorne's hand. "You must stay. I have to speak to you. Reverend Berridge, take Dr. Phillips away from us for a moment, please."

Fearful that Lord Thorne would vanish without seeing her again, Olivia refused to release him. She must understand his meaning. She must know why he had accused her mother of such . . . such . . .

"The babies," she implored. "Please, sir. You must explain yourself."

Lord Thorne cleared his throat. "It is irregular, I realize, for such a private conversation to occur, Reverend Berridge. Yet you can see that Miss Hewes's distress will not be relieved until I have satisfied her questions."

"Of course, sir," the minister said. "Certainly, under the circumstances, we must do all in our power to calm this poor injured young lady. We shall all await you in the sitting room."

"I thank you, sir." Lord Thorne stood as the three left the

room, Mrs. Berridge clearly uncomfortable about the arrangement and looking back over her shoulder to make certain nothing was amiss.

When they were gone, he drew a chair near the settee. "Now then, dear lady," he said, "how may I ease your suffering?"

Nine

"YOU BLAMED HER." Olivia spoke softly, unable to blink away the tears that filled her eyes. "You blamed my mother for the loss of her babies. I heard how you accused her."

"I was wrong to reproach Lady Chatham in such a manner." Lord Thorne bowed his head. "I confess, I was angry, and I failed to control my tongue."

Olivia wished she could bring herself to forgive the man, but his words still rang in her head. She despised the sound of raised voices. Throughout her childhood, she had listened to her mother and father shout at each other. Sometimes she heard the crash of breaking glass or the thud of furniture falling to the floor. Always her parents had kept their fury behind the closed door of their bedroom. Yet the tension between them seeped out through the corridors of Chatham Hall and into the hearts of their children.

What had been the root of their anger? Why had they married and then despised each other so? Had they ever loved each other?

The memory of her own anguish at the sound of her parents arguing brought fresh tears. Unable to find her handkerchief in the tangle of her wet gown, Olivia wiped her cheek with the back of her hand.

"I heard how you accused my mother," she managed. "That is when I knew I must come after you. I had to know . . . I must . . ."

"Please, Miss Hewes," Thorne murmured, "I cannot bear to see you weep. It was very wrong of me—"

"Aye, but you were correct in what you said." She shook her head, and her voice fell to a whisper. "How did you know?"

"I did not know. I only supposed."

He took her hand again and pressed it between his. For a moment he did not speak, as if turning over the words he might say. His fingers were strong and warm around hers, and she found that his touch made her tears fall all the harder.

"Gossip is a tragic human failing, Miss Hewes," he said gently. "I avoid it, yet I fear it is inescapable no matter where I go. Rumors, tales, stories. People do love to talk. From my childhood, I heard accounts of your mother's affinity for strong drink. I believed the charges, of course, for as a boy I was surrounded by my parents' love and affection, and I believed everything I was told. As I grew into a man, I began to sift through my experiences—learning right from wrong, good from evil. I learned that people will cheat and betray and willfully harm others. And I learned that they will lie. At university, under the tutelage of an exceptional gentleman, I became a true Christian—an ardent follower of Jesus Christ and His teachings—and I further worked at sorting out right from wrong. Yet in all this moral education, I never questioned what I had heard about the incorrigible clan whose land bordered our own. About the Chathams."

Olivia gasped. "Incorrigible? Upon my word—"

"Hear me now, please." He settled her again on the pillow and drew a handkerchief from his pocket. Before speaking further, he dried the tears from her cheeks and tucked the scrap of linen into her hand. "When my father met his tragic end and I became baron, I realized I had to begin to think more seriously about all things, including my neighbors. By now steeped in Scripture, I wondered how it could be righteous to live out the remainder of my life filled with hatred for a family I had never even met. And then . . . that day in church . . . I saw you."

Olivia looked into his face, absorbing the depth of feeling behind his words. "You were very good to me, sir."

"Dear lady, from that moment, I could neither eat nor sleep without thinking of you. I became resolved that I must make peace between our families. I attempted in every way to heal the rift."

"You sent me your lye."

"It was not enough. I longed to make an easy and amiable friendship between us. And not with you only, for I wished to build a civil acquaintance with your mother. And of course your brother . . ." He paused.

"You have been kind to Clive."

"He is a good lad, charming in his ways, and I wanted nothing more than to console him today when I found him at the stream. He told me you have been unwell."

"Since my father's death . . . perhaps even before that . . .

I have suffered an occasional stomach malady. Times of unrest in our home, trouble at the mill, Clive's many illnesses—these and other difficulties in my life seem to bring it on."

"I believe you are in great need of peace."

"I am indeed. But who is not?"

"And today I brought yet another calamity to trouble your health. I thought . . . I hoped . . . that in returning your brother safely to Chatham Hall, I might take the opportunity once again to try to forge a peace."

"Mama was shocked to see you in our home, and rightly so." Olivia felt the tears well up again. "But she spoke out of turn. She was unkind."

"Were I a better Christian, I might have shown her a greater forbearance. Instead, I retaliated by bringing to light a rumor that I had heard so many years before. I regret doing so, and I deserve her censure."

Olivia debated speaking from her heart to a man who was supposed to be her enemy. At this moment, she could deny everything to him. She could call reports of Lady Chatham's drinking false and declare her mother sound and sane. She could lie.

Gazing into his eyes, she read the honesty and compassion in their blue depths. "My mother does imbibe too much of strong spirits," she whispered. "Her preference is sherry."

His hand tightened on hers. "I am truly saddened to hear this. I assure you, I will never speak of it to anyone."

"But you did more than accuse her of drunkenness. You said she bore the blame for the death of her babies. You said—"

"Yes, I said it, but I did not know. I had no facts, Miss

Hewes, and I was wrong to say what I did. I have only heard talk that she had lost babies. Rumors that there were deformities—"

"Truth." Olivia said the word and then buried her face against the pillow. Unable to hold back her sobs, she poured out her grief. "They died, one after another, and she drank all the more, and they did die, all of them until . . . until poor Clive . . ." She raised up and took his hands in hers again. "And was it the sherry? Oh, please! Please, you must tell me the truth!"

"Dearest lady." He folded her in his arms and drew her close against his chest. "Here is all I know. When Mr. Buckland spoke of the gin babies, I confess I did think of your mother and all that I had heard through the years. Not long after the unfortunate events of that night, I wrote a letter to my attorney in London—citing no specifics—and I asked him to investigate Buckland's allegations. Shortly, I received his answer."

"Tell me." Olivia wept, her face pressed against his neck. "You must tell me everything."

"My attorney wrote that indeed there had been a great gin problem in the last century. It seems the price of the stuff fell so low that our country suffered what was known as a gin epidemic. Not more than fifty years ago, Miss Hewes, annual consumption had grown to eleven million gallons."

"So much!" Stunned, Olivia lifted her head.

"But the material point is this: Having observed the detrimental effects of drink upon England's citizens, the College of Physicians drafted a letter to Parliament to voice their concerns. I believe it is that letter to which William Buckland referred."

"What was the conclusion of the physicians?" At her question, she read the wariness in his face. "I am well enough to hear the truth, sir. Speak plainly."

"They reported the fatal effects of the frequent use of distilled spirits."

"Fatal . . ."

"They determined that the drinking of spirits while pregnant caused weak, feeble, and distempered babies. Rather than an advantage and a strength to their country, they believed these children must certainly become a burden."

Olivia reflected on her brother. Clive could never be called a burden. But would he ever grow into a man who could fulfill his role as baron? Could he ever be relied on to oversee the manor and care for his tenants? *Weak, feeble, distempered*—these words described the boy completely.

Olivia returned her attention to Lord Thorne. "What was done to repair the situation?"

"Parliament dealt with the gin epidemic by raising the price of the liquor, but they did little to address the medical crisis. Though the college had expressed concern that there was too little appreciation of alcohol's influence on the conceptus, nothing came of it."

"But I can see by your face that you know more."

"There are those physicians who continued their observations. Buckland mentioned a Frenchman by the name of Dr. Lanceraux. This gentleman has been studying babies born to women who have consumed strong spirits during the length of their confinement. My attorney wrote to Lanceraux and received a letter summarizing the man's observations. I can bring you the letter, Miss Hewes."

"No, you must tell me everything now, for I cannot wait

another moment to know the truth. How did Dr. Lanceraux describe the children?"

"He stated that the infants often die of convulsions or other nervous disorders. If they live, they may become idiotic or imbecile."

"Oh, dear heaven . . ." She pressed the handkerchief to her cheek. "Go on, sir. Go on."

"Dr. Lanceraux has observed that children born in such cases tend to have certain characteristics. The head is small. The physiognomy—by which one can determine temperament and character through physical features—shows a vacancy. The child evidences a nervous susceptibility often bordering on hysteria. Convulsions and epilepsy may be seen. These, Dr. Lanceraux concludes, are the sorrowful inheritance that the drinking woman bequeaths to her children."

Her heart breaking, Olivia wept into her handkerchief. "Then it is true. All of it."

"We cannot be sure."

"Indeed, we can, for this is the perfect description of my poor brother. All his life, Clive has been ill and weak. He suffers convulsions and hysterics to the point that we sometimes fear he may die. His head is small, and his appearance is so different from that of the rest of our family that . . . that . . ."

A memory of the words shouted between her parents came to Olivia, one she had not thought of in the years since the death of Lord Chatham. "My father," she said softly, "did not believe Clive was his son."

"Surely not."

"Yes, for my father was a tall man and very robust, and my

mother was the picture of health in her youth. But Clive has always been tiny, appearing far too young for his years. Even his eyes are small, with drooping lids and such weakness that he must wear spectacles at all times. The look of his face has never matched that of my parents, who were called handsome even by strangers. But poor Clive has a flat face, a short nose, and such a small, unimportant chin."

"The look of a child cannot always determine his parentage. I am dark-haired while my younger brother, who serves as a missionary in India, was flaxen as a child. Even now, his hair is light."

"A missionary? I had always heard he was in trade."

"There, Miss Hewes, you see how rumors can run rampant. You must not put great trust in them—nor even in this information from Dr. Lanceraux. Perhaps it is mostly conjecture on his part."

Olivia nodded, wishing rather than believing he was correct. "But you know . . . Clive has great difficulty in learning," she said. "I may teach him a thing and feel certain he knows it—and the next day he can remember nothing I said. My brother, sir, does not read with ease. Nor does he count well."

She watched for his reaction, willing that he might understand the deep significance of her words.

"And yet your manor is in able hands." Thorne tightened his hold on her hand. "You are not the first woman in the history of England to capably manage land, livestock, and tenants."

"I am the most poorly trained."

"Yet you do well. I have heard that despite your lye problems, your wool began to arrive at the worsted mill just a day or two after mine. John Quince told me he was hard-pressed to recall seeing finer and whiter wool than yours."

She smiled. "And I am quite sure our miller will tell me the same thing about your wool."

"Aye, for he must do all he can to pay us the lowest possible price. But, Miss Hewes, now you and I must bring our conversation to an end lest we jeopardize the excellent reputation of our vicar. May I be assured of your health?"

"I am well enough. My head hurts, but the pain is not as great as that in my heart."

"For that I make my apologies. If not for my outburst today, you would never have had to bear such a burden."

Nodding, she returned his handkerchief to him. "And yet, sir, I have been kept from the truth for too long. These secrets have never served my family well. Perhaps now I may know better how to proceed."

"Then I shall bid you farewell, with one final request. May I call on you again, Miss Hewes?"

Olivia's gaze followed the gentleman's tall form as he rose from the chair. She should deny his request. In short order, her mother would make an appearance at the vicarage. Others in the town would come to visit and offer their good wishes. The last thing anyone should observe was a Chatham deep in conversation with a Thorne.

She looked beyond him to the window, through which the last rays of sunlight now poured. "The rain has stopped," she said softly. "I trust you will find your way safely home, Lord Thorne. And safely back again."

A broad smile lit up his face. "As you wish, dear lady."

"I could not rest until I had made certain of her well-being."

The echoing voice from the foyer of the vicarage sank like a stone into the pit of Olivia's stomach. Two days had passed since her fall from Nelly, and already it seemed she had been besieged by nearly every man, woman, and child in Otley.

For most, the occasion had meant a brief visit, an offer of flowers or fresh fruit, and a politely worded condolence. But for others, Olivia's confinement provided the perfect opportunity for oration. Seated beside their minister's fire, they opined to her on every matter that affected them—their families, their crops, their business, their religion, and their village.

At least the miller was not likely to talk about the controversy plaguing the church. Everyone, it seemed, had formed an opinion on the subject of biblical literalism. Now they were dividing into two camps and threatening all manner of hostility. Some even advocated forming a new body— a church of their own making that would forbid anyone to believe differently from themselves. But John Quince was a man of business, a self-important fellow who inserted himself into every event that could affect his dealings. He had little interest in matters of faith, and as far as Olivia could recall, he never talked of such things when he called upon her mother.

"Ah, there she is," Quince said as Mrs. Berridge led him into the drawing room. "My dear Miss Hewes, how very pale you look today. I am told you suffer a great deal with your head and back. Please accept my most sincere sympathies."

"Thank you, sir." Olivia could not rise from the settee, for the entire length of her back had been badly bruised in her fall. Dr. Phillips had ordered her to recline at all times until he declared her fit to rise without assistance. She hardly objected, for she was very sore, and her spirits had fallen so low that she could not make herself want to leave the comfort of the fire and the layers of blankets that covered her.

"Shall I ring for tea?" Harriet asked.

"For myself, I am nearly ready to float away on tea," Olivia said. "We have had callers all day, Mr. Quince, as you can imagine."

"Indeed, I can." He seated himself without taking her hint. "I should welcome a cup of tea, Mrs. Berridge. A brisk breeze blows down from the Chevin, and I am chilled through."

"Of course, sir."

As she disappeared, Harriet gave a look of exasperation that brought a smile to Olivia's lips. Her one solace in this misery was the company of the dear young woman whose companionship cheered her heart. Harriet and Nigel Berridge kept a household so warm and cozy, so filled with goodwill and love that Olivia began to wonder if she would ever wish to leave them. Though they had no children, Harriet confided that it was their dearest wish to conceive, but God had not yet seen fit to bless them in such a way. They took great delight in sharing their home with a guest.

"When I was first told of your accident," Mr. Quince began, leaning back in the chair and setting his tall hat on the table, "I could hardly countenance the thought of it. And the rain! It is a great wonder that you have not caught a nasty cold."

"I am in good health other than my bruises," she said.

"And you, sir? How are things at the worsted mill this summer?"

His face darkened. "I am sorry to bear you bad tidings. I fear your difficulty in obtaining lye must have led your shepherds to great haste in washing your flocks, Miss Hewes. The wool is very sandy."

"How odd. Lord Thorne told me not two days ago that you had found my wool to be exceptionally fine this year."

The man's brows lifted. He ran a finger around his collar. "Lord Thorne spoke to you? I had heard that he . . . that you were . . ."

"He was my rescuer after I fell. When he carried me here, we had a moment to speak in private. He told me you had complimented my wool."

"I cannot imagine why he would have thought so, for I assure you, I was sorry to have to judge it so poor. But come, Miss Hewes, you know I am a fair man and will give you a good price for your wool. Have I not always treated the Chatham family well?"

"You have, sir. We both have benefited from our relationship." She drew her shawl more closely around her shoulders. Quince was a handsome man with a grand profile and locks of thick dark hair threaded with silver. He had never married, turning all his attention instead to his worsted mill. His wealth had allowed him to purchase a great deal of land adjoining Chatham manor. Rumor had it that he was in the process of building himself a large house and gardens, constructing a waterworks, and laying out a fine road. Olivia had come to view him as a shrewd tradesman, one who had caused her family much anguish over the years.

"Teatime!" Harriet bustled into the room, her maid following with the usual silver tray. "I am sorry not to summon my husband to greet you, Mr. Quince, but he has gone out to visit the sick this afternoon. The Hedgleys have got the chicken pox, and all of the children are covered in spots top to bottom." She flushed. "Perhaps I should have said head to toe."

Olivia giggled, but Quince's solemn expression never altered. "I am not familiar with that family, madam."

"Old Mr. Hedgley is the head gardener at Longley Park." Harriet paused in pouring the tea. "I sometimes forget that my husband and I minister to those from all walks of life. The Hedgleys are a common family, but a most honorable one."

"Ah, I see." He took his cup and turned away from Harriet. "Miss Hewes, has your mother been well enough to visit you?"

"Not yet, sir, but I hope I may see her soon. She ordered my clothes sent down from Chatham Hall, of course."

"I have been sorry to find her so very ill these past months. Does she improve at all?"

Olivia bristled slightly at the question. Was he hoping to learn of Lady Chatham's impending death? "My mother feels better at times," she said. "We are all quite well enough, I assure you."

"And your brother, young Lord Chatham?"

"He is much as he always was."

"We do not see him in town."

"No." She forced a smile and turned to Harriet. "I suppose I might feel up to a crumpet. May I help myself?"

"Of course, dear Olivia." Harriet reached for a small dish. "You must try my honey. We have our own bee skeps here in the garden, you know. I never thought I should like bees, for they can be so—"

"Lord Chatham has not yet come of age, I believe," Quince cut in. "He is seventeen, is he not?"

"Sixteen, sir. Their buzzing can be unnerving," she told Harriet. "One cannot help anticipating a sudden sting."

Harriet glanced back and forth between her two guests as if uncertain whether to speak again. Finally, she brightened. "I believe I hear my husband coming up the path! He always whistles when he is out walking. If you will excuse me for a moment, I must see to a dish of cold meats and some bread, for he missed his luncheon altogether." She hastened from the room.

Annoyed that Mr. Quince had been so rude to his hostess, Olivia bit into her crumpet and regarded him through lowered lids, wishing he would go away and tend to his milling. Though her stomach had calmed in the peace that permeated the vicarage, she felt exhausted from the stream of visitors, and she longed for time alone to reflect further on the information Lord Thorne had given her. Perhaps she might even discuss the situation with the Berridges.

Reverend Berridge, though overly fond of making lengthy sermons, was a wise man. He was well educated, and he appeared to take a great interest in the daily affairs of his congregants. This quality, in Olivia's opinion, rated him far superior to most of the ministers who had been assigned to Otley Church. Their focus had been the penning of eloquent speeches and the practice of high rhetoric. They had loved equally well the business of the church—the assimilation of funds, the maintenance of the cemetery and the building, the appointments and meetings of their deacons and elders. Few took the time or trouble to shepherd their flock, instead leaving such matters to those beneath them.

Not only did Olivia admire Nigel Berridge, but she had come to adore his wife. If Olivia had been blessed with a sister, she could not have wished for one any different from Harriet. Indeed, this sweet couple would have no qualms about sitting down with their guest and letting her pour out the questions in her heart.

Should Olivia give her mother the devastating information she had learned? Might it finally put a stop to Lady Chatham's drinking? Or would it lead her to deeper despair and a greater reliance on her sherry? And what about poor Clive—

"Miss Hewes, may I take this moment of privacy to speak to you regarding a matter of some delicacy?" John Quince set down his teacup. "I have a request of a personal nature to make of you."

Now it would begin, Olivia thought. He would mention the growing rift in the church and ask her to attend a meeting. Or he would bring up some other controversy that hindered his trade and beg her participation in resolving it. She shifted on the cushions, preparing herself for yet another lengthy discourse from a citizen.

"Yes, Mr. Quince," she said. "Of course I am happy to hear you."

"I am honored." He rose from his chair and came to her side, kneeling on the floor and taking her hand. "Miss Hewes, I am cognizant of the superiority of your breeding and the connections of your esteemed family. Surely you have every hope of attaching yourself to a man of similar rank. But I am unable to deny my ardor any longer. Madam, your beauty and grace have overwhelmed me these many years, and I cannot endure the agony of my passion for you! Please say you will relieve my suffering and consent to become my wife."

Olivia's mouth parted in utter surprise, and she found she could not speak a word.

"Before you answer," he went on, apparently unaware of her shock, "allow me to lay before you the particulars of my request. Miss Hewes, not only am I afflicted with the agony of my love for you, but I have become sensible to the dire straits in which you have found yourself. Since the death of your beloved father, you have had the assistance of only your steward, Mr. Tupper, in the management of the Chatham manor. Forgive my boldness, but I am aware, too, of your poor mother's continuing ill health. And . . . I regret to confess . . . I have heard that your brother is not much—"

"Sir, I am most opposed to rumormongering," Olivia exclaimed. "And I beg you to—"

"But of course you do not wish these matters to be made public. I assure you, I would never repeat a word of it. Yet my business dealings with your family are such that intimate information may be passed to me. And I cannot think to continue a moment longer with knowledge of the heavy burden you bear. Allow me, madam, to become your husband, and I assure you that you and your family will be provided for in the very best possible manner. Your mother will be examined by the most skilled physicians in the land. Your brother will be accorded the greatest of respect and opportunity. All that I have at my command will be at your service. Please, Miss Hewes, I keenly beg you to accept my petition and consent to marry me."

Olivia stared at his bent head, the tops of his pink ears, his large white hand clamped upon hers, and she could hardly think how to respond. Never in all her years had she given the slightest consideration to marrying John Quince. He was the town miller, nothing more to her—a man she passed in church and spoke to at meetings in her father's library. Though pleasant of appearance and well respected, he had never provoked romantic feelings in her—not in the least.

"Sir, I—" she drew her hand from his and tucked it under her blanket—"I fear you present your request at a most inopportune moment. I am hardly well enough to rise from this settee, let alone calm enough of mind to consider such a sudden and unexpected marriage proposal."

"I am too aware of the awkwardness of this setting, madam. But when I heard of your unfortunate accident, I immediately saw the peril of your situation. Should you become disabled in any way, your mother and brother must suffer terribly. I permitted myself to delay coming to you for two days, taking time to weigh the suitability of my proposal and to study the matter from every angle. At last, I concluded that I must see you and lay out my humble petition."

"But I am unable to give you an answer, sir, for I have not had the luxury of contemplating such a match, as you have."

"Is there time for such a luxury, Miss Hewes? I think not, for surely you know that your manor hangs by a thread! Your wool has not been profitable these past three years. Indeed, it has pained me greatly to have contributed to your family's suffering. Yet, in those days, I confess I thought only of my business. Madam, surely you can perceive the fortunate results of an alliance between us. From the moment of our union, I shall throw all my efforts into breeding Chatham sheep to be the finest in Yorkshire. Chatham wool will go through my worsted mill before any other. All proceeds will be turned back into Chatham coffers. There can be no question that this arrangement will bring you every security and happiness imaginable."

Olivia felt suddenly so hot that she thought she might suffocate. He was right, of course. Absolutely correct. His proposal offered a way out of all her problems. How could she deny him her hand? And yet the thought of marrying a man she did not love was all but unbearable.

"Sir, I do appreciate your offer," she tried. She brushed a hand over her heated forehead. "It is most kind. And reasonable."

"Of course it is. You must agree to it at once. Say you will accept my hand, and I shall speak to your mother directly."

"But I . . ." She knotted the blanket in her fists. "Please, sir—"

"My dear daughter!" At that moment, Lady Chatham herself stepped into the drawing room and threw open her arms. "Olivia, darling! And Mr. Quince! How good of you to call on my poor, sick child!"

"Mama, you have come at last." Never in her life had Olivia been more happy to see her mother.

Ten

"LIVIE!" CLIVE RUSHED through the door of the vicarage, skipped past his mother, and ran to the settee. "Oh, Livie, where have you been? We missed you dreadfully! You were very naughty to go riding in the rain!"

Olivia laughed in spite of herself. Hugging her brother, she kissed his forehead. "Dearest boy! You do not know how happy I am to see you."

"Oh, yes I do, for I am just as happy to see you!" He kissed her three times on the cheek and then wedged his thin frame onto the settee beside her. "Who is that man?"

"He is Mr. John Quince," Olivia said. "Mr. Quince owns the worsted mill in Otley."

"I know him."

"Perhaps you do, for he has called on Mama."

"Lord Chatham," the miller said, bowing. "Good afternoon."

"I have seen you before." The boy's small face pinched into a scowl.

Olivia elbowed her brother to prevent him from saying

something untoward, as he had been known to do on occasion. "How have you been keeping yourself busy since I went away, Clive?"

"I have had no fun at all," he told her. "Mama will not even allow me to go fishing, though I told her I know how to find the bait. That kind gentleman told me what to look for. The bait is blue and yellow! Or is it green and yellow? Or black and . . . ? What is it, Livie?"

"I am sure I do not know," she said.

"It is caterpillars."

"Really? Oh my."

"They live in the hedgerow, but it is a secret."

"I shall never tell anyone. Truly, brother, you ought to wait until I am well enough to take you to the stream again. You must obey Mama, for she knows what is best for you."

"But I want to go fishing now! I adore it! Fishing is my very favorite thing."

"Of course it is." Smiling, Olivia turned to her mother. "And how are you these days, Mama? I think of you very often."

"My dear girl, I suffer greatly. Of late, I have endured a nervous tickle just behind my eye." She had seated herself in a chair near the fire. The hem of her embroidered green skirt was spread out around her feet, and her high-crowned bonnet nodded as she spoke. "The pain begins the moment I wake in the morning, and it pierces straight through my head like a knife. Then it settles into the most infuriating, niggling little twitch. I can hardly bear it, I assure you."

"Poor Mama, I am sorry to hear this." Olivia hoped John Quince would realize that his presence was no longer welcome, but he seemed unaware of her desire for family privacy. Perhaps she might gently acquaint him with the truth. "Mr. Quince, it was good of you to call on me. I am sure we shall have opportunity to speak again after I am recovered."

"Indeed, I believe we must," he said, fixing her with a piercing stare. Then he raised his eyebrows and turned to her mother. "Lady Chatham, I find your daughter in high spirits today, though I believe her complexion remains too pale."

"Exactly so," the elderly woman replied. "She ought to come home, I think. One can never be fully comfortable except in one's own domain. I myself suffer far worse from my head when I am out. In church, I can hardly endure the light that streams through the stained-glass windows. All those colors! It is truly painful to bear. And while riding to town, I find the carriage jostles me dreadfully. Upon my honor, I confess there are times I believe my poor head will split right in two!"

"This is sad news," the miller said. "I did not know you endured such agonies, my lady. Has a physician been summoned to examine you?"

"My dear late husband sent for a man from London, but I do not believe he was at all familiar with my sort of pain. He made such silly comments that I could not begin to take them seriously."

"But you really ought to be seen by someone."

As Mr. Quince and her mother discussed the subject of Lady Chatham's health at great and painstaking length, Olivia drew her brother more closely into her arms and shut her eyes. Not two days ago, Lord Thorne had sat in that same chair near the fire. His long legs stretched beneath the tea table, and he spoke so kindly to the Berridges. Olivia had to wonder if her mother had even greeted the couple, who now sat side by side on a bench and looked as though they were reluctant to open their mouths. Despite their exclusion from the conversation between Lady Chatham and John Quince, the Berridges were perfectly at ease with each other. Harriet leaned against her husband's arm, while he regularly reached to make certain his wife's shawl did not slip from her shoulder.

How could Olivia ever think of marrying such a man as John Quince? Oh, he would make her an ideal husband in most ways. He wanted nothing more than to elevate himself in the world by marrying a titled woman. And the Chatham family finances could only benefit from his prosperity. He would be solicitous of Olivia's mother—so eager to please, in fact, that he would no doubt order sherry by the cask. He would immerse himself in the management of the Chatham lands, taking pleasure in everything Olivia found so difficult. No doubt Chatham manor would turn a handsome profit from this year forward. Even her brother must be happy enough, for Mr. Quince would take on every responsibility that should have been Clive's.

One day, there would be children, and eventually a truly capable Baron Chatham could inherit the land. But the idea of this man touching her . . . kissing her . . .

Olivia fought the lump that rose in her throat. What was the lot of a lady born to such a great family, after all? She must learn the womanly arts, becoming accomplished in embroidery, painting, singing, playing the pianoforte. She must carry herself with deportment in all social occasions. She must dress in the finest gowns and make certain that her hair was coiffed with perfect plaits and curls. And in the end, she must marry the right man and bear him children—as many boys as possible.

What right had Olivia to wish for love? She had never witnessed that emotion expressed between her mother and father. Their marriage had been planned by their parents, an arrangement that had brought a fresh infusion of funds to the Chatham coffers. Why should Olivia expect anything different? One could hardly hope for such a contented union as that of the Berridges.

Lord Thorne, of course, would leave such matters in the hands of God. He believed that his Maker directed every step of his life's journey. If that were true for Olivia, she certainly had little for which to thank Him. Now He had placed the miller of Otley as her lone prospect for a husband, and she must decide whether to marry him. Randolph Sherbourne, on the other hand, would benefit from his title of Lord Thorne by marrying the daughter of a count or maybe even an earl. They would live out their days happily overseeing their manor, rearing hordes of pleasant children, and trusting God in all things. Could anything go awry in such a delightful scene?

Perhaps if Olivia prayed every morning before stepping out of her bed—as Lord Thorne did—she, too, would have a happy life. She had never attempted such a daily evidence of faith, turning to God only when she felt she could not manage her affairs on her own. And even then, nothing miraculous ever happened. So, what was the point?

"Are you sleeping, girl?" Her mother's shrill voice stirred Olivia from her thoughts. "You have callers! You must engage us!"

"Mama, I am sorry."

"Livie is tired," Clive said. "That man should go away."

"Young man!" Lady Chatham rose halfway from her chair, preparing to soundly reprimand her son.

But John Quince stood at the same moment and made a deep bow. "Indeed, it is time I am off. I have tarried far too long away from my affairs. Even now I am reluctant to part from you, but so it must be."

"Do come to call on us at Chatham Hall," the older woman said. "We could not wish for a more solicitous guest."

He smiled. "Certainly, madam. And, Miss Hewes, may I offer you my best wishes for a speedy recovery?"

"Thank you, sir." She tightened her arm around her brother. "Good day."

"Miss Hewes, I do hope you will consider the request I made of you this afternoon. I shall call upon you at the soonest possible moment to receive your answer."

She swallowed. "I shall send word, sir, when I am fully recovered and able to address the matter."

"Certainly." Favoring her with an even grander bow than the one he had given her mother, Mr. Quince took his leave.

Lady Chatham had hardly sat down again before she began to question her daughter. "What request did he make of you?" she demanded. "Was it a business matter? Or was it of a personal nature?"

"Mama, you can hardly expect me to speak of such things in a public place."

"Indeed I can! You must tell me at once. What does he want of you?"

"Mama, please—"

"No, daughter, I insist upon knowing. There is nothing he could say that our vicar cannot hear. He is a man of God and will not speak of it again. Am I correct, sir?"

Reverend Berridge straightened. "Certainly, Lady Chatham, I never repeat anything—"

"There, girl. You have his oath on it, and now you may speak plainly. Do not hold back a single word of what was spoken between you and Mr. Quince, for I must hear it all."

"It is a subject for me to consider and not for anyone else—"

"Speak! Do not force me to grow angry, child, for then my head will begin to pain me again, and I may be unable to bear the agony of it!"

Olivia clenched her teeth. "Very well. Mr. Quince has asked for my hand."

"He wants to marry you! And what did you answer him?"

"I gave him no answer. I am not in a condition to think clearly about a matter of such great import."

"But he has asked you—that is the material thing! You can tell him yes soon enough." She laughed and hugged herself warmly. "Oh, this is excellent! What a good fellow he is. What a perfectly amiable gentleman."

"Mama, how could you have considered my marrying Mr. Quince before now?"

"How could I not? I have considered every eligible man from here to London."

"Eligible? Mr. Quince is in trade! He has no title!"

"But he has wealth—and a good deal of it. I have heard it rumored that he has ten thousand pounds a year. Maybe more! Think of it, Olivia, that much money can only mean our comfort and happiness forever."

"Are you serious in this, Mama? But you have always said I must wed someone from London. You and Papa used to—"

"Oh, hang your father! What did he know about anything? He never understood how it ought to be, for his thoughts were always on his silly sheep. My own dear father taught his children the value of a profitable marriage. You can be sure he never would have considered allowing any of us to be poor. He was a wealthy man himself, and he made profitable arrangements for all my sisters and brothers. When it came to me, he found a man with both a title and money. Or so he thought. He did not know how close the Chathams were to ruin."

"Mama, please! You must keep silent on such personal matters. We are not near to ruin." She glanced at the Berridges. "We have experienced some difficulties these years since my father's death, but certainly we are rich in land and livestock and—"

"Yes, that is all very well," Lady Chatham interrupted. "But what about money? One cannot go on forever without it. I like Mr. Quince very much indeed. He is an honorable man, and he will make you a good husband. Surely you can see how advantageous such a union must be for us. Why, our wool will never again be judged of poorer quality than that of those horrid Thornes!"

"Do not say that name in my presence," Clive spoke up. "I hate that family!"

"Shh, Clive. Oh, dear." Olivia sighed. "Mama, please, I am very tired and still weak from my injuries. You must allow me to rest."

"You ought to come home, child. You will rest better in your own bed."

"Will I, Mama? Do you know everything that is best for me?"

Lady Chatham glared at her daughter. "What did you say?"

"Please go home, Mama. I shall return to you as soon as Dr. Phillips gives me permission to travel."

"Olivia, I am ashamed of you!" Her mother stood. "Such a self-serving speech. Such a bold demeanor. Truly, you are the most ungrateful child."

"No, I am," Clive said. "That is what you always say about me, Mama. I am the most ungrateful child. Me."

"Come, boy!"

Without bidding her daughter or the Berridges farewell, Lady Chatham strode from the drawing room. Clive gave his sister a quick peck on the cheek and hurried after his mother.

Leaning back into the cushions, Olivia let out a groan. "Oh, dear," she murmured, sensing herself at the brink of despair.

"May I help you, Miss Hewes?" Harriet Berridge asked, standing. "Would you like some . . . some tea?"

Olivia shook her head. "Not even tea can soothe my tattered nerves, dear Harriet," she said. "I fear that I may come all to pieces at any moment."

Reverend Berridge rose from the bench and moved to a chair near the settee where she lay. "Miss Hewes, I sense that Mr. Quince's proposal of marriage has given you a great shock today. May I . . . would I be amiss to ask if I might pray for you now?"

"Now? Here?" Olivia could not have been more surprised. "I . . . I suppose so."

Harriet took another chair and bowed her head as her husband began to pray.

"Dear Lord," he said, "our guest, Miss Hewes, whom we have come to cherish as a sister, endures pain of body and agony of soul. You have called Yourself by the name Jehovah Rapha, the God who heals. We petition You now to lay Your healing hand upon Miss Hewes. Restore her body, Father, for she is weak and weary. She has been giving of herself to others from the moment she was laid here on our settee by Lord Thorne. So many people from town have come to see her, Father, and she has kindly listened to them all. And so, dear Lord, we pray that You might give our poor sister rest and healing of body.

"Furthermore, holy God, we pray for a quietude to descend upon her spirit, that she may hear Your voice in this important matter of whether to marry John Quince. Speak to her plainly, please, and show her Your divine will. Teach her, dear Lord, to lean upon You and to trust You. Allow her to understand that You are with her in all her days—the good ones and the bad. Show her Your love, dear Father, for she carries such a weight. And it is in the name of Jesus Christ, our Savior and Lord, that I ask all this. Amen."

"Amen," Harriet said.

"I thank you, sir." Deeply touched at this gift of prayer on her behalf, Olivia searched for her handkerchief. "Do you often pray at such times as this?"

"I make a great attempt to pray always, even when the words are not consciously formed on my tongue."

"He prays always, too," Olivia murmured, gazing at the fire through tear-filled eyes.

"Of whom do you speak?"

She shook her head, fighting emotion.

"Lord Thorne," Harriet put in. "I imagine she means him."

Olivia glanced at the young woman in surprise. "How did you know?"

"I took note of the way he looked at you when he carried you into our home. Such great tenderness he feels for you. I am sure he has spoken to you of many things, Miss Hewes."

"Please, Harriet," she said, her voice barely above a whisper. "I have asked you before, and now I must insist that you call me Olivia. We are far too intimate here for formalities."

"Very well," Harriet agreed. "Nigel believes . . . Olivia . . . that Lord Thorne is a great man of God, for all his actions reveal his deep faith."

"Actions? What does he do?"

Reverend Berridge spoke up. "He gives generously to the church in support of our labors to feed and clothe the poor of Otley and the whole of Lower Wharfedale. He sees that the ill are tended to. Did you know that when Dr. Phillips could not find the cause of Mrs. Winn's pain, Lord Thorne ordered a doctor brought up from London in his own carriage to have a look at her?"

Harriet picked up the narrative. "It was a cancer, and she died, the poor creature—and all those children were left without their dear mama. But that fine doctor stayed with her the whole time, right to the end, giving her laudanum to ease her pain. It was done at the order of Lord Thorne and paid for by him too, of course. Indeed, I believe he has called on nearly every family in the town at one time or another."

"Lord Thorne himself calls?" Olivia could hardly believe this news.

"Oh yes," Harriet said. "He is too kind. He paid for a crew of men to come over from Leeds and repair the town's waterworks, even though his own water comes from a stream on his lands. And do you know—he has allowed strangers to stay the night at Thorne Lodge? Strangers! Think of that."

Olivia *was* thinking of it. She found it impossible to reconcile such generosity with the evil reputation her mother had laid on the man. No wonder he had bristled at Lady Chatham's accusations. He had given of his wealth, his time—even his home—to assist those in need. Yet he was called a cheat, a liar, a murderer!

"Anyone who would do such godly things," Harriet went on, "must be very close to God. And drawing close to God can only come of much prayer and study of Scripture. That is why I imagined that you referred to Lord Thorne when you spoke just now, saying he prays at all times."

"Indeed, I did. He told me he prays before ever setting one foot from his bed."

"Do you not pray often, Miss Hewes?" Reverend Berridge asked.

"Hardly ever. The prayers I have said were rarely answered, so it seemed pointless to cast more words into the empty winds."

"But Jesus clearly instructed us to ask, and we shall receive. We may not receive precisely what we asked, dear lady, but God acts in His wisdom, not ours."

"Nigel and I have learned," his wife inserted, "that God gives us what we need. Sometimes what we need is not at all what we asked for. It is possible that we may need a dose of strong and unpleasant discipline. Often, the way God disciplines and trains those He loves is through adversity."

The minister spoke again, and his voice took on a sermonizing tone. "You have only to look in the Bible to see examples of that. The Israelites were forced to wander in the desert forty years for God to subdue their stubborn and willful hearts. Samson was blinded and enslaved to teach him submission to God. And even David—"

"Yes, Nigel, darling," Harriet said, patting her husband's knee. "And I wonder if our dear guest's difficulties . . . the mishap on her horse . . . a proposal from Mr. Quince . . . even Lady Chatham's visit today . . . perhaps they are intended to help you, dearest Olivia."

"Help me? How is that possible?" But even as she said the words, she knew that her presence here in the home of this amiable couple had blessed her more richly than she had ever imagined possible. For the first time in her life, she felt truly befriended. And she had witnessed genuine love between a husband and wife in a way she had never seen before.

"It is not for another man to tell you what you are to learn," Reverend Berridge explained. "In order to grow, madam, you must uncover the truths about God for yourself. But I assure you, He has not abandoned you. He hears every word you whisper. And when you are too anguished to pray, His Holy Spirit makes intercession for you with groanings which cannot be uttered."

Olivia contemplated his words. "Do you mean to say that

I may somehow benefit by this offer of marriage from a man I cannot love?"

"But of course!" Harriet said. "It is not the answer you give that holds the greatest weight. The important thing is how you go about determining your answer. Will you make Mr. Quince's marriage proposal a matter of prayer, searching the Scripture and bending your knee in supplication before God?"

Olivia gazed into the fire. "I confess . . . I have always done what I thought right. I have relied upon myself for all things."

"You must be very weary indeed, dearest friend," Harriet said. "As Christians, we are taught to bear one another's burdens—not our own. I cannot imagine anything more tiring than toiling under the weight of my own cares."

"I do not think I am a good Christian." Now Olivia could not keep back the tears of misery. "I am afraid I do not like God very much. If He is in charge of my life, I cannot help thinking He has made a great bungle of it!"

"But you have not let Him take control," Harriet said. "Olivia, why will you not surrender to Him? It is not so difficult as you might imagine. Let Lord Thorne's example be your guide. Before you rise each morning, pray for God's direction. Pray throughout the day. Lean on Christ in all things. And when adversity comes, trust that He will use it to mold you into a better woman—a creature more useful and beautiful, a woman more fully able to glorify Him."

Olivia nodded. "I should like very much to do this. But you do not know the half of what I bear."

"Are your burdens too heavy for the shoulders of almighty God?" Reverend Berridge asked. "He created you and the universe around you. He knows about your mother. Your brother. The difficulties surrounding the maintenance of your manor. Mr. Quince's marriage proposal."

"And the fond attachment between yourself and Lord Thorne," Harriet inserted.

Her husband continued. "Certainly these troubles are nothing to those of Joshua, who faced the walls of Jericho—"

"Harriet, what did you say?" Olivia cut in. "Did you say there is an attachment?"

"Of course. It is obvious to anyone with sensitivity to such matters."

"What is obvious?" her husband asked. "Who has an attachment?"

"Olivia and Lord Thorne. They admire and adore each other. They are wildly in love."

"Harriet!" Olivia and Nigel cried at once.

"I only say what I see. It was obvious to me from the moment he trod on your gown in church, Olivia. The look in his eyes . . . the flush on your cheeks . . . you were both transported!"

Olivia and her minister sat staring at Harriet, neither able to speak a word. Finally, Harriet shrugged. "Perhaps I was mistaken, though I think not. But we have chatted long enough to bring our poor guest to the brink of tears. Come, Nigel darling, let us retire to the library, for you have only read me the first six pages of your sermon, and I have no doubt of there being a good deal more of it by now."

"Yes, there is, Harriet, my dear." He stood. "I felt it expedient to deliver some rhetoric on the situation of the woman caught in adultery, for I believe that event may contain

Christ's definitive teaching on the subject of peace. Blame and accusation cannot be countenanced—especially among Christians. We are all of one family and—"

"Take your rest, Olivia dear," Harriet whispered, tucking in the blanket. She merrily rolled her eyes in the direction of her husband. "Love may be essential to a happy marriage, but patience is also welcome."

As they left the room, Olivia sank down into the cushions and closed her eyes. The fire crackled on the grate, and a gray cat leapt onto her stomach and began to purr.

Eleven

"RANDOLPH, YOU CANNOT prevent this discord in the church." William Sherbourne matched strides with his elder brother. "It has already grown far too violent, and your hope of forestalling a division of the congregation is futile."

"My hope may be futile," Randolph replied, "but my faith is not."

On such a fine summer morning, Randolph had suggested that he and William walk from Thorne Lodge down the dale to Otley for the town meeting. Just ten miles north of Leeds, the busy market town nestled comfortably in the verdant valley of the River Wharfe. The surrounding fells rose as high as five hundred feet, providing the brothers pleasant views of the rolling moorlands and the mount known as the Chevin, which ran in an east-to-west ridge south of the town.

Crisp and fresh from the rain, the breeze bore the fragrance of pink and white roses that grew wild along the banks and hedgerows that lined the country lane. Cowslips, bluebells, and meadow buttercups lifted their bright faces to the sun, while orange-tipped butterflies and red-tailed bumblebees sipped at nectar. Wrens, blue tits, and dunnocks paused in their nest building to watch the two gentlemen who strolled along, deep in conversation.

"I admire your determination to make peace," William continued, "but you must accept that it is not to be. If these people wish to form a new church—or two or three, for that matter—there is nothing you can say or do. You have no authority to stop them."

"But I can try," Randolph said. "I can, and I must."

"If only Reverend Berridge would make a definitive statement on the subject. He refuses to mention William Buckland's lecture, and he will not give his opinion on Creation and the Flood—"

"Except to say that he believes them both to be true events," Randolph cut in.

"Yes, but he ought to address the infallibility of Scripture! That is the crux of the trouble, and he ought to say what he thinks about it. All he has done thus is to give one lengthy sermon after another on the topic of peace."

"He does run on."

"If he continues to avoid addressing the subject directly, both sides are likely to flee the church. Then he will have no one left to hear him preach."

Randolph mulled over his brother's assessment and concluded he could not agree with it. "I believe our vicar is wise not to take this into the pulpit, William. If he speaks in support of either party, he must offend half his congregants."

"But as it is, he appears to be of two minds. How can it be

good to have a minister who will not stand on a clear theological statement?"

"Theology, my dear brother, is a most difficult arena in which to live one's life, and I do not envy poor Berridge. The Bible is the Word of God—there can be no doubt of that. It is wholly true, infallible, without fault or error. Yet not every word of it is perfectly clear to human understanding. God knew exactly what He meant when He inspired the writers of Scripture, but man—who is all too fallible—has managed to mistake portions of it. Christ's own people failed to recognize their Messiah when He walked among them. They had misread the Scripture, you see, and they were expecting a military conqueror, not a carpenter's son who would be born in a stable and die on a cross."

"I hear what you are saying, Randolph." William plucked a daisy from a clump growing by the roadside. "But ministers have studied the Bible. It is their life's labor to instruct us on what the Scripture means."

"And so they do—to the best of their ability and education. But they are not God, and they cannot know everything front to back and top to bottom. Nor are we to be so gullible as to swallow everything they say as if God Himself had spoken it. Though forgiven and redeemed, our ministers are as human—and therefore as fallible—as you and I."

"But the Bible is not."

"No, indeed, for it is completely perfect and correct. You must understand, William, that certain matters are stated plainly in the pages of Scripture. Other issues must be dealt with in the conscience of the individual. Christians are to have no mediator between themselves and God. The Holy

Spirit has been given to us as Counselor. It is He, and not Reverend Berridge, who holds authority in the hearts of the people of Otley Church, and it is He who must be consulted in every matter relating to Scripture."

William tucked the daisy into his lapel as the brothers entered the town. Randolph always enjoyed venturing into Otley. It was a pleasant place, with many good stone houses, two cattle markets, several shops selling agricultural supplies, a fine blacksmith, and a printer. The Market Cross provided a covered area with tiered stalls from which farmers' wives sold fruits, vegetables, and fresh meats. The Cross Green sported a fine maypole. Every May Day since long before Randolph was born, young girls had decorated the pole with ribbons and danced about it in celebration of the return of spring.

As he and William passed through the town, Randolph greeted several men he recognized as laborers in the worsted mill or tenant farmers on his manor. They doffed their hats in respect, and their wives made hurried curtsies. Troubled to see so many people hurrying toward the Assembly Hall for the meeting, he lifted up an ardent prayer that no violence would erupt.

Randolph could not help but wonder if the Chatham family would make an appearance. After leaving Miss Hewes in the care of Reverend Berridge and his wife, he had been delayed in calling on her again. On returning to Thorne Lodge, he discovered that the Bryse sisters, with William's sanction, had invited a party of their friends from London for a visit. It was meant as a surprise, which it was, though he could hardly call it a happy one.

Most of his guests were ladies, and it seemed all were bent

on creating a good impression and taking up as much of his time as possible. They insisted on demonstrating their talents at the pianoforte, singing far too often, painting his portrait, inviting him to take strolls in the garden, and obliging him to row any number of them about on his lake.

When he was able to escape and hurry back to Otley, he learned that Miss Hewes was already gone. She had rested in the Berridges' home only two days. On her third morning of confinement, her mother had sent a carriage down from Chatham Hall. Nothing anyone could say could prevent the footmen from trundling her away in it and hurrying her home.

Now, nearly three weeks had passed with Randolph neither seeing nor hearing of the young woman. She did not appear in church on Sundays, and no one had received any report of her health. As he had last taken his leave of Lady Chatham under the worst possible circumstances, Randolph did not dare to send a letter or make any further inquiries about her daughter.

"Lord Thorne!" John Quince stepped forward to greet the baron as he and his brother climbed the stone steps to the Assembly Hall. "And, Mr. Sherbourne. How delighted I am to see you both here this morning. Such a fine day to be out walking."

"Indeed it is, Mr. Quince," Randolph replied. "We seem to have quite a crowd here. I understand you have taken it upon yourself to moderate the proceedings."

"I freely offered my services to Reverend Berridge, for he deemed it an importune task for a man so deeply invested in the issue as himself."

"But I am told that you have allied yourself with one faction in the troubles, Mr. Quince. Might it not be wise to employ an impartial moderator?"

"Who can be found to fit such a description, sir? Every man in the town has taken a side, it seems. No, after consultation with Reverend Berridge, I determined that I could fill the role competently. I am an employer of many, and if I may boast a little, I shall say that I am well respected."

"I believe you are, my good man."

The miller smiled. "The minister is to speak first regarding his position. And of course, you, sir, are welcome to share your views, if you wish."

"Yes, Quince, I am quite certain I shall take that opportunity." Randolph stepped into the large room and scanned the crowd. "I wonder if the Chatham family have come down from their house."

"No, sir, I do not expect to see any of them, for they are all quite ill, you know." He tipped his head. "I recently had the pleasure of condoling with Miss Hewes."

"Did you? And how did she appear?"

"Very pale and weak, my lord. I believe her misadventure damaged her health greatly. She confided in me that she regretted going out on her horse that day, for she believed it had been a most foolhardy action."

"I see." Annoyed that the man seemed to have had a rather intimate conversation with the lady, Randolph suppressed a scowl. "You spoke at some length with her, did you?"

"Very great length, sir. Miss Hewes was most eager to see me, I assure you."

"I did not realize you were such great friends."

"Oh yes, indeed. Her parents and I have been associates for as long as I have known them. And for some time now, Miss Hewes herself has regularly summoned me to her side. She wishes me to advise her on matters of business, you understand. I daresay we have become good friends over time. Such is our relationship, in fact, that we do not hesitate to venture beyond talk of wool and sheep—and into subjects of a most personal nature."

"Randolph, do you mean to sit down?" William interjected. "Or shall we stand about here all morning? I believe the meeting is to begin at ten sharp. Come, I shall find us places at the front of the hall."

"A personal nature?" Randolph said as his brother walked away.

The miller tipped his head, a smug smile on his lips. "Dare I confess, sir, that Miss Hewes and I have an understanding? We are . . . I shall say . . . happily discussing our future together. I realize it is an unexpected attachment, and yet it is to the very great benefit of both parties."

"Upon my word," Randolph managed, "I am astonished."

"Oh, but have no fear, sir! I see by your reaction that you believe this agreement may play havoc with your own business at my mill. Certainly, I assure you that nothing could be further from the truth. You will always have the best service I can provide. To be honest, your wool is far superior to that of the Chathams, and I shall have no qualms about purchasing as much of it as possible each year."

Stunned, Randolph stared at the man who was bowing politely before him. Though he knew he should respond, he could think of nothing at all to say.

"I fear I am already late in calling the meeting to order," the miller said. "Do excuse me, sir, I beg you."

"Of course, Quince. Go along with you."

Randolph watched the fellow hurry away, his coattails bouncing behind him as he made for the dais at the front of the assembly. An understanding? An attachment? With *her?*

Impossible!

Miss Hewes would never agree to such madness. Quince was the town miller! He was in trade and had no title!

Certainly, this could not be true. She deserved far better. Quince was at least twenty years her senior, and he had never shown the slightest interest in anything beyond his blasted worsted mill. Miss Hewes was a beautiful and eligible young lady who could have any man she chose. She stood to inherit a fine manor and a large manor house, and her mother would expect her to wed someone equal in society.

Marry the miller?

No!

His mouth suddenly dry and his heart hammering, Randolph made his way to the front of the room as John Quince called the meeting to order. Taking the empty chair beside his brother, Randolph swallowed against the lump of disbelief in his throat.

"Did you hear what he said?" he whispered, elbowing William.

"Who?"

"Him! Quince. He has an understanding with Miss Hewes. An attachment!"

William frowned. "Shh. You disturb the proceedings."

"He said they are planning their future together."

"Well, what of it?"

"They mean to marry!"

"Randolph, honestly. Do keep your voice down." William nudged him. "Look, Berridge is to speak. Let us hear what he has to say for himself."

Randolph tried to make himself listen to the minister, but he found it impossible to concentrate. As predicted, Berridge chose the topic of peace on which to base his comments. Scripture after Scripture rolled like marbles from the man's tongue, all his words exhorting those assembled to turn away from strife and to unite in harmony.

Randolph dutifully heeded at least two full minutes of this recitation before his thoughts strolled off in their own direction. Miss Hewes was to marry John Quince? Preposterous! And yet it must be true. Quince could never make such a pronouncement were it not factual. But why would she agree to an arrangement so unsuited to her station in life?

Randolph tapped his fingers on his knee, irked at the very thought of the alliance. Of course, it would cause him many problems in regard to his wool, and he knew he must immediately begin to seek other worsted mills with which to do business. Though Quince had said he would continue to purchase from Thorne, he would surely give over all his time and energy to milling Chatham wool. That manor would be his own now—along with all its wool—and he must do everything in his power to turn a high profit from it. What an astounding turn of events.

But this hardly consumed the bulk of Randolph's thoughts. It was Miss Hewes herself who perplexed him. How could she do such a thing? Did she love the miller? Quince would lead

Randolph to believe that he had an intimate friendship with the woman. Yet in public they rarely spoke, and in all Randolph's conversations with Miss Hewes, she had never mentioned any attachment to Quince.

No, it must be a business arrangement. She recognized her own lack of confidence in managing Chatham manor, and she welcomed Quince's offer to take the reins. Perhaps Lady Chatham had set up the whole thing on behalf of her son. By the time young Clive came of age, the miller would have taken complete control of the situation, and Quince could see that all went well until he and his wife bore a son to take the title. It made good sense, though it seemed a drastic solution.

The material point, in Randolph's opinion, was that of the marriage itself. Would Miss Hewes really consent to wed a man like Quince? Would a creature who was so young and beautiful actually allow him to—

"And now we shall hear a word from our esteemed neighbor," Quince announced loudly from the dais, "the Right Honorable Lord Thorne."

As people began to applaud, William prodded his brother. "Randolph, they await you," he whispered. "You must speak."

Feeling slightly off balance, the baron stood and took the dais. "My dear friends," he began. He paused, trying to think what to say next and wishing mightily that he had listened more closely to Reverend Berridge. "Our minister has spoken clearly on the matter before us. We must build a bridge of peace in Otley. I cannot support any division in the church. Nor will my family in any way lend our resources or our name to an action that separates the body of Christ."

He looked out across the sea of faces gazing up at him in

expectation. Most of the people here relied on him or on the Chatham family for their livelihood. Many were tenants of his manor; they rented land and housing on his property, or their trade depended on him. Despite their dependency, they were individuals who had the right to choose their own form of worship. He might control their purse strings, but he did not own their hearts and souls.

"I am," he continued, "most painfully aware of the effect that divisiveness has had on the town of Otley in the past. My own family, I regret to say, has played a part in sowing seeds of discontent. Long before I was born, these seeds were planted. Throughout the centuries, they have produced a bountiful crop of pain, sorrow, and suffering. My family has tended and nourished this growing crop and has been harvesting from it for many years."

As he spoke, he saw heads nodding in acknowledgment. Some of the farmers whispered to their colleagues, and wives gazed at him with understanding in their eyes. He had to believe that these people did not truly desire a division in the church, and he took new hope that something he might say could put an end to the rancor.

As he opened his mouth to continue speaking, he noted a small disturbance near the open door. Miss Hewes stepped suddenly into the hall, and every head turned in her direction. At the sight of the young lady, Randolph had to clutch the sides of the podium for support. Clad in a gown of the finest gold jaconet and a dark green pelisse with puffed sleeves, she wore the air of a royal princess. Her bonnet, trimmed in silk ribbons and fine gray ostrich plumes, revealed eyes as bright as he had ever seen them. She caught his astonished stare and made him a quick smile and a little curtsy as she slipped onto a chair near the back of the room.

"And so," he tried, wondering what on earth he had been talking about. "So . . . I wish to say . . . that . . . that I believe division can do none of us good. The church must find a way—all of us must find a way—to be at peace. We are not so far apart, are we? Not in values and beliefs. Not in motivation or understanding. Nothing must be allowed to separate us, then. God does not want His people to be divided. Christ taught that we are all members of one body, each with a valuable purpose. I believe, therefore, that the church—and indeed, the entire populace of Otley—ought to do all in our power to avoid separation. We must come together in unity. To that end, I pledge on behalf of the Thorne family, my every effort toward reconciliation. We give ourselves wholeheartedly toward the establishment of peace and . . . if I may be so bold . . . toward the hope . . . of unity."

As a smattering of applause began, he bowed. Clearly the people were dissatisfied with his message, and he heard several comments to that effect as he stepped away from the podium. They did not want peace, some said. They wanted a new church. They wanted victory, others called out. The miller moved to take up his former position as moderator, but Olivia Hewes now made her way to the front of the room. Randolph paused at the edge of the dais, reached out to her, and offered his hand.

She set her gloved palm in his, allowing him to assist her up the step onto the platform. "Thank you, my lord," she said softly.

"Miss Hewes, I am at your service." He breathed in the

sweet scent of garden heliotrope on her skin. "I hope you are feeling better."

"As you see, sir." Without a further word, she walked past him and took a place behind the podium.

Randolph was left with no other option but to return to his seat and gawk at this mystical beauty who had promised her hand in marriage to the town's miller.

She moistened her pink lips and surveyed the audience for a moment. "My dear friends," she began, her voice strong but melodic. "How happy I am to find you gathered here for the purpose of discussion. I speak for my mother, the Right Honorable Lady Chatham, widow of the late Baron Chatham of Chatham Hall, when I state that our family shall in no way support any division in the church. We shall give no financial assistance toward the building of a new edifice, nor shall we lend our name or backing to any new organization of a religious nature."

The rumble of dissent in the hall grew louder. But she continued speaking. "The Chatham family supports Reverend Berridge in his desire for peace and unity. And—" here she looked straight at Randolph—"and I speak for myself when I say that we shall join together with the Thorne family—"

At this, the crowd erupted. Murmurs mingled with cries of disbelief. People leapt from their chairs.

"No unity!" someone shouted. "We shall have our way!"

"Silence, you heathen!" another railed.

"The church must divide! Cast out the dissidents!"

Quince raced to the podium. "I beg you all to sit down!" he thundered. "Let us talk about this matter—"

"Infidel!" a man roared. "You are their leader, Quince, and we shall not hear a word from your lips!"

"No, you are the pagan here, Martin!" a woman called out.

"Keep the women in silence!" another cried.

"Now then, everyone—," Quince tried again, but he was too late. The rumble grew to a roar, and a shoving match broke out in the back of the hall. A woman screamed as the crowd began to rush toward the front of the room.

Randolph hardly had time to react, so swiftly did the animosity escalate to violence. He and William both recognized their peril at once and sprang to their feet. But Randolph could think only of Miss Hewes. She held her position on the dais, seemingly paralyzed as the throng pushed their way toward her. John Quince tugged at her elbow, shouting at her to step away.

"I join with the Thorne family," she cried loudly, "in calling for peace! Please! Let us have peace!"

"No peace!" a man shouted. "No peace!"

"Let the heretics be driven from the church!"

"Burn them!"

"We shall have our say!"

"Call the constable!"

Surrounded, pressed on every side, Randolph elbowed his way through the swelling crowd toward the dais.

Still at his side, William clamped his hand around his brother's arm. "Come, Randolph!" he cried. "Through the side door!"

"But Miss Hewes—"

"Hang Miss Hewes! Let Quince save her!"

The throng pushed Randolph toward the wall even as he

struggled to reach the dais again. He must rescue Miss Hewes. She could be harmed by this rabble. Even killed!

He edged around two men who were slugging each other with balled fists. People grasped his coat, pulled at him, shouted in his face. Just as he reached the dais, he saw Quince grab Miss Hewes by both arms and drag her to the back of the platform. The miller tore open a pair of velvet curtains and stepped between them, the woman captured firmly in his grip.

Randolph fought his way toward the two. "Miss Hewes!" he called as he made his way across the dais.

He ripped apart the curtains to find an open door. As he ran through it and down the back stairs of the Assembly Hall, he caught the flicker of Miss Hewes's green pelisse flash around a corner. He followed her, his heart hammering in his chest.

"Miss Hewes!"

But when he burst out at last into open space, he recognized the miller's carriage already drawing away from the hall. Planting one hand on the stone wall and gasping for air, he watched the team of horses in full gallop as they pulled the rig toward the road. Quince had saved her. He would take her home, where he would be welcomed by Lady Chatham as the savior of the day. Blast!

"Randolph, there you are!" William trotted up, his own coat torn and his hat missing. "By george, you are a fool!"

"What do you want, William?" Randolph barked in return. "Can you not see I wish to be alone?"

"Alone? You wish to be with her!"

"And what of it?" Randolph turned on his brother. "She is the most beautiful, the most intelligent creature I ever beheld.

And this day, she makes public her commitment to stand alongside me in a bid for peace! Am I to ignore that, William?"

"If you are smart, you will. But clearly you are not. In fact, you are an idiot!"

"You insult me, brother?"

"Indeed, and I shall do so for as long as it takes to hammer some sense into your thick, besotted brain." William clamped a hand on Randolph's shoulder. "The woman agrees to stand with our family in this bid for peace—not to stand at the altar and marry you! In that, she has consented to the miller."

"Impossible!"

"It is true, Randolph, and you must accept it. Perhaps you will have your wish and make peace with the Chatham family. But look what your silly dream has brought to the town."

He pointed behind them toward the Assembly Hall. Through the windows, Randolph could see the figures of men pummeling each other, chairs thrown, and lamps snuffed out one by one in an attempt to prevent a fire. The melee spilled out into the street, women screaming as their husbands battled each other. Children wept, and people rushed from shops and houses to witness the spectacle.

"They do not want peace," William said. "It does not suit them, you see? It is not in human nature to like peace overmuch. As a species, we greatly prefer war."

"This is insupportable!" Randolph growled as he watched a man smash his fist into another's jaw. "I shall—"

"You will do nothing, for you have no power to stop them. They want to hate each other. They have drawn their lines, and there is nothing you or your precious Miss Hewes can do to prevent the battle."

For a moment, Randolph stared in disbelief. "They fight in this manner—over the church!"

"Not the church. Religion, my dear brother. It is a lovely excuse to fight. People have been doing it long before now, and they will continue long after we are dead and buried. Crusades, holy wars, inquisitions. Oh, mankind loves to make war at the foot of the Prince of Peace."

Randolph studied his brother. "William, I believe I truly am a fool, for in this, you are the one with all the intelligence."

William grinned. "Little brothers sometimes know a thing or two."

"What are we to do?"

"We are to go on being Thornes, that is all. Let them fight it out; let them form two churches—or even three, if they wish. In another hundred years or less, they will find a new reason to divide themselves again. It is the way of things."

"It is the wrong way."

"Perhaps, but we cannot stop it. We are Thornes, and that is all we know. We shall continue to attend Otley Church as we always have. We shall sit in the west, the Chathams will sit in the east, and perhaps we shall have our little peace—and look at one another or speak to one another now and then. Great changes such as this are possible, you know."

"It is a very small change."

"Big enough for Otley, brother." William slung his arm over Randolph's shoulder. "Let Miss Hewes marry the miller. He is an insufferable chap, but he will infuse their coffers and give her enough sons to carry on the line. You, meanwhile, must find a lovely and eligible young wife of your own."

Randolph allowed William to lead him toward the road. They would take a backstreet through the town and set their course safely for Thorne Lodge. When they arrived at the manor house, the Bryse sisters and their bevy of silly friends would be there to greet them. Randolph supposed he really ought to take a closer look at the young ladies.

~ *Twelve* ~

"YOU MUST TELL him your answer today, Olivia." Eyes closed and little finger raised in an elegant manner, Lady Chatham took a sip from her sherry glass.

Her daughter and son sat across from her on a settee. A porcelain tea set in a pink rose pattern adorned a round oak table draped in fine white linens. As it was a warm summer afternoon, the servants had not lit the fire, and the long drawing-room windows stood wide open. Despite Lady Chatham's worries that a chill might give her a headache, Olivia relished the breeze that drifted down from the Chevin and across the purple moorlands, carrying with it the heady scent of loam and wildflowers.

"You cannot go on making the poor man wait and wait," the older woman continued. "I have already given him my blessing—"

"You have done what?" Olivia cried, setting her teacup into its saucer with a loud clink. "When?"

"Oh, he came to me some time ago." She brushed aside the

question with her hand. "I cannot remember the exact day, but Mr. Quince called here to bring me news that he deemed significant."

"What news?" Olivia demanded. "I must hear it at once."

"He was reluctant to speak in any way that might cause me to suffer—such a solicitous gentleman! Only this did he say—that he had been given information concerning the coming nuptials of a certain man whose business interests are in competition with my own. That man is to wed within the year, Mr. Quince told me, and the woman who has captured his heart visits his residence even now."

Olivia held her breath. He must have meant Lord Thorne. And that young woman—what was her name? Olivia had seen the lady and her siblings at Mr. Buckland's lecture, and they had accompanied the Thorne brothers in church on several occasions. Bryse, that was the name. But could this rumor of engagement be true? Olivia had heard nothing—no word from anyone else on this subject.

"I knew of whom he spoke, certainly," Lady Chatham continued, "and I was most displeased to think of that family producing yet another generation when my own daughter has failed to form a profitable attachment. And Clive's prospects offer little hope either. My spirits sank very low, indeed. Then in the next moment, Mr. Quince told me of his intentions toward you! How could I be anything but glad? Of course I gave my blessing. His offer is generous and most welcome."

"It is not welcome to me, Mama." Olivia stared at her mother in dismay. "I do not love John Quince, and I have not yet agreed to marry him. How dare you give him your blessing?"

"How dare I? I am Lady Chatham. I dare anything I jolly well please!" A dismissive wave of her hand caused the sherry glass to topple over, spilling the dark wine across the white tablecloth and onto the Turkish carpet. "Now look what you have done, Olivia! Clive, fetch me another glass; there's a good boy."

"No more sherry, Mama," Olivia declared. "No more until you have explained yourself! Have you no thought for my feelings on this matter? Have you no regard for me at all?"

"Not in terms of carrying on the line—none whatever!" She reached with a shaking hand for the glass that Clive had hurried to bring her and filled it from the crystal decanter. "I think only of Chatham."

"You think of yourself!" Olivia slapped her napkin onto the table. "You think only of yourself, Mama, just as you always have. Just as everyone in this town does!"

"And you? Do you not think only of yourself, daughter, when you even consider refusing the good miller's offer of marriage? Quince promises us comfort and security for the rest of our lives. He promises the continuation of our line. He promises protection for your idiot brother, who will never be well enough to do his duty—"

"Mama, please!" Olivia gasped as Clive stiffened and burst into tears. "Guard your tongue, I beg you."

"Why should I? You did not guard yours when you went into town and told the whole world that we wished to join with the Thornes in a bid for peace! Did I ever say that to you? Did I?"

"No, but I—"

"You caused a riot with your selfish remarks! The Assembly

Hall nearly caught fire. Three people suffered grievous wounds. And the poor minister was almost torn to bits! What do you say to that?"

"I have told you how very bad I feel about what happened that day." Olivia put her arm around Clive, who was sniffling miserably. "I never intended—"

"You never intended anything but to have your way! You threw all our tradition to the wind! You tossed away everything your family has stood for these many centuries!"

"But, Mama, you *did* say we would not support division in the church."

"Of course. But we shall stand on our own in this. We must never join with that family in anything, for the town functions well enough divided into two camps who serve each of us loyally." She paused. "Oh, see to your brother before he chokes himself to death!"

Olivia patted Clive on the back. "There, there," she told him softly. "It is not so bad."

"I am an idiot, Livie," he sobbed, "and that is very bad. I do not wish to be an idiot! It is not my favorite thing!"

"No, indeed."

He laid his head on her shoulder. "I am a bad boy."

"You are not a bad boy, Clive. Nothing that has happened to you is your fault." She looked up at her mother as rage flamed anew in her chest. "Mama, please speak more kindly to your son. He hears and understands what you say."

"He understands nothing. And you are as witless a child as he! A simpleton! Marriages are not made for love. Heaven forbid! If so, we should all go about besotted and silly, and we should never accomplish anything. Besides, love cannot continue beyond a year or two at the most. I once fancied myself in love with an officer—how handsome he looked in his regimentals! But nothing came of it. Our passion soon faded away, and I agreed to marry your father, which was the right and proper thing to do."

"But the Berridges love each other. And they have done so for many years."

"Commoners such as our vicar and his frumpish little wife have nothing better to do with themselves than wallow about in such folderol! We have graver matters to attend to. We have a manor to oversee and a family name to protect. You must marry Quince and bear him sons, and the sooner you begin to do your duty, the better."

Olivia sat in silence, stroking her brother's soft brown hair and listening to his shallow breathing. Clive had not been well lately, and once again she knew the clutching fear that he might perish from one or another of his various maladies. How could she bear to go on living without her brother? Of all the people in her life, this thin, sickly boy was the only one she truly loved and needed.

In the comfort of the Berridges' home, Olivia had made a conscious decision both to seek and to obey God. Not only had her bruises healed in the month since, but to her surprise, she had discovered that a growing reliance on her heavenly Father had eased her fragile stomach. When trials came, she tried very hard to recall dear Harriet's instruction. God always gives us what we need, her friend had said, though sometimes what we need is not what we have asked Him for. Through adversity and suffering, He trains those He loves.

Olivia believed she must be very much loved, for her adversity in this life had been great indeed. Now she must add to her woes this news of Lord Thorne's impending wedding. How could she accept it? And yet she had no choice but to include this new sadness in the list of heartaches over which she daily prayed.

Alone in her bed at night, she had made every effort to know God in the way the Berridges had explained Him to her. She had begun praying again in earnest, trusting what her minister had said—that she must uncover His truths for herself, and that He heard every word she whispered. And like Lord Thorne, she had refused to set one foot from her bed each morning without spending a few moments committing herself and her day to Christ.

Now she looked at her mother and tried to see Lady Chatham with eyes of godly compassion. But frustration grew like a thorny shrub around Olivia, and she felt as if she surely must choke upon it.

"I shall not marry John Quince only because you require it of me," she said, carefully measuring her words. "I shall marry him if I feel this is God's plan for my life."

"God's plan? God's plan?" Her mother tipped her glass and swallowed the last of the sherry. It would not be long before the effects of the drink would begin to show. "What has God to do with this? Marrying Quince is your responsibility, Olivia! You must marry him! I insist upon it."

"I have prayed about his offer, Mama, and I have searched the Scripture. But I do not have an answer."

"What answer do you need? What is the question? What are you saying?" She was bright red in the face, and she smacked the table with her palm. "Marry him! I command you to marry him!"

Clive began to cry again. "Yes, Livie, do marry him! Please!"

"Oh, Clive—"

"Please, Livie! Please do it so Mama will be happy!"

"You will marry Quince whether you like it or not, because I have given him my word on it!" Lady Chatham trembled violently as she spoke. "I promised him you would become his wife! I said it! I said it, and you will do it!"

"All right!" Olivia burst out, covering her ears with her hands as Clive's sobs escalated into screams. "I shall do it, Mama. I shall marry him!"

"Go, then! Go and tell him!"

"Mama, not now, for it is teatime, and . . . and—"

"Now, or the devil take you!" Lady Chatham stood and hurled the empty sherry decanter at her daughter. The bottle glanced off the corner of the settee and fell to the floor, shattering into a thousand crystal shards. "Do it!"

Olivia leapt to her feet. "All right, Mama. I am going!"

Clive rolled onto the floor and began to fling himself to and fro, his skinny arms and legs slamming into the furniture. Tears flooding her eyes, Olivia lifted her skirts and ran from the room. She snatched her bonnet and shawl from the hooks near the door and raced out into the summer afternoon.

Randolph studied Beatrice Bryse, who was stirring her tea and condoling with her sister. They were sad, they declared to one another in mournful voices, for their friends had all gone away, and the house now felt quite empty.

Beatrice wore an orange gown of shot silk with a low neckline, a high waist, and tight sleeves. Her glossy curls were crowned with her favorite turban, a grand gold spectacle trimmed in tall quail feathers. A chain dripping with pearls graced her neck, and it matched the earrings that dangled from her earlobes.

The elder Miss Bryse was not unhandsome, Randolph had decided, though he found it difficult to warm to Beatrice. Since learning at the Assembly Hall that Olivia Hewes planned to marry John Quince, Randolph had determined that he too ought to set his mind to the task of marrying. But was Beatrice Bryse the woman God intended for him?

Certainly he could find little to discourage such a notion. She had been brought up in a good family, and her reputation was excellent. Not a hint of scandal had ever been associated with her name. Several eligible men had vied for her hand without success. Educated in the womanly arts, Beatrice produced endless canvasses of still-life arrangements, moody landscapes, and children gazing wistfully into some unseen source of golden light. She carried reticules that she had beaded herself, and she was known for her skill at trimming bonnets and turbans—though Randolph found himself indifferent to ostentatious millinery. Adept at whist and other card games, she often won but was careful not to crow about her victories. She spoke French very well, and she was often seen reading sermons and other books of high moral content. She loved her sister and brother, rarely complained or argued, and liked very much to sit about smiling and making herself appear as pleasant a person as possible.

Indeed, Beatrice *was* pleasant, Randolph thought as he evaluated her over the rim of his own teacup. Very pleasant. And what man would not wish for a pleasant, educated, amiable wife? Moreover, she came from a wealthy family and would bring a substantial yearly sum into her marriage. What could be better than this?

He ought to do it, Randolph told himself. He really ought to take her for a walk through the gardens, set himself down on one knee, tell her that he was violently in love with her, and ask for her hand in marriage.

But he did *not* love her. Not in the least.

Setting down his cup, he shifted in his chair. Such a paltry and inconsequential thing as romantic passion should hardly matter under the circumstances. Beatrice was admirable in every way and would make him a good wife. That ought to be enough.

"Are you not quite bereft, sir?" she asked, turning to him with great sad eyes.

"Bereft? On what account?"

"Why, that all our lovely friends are gone away to London again!" She glanced at her sister. "Caroline, I fear Lord Thorne has not been attending to our conversation at all."

"No, indeed, for he is much occupied with his own thoughts." Miss Caroline smiled. "I believe he observes you a great deal, Beatrice. Come, my lord, tell me what you think of my sister."

"Oh, Caroline!" Beatrice exclaimed, sending her quail feathers into a wobble. "Such a question! Do you not think it a very impertinent question, Mr. Sherbourne?"

William and Captain Bryse had been studying maps at a

long table in the drawing room, and now the men moved to the gathering around the fire.

"I should like very much to learn my brother's opinion of Miss Bryse," William said.

"As should I." The captain took a chair near his sisters. "I believe we have been here at Thorne Lodge long enough for you to draw some conclusion as to the nature of Beatrice's character and form, Thorne. Come, man, give us your thoughts."

"Rather a public setting for such a pronouncement, I should think," Randolph said. He regarded the young lady. "I find Miss Bryse to be a most amiable and accomplished woman. I doubt any would disagree with me on that."

"No, indeed, for my sister is among the most accomplished I have ever known," the captain said.

Caroline Bryse took Beatrice's hand. "Do you admire her skill in the millinery arts, sir?"

"Well, yes," Randolph replied. "Her hats are striking. Lots of feathery bits stuck about here and there."

Beatrice chuckled. "Lord Thorne cannot know much about the latest fashion in millinery, sister, for he rarely goes into London to mingle with women of style and substance."

"No, but he is quite a judge of art, I am told. How do you like my sister's paintings?"

"They, too, are . . . good. Very good. She makes much use of color and light . . . and fruit."

William laughed. "Truly, you are not out in society enough, Randolph. Miss Bryse is highly regarded by one and all for her fine paintings and her most elegant hats. She has developed a marvelous singing voice as well."

"Ah, yes." Randolph recalled the numerous songs in high soprano that had filled his hall each night. "Quite robust."

"Robust?" William said in surprise.

"Hearty singing. Very hearty indeed." Randolph realized he was actually beginning to squirm a little. "Captain Bryse, do you fancy shooting in the meadow this evening? I believe we might find a great many pheasants near the stream at this time of year, for it has been rather dry of late."

"He changes the subject," Beatrice said. "Mr. Sherbourne, I fear your brother does not like me overmuch."

"Yes, I do," Randolph cut in. "I like you a great deal, Miss Bryse . . . in that you are accomplished and pleasant and quite acceptable in every way. I simply would prefer to discuss my opinions in a less open fashion."

"Then perhaps you might wish to discuss them in private?" She smiled sweetly. "Shall we take a turn in the gardens, sir? I believe the lavender is coming into bloom, and I am greatly fond of that fragrance."

"Yes," he said, making up his mind at last. "Yes, that is a fine idea. We shall walk in the gardens together, Miss Bryse, and there we may discuss whatever it is we have to say to one another."

Squaring his shoulders, Randolph stood and held out his arm. Beatrice glanced at her sister before slipping her hand through his arm and taking her place at his side. As they strolled through the drawing room toward the French doors that led into the gardens, Randolph fought down the sudden panic that gripped his throat like a vise. He ought to do this. He really should ask her to marry him. It was the right and sensible thing to do.

God had placed Beatrice Bryse into his life in such an obvious manner, Randolph reasoned as they descended the stone steps. He could not find a single thing about her of which to disapprove. She was well respected, talented, and in every way perfect. She would make him a fine wife indeed. Very fine.

"I have heard some news," she commented as they started down a gravelled path between two formal garden beds lined with boxwood. "It seems that the town miller has engaged himself to your neighbor, Miss Olivia Hewes."

At that lady's name, Randolph's muscles tensed. He forced his legs to continue walking. "Yes, I believe he has."

"But perhaps it is only a rumor, for so imprudent a match seems unlikely—even for such a peculiar family as the Chathams."

"It is not a rumor. The mill owner, John Quince, told me that Miss Hewes has consented to marry him. It appears they have become intimate through their business connection."

"How sad for you, sir, for I believe you admired her very much at one time."

Randolph paused at the end of the path and surveyed the slope of lawn that ran beyond the garden down to the road. "I do admire Miss Hewes. I have great hope for a peace between our families."

"It was not a romantic attachment between you, then? For I thought it must be so."

"We had no such understanding." He glanced at Beatrice. "I do not like to think of myself as romantic in any way, Miss Bryse. I am a God-fearing man. Rather than heeding to the whims of my heart, I consult my Lord in all matters, through prayer and the study of Scripture."

"And what does God tell you about yourself, sir? Has He written in some obscure verse the name of your future wife?" She giggled. "Does He say in Habakkuk or Ezra that Randolph Sherbourne, Lord Thorne, is to wed Miss So-and-So or to take Lady Such-and-Such as his bride?"

"I believe He is not quite so specific as that."

"No indeed. But if you will not consult your heart, and if your Bible cannot point you the way, perhaps your head must be the master in this case."

"Both my head and my heart—indeed my body and spirit as well—are under submission to God, madam."

He again started forward, following the path in a line parallel to the road. This was why he could not marry Beatrice Bryse. She did not understand him. She would never share in his quest for spiritual growth. To her, it was all a joke. A lark. Her whole world was hats and card games.

"Oh, look," she cried suddenly. "I believe that must be the young lady herself. Miss Hewes is walking down the road, just there."

Randolph spotted her at once. In a straw bonnet and a white morning gown, she was moving as if in great haste. Her pale blue shawl had fallen away from one arm and was trailing in the dust as she hurried down the road. It was all he could do to prevent himself from running to her assistance.

"She certainly dashes along," Beatrice said. "I believe she has urgent business in Otley."

"Yes, she must."

"Only one object can propel a gentlewoman to race at such a speed, and that is the quest of love. I daresay Miss Hewes must be running to the worsted mill to meet Mr. Quince."

Randolph tried to make himself breathe. Beatrice had to be right. What other duty could call the young lady so urgently? Any other appointment would take place in the library or a drawing room at Chatham Hall. But clearly Miss Hewes flew on winged feet to see someone—and that person could only be Quince.

"Shall we call out to her?" Beatrice asked. "She must hear us from this place."

"No, I do not think it wise—"

"Ho, Miss Hewes! Miss Hewes!"

The woman stopped on the road and swung around. She set her hand against her brow and peered at the couple who stood arm in arm at the edge of the garden that fronted Thorne Lodge.

Beatrice lifted a hand and waved. "It is I, Beatrice Bryse," she called down. "And Lord Thorne. We are out for a walk."

Miss Hewes dipped a curtsy. "Good afternoon to you both," she answered.

"Where do you take yourself in such a rush?" Beatrice asked. "I do hope nothing is amiss at Chatham Hall."

"No indeed. We are all well." She twisted her fingers together for a moment. "I go to the worsted mill. I have a matter of urgent business with Mr. Quince."

"Ah, very good!" Beatrice elbowed Randolph and chuckled. "Best wishes to you, then, Miss Hewes. And to Mr. Quince. Both of you."

Again, the young lady bowed and then hurried off on her errand. Randolph watched her go, dismay flooding his chest. She would marry the miller. She would submit herself to a sensible if loveless match in order to save her family. She would do her duty—as must he. As must every man of property and breeding. God's will was obvious. It could not be more apparent.

Forcing himself down onto one knee at that moment of clarity and insight, he took Beatrice by the hand. "Miss Bryse," he said, bowing his head, "it has become obvious to me that you are the woman with whom I am to share my life. I beg you, then, to relieve my suffering and consent to be my wife."

It was not a pretty proposal, and he knew he ought to have planned it out better. But there it was. What more could he say? He could not lie to her by making avowals of love and passion. He could not tell her that he adored her every smile, was smitten by her beauty, and felt the room shift at the very sight of her sweet form. He could say only this and nothing more.

Looking up at her, he saw that she had begun to weep. Well, this was the way of it. Women wept when proposed to, and now Miss Bryse would make her acceptance speech.

"Sir," she began, "from the bottom of my heart, I accept your proposal. It has been my greatest dream and my fondest hope from the moment I first saw you that we might form an attachment of the most intimate sort."

"Very good, then," he said, making to rise.

"For I believed that destiny had drawn us together. That Cupid's arrows had pierced not only my heart, but yours as well. That Eros had schemed to set our souls ablaze with passion, and that we could neither turn away from nor resist his beckoning."

"Indeed," Randolph said, getting to his feet.

"You are, sir, the very best of men," she continued. "The handsomest and most gallant, and I have loved you with my whole heart almost from the time your brother first spoke your name aloud in my presence. He said, 'Miss Bryse and Miss Caroline, I beg you to accompany me to Thorne Lodge, for there my brother languishes. He is bereft of companionship since our poor father's untimely death. You must come with me and give solace to my dearest brother, Randolph.' And on hearing that name, sir, my heartstrings sang with joy! May I call you Randolph? For nothing could give me greater pleasure."

"Well, yes. I suppose that would be appropriate." He drew down a breath. It was done. "I shall write to your father directly and ask for his blessing on our union—"

"Write to him? But will you not go into London? Surely you must know that he would insist upon meeting you. And my mother will wish to make an interview of you."

"An interview?"

"Of course, sir, to confirm that all is as it should be."

"What could possibly be amiss? I am a baron's son and now a baron myself. My properties are well documented, and my reputation is free of any blemish."

"But, Randolph darling, you can have no objection to meeting my parents—for soon they will be your own." She smiled sweetly. "And we must see to the house."

"Which house?"

"You must purchase a house in London, of course. Oh, Thorne Lodge is handsome enough, I grant you, but a lady of my breeding cannot stay in the country during the Season. It is not done. And you will want to attend balls and parties with me, surely, for all my friends must make your acquaintance. We shall go to St. James's, as well, for I am often at Court when I am in town."

Randolph looked into her pale blue eyes and felt the vise around his neck tighten a notch. "As I believe I have made clear, Miss Bryse, I am not fond of town. My manor and all my occupations are in Yorkshire. Here is where you and I shall reside, here we shall entertain our guests, and here we shall raise our family."

"Of course we shall." Her vacant expression held not a grain of comprehension. "Do you like Belgravia? Or do you prefer Grosvenor Street?"

"I do not intend to purchase a house in London, madam," he said bluntly.

"I have several friends who live in Berkeley Square. It is becoming quite the fashionable address these days." She slipped her arm through his. "You must understand, Randolph darling, that I cannot think of living only in the country. Certainly it is lovely here, but what is one to do all the time? Indeed, Caroline and I have mourned greatly the absence of our friends and companions, as you well know. Without my dear sister's companionship, I should have been quite desolate. You would not deny me solace and entertainment when we are married, would you?"

"No, but—"

"I thought not. I shall direct my inquiries immediately." She rose on tiptoe and pecked his cheek. "Oh, we shall have such a happy life together! And our wedding will be a most wondrous event. When we go into town tomorrow, I shall order my clothes—"

"Tomorrow?" He paused. "But I cannot go to London until the harvest is ended."

"Harvest? Do you speak of the autumn, sir?"

"You did not suppose we could marry sooner than that."

"I had hoped to wed by August at the latest."

"Madam, during the month of August, my men will be fully occupied in reaping my fields of corn, barley, and rye. Following that, they must thresh and winnow—both under my direct supervision. I shall oversee the choosing of the seed corn, after which the remainder must be milled. The men will be cutting bracken to litter cowsheds, stables, and pigsties. And this is to say nothing of my sheep. At Lammas, on the first day of August, all milking must stop at once, as the—"

"Please, sir!" She held up a hand. "Say no more to me of these vulgar occupations, for I am a lady and not bred to them. To my ears, the words you speak ring common and very low. I understand that you enjoy the overseeing of your manor, and I shall be glad of the financial result of your labors. But I beg you never to discuss such matters with me or my friends, for they detract significantly from the fine effect of your elegance and education."

"But this is what I do! This is what occupies me!"

"Let us not quarrel on this, my darling Randolph." She laid her head on his shoulder. "Rather, let us hurry into the house to inform our siblings of the happy news of our engagement. Thence, I shall remove myself to my room to pack my trunks. Tomorrow morning, Caroline and our brother will journey with me to London, and you must follow as soon as possible. When you have come, you will meet my parents and see to the purchase of our town house. We shall set our wedding date and proceed toward our future bliss with all expedience."

Randolph took a last look at the road before stepping into the parlour again. He could not see Miss Hewes now, and he imagined her engaged in a similar conversation with John Quince. Surely she would not race off to London to buy a house. No, indeed, she and her miller would make themselves quite content at Chatham Hall. Yorkshire would be more than enough to satisfy them.

So his future bliss was all arranged, Randolph realized. Why did he not feel happier about it?

Thirteen

OLIVIA GLANCED BACK over her shoulder at the elegant young couple who strolled along the garden path below Thorne Lodge. How well suited they appeared, she in a shimmering bronze gown and he in tall leather boots and a dark coat. "We are out for a walk," Miss Bryse had called—as though it were their daily custom, and no doubt it must be so.

The young woman and her sister and brother had been staying at the manor house many weeks. Clearly she had formed an intimate attachment to Lord Thorne. How she leaned against him, her head tipped toward his shoulder! How he clasped her arm so warmly in his! It could not be long before the announcement of their coming nuptials was printed in the newspaper.

Her chest tight and aching, Olivia forced herself to turn the corner into Otley.

"Why, Miss Hewes!" Harriet Berridge cried as she stepped

through the vicarage gate onto the road. "This is a surprise, for I was just on my way to Chatham Hall to call on you!"

At the sight of the young woman's bright face and beatific smile, Olivia could not hold back her heart. "Dear Harriet, how I should love to see you, but I must hurry to the worsted mill."

"To the mill, Olivia?" Harriet's brow narrowed. "But you look most distressed. Truly you are quite out of breath, and your cheeks are very pink."

"No, I am . . . I am all right." Olivia lowered her head. "I am as well as can be expected under the circumstances."

"Which circumstances are these?" Harriet asked as she neared and slipped her arm through Olivia's. "Is something amiss at Chatham Hall?"

"No more than usual. But today, my mother has instructed me to accept Mr. Quince's marriage proposal, and I must complete my task at once."

"I see." Harriet paused. "Surely you can step inside the vicarage for a moment to catch your breath. I believe you have run all the way down from the manor house."

"I have, Harriet, for Mama is in such a state."

"Come with me, dearest friend. I insist upon delaying your outing to allow you a brief respite. If your mother protests, you must give me all the blame." Harriet drew Olivia down the short path and into the cool interior of her home. "Let me take your shawl. You are frightfully warm. And such pantings as these! I fear you may swoon."

"I never swoon, Harriet. I abhor such affectation." Olivia allowed the young woman to lead her into the drawing room, where she once had passed such pleasant hours. "But you are correct in assuming that I am distressed. May I take my former place upon your settee?"

"Please, and I shall call for refreshment at once. We have made lemonade this very morning."

As Harriet bustled out of the room, Olivia sank onto the settee and let her gaze linger on the chair where Lord Thorne once had comfortably reclined. His words to her on that rainy day had been so kind, so admiring. When he told her what he had learned about the gin epidemic and what Lady Chatham's excessive drinking might mean for Clive, his voice had been filled with concern for Olivia's well-being.

But he had not returned to the vicarage to call on her again, and now she understood the reason. He must not absent himself too long from Miss Bryse. Certainly he could never speak to any other woman in such a private manner as he had done with Olivia, his chair drawn so close . . . his hand warmly clasped around hers . . . his blue eyes gazing with such compassion . . .

"Now then," Harriet said, entering the room bearing a tray, two glasses, and a full pitcher of lemonade. "I told Sukey I should be happy to carry the lemonade in to you myself, for she was churning in the buttery, and I have no objection to such a welcome task. Here, my friend, take a glass and drink it down. And do give me your bonnet at once."

Olivia hesitated for a moment before untying her ribbons and handing over the bonnet. As she did, she discovered that in her race down from the manor house, her hairpins had slipped out, and her careful twists and knots had all come loose. Choosing to delay repairs to her coif, she allowed her hair to spill onto her shoulders as she gulped down the lemonade and tried to calm her breathing.

"Have you made up your mind to accept Mr. Quince then?" Harriet asked. "Is this why you ran down the road to Otley?"

"I have no choice in the matter. Mama has already given him her blessing."

"What? Before you have accepted him?"

"The agreement was settled between them some time ago. Now it is only left to me to make the engagement formal."

"Dear Olivia, my husband and I have prayed for you each day since you left us. We did not believe it would come to this."

Touched, Olivia took her friend's hand. "I have prayed, too, but nothing can be done to alter my course."

"So, you do not believe it is God's will that you wed Mr. Quince?"

"I cannot say what His will is. I have prayed and read the Scripture, as you instructed me, but I do not receive any answer."

"Have you searched your heart? God's voice often whispers through our heartstrings, my dear."

"My heart . . ." Her voice was almost a sob. "Oh, my heart . . . cannot be happy. My heart longs for a different man, dear Harriet. But I can never have him."

"Why not?"

"Because he has asked for another woman's hand in marriage. Lord Thorne is to wed Miss Bryse."

"Indeed? This is news to me. He has never spoken a word of it to my husband."

"But why would the baron tell anyone but his most intimate friends until the news is published?"

"I should think he would have mentioned it, for Lord Thorne comes regularly to confer with my husband. He and Nigel walk in the garden behind the vicarage, and they talk of many things. I believe their conversation usually turns to the trouble in the church . . ." Her voice fell away for a moment. "But they do speak of other subjects that interest them both."

Olivia set down her glass. "When did they become such fast friends?"

"Lord Thorne came here to see you the day after you went home—"

"Did he?"

"Indeed, and he was most astonished to find you gone away from us so soon. He had very much wished to call on you before that, but it seems a great number of ladies had come up from London at the request of the Miss Bryses. Much to his dismay, he told us, these ladies occupied him utterly until the hour he could escape them. Immediately, he came down to inquire after your well-being. Not finding you here, he instead spoke at some length with Nigel. And from that day on, he has come to the vicarage at least twice a week. Indeed, he often dines with us as well."

"I had no idea of this."

"Yes, and he always asks after you."

Her distress rising again, Olivia stood and clenched her fists. "Oh, do not tell me this, Harriet, for it does me no good to know that he may be thinking of me warmly. She has won him! She has captured his heart! That prickly Miss . . . Miss Bryse! And there is nothing to be done—"

"Olivia—"

"With all her quail feathers and fancy gowns! And her silly, ridiculous—"

"Miss Hewes!" Harriet leapt up and clamped her hands on Olivia's shoulders. "He is here."

"What?"

Slowly, Harriet turned her friend around, and Olivia discovered that Lord Thorne himself stood staring at her from the foyer, not ten paces away from the drawing room. At the sight of him, all her blood rushed at once from her head to her feet in a great wave. And before she could prevent it, she swooned.

"It was the running," Harriet said, fanning Olivia as she lay crumpled on the carpet. "That, and the cold lemonade."

"And the heat." Lord Thorne knelt beside her, his blue eyes warm. He laid his palm on her forehead. "The afternoon is very hot."

"You are breathing hard, too, sir. Did you run down from Thorne Lodge?"

"I hurried, yes, for I wished to speak to your husband on a most urgent matter."

"Not to Miss Hewes?"

"Miss Hewes? No, for I had no idea she had come here. She told us she was going to the worsted mill."

"Oh, the mill!" Olivia gasped out, struggling to sit up the moment she remembered it. "I must go! I told Mama . . . I said I would—"

"Dear Olivia!" Harriet caught her shoulders. "Please do not distress yourself again."

Sinking back onto the floor, Olivia shut her eyes in utter humiliation. She *never* swooned, and she reviled those silly females who made a regular practice of it. Now she lay sprawled out on the carpet with her skirt twisted about her ankles like some fluff-headed ninny! And all in front of him! Oh, heaven . . .

"Mrs. Berridge, I should like to lift her onto the settee," he said, his deep voice sliding like honey through Olivia's bones. "And perhaps we ought to send for Dr. Phillips."

"No, please!" Olivia caught his wrist. "I beg you, no. I am all right, truly. It must have been the lemonade."

"I have heard that a blow to the head—such as you received in your fall from the horse—may lead to complications afterward. I believe those who have suffered in such a way are more likely to be rendered unconscious again. Dr. Phillips could—"

"No, sir, I cannot speak more plainly on this. Do not call the doctor." She groaned in embarrassment. "I am really quite, quite fine."

At that, his mouth tipped into the hint of a grin. "I believe I have seen you looking finer, Miss Hewes."

"You have seen me worse as well," she said. "I cannot believe that twice—twice!—I have fallen insensible in your presence. This is not my habit, I assure you."

"I hope not. I like you much better as you were the last time we met. You looked positively regal then, Miss Hewes."

She moaned again. "You refer, I suppose, to the day I caused the riot at the Assembly Hall."

He laughed. "You do stir things up, dear lady. Come, let me assist you onto the settee so that you may collect yourself."

To her chagrin, Olivia had no choice but to let him slip his arms around her and lift her easily to her former place. Oh, her hair was all atumble, her face flushed, and her gown a wrinkled mess! And this was nothing to the rash words she had been speaking when he stepped into the vicarage. Had he heard what she said about his intended wife? If there was an uneasy peace between them before, it must surely vanish altogether now.

"There you are," he said, releasing her gently against a pillow. He brushed a strand of hair from her cheek, his fingers lingering for a moment on her heated skin. "I am sorry if I startled you, Miss Hewes."

"You did, sir," she said, breathing the scent of his hand, the leather from his gloves, and perhaps some vague hint of cologne. "You startled me greatly."

"It was not my intent."

She longed to tell him that he startled her every time she had seen him from the very first day she laid eyes upon him in the church. She wanted to say how even now the very sight of him sent waves of delighted shock down to the tips of her toes and out to the ends of her fingers. He could barely enter a room without her heart nearly hammering straight out of her chest and her breath catching in the back of her throat. And when he spoke, oh dear, every word sounded somehow mysterious and fraught with magic.

"Ah, here is my husband, at last!" Harriet exclaimed happily. "Nigel, this is such a to-do, for I was on my way to Chatham Hall, when who should round the corner but Miss Hewes! And then what do you think? She and I were speaking about Lord Thorne, when at that very moment, he stepped into the house!"

"My goodness, Harriet, what have you done to our poor guest?"

"She swooned!"

Olivia sighed. "It was the heat of the day in contrast to the chill of the lemonade."

"Pardon me," Thorne said, "but I understood it was because I stepped into the house and startled you."

"Miss Hewes, you must humor my friend," Nigel Berridge said with a laugh. "There is little a man likes more than to be swooned over by a lovely woman."

"Truly, I am not the swooning sort," Olivia protested. "It was merely the heat."

"I am with Berridge in this—and I shall not so easily surrender the privilege of being swooned over," Thorne announced. "Miss Hewes, I insist that you collapsed the moment you saw that I had intruded upon your conversation. A conversation about me, I am told. May I inquire as to what you and Mrs. Berridge were saying at that moment just preceding this particular swooning?"

Olivia glanced at Harriet, who suddenly blushed a bright pink.

"We were talking of you, Lord Thorne, and . . . of you and Miss Bryse," Harriet said. "Olivia tells me you are engaged to marry her."

The baron's brows lifted in surprise. "But I have only just now proposed. How could you possibly know about it already?"

"Mr. Quince told me of it some time ago." Olivia frowned. "You asked her only today?"

"Not half an hour ago."

"But Mr. Quince said—"

"Upon my word, I should not believe a word from that

man's mouth!" he spat, rising in agitation. "He tells you that my wool is better—and then he turns around and insists to me that yours is superior! And as for the strife he has stirred up in the church, I can say I have never met a more self-centered, abominable—" He stopped speaking and clamped his mouth shut.

Reverend Berridge cleared his throat. "Yes, well . . ."

"Forgive me," Thorne said. "Berridge, you can see that your efforts to help me tame my tongue have had little effect. I apologize most sincerely to each of you. Miss Hewes, to you especially, I—"

"No, please. It is all right, sir. I am not offended."

He paced to the fireplace and set his arm on the mantel. "Miss Hewes, it has been my practice from the first moment we met to offend you. I find that when I am in your presence, I speak with such fervor and such animation that all my Christian principles fly straight out the window. I have repeatedly spoken harshly to your mother, and by that offense, I have harmed you. Now, once again, I have blurted out the most thoughtless and hateful—"

"Please, sir, you are too hard on yourself. You speak your feelings honestly, and I cannot condemn you for that. My mother has provoked whatever response you gave her."

"No, I cannot accept this excuse. Our minister will testify that this willful shouting out of my angry thoughts is my greatest flaw. He has made every effort to assist me in submitting my tongue to the control of Christ—all in vain. Is this not true, Berridge?"

Reverend Berridge looked from Thorne to Olivia to his wife, then cleared his throat. "Yes, we have discussed the matter."

"Miss Hewes, please accept my apologies for the harsh words I spoke in regard to the character of your intended husband. Mr. Quince is a man of great business acumen, and his worsted mill has—"

"My intended husband?" Olivia turned to her friend. "Harriet, you told him!"

"I did not!"

"But you must have, for other than my mother and Clive, only you knew of his proposal!"

"Olivia, no," Harriet said, "neither Nigel nor I have said a word on it to anyone!"

"Quince told me himself," Thorne spoke up. "The afternoon of the meeting at the Assembly Hall, he broke the news."

"I see." Olivia's shoulders sank as she realized that if Lord Thorne knew of John Quince's proposal of marriage, so must everyone in Otley.

"But I cannot think why Quince told you that I was to wed Miss Bryse. I had not decided on the matter until today."

"Perhaps he surmised it. She has been staying at your house a long time."

"Surmising is very different from knowing."

"Yes, it is."

She looked into his eyes and knew they were speaking the same words that were written across her heart: John Quince was a liar. He would lie and cheat and manipulate everyone and everything to achieve his aims. He had told Lady Chatham that Lord Thorne intended to marry in order to convince her that Olivia ought to do the same. Then he had made his case for being the logical choice.

"Well," Reverend Berridge said. "Hmm."

"Would you like some lemonade, Lord Thorne?" Harriet asked. "I do not think it so cold that you yourself would swoon."

"Thank you, madam, but no. I came down to the vicarage just now to have a word with your husband, if I might. In the garden."

"Yes, indeed." The minister brightened. "Let us walk in the garden, shall we? A grand idea!"

"Excuse us," Thorne said, bowing to Olivia.

"Of course, sir."

When they stepped out of the room, she fell back onto the cushion and rubbed her eyes. "Oh, Harriet! Only just now! Just now he proposed to her, and surely she accepted. To think that somehow it might have been prevented! But, of course, it could not be prevented, for who better for him to marry than that horrid, prickly Miss Bryse? He could not even think of me, certainly not, for I am a Chatham, and why should I ever suppose that he even liked me beyond—"

"Olivia, you are babbling," Harriet said.

"I am not babbling, Harriet. I am merely distressed, because he only just now asked her! Within the past hour, and it must have been while I was walking near them on the road, and they were in the garden together, she in that ridiculous gold turban and—"

"Olivia." Harriet moved to the settee and sat down beside her friend. "The wise thing to do now is—"

"Pray, yes, I know, but how can I pray when everything in my life is so utterly horrid and impossible! I should have walked straight up the lawn right into the garden and said, 'You do not deserve him, Miss Bryse, for you do not know his heart as I do, and you have not seen him as I have, and you will never, ever love him as much as . . .' Oh, Harriet!"

"Dearest Olivia . . ." She smiled sadly. "Whatever will you do?"

Olivia paused for a moment, her thoughts reeling. "I know what I shall *not* do, Harriet. I shall *not* marry John Quince!" She sat up. "I shall go home and tell my mother at once. Never shall I marry a man who is of such ignoble and deceitful character! I shall tell Mama, and then I shall come down to town again and tell Mr. Quince. Or the other way round. Which should I do first, Harriet?"

"I think you ought to tell your mother." She laid her hand over her friend's. "But, Olivia, what will you do if she insists? Can you bring yourself to tell her that this is not God's will for your life? Can you make yourself stand up to her rage?"

"I must." She knotted her fists together. "Harriet, my world spins completely out of control."

"No, Olivia. God controls everything. His power is absolute."

"Yes, but He has given me some wisdom and strength, has He not?"

"Certainly, and He expects you to use it as did Solomon and David and all His saints. Yet we are to remain always under submission to Him. We are not to act in our own strength—but in His."

"I must use His strength to face my mother. When I was a child, I existed in a world of books and solitary pastimes. My parents' marriage was so fraught with animosity that I withdrew from them as much as possible. With my father's death, I became the caretaker, not only of Chatham manor but of my mother and my brother. Yet I have continued to be ruled by my mother as if I were still a child. And ruled not by her—but by her drink! That is what dominates our home, Harriet. It is the sherry! It holds power over not only my mother but over my brother and me as well."

"I believe you speak the truth, Olivia."

"I refuse to be ruled by a bottle any longer. I wish to live as you and your husband do, Harriet—under the rule of God Himself, and Him only. I cannot allow my mother's affliction to destroy us. With God's strength, I must face her. I may never be able to prevent her from drinking—as I have tried so desperately to do these past many years—but I must protect my poor brother and myself from the harm her drinking causes us."

"This is true wisdom," Harriet said. "May I give Nigel this information, that both of us may pray earnestly on your behalf?"

"Please do, Harriet. I shall rely upon your prayers, for it will not be easy to step out from under the dominion of that sherry bottle."

"And you are certain in this matter regarding Mr. Quince? You will not marry him?"

"No, indeed. It is a match made for the wrong reasons with the wrong man. Though I might wed him and pray for God to make some good come of it, I should prefer to face my mother's wrath and remain unmarried all my days. God has given me the care of Chatham and my family, and I cannot believe He thinks it best for me to unite myself and all my responsibility to a man whose character is so low."

"Olivia, you astonish me in your strength." Harriet

embraced her friend. "Truly, I do believe that you have been making every effort to find a closer communion with our Lord, for your words and your actions give evidence of it."

"I try, Harriet. I do try." Olivia stood from the settee. "Until I met you and . . . and Lord Thorne . . . I had never seen true Christianity in action. I did not understand it. I thought God had made Himself available solely for my benefit—and I believed that He was performing very poorly indeed on my behalf! Now I see that it is the other way around altogether. I am put here on earth to serve Him. I am to submit myself to Him, to do His will, to attempt to grow in greater understanding of Him."

"Oh, my dear friend, God is answering my every prayer for you. I am so happy!"

Olivia made for the foyer. "Do not cease praying, Harriet, for I am far from where I ought to be in my knowledge of Christ."

"As are we all," Harriet said. " 'For now we see through a glass, darkly.' Only in heaven shall we know Him face-to-face."

Giving her friend a parting hug, Olivia felt her heart lighten. "Do the men still walk in the garden? I must not encounter Lord Thorne again."

Harriet stepped to a window and peered out. "They talk at the far end of the rose beds near the wall. Their discussion is very animated, and I believe it must continue for some time. You are safe to go away now."

Olivia reached for her bonnet and shawl, but as she did so, she noticed the basket that her friend had been carrying when they met earlier on the road.

"Harriet, why were you coming up to Chatham Hall?" As she spoke, Olivia realized that to this moment, all their conversation had been centered upon herself. Not once had she inquired about the Berridges, about the church, or about anything at all beyond Olivia Hewes herself.

"It was nothing of great importance to you," Harriet said. "I had some jars of good honey from our bees, and I—"

"No, indeed, for you meant to tell me something. Harriet, speak plainly. Come, we shall sit here on this bench, and you must be frank. What is on your heart?"

At this, the young woman's face fell solemn. "I do not wish to burden you further."

"Honestly, Harriet! How are we to be friends if all our discussions are directed only upon me? Certainly I am selfish enough to welcome it. But that is not true friendship—not the sort of holy fellowship that God intended of us. Indeed, I have just read about such Christian love in the thirteenth chapter of Corinthians, and I am working to commit that Scripture to memory. Please, I beg you to speak plainly with me."

Harriet nodded. "I have very happy news . . . and news of the worst sort imaginable."

"What has happened?" Olivia took her hand. "I cannot think what you have to tell me."

Fourteen

AS THEY SAT on a bench in the foyer of the vicarage, Harriet Berridge's blue eyes focused on Olivia. "The good news is this," she said softly, as a shy smile filtered across her lips. "I am to have a baby."

"Oh, Harriet!" Olivia threw her arms around her friend. "This was your fondest wish. I am delighted for you!"

Harriet gave a laugh of delight as they embraced. "Nigel and I have been praying about this ever so long. I believed I might never conceive, and yet God has seen fit to bless me at last. Olivia, I have never been so happy in all my life!"

"When will your baby be born?"

"In the autumn. October is most likely, we think. Dr. Phillips has examined me, and he believes it probable."

"But that is not far."

"No, for I told no one—not even Nigel—fearing that it could not be true, hiding evidence beneath the fullness of my skirts. Only recently, I could deny it to my husband and myself no longer, and Nigel urged me to speak to Dr. Phillips. He has confirmed my hopes."

"The birth of your baby will be a glad day, indeed. I do believe all of Otley will share in your happiness." Olivia saw Harriet's expression grow somber again. "But surely nothing can dampen this wonderful news, dearest friend. What else has happened?"

"It is the church." She took out her handkerchief. "I am sorry to cry. It seems lately that is all I do."

"What woman does not weep on occasion—especially one in your condition?"

"You see, Olivia, someone has written to the bishop. A letter has gone out regarding the troubles in the church here." She blotted a tear from her cheek. "My husband has been denounced. The writer of this epistle recommends that the bishop remove Nigel from his position of vicar of Otley. And now Nigel is summoned for an inquiry on the matter."

"Oh, dear!"

"We believe it cannot be long before we are sent away!"

"No, Harriet!"

"Yes, indeed, for how else can the matter be resolved? Nigel has refused to give credence to either side in this argument. He speaks only on peace."

"Peace, yes, he speaks on nothing else."

Harriet gave a sad chuckle. "He cannot get past it, for he has such a strong conviction that this is God's will. The church, as the body of Christ, must not be divided."

"But the body of Christ is greatly divided already, Harriet. Here in Otley, we have Methodist chapels at Green Lane and Nelson Street. The Congregationalists are talking of building a small church. And of course the Catholics were here before any others."

"But we cannot believe that strife-filled division is God's plan for His people. Certainly some prefer to worship in one fashion and some in another, and for this reason the various churches may be acceptable. But not the fighting, Olivia! Not the constant arguing and contention and discord. Such quarreling can be pleasing only to one. Indeed, I believe Satan claps with glee when he sees God's people behaving so abominably toward each other."

"And God weeps."

"Certainly, for we have defied Him. This was not how He intended His church to behave. Nigel tells me that during the time of the apostles, all the body were one—worshiping in unity and accord. But first Rome split away and became separate. Then, during the Reformation, another split occurred. And from that time until now, we have been dividing and dividing so rapidly that Nigel fears when Christ returns all He will find left of His body is tiny crumbs!"

"But surely many of these divisions occurred for positive reasons—as Christians have worked their way toward a closer understanding of Scripture and truth."

"Closer, Olivia? Or farther?" Harriet sighed. "It is not so much the fact of many divisions that troubles Nigel. This cannot be changed. What disturbs him is the way these divisions affect God's people and their witness to unbelievers. How unpleasant we must appear as we sling mud at each other! How unlike Christ we must look to those who read in the newspapers about our anger and our hatred of our own brothers!"

"And as we cast stones at our own minister," Olivia added.

Harriet nodded, pressing the handkerchief against her damp eyelashes. "Poor Nigel," she said softly. "He cannot sleep at night. He talks of nothing else but this problem. Indeed, he is so wounded as to be quite broken in two by it all, and I fear his health may soon suffer. He paces the floors. He studies his Bible day and night searching for some solution. Yesterday morning, when he read the bishop's summons, Olivia, he went into his study and did not come out for nearly the whole day. He abandoned making his calls on the sick, refused to see visitors, and turned away all food. He would not even take tea."

"Oh, Harriet, this is too appalling." Olivia lifted her chin in anger. "Well, if some in the congregation are so unhappy, why not let them form their own church? If they cannot be content, let them go away and do whatever they wish."

"But neither side is happy, Olivia. Each prefers the other to leave. Each believes they have the right to stay and worship in the building that is already present. Each insists that the other must give way in this matter. And both are very unhappy with my poor husband."

"But who wrote the letter against our minister?"

"We do not know. We know only that a complaint was made and Nigel has been summoned before the leaders of the church. It is clear that we must be reassigned and move away and leave Dr. Phillips and you and Lord Thorne and all our friends and—oh, Olivia!" She bent over and wept into her handkerchief, her shoulders heaving with sobs.

Olivia wrapped her arms around the dear woman and murmured words of sympathy. But even as she comforted

Harriet, fury built inside her chest. Something must be done to end this madness!

Reverend Berridge was surely the kindest and most servant-like of all the ministers who had ever been assigned to the church in Otley. He could not be faulted in any way. Even his refusal to take sides in this conflict must be viewed as admirable.

Yet what could be done? Olivia could write to the bishop, but she had little authority in that realm. She had tried already to speak publicly to the town—and had set off a riot. All the same, she must do something. She must.

"Harriet," she said gently, "calm yourself, I beg you. Such distress cannot be good for your welfare and that of your child. You must go up to your room and lie down at once. You have wisely instructed me to place all matters in the hands of God, and now you will have to obey your own counsel."

"I try, Olivia, truly I do. But in this I am so weak."

"When we are weak, then His power may be manifest—is this not a theme on which your husband spoke to us before the troubles began? And yet you and I agree that God has given us wisdom and strength to use for His glory. Harriet, I promise I shall do all that I can to assist you."

"Thank you, my dear friend. I do not deserve such kindness."

"You deserve that and much more. Be assured that I shall not rest until I have done everything in my power to see that harmony is restored." Olivia looked up at the Chevin, whose rounded peak could be seen through the open door of the vicarage. The mount rose over the town like a comforting bulwark. "I have lived the whole of my life with strife, Harriet, and I have had quite enough of it. 'I will lift up mine eyes unto the hills, from whence cometh my help. My help cometh from the Lord, which made heaven and earth.' The Lord will help us. We must trust Him."

Harriet reached out and squeezed her friend's hand. "And now you must hurry home, Olivia. Your mother will be waiting for you."

"It seems I have more than one dragon to slay these days," she said, smiling. "And so, tallyho! I am armed and willing to fight the good fight."

"I shall pray for you."

The women stood and embraced once again before Olivia donned her bonnet, drew her shawl over her shoulders, and hurried out the door. Almost as soon as she stepped onto the road, however, her thoughts turned from the problems in the church to that of her failed assignment. Her mother would be furious when Olivia returned home to report that she had not gone to the worsted mill, had not accepted John Quince's marriage proposal, and had come away with a decision to marry neither that man nor any other.

The more she thought about this choice, the more Olivia sensed it was the correct one. God had entrusted her with the future of Chatham manor, and she must do her best to fulfill her duty in a godly way. How could marriage to a deceitful man please her heavenly Father? It could not, and she would not do it.

She rounded the corner of the vicarage and headed toward Chatham Hall, her head bent low as she considered how she could best approach her mother. Not only must she speak plainly, but she must not give way, no matter how Lady Chatham railed against her. Furthermore, Olivia would need to make renewed efforts to find a younger, more able steward to replace Mr. Tupper as soon as possible. If she were to live out her life as the sole caretaker—

"Miss Hewes, our paths cross once again." Randolph Sherbourne stepped through the garden gate of the vicarage and bowed.

"Lord Thorne! But I thought you were . . . Harriet said that you and Reverend Berridge were . . ."

"I am sorry to startle you," he said, a warm smile spreading across his face and crinkling the corners of his blue eyes. "Berridge and I ended our conversation, and I lingered a moment until I heard your footsteps on the road. With your permission, I wish to speak to you on a most important subject."

Olivia tried to hide her discomfort by making him the best curtsy she could muster under the circumstances. "Sir, I . . ." She let out a breath. "I must speak frankly. It is not right that we be seen together in such a casual manner and without chaperone. Truly, I cannot stay—"

"Please hear me out. I may not call on you at Chatham Hall, and although you would be welcome at Thorne Lodge, I fear you will never come there. If we are to speak, it must be so—as if unplanned and unexpected."

"It *is* unexpected and, I must confess, unwelcome," she said, starting along the road again. "I am in as great a rush to return home to Chatham as I was to leave it earlier. I have no time for—"

"I thought you intended to go to the worsted mill."

She paused, surrendering for the moment to his persistence. "I have changed my mind, sir, as you see."

"Aha."

"It is a woman's prerogative, is it not?"

He smiled. "Certainly, and a man's as well. We humans are fickle creatures."

"I do not find you fickle in any way, Lord Thorne. You completed your education, assumed management of your manor, and now you set your course for marriage to Miss Bryse." She arched one eyebrow at him. "I cannot see that you waver at all in your path, sir. Indeed, you are quite single-minded."

"I conclude by your tone of voice that you may be slightly annoyed to learn that I have asked for Miss Bryse's hand."

"What does my opinion matter? You may do whatever you like."

"As may you."

"Yes, that is true. Although lately, I make great effort to subject my own will to that of God."

"Berridge mentioned this to me. I must say, I was very happy to hear it. And how does your effort succeed?"

She considered the question for a moment. "It would be easier to hear God's voice had I not quite so many human voices shouting at me all the time."

He laughed, a warm rich sound that soothed the ruffled edges of her heart. "Well put, Miss Hewes," he said. "And those shouting voices set me in mind of our dear church—which, I fear, must become the topic of our conversation." He held out his arm. "May we walk together again? I am happy to see you as far as your gate, though we shall pass by mine along the way."

Olivia began to understand that he would not be deterred,

so she accepted his offer and put her hand through the curve of his arm. Though she felt uncomfortable at being sought out by him when she had tried to avoid a meeting, she could not deny how very easy it was to walk beside this man. Their stride fell into a pleasant rhythm, and the sound of their boots on the stony road made a perfect beat.

Embarrassed by the cascade of hair that streamed from beneath her bonnet, Olivia realized that she had made a fool of herself more than once before this gentleman. Her effort to pursue him on horseback had landed her flat in the mud. Her words at the Assembly Hall had incited half the town to assault the other half. And today, she had swooned. Oh, it was all too mortifying to remember!

But why should she worry at all about her appearance in his presence? Lord Thorne had attached himself to Miss Bryse. Nothing could be done to alter that, and so Olivia must set aside her girlish silliness over him and concentrate on more serious matters.

"Mrs. Berridge told me she is expecting a baby," she remarked, electing to begin the conversation herself. "She says also that the bishop has summoned her husband to an interview."

"I see her friendship with you is as honest and forthright as her husband's is with me."

"I could not wish for a dearer companion than Harriet. Truly, she is the very best sort of person, and she does not deserve such misery during a time that should be so filled with happiness."

"Did she tell you who wrote the letter to the bishop?"

"No."

"Nor would Berridge admit the man's name—if he knew it."

"In spite of everything, the Berridges condemn no one."

"They are good people, and I value my friendship with Berridge almost as highly as I value that of my two brothers. Never have I received such godly counsel as when I am in conversation with my minister. He measures his words, and he will not speak unless he is certain his advice is wise. Despite the short duration of our relationship, he has advised me on a great many matters—from personal decisions to those that stem from my position in the community."

"Personal decisions?" she said. "I believe he and his wife were as stunned as I to learn of your very recent engagement to Miss Bryse."

The moment she had spoken the words, Olivia wished she could take them back. Oh, why had she mentioned that insufferable woman again? Why did she have to let him know she cared! It did not matter—it could not matter—whom he chose to wed!

"I did not consult with Berridge on the matter of my engagement," Thorne admitted. "It was a decision that came to me . . . well, it came quite suddenly."

"I see."

"But I have discussed it with him now."

"Oh."

"Yes."

He fell silent, as did she. They passed the gate to Thorne Lodge, and Olivia thought about urging him to leave her and go his own way. But she could not deny how very much she enjoyed his company. Despite the vast gulf between them, she found that she liked this man. He was easy to talk to, kind and honest, and she trusted him completely. How odd it was to think that once she had imagined him as vile and evil, the very worst sort of villain. Now, she truly must confess, she believed him to be the most admirable—and certainly the handsomest—man of her acquaintance.

"Perhaps it is not my tongue that should be reined," he said, "so much as my willfulness. I am rash."

She laughed at this. "Rash! I can hardly agree with this assessment of you, sir."

"I speak before I think. I act before I think."

"And who does not? I have said and done many things, only to regret them and seek counsel afterward."

"It is not counsel that must be sought so much as a method by which to mop up the damage one has caused."

Olivia wondered if he were speaking of his hastily proposed engagement to Miss Bryse. Did he now regret his action? Or was Olivia only hearing what she wished he would say?

"If you speak of your harsh words to my mother, sir," she said, "you must grant yourself ease. Lady Chatham, I fear, provokes a strong response from many."

"I see."

"And if you meant the church . . . well, I am the one who caused the melee at the Assembly Hall. I continue to rue the effect of my words there, yet I do not see how I could have spoken them better."

"You spoke very well, I assure you. But the people do not wish to hear that your family and mine may become united about the problem in the church. It would be better for you to choose one side and I another."

"Is this your advice to me?" she said, her face flushing with heat. "Because I assure you that I shall never align myself with either faction in any way that might cause pain to the Berridges! If you do not wish to be united with me, that is—"

"No, I do," he assured her. "I do wish it. I wish to be united with you."

"Oh."

"Very much."

Olivia looked up at him to find his blue gaze riveted to her face. Suddenly, the evening felt stifling. Her mouth went dry and she could hardly draw breath. "In the . . . in the matter of the church, of course," she mumbled.

"In all things."

"Well, certainly, and you mean . . . the town. We should, I think . . . yes. We should make peace. A sort of agreement between us."

"A promise," he said. "A promise to speak often. About everything."

"Regarding the town, of course. And the church." She forced herself to try to think clearly. "The shopkeepers and traders who do not welcome our commitment to harmony must find a way to adjust themselves to it. We could meet with them, perhaps, and work out a compromise. And as for the church—"

"I believe we should sit together."

"In the same pew?"

"Exactly."

"But there is only one of me, and you have your brother and the Bryses—"

"We shall ask Harriet Berridge to accompany you. She always sits alone in the shadows, and that should not be so."

"Which pew?"

"At the front."

"Dear me."

He grinned. "Yes, we shall sit together in church, Chatham and Thorne. And we shall write together to the bishop, shall we?"

"Definitely. I had thought to do so already."

"Very good. Write your letter, sign it, and send it on to me. I shall add my own thoughts, affix my signature and my seal to it, and post it directly."

Olivia could not hold back the bubble of joy that welled up inside her. "We ought to have a tea! A peace tea. Harriet suggested it some time ago, but I knew it could not be held at Chatham."

"I should be pleased to sponsor such an event. Will you come across to Thorne?"

"Let us have it at the church. We shall invite only the leaders of the two factions—a small party."

"Excellent."

"Then we shall both make our speeches again, and this time we are sure to meet with success."

"Will you commit to pray with me, Miss Hewes?"

She glanced at him in surprise. "With you?"

"Separately, of course. And now. Together."

They had arrived at the gate to the Chatham manor. He faced her and took both her hands in his. His eyes searched hers. "Miss Hewes, until I met you, I had never known a woman whose company I could enjoy so thoroughly or whose speech could delight me so completely. I thank you for your . . . for your friendship. For your willingness to set aside the hostility in which both of us were brought up. For your kindness and gentleness and—"

"Oh my, yes, thank you, but it is very late," she said suddenly, fearing that if he went on much longer, she would sink into his arms and beg him to hold her. "The sun begins to set and—"

"I am sorry to delay you." His hands tightened around hers. "May I beg one further moment to pray with you?"

"Of course, sir."

She bowed her head and listened as he dedicated to God their vow of peace. He lifted up the Berridges, asking for a large measure of mercy and grace to be poured out upon them. And then he prayed for Olivia herself. When he spoke her name, she could not refrain from opening her eyes and gazing upon this man who so humbly petitioned his Father on her behalf.

Lord Thorne had removed his hat, and his brown hair sifted in the gentle breeze. The gold of the setting sun lit his skin to a fine bronze hue, outlining the curve of his jaw and the ridge of his nose. How could there be such a man in this world? Was it possible that he truly could be so noble and bold—and yet so humble? Had she finally met someone with whom she could share her heart in a way that she had never relinquished it before? And yet this must be only a friendship between them. Only a warm acquaintance.

Oh, dear God, she prayed silently. *How my heart aches! And how it sings!* She lifted her eyes to the pink-and-yellow-streaked clouds and fought against the tears that threatened. *Teach me how to let him go. Teach me how to be thankful for what he is to me—and not to ask for more. Give me strength, I pray!*

"Amen," he said.

She echoed the word and then removed her hands from his. "Thank you, sir, for your graciousness. I shall never forget it."

He lingered for a moment, his eyes on her face, then he made a quick bow. "I delay you too long, Miss Hewes. Forgive me."

"Good evening, my lord."

She curtsied quickly and stepped through the gate. Before he could speak again, she lifted her skirts and hurried down the road.

"A tea with the Chathams?" William tossed down his cards and stood. "Honestly, Randolph, what will you do next? Marry me off to Miss Hewes?"

"You? Certainly not." Randolph set down his own hand with relief and rose from the table. "I should think *you* the worst possible match for her."

"My dear Randolph had hoped to wed her himself, I think," Beatrice Bryse said, "until he proposed to me this afternoon." She laid her cards down with a sigh. "It seems we never do get to the end of a game before you begin to argue with your brother, darling. We shall have to amend that habit once we are married."

Randolph turned on her in annoyance. "I have never liked cards, madam, and I doubt I ever shall. Such games are a tedious waste of time, in my opinion. I should much prefer to read a good book."

Beatrice raised her eyebrows at her sister. "Do you see how he speaks to me, Caroline? And we are only just engaged!"

"Perhaps his conversation with Reverend Berridge has set him in a foul humor." Caroline stood and accompanied Beatrice to the fire. "Come, Lord Thorne, you must tell us all that transpired between you and the vicar, for you were away ever so long."

"Indeed, we quite despaired of you," Beatrice said. "I feared we should be abandoned at dinner, and I myself would have been disheartened to think you preferred the company of a minister to that of your future wife."

"No, of course not," Randolph said, omitting that his attention had been even more agreeably occupied that evening before he returned home. "I never intended to stay away so long. But I had a great many things to discuss with Berridge."

"Why does he think a tea may accomplish anything?" William asked. "And why have it at the church?"

"Indeed," Beatrice concurred, "why have tea at all? Certainly, you cannot expect me to return from London to arrange everything. I shall be immersed in wedding preparations, darling, and I shall never be able to—"

"You will not have to undertake any of the planning, Miss Bryse," he cut in. "Miss Hewes and I discussed the matter, and we have agreed that the tea is to be hosted by both of us together."

"Miss Hewes!" The exclamation arose in a chorus from everyone in the room.

"When did you see that woman?" Beatrice demanded.

"Upon my word!" William exploded.

"A secret rendezvous!" Caroline cried.

"Insupportable," Captain Bryse concurred.

"We laid out the plan this evening," Randolph said. "And it was far from a secret rendezvous. To my surprise, I discovered that Miss Hewes had not gone to the worsted mill but was residing at the Berridges when I arrived there. She and I reviewed the situation in the church and agreed to the tea. It is, we believe, the most reasonable and efficient scheme by which to resolve the issues dividing the congregation."

"A tea party with Miss Hewes!" William slammed his palm down on the mantel. "Have you quite lost your senses, brother?"

"I am in perfect possession of my faculties, and I suggest that you begin to work at adjusting your own. Chatham and Thorne are no longer at enmity. On the contrary, we are friends—as were our early ancestors who fought side by side on behalf of their king. As with the church, division and animosity were never the original intent of our forefathers."

"You have a high opinion of yourself, brother," William declared. "You believe you may repair both chasms, do you? You will bring Chatham and Thorne together as well as heal the rifts in the church? I am impressed."

"I have no such lofty ambitions on my own account, William. But I do believe that healing is the will of God. With His help, I have succeeded already in cementing a friendship with Miss Hewes and—"

"Miss Hewes is hardly representative of the Chatham family. You must apply to her mother for that! And as the young lady is to wed herself to the town miller, I should think you soon will have to gain his approval for your efforts to make peace."

"Miss Hewes has taken her father's place at the helm of the

Chatham family, and it is with her that I have made my peace. As for that . . . that other matter . . . her future marriage . . . it can have little effect on the respect and honor accorded her. John Quince will never be a Chatham, and the manor will be under his management only until they have a . . . a child. A son. Yes, and that child will inherit Chatham, and with him we shall continue in peace."

"Surely you cannot suppose that Quince will allow you and his wife to—"

"Quince matters nothing to me!" Randolph barked. "It is Miss Hewes alone for whom I care."

"Oh my," Caroline said, slipping her arm around her sister. "This is very strongly worded, sir!"

"I refer to business dealings, of course." He had taken his fill of this company, Randolph decided. "If I have any say in the matter—and I certainly do—there will be peace between our families, and there will be peace in the church."

William spoke up. "But I cannot see how—"

"And furthermore, there will be a tea!" Unwilling to hear continued protests, he snatched a thin volume from a table beside the settee. "Excuse me. I must retire early. I have some important reading to do."

As he stalked out of the room, he heard Caroline exclaim, "Beatrice, he has gone off with your book of French wedding gown designs!"

To the sound of their giggling, Randolph climbed the stairs to his bedroom.

Fifteen

EAGER TO BEGIN THE DAY, Olivia threw open her bedroom window and drank down deep breaths of the heady fragrance of lavender, roses, and honeysuckle that drifted up from the garden below. Beyond the neatly trimmed lawn of Chatham Hall, the wild heather had come into bloom, spreading its vibrant purple carpet across the moorlands. Bracken, gorse, and crowberry flourished among the tufts of feathery blossoms. Patches of green sphagnum moss and white cotton grass marked the boggy areas, while pale gray gritstone rocks warmed in the sunshine. In the distance, a male red grouse skimmed low over the horizon. His down-curved wings stretched wide, and his cry, "Go back, go back!" echoed across the landscape.

Olivia laughed as she leaned on the windowsill. "No, I shall not go anywhere, Mr. Grouse! For I am just like the wild heather, with my roots dug down deep—and here in Yorkshire is exactly where I am meant to stay."

The morning could not be brighter or her spirits more

elated. She had returned home from Otley the evening before to find her mother already abed with a headache—an event that Olivia found she could not regret. At dinner, she and Clive had chatted about fishing, and he recounted his ride through the rain on Lord Thorne's horse. Clive did not often recall the people he had met, and Olivia found herself oddly pleased that this man had made such a favorable impression on her brother. After playing a counting game beside the fire, they retired to their rooms, and Olivia had been left alone with her thoughts.

In all her memory of yesterday, she could think of nothing to displease her. Oh, her mother had shouted at her—but that was far from rare. And, of course, she had swooned at the Berridges' house. But elegant women often collapsed from one delicate affliction or another, and so she could not bring herself to feel too greatly ashamed after all.

There was the matter of Lord Thorne's engagement to Miss Bryse, but Olivia refused to permit even that to dampen her mood. She did not need him or any other man, she reminded herself when regret or sadness threatened to rise like an ugly wart inside her. Her heart would not break over the loss of someone whose affection she had never possessed. Nor would she pine away, as silly women sometimes did on such occasions. No, indeed. Like the heather, she would survive the chilly dark days of every winter, and she would lift her head to bloom again in the summer sunshine.

A great peace filled Olivia's breast, and it had lasted from last evening straight through the night until this beautiful morning. She attributed it to God, for only He could have brought her such comfort. His Holy Spirit, who was called

Comforter, abided within her. She sensed His presence, and she knew that no matter what came her way, He would lend her His holy sufficiency.

How odd that the prospect of peace with the Thornes and harmony in the church had slipped into her own heart. Peace, it seemed, was as contagious as rancor!

She plucked a cluster of gardenia blossoms from the vase on her morning tea tray and nestled it in the curls above her ear. Shivering with the bright fountain of confidence that welled inside her, she left her bedroom and started down to breakfast. She meant to make the most of this day.

This morning she would pen her letter to the bishop. Her words about the Berridges would ring with admiration. She would cite specific examples of her minister's acts of servitude on behalf of his congregants, and she would praise his sermons for their aptness and grounding in Holy Scripture.

After sending the letter on to Thorne Lodge, she must take her luncheon and then meet with Mr. Tupper. On this day, Olivia had decided, she would tell him of her plan to find him an assistant. The two men could work side by side until Mr. Tupper felt confident in the other's ability to oversee the manor. Of course, Olivia would assure her faithful steward that all his continuing needs would be adequately met upon retirement from his position, including the maintenance of his cottage along with a regular yearly sum.

After that, she would take tea with her mother. At that time, Olivia would disclose her decision not to marry John Quince. She would insist that she much preferred to live out her life alone. If Clive were capable of marrying when he came of age, she would help him choose a good wife. If not, she would then take it upon herself to select a husband. Olivia had made up her mind to apply to her mother's sisters in London for assistance. Her aunts moved in the highest circles of society, she was told, and they would help her find a worthy mate, if indeed it came about that she must marry someone.

But—and she meant to make this very clear to her mother—she did not *want* to marry anyone. Such a sacred union ought to be made for more than the procreation of heirs. There ought to be love.

As she descended the stairs to the breakfast room, Olivia recalled that only last week she had read the teaching of the apostle Paul on this subject in the fifth chapter of the book of Ephesians. A husband was meant to love his wife as Christ loved the church—willing to give up his life for her, to love her as he loved his own body, and to be united with her as one flesh.

Mr. Quince certainly did not love Olivia in this way. Not in the least. Nor could she respect him, as St. Paul also taught in that passage. A true Christian marriage between them could not be. It must not be. If Olivia must someday marry in order to continue the Chatham lineage, she would marry only where love and respect could be expected to grow. And to this moment . . . forever, she feared . . . only one man was capable of igniting such feelings within her.

Stepping into the breakfast room, she saw that her mother had preceded her. Lady Chatham sat at the head of the table and picked at her breakfast. Her white mobcap, trimmed in frothy lace, billowed around her head, making her sallow complexion look all the more yellow and her thin lips even tighter. She wore a dark brown taffeta gown, and over it, a finely embroidered silk shawl, pinned together with a large cameo brooch.

Hardly lifting her head, she greeted her daughter. "You spoke to Mr. Quince yesterday, I assume," she began.

Olivia swallowed the instant surge of dismay. "I went into Otley, certainly," she said. "Where is Clive? Has my brother come down to breakfast already?"

"How should I know the whereabouts of that boy? I have only been out of my room this past quarter hour myself. And what did Quince say to you? Did you set the wedding date?"

Olivia poured herself a cup of tea. "Mama, I should prefer to discuss the subject this afternoon. My thoughts are greatly occupied with other matters." She dropped in two lumps of sugar. "How are you feeling today? I hope you do not have a headache."

"Oh, I do, certainly I do." She winced. "I had hardly opened my eyes when I felt the pain strike me like the blow of a hammer upon an anvil. The silly maid had opened the curtains, and the sun came pouring in upon me, heating me, blinding me, searing my brain until I thought I should weep from the agony of it!"

"Poor Mama. I am so sorry to hear this." Such recitations of woe had been her daily fare for so many years now that Olivia was able to respond with little effort. She did sympathize with her mother's pain, but she suspected that if Lady Chatham would only cease her preoccupation with drinking sherry, she would feel ever so much better.

"It spreads all across the forehead, you know," the woman

continued in a wavering voice. "It is something like a dense fog or a pillow that settles there. So heavy!"

"Oh, dear me," Olivia said, buttering her toast as she spoke. "This is too sad."

"Aye, it is, for nothing will lift it! And the smallest sound crashes through my brain like a horn at foxhunt. You have never known such racking pain. The briefest whisper from my lady's maid sends me into such torment that I do believe my head must break in two!"

"This is dreadful!" Olivia said, chewing her toast and wondering if Lord Thorne was awake by now. He would be breakfasting with the Bryses, of course. Miss Bryse must be ecstatic over her success at winning him. No doubt she would plan a magnificent wedding.

"The only thing that can ease me is a sip of sherry," Lady Chatham said. "One sip, and I begin to feel the pain recede a little."

"Aha," Olivia murmured, contemplating whether Lord Thorne and his bride-to-be would hold the ceremony in the Otley Church or if it must take place in London.

"But not enough! For as I am dressed, the torture continues. This morning, I thought I should be ill from it. Indeed, I ordered my lady's maid to bring me a bowl, lest I should need it."

"Appalling!" London probably, Olivia thought, for Miss Bryse's family would wish for their society to witness the grand event.

"Coming down the stairs, do you know, I nearly swooned!"

"Oh my." And no doubt they would purchase a house in London, too, for Beatrice Bryse would wish to stay near her family and friends as often as possible. So it was likely that Lord Thorne would be gone away from his home on regular occasions, and Olivia would rarely even pass him in the street or see him at church.

"It is all I can do to force myself to eat! This toast is as dry and tasteless in my mouth as a piece of blotting paper. And when I think that all this day I shall have to endure the creakings of my bones and the poundings inside my head and the staggering palpitations of my heart . . . oh, it is too much!"

"This is horrid for you," Olivia said, wondering if he would even bother to undertake the tea party after all. Perhaps when he returned home from the Berridges' house yesterday, Miss Bryse convinced him that it was a bad idea. Beatrice could not wish to promote any activity that would draw his attention from their wedding plans.

"And so here I sit, hardly able to lift my spoon to the porridge. It is indeed the direst of plagues! My only happiness will be in your situation. And now I insist that you tell me all that transpired between you and Mr. Quince."

There could be no question that the two families would never meet as friends in church. And as for sitting together—

"Olivia!"

"Yes, Mama?" She looked up from her plate of eggs and kippers. "I am sorry. Did you say something?"

"The engagement to Quince, of course! Tell me at once how you settled it."

Oh, dear. Olivia set down her knife and fork, and blotted her lips with the linen napkin. She had preferred to address the matter at tea, but she could see her mother would not be deterred. Very well, so it must be.

As she arranged her napkin in her lap again, she lifted up a prayer for wisdom and confidence. Then she set her focus on her mother. "I have not yet spoken to Mr. Quince," she said. "But when I do, Mama, I mean to refuse his proposal."

Lady Chatham's brow furrowed. "I beg your pardon?"

"I have decided not to marry John Quince. He is not a man of honor, and I can neither respect nor love him. To accept his offer would mean dooming myself to a life of great unhappiness and a union fraught with discord. I have made up my mind to reject him."

"Reject him!" She threw down her own napkin. "Reject him! A man who can offer us every security, every promise of a happy future? No, you will not reject him! I have given him my word, and that will stand!"

"Dear Mama," Olivia said as calmly as possible, "I do not mean to dishonor your wishes, but I must obey my conscience. Mr. Quince is not a godly man—"

"He goes to church every Sunday!"

"But he is deceitful—"

"I hardly care whether he is the wickedest man in the kingdom! You will marry him!"

"Mama, be reasonable, I beg you. I cannot agree to—"

"You have no choice in this!" She pushed back her chair and rose to her feet. "You will marry him, and if you do not set the date at once, I shall do it myself!"

Olivia stood as well, her peace fleeing like sheep before a marauding wolf. "Mama, I shall not wed John Quince. You need have no fear for your security. I mean to arrange everything—"

"Everything is already arranged!"

"I intend to employ a younger steward who can assist Mr. Tupper in the management of the manor."

"Certainly not! We cannot afford two stewards."

"Indeed we can, and I promise I shall do all in my power to prepare Clive for the possibility of marriage."

"Oh, come now! Clive will never have any hope of securing a wife. No, young lady, that task must fall to you, and John Quince is—"

"If it falls to me to marry, Mama, I shall apply to my aunts in London for assistance. I am certain that they—"

"My sisters? You believe my sisters will help you?" She laughed, and then just as quickly winced and clasped her head in agony. "Oh, dear heaven, my brain! My head!"

"Mama, please, take your chair again. We must discuss this calmly, and we shall surely—"

"No! No, indeed! There is no discussion to be had." Holding out a hand to steady herself, she started around the table toward her daughter. "I ordered you yesterday to go to him, and you said you would. You lied to me! You are no better than a Thorne! You are nothing! Nothing but a silly . . . a silly child, and your purpose in life is to . . . to wed Quince, yes, and breed a son to inherit this . . . this silly . . ." She swayed, clutching her head. "What was I saying? Silly . . . but no . . . this is all I have lived for. All I ever wanted . . . was . . . was . . ."

"Mama, do sit down." Alarmed as the woman stumbled forward, bumping into the table and knocking over glasses with her hand, Olivia reached out. "This agitation cannot be good for your health, Mama. You must sit and—"

"Go to him now!" Lady Chatham snatched a knife from the table and pointed it at her daughter. "Do as I say!"

"Mama!"

"Do it now!"

"Dear Mama, you are not yourself. Truly, I insist that you sit down and take some tea. Your face is very pale!"

"I have made a plan, and . . . and I shall see . . . silly . . . sill it . . ." She stepped closer, the knife held menacingly. "Go on! Go to him immediately."

"If I go to Mr. Quince now, I shall go to inform him of my refusal. I am a grown woman, Mama, and I must follow my conscience. Do put down that knife, I beg you, and let me bring you some tea."

"No tea!" She slumped suddenly against the table, dropping the knife to the floor and brushing the mobcap from her head. "No taaa . . . fetch my salling . . . my salling smelts—"

"Smelling salts?" Olivia reached out for her mother as the woman crumpled onto the tabletop. "Oh, Mama! Please, someone help! Thomas! Fetch the smelling salts!"

"Go . . . mill . . ." She began to slide to the floor. "Mah . . . mahwah . . . mahwah Quant . . ."

"Dear Mama!" Olivia caught her mother under the arms as a maid came running into the dining room with the vial of smelling salts. "Send for a footman to assist me here, Mary! And Dr. Phillips! Tell Thomas to go for him at once!"

As the maid set the vial on the table and hurried away, Olivia struggled to lift her mother into a chair. How could such a small creature weigh so heavily in her arms? It seemed as if Lady Chatham had no strength at all. And how she babbled! Her mouth moved up and down, but nothing of any sense came out of it.

"Here, Mama," she said, snatching up the salts and uncorking the lid. "Breathe in. There you are."

But unlike in the past, this time the powerful scent of ammonium carbonate in a perfume solution did nothing at all to rouse Lady Chatham from her swoon. She lay draped on the chair like a rag doll, her eyes rolled back in her head and her arms limp.

Terrified, Olivia shook her mother's shoulders. "Mama, what is the matter? You look very ill! Your skin . . . you are so yellow!" She knelt at her mother's feet and rubbed her hand. "Please speak to me, Mama, I beg you!"

As tears filled her eyes, Olivia heard several footmen burst into the dining room. They surrounded Lady Chatham, all talking and shouting at each other, some giving commands, others making suggestions, and Olivia found herself eased aside onto a chair. In unison at last, the footmen carried the older woman out of the room and up the stairs to her own bedchamber.

Left alone for the moment, Olivia stared at the knife her mother had held. It had fallen to the floor and was lying near the table leg. Trembling, she bent and picked it up. Had her mother really intended to do her harm? Was this marriage to Quince as important as that? And had Olivia's refusal caused the terrible malady that had stricken Lady Chatham?

"Madam." The head footman entered the room and bowed. "I have sent Davies to town to summon Dr. Phillips. Lady Chatham lies abed, tended by her lady's maids. May I be of any further service to you?"

Olivia stared at the elderly man, her mouth agape. "What has happened to my mother, Thomas?"

"I cannot be certain, madam."

"No, of course not." She swallowed and set down the knife. "I fear she is very ill."

"If I may be so bold, I should say that I suspect . . . well, we all think . . . that is, it appears to be apoplexy."

"Apoplexy?"

"A fit of apoplexy, aye. My own mother was taken by such a stroke. It came upon her quite suddenly. She did not last long after that, madam, and I might suggest that you ought to . . . you might want to . . ."

"I should go and see her, yes, of course. Please help me, Thomas." Olivia reached for his hand. "Where is my brother?"

"I have not seen Lord Chatham this morning," he said, helping her to her feet. "I am told he still keeps to his room."

"See that he stays there until the doctor is come and gone. Tell Mary to take his breakfast up to him."

"Yes, of course."

They started for the door. "Oh, Thomas, I fear my mother may perish!"

He patted her hand. "Indeed, madam. Her condition appears grave."

Randolph did not expect to see Miss Hewes that Sunday morning, but her carriage pulled into the churchyard promptly at ten. Relieved, he let out a breath and beckoned his brother.

"Come, William. We shall occupy a different pew today."

He strode toward a long, ornately carved wooden bench near the front of the church. "You must take your place beside me as usual."

"Sit here, Randolph? In the middle?" William caught his brother's arm. "But the Thorne family occupies the western side of the chapel."

"No longer. Miss Hewes and I have agreed to the change."

"Miss Hewes?" He scowled as he accompanied Randolph. "I shall not sit with the Chathams, if that is what you intend."

"Indeed, you will. You will sit on my left hand as you always do, and if you cannot be polite, you will keep your mouth shut."

"Upon my word!"

"Upon *my* word, William, we shall have peace. Now sit down!" Randolph could feel every eye in the church on him as he stepped into the unfamiliar place. No doubt he was unseating some other family from its traditional pew, but so it must be. Everyone in Otley would be required to shuffle a little as these changes occurred. It would be a sort of dance—not necessarily a happy one—that would shift people into new positions. Feathers might be ruffled and necks stretched out of joint, but eventually harmony would reign.

"If Miss Hewes were any sort of decent daughter, she should have stayed at home with her mother," William whispered as they watched the young woman walk the aisle toward them. "Lady Chatham is said to be on her deathbed."

"A rumor." Randolph squared his shoulders in anticipation as Miss Hewes greeted well-wishers on the eastern side of the church.

Radiant in a straw bonnet trimmed in blue ribbon, she wore

the gown made of the fabric he had sent her. A good sign, he thought. But would she join him? Or would she succumb to tradition and take the Chatham family's usual place?

"Hardly a rumor, Randolph," William said. "Our butler heard it from his brother, whose wife's sister is married to Dr. Phillips himself. Just two days ago, the old woman was stricken dumb with a fit of apoplexy. She is so consumed with jaundice that she is quite as yellow as a daffodil."

"Quiet, brother!" Randolph hissed. "If Lady Chatham is ill, that is all the more reason for us to be polite to her daughter. Look, she comes."

To his relief, Miss Hewes spotted him and smiled sweetly. Then she lifted her skirts a little and stepped into the pew. He had planned to make a gallant bow, but instead he stood dumbstruck as she curtsied before him. How lovely she was . . . how shining her dark brown eyes . . . how full her pink lips. And what was that fragrance that drifted toward him as she moved ever closer?

"Good morning, Lord Thorne," she said in a low voice. "And, Mr. Sherbourne, good morning to you as well."

Randolph executed his bow and elbowed William to do the same. "Miss Hewes, we are . . . we are very happy to see you."

"It is a lovely day, is it not?" she asked.

"Very lovely. Yes, indeed. And you also . . . are . . . very lovely." Randolph heard his brother's soft snort of derision at this weak attempt to pay a compliment. He would have to do better. "I see you come alone. Will Mrs. Berridge join you?"

"I hope she means to do so," Olivia said. "I have asked her to sit with me today."

"And Lady Chatham? Does she come to church also?"

At this, her eyes lowered, her lashes casting dark shadows across her cheeks. "My mother is ill, sir."

"I am sorry to hear it. Very sorry indeed. I hope she may recover soon."

"Thank you, but I . . . I fear it is unlikely." She glanced to the side, clearly as aware as he of the scrutiny of the congregation. Lowering her voice even more, she leaned near him. "Dr. Phillips believes my mother has suffered a fit of apoplexy. She cannot speak clearly, nor is she able to move her right leg or arm. In addition, sir, she endures a severe case of jaundice."

"Her health must be greatly compromised by this."

"Very much so. We fear her liver begins to fail." Her lower lip trembled, and she drew a handkerchief from her reticule. "I should thank you very much, sir, if you would pray for my mother."

"Indeed, Miss Hewes," he said, reaching for her arm. "Of course I shall pray for her. And for you, as I have done already. May I help you to sit down, dear lady?"

"Thank you." She leaned into him slightly, allowing him to settle her onto the pew. "I do not mean to make a spectacle of myself. I have every intention of carrying through with our plan, sir. Have you spoken to Reverend Berridge about the tea?"

"Yes," he said, seating himself beside her. "He thinks it a capital idea, of course. We have set the tea for this coming Wednesday, if that is not too soon for you."

"It cannot come too soon, sir. I am told the unrest in town grows stronger by the day. The night before last, someone threw a stone through the Berridges' window."

He stiffened. "Berridge said nothing of this!"

"He would not, of course. Harriet told me only because I discovered her weeping yesterday afternoon. She had come up to Chatham Hall to call on me, and I left her alone for no more than ten minutes. When I returned, I found her in tears, and I implored her to tell me everything. I have not had time to write a letter to the bishop on behalf of the Berridges, for every moment is consumed with caring for my mother."

"And Lord Chatham? How fares your dear brother?"

"Not well." She shook her head. "Clive is confused. He cannot comprehend what has happened."

"It is difficult for anyone to understand the illness of a parent."

At this, she looked up gratefully. "You speak truth, sir. I struggle with it myself. Had I not the comfort of Harriet's faithful companionship during these days and the assurance that God walks with me through this shadowed valley, I doubt I could endure it."

"Reverend Berridge told me recently that such shadows are actually the wings of the Almighty, beneath which we may hide ourselves in the assurance that He watches over and protects us. I have found that image to be—"

Randolph felt his brother's elbow in his side, and he glanced around to find John Quince stepping into the pew. The man wore a dark look, his mouth drawn into an unhappy line as he edged toward them.

"You are in for it now," William whispered. "Fraternizing so freely with the miller's intended. I hope you brought your knife along."

"Nonsense." Randolph stood to greet the man. "Mr. Quince, good morning."

The miller bowed. "Good morning to you, my lord. And to you, Mr. Sherbourne." His eyes fastened on the young woman, who stood quickly and curtsied. "Miss Hewes, you are looking well."

"Thank you, Mr. Quince, but I confess, I suffer greatly beneath the onus of my mother's ill health."

"As I feared," he said. "I mean to call on Lady Chatham today—this very afternoon, if I may be so bold."

"Thank you, sir, but she is unable to receive visitors. She keeps to her bedchamber."

"How very sad for her." He bent his head for a moment. "But you must require some diversion from this constant burden, madam. I should be most pleased to offer you respite and solace. Please tell me when I may stop at Chatham Hall, and I shall be eager to do my part to cheer you."

A flash of envy seared Randolph's chest as he thought of the ease with which such a man—any man but himself, for that matter—could pay a visit to that house. But he quickly suppressed it. Miss Hewes had agreed to marry Quince, and the miller had both the right and the duty to attend her at this difficult time.

"I thank you, Mr. Quince," she said, offering him a small smile. "But I fear your offer of succor must be in vain. My hours are consumed with meeting my mother's needs while continuing to oversee the manor. When my mother and I are able to accept callers, sir, I shall send word to you directly."

He nodded. "Of course, madam."

Startled by Miss Hewes's reply to her intended, Randolph was distracted when the miller turned to him.

"I observe that your fiancée has departed your abode, sir," he said. "I am sorry to hear this. Miss Bryse has gone away to London, I suppose."

"London? Ah—indeed she has. With her brother and sister."

"She must be much occupied with preparations for the wedding."

"I suppose so, yes."

"Very good, sir. And I imagine your future wife is most encouraged by the accord worked out between you and Miss Hewes, for I observe that you both choose to break from tradition today and take a pew together."

"Miss Bryse has no opinion on the matter," Randolph said. "I sit where I please."

"But I do have an opinion," William spoke up. "I think it highly irresponsible and thoughtless to—"

"Thank you, brother," Randolph cut in. "Mr. Quince, I am sure you will be happy to join us here after you and Miss Hewes are wed. I am certain in fact, that her wise decision to promote peace—"

"Wed?" The young woman at his side interrupted him. "Lord Thorne, I am afraid you are mistaken in your supposition that I am to marry Mr. Quince."

"But he . . ." Randolph glanced from Miss Hewes to the miller. "He told me you had agreed to his proposal."

"I beg your pardon, but I said nothing of the sort, sir." As a fine sheen of perspiration broke out on his forehead,

Quince produced a white handkerchief and dabbed at his brow as he spoke. "I informed you that Miss Hewes and I have enjoyed much discussion about our future. I do plan for us to marry, of course. Lady Chatham is most eager to see the attachment formalized—"

"But I am not, sir," Miss Hewes said. "I am not eager to accept your proposal, sir. Far from it."

"I beg your pardon?" His hand paused in blotting. "What can you mean?"

"Only this, Mr. Quince. I refuse your proposal of marriage. I am sorry to make my position known in so public a place, but you have forced the issue. I thank you for your offer. It was welcomed by my mother, as you stated. Yet, after much consideration and prayer, I have concluded that marriage to you is not God's best plan for me or for Chatham, and I must kindly refuse you."

With that, she sat down.

Randolph stared at the miller, whose face suddenly flushed a bright red. Then he glanced at his brother, who was struggling to hold back a grin. As he cleared his throat, he saw Reverend Berridge ascend to the pulpit and spread his arms.

"As David spoke in the fourth psalm and the eighth verse," he announced, "'I will both lay me down in peace, and sleep: for Thou, Lord, only makest me dwell in safety.' Let us be seated and bow our heads in meditation upon the Word of the Lord."

Randolph sat down beside Olivia Hewes and tried to still the hammering of his heart. Her hands were clasped together tightly, and he discerned a slight tremble in her breathing. Against her mother's wishes, she had refused John Quince!

How bold of her. How daring. He wanted nothing more than to take her in his arms and plant a congratulatory kiss on those beautiful pink lips!

But he had promised himself to Beatrice Bryse. He had done what seemed at the time to be the sensible thing . . . the right thing. So why did his chest ache and his brain pound with recriminations? Because his action had been neither sensible nor right. His marriage proposal had come of an explosive reaction to seeing Miss Hewes on her way to visit the man he had assumed was her fiancé.

Randolph's rashness in word and deed had brought him to this end! Nothing now could undo it. His own lack of control, his impulsiveness, his failure to submit to the authority of Christ—these combined had swept him into a future that must be filled with discord and acrimony.

"I shall speak my message this morning on a subject that by now should be familiar to all of you," Reverend Berridge intoned from the pulpit.

Beside Randolph, Olivia Hewes lifted her head. Joining with her minister, she whispered the word in a sigh. *"Peace."*

Sixteen

Olivia sat beside her mother, clasping a frail hand and gazing into rheumy eyes so saturated with yellow pigment that they were almost unbearable to observe. Dr. Phillips had come to call on Lady Chatham the evening before, and he predicted that her passing could come at any time. Olivia realized that her mother's absence would make some aspects of life simpler. But she found her heart weighed heavy at the thought of losing this woman who had exerted such an influence in the community.

"Mama," she said softly, "how do you feel this afternoon?"

As always since her attack, Lady Chatham mumbled unintelligible words of response, her tongue and lips thicker than they had ever been when affected by her abuse of liquor.

Olivia stroked a hand along her mother's arm. "Did I tell you that I am going into Otley today?" she asked. Then she paused and waited for an answer, forgetting for a moment that the conversation was one-sided. "The church is hosting a tea. Reverend Berridge makes another attempt at peace in the congregation."

She elected not to tell her mother that Lord Thorne would be in attendance. John Quince would be there as well, but Olivia could not bring herself to inform Lady Chatham about their encounter in church. Olivia's strong words on the subject of marriage had brought on this fit of apoplexy that had so greatly afflicted her mother. Indeed, Olivia held herself partially responsible for that terrible event.

She might have blamed herself entirely if not for Harriet Berridge. Lady Chatham's current condition was primarily a result of her excessive consumption of hard spirits, Olivia's friend reminded her, and had not been caused by a simple argument between a mother and daughter. Dr. Phillips concurred with that analysis, explaining to Olivia that regular overuse of alcohol afflicted the health and often led to diseases of the liver and fits of apoplexy.

"I hope you will not mind my being gone, Mama," she said gently. "I shall hardly be away more than two hours, and Dr. Phillips has consented to sit with you during my absence."

She reached out and tucked a wisp of hair back under her mother's white mobcap. "Clive will be here, too, of course. I have agreed to take him fishing this evening when I return from the tea. He is determined to catch something delicious for your dinner, Mama, for he cannot think . . . he cannot think how to please you more."

As she spoke, tears filled her eyes at the realization that her mother could no longer enjoy Clive's fish or any other solid food. Indeed, she barely swallowed sips of cool water—and winced horribly at that. Lady Chatham muttered something as Olivia drew her handkerchief from her reticule. Despite all the years of wishing that her mother would rein her sharp tongue, she now would give anything to hear a single word of sense from the woman's lips.

"Clive wishes to see you more often, Mama," Olivia whispered, "but he grows so angry and frustrated when I allow him into your bedchamber that I must keep him away. I cannot think how to explain . . . how to tell him . . ."

She could not speak of her mother's impending death, and so she wept into her handkerchief for a moment. But this would never do. Lady Chatham needed to spend her final days in comfort and assurance that all was well. Yet how could it be well, when Olivia had little confidence that her mother would spend eternity in the presence of God? A person's immortal soul could be saved by grace alone. Yet Christ, as well as the apostles Paul and James, had taught that people's faith must be evidenced in their works, in the fruit of their life. If that was true—and Olivia had no doubt of it—then Lady Chatham had little to recommend her to the Almighty.

Again, Olivia thought of how different life here at Chatham Hall must be without her mother. Clive would surely be inconsolable. Their meals and afternoon teas would be so quiet, so empty of conversation. Though the weight of the manor had fallen on Olivia's shoulders in recent years, she had always known that her mother's firm presence held ultimate sway both in the manor and in the town. How could she ever take Lady Chatham's place?

A rap on the door drew Olivia's attention away from her heavy thoughts. One of Lady Chatham's maids ushered Dr.

Phillips into the darkened bedchamber. The gentleman took one look at his patient, and his face grew somber.

Olivia read his expression immediately. "Perhaps I should not go into town, sir," she said. "I fear my mother is too unwell."

Dr. Phillips regarded Lady Chatham again; then he drew Olivia aside and spoke to her in a low voice. "Your mother is very ill, but she remains conscious. I believe she will not succumb today, madam. Jaundice of the liver commonly precedes the general failure of all internal organs. This failure is accompanied by a period of torpor leading to insensibility and, finally, to coma." He paused. "Miss Hewes, may I speak frankly?"

"Of course, sir."

"Upon leaving my home, I observed several leading gentlemen of the town gathering at the church. Lord Thorne himself had arrived already and stood at the door to greet them." He glanced at Lady Chatham, then returned his attention to Olivia. "Your mother's influence will not long be felt in Otley. But you and Lord Thorne hold the future of our church in your hands. Miss Hewes, I believe you should go to the tea."

Olivia nodded, understanding the sincerity with which he spoke. She stepped to her mother's bedside and gently kissed the pale, cold forehead. "Dearest Mama," she said, "I must leave now. Dr. Phillips has come to sit with you. Try to rest." Pausing a moment, she bent and spoke in her mother's ear. "I love you."

As she hurried from the room, Olivia realized she had never spoken those words to her mother in all her life. Nor had she ever heard such an expression of affection from either of her parents. Love had not been cultivated at Chatham Hall, and Olivia had to wonder if the animosity that had begun with her ancestors so many centuries before had seeped down through the generations and into the very fiber of her own family. Did hatred breed hatred? Did anger give birth to rage? Did bitterness run through her veins like some diseased sap through a vine?

Stepping into her carriage, Olivia looked up at the gray stone walls of the manor house. Had these vines of unforgiveness led to the hostility between her parents? Had they caused her mother to drown her pain in drink? Had years upon years of rancor finally culminated in the birth of a child so physically and mentally hampered that the continuation of the family's lineage hung by a thread? And had all this evil crept out of Chatham Hall across the moor to Thorne Lodge and down into the very crevices between the cobblestones that lined the streets of Otley—causing hatred between families and division in the church?

Olivia knew in her heart that the answer was yes. But how could she—a single woman without family, resource, or training—hope to make any difference? Threading her fingers together in a tight knot, she prayed for help. She could not do this. Nor did she want to do it alone. This healing could only be brought about by one. By God Himself.

When the carriage pulled to a stop in the churchyard, Olivia took a moment to settle herself. She checked her bonnet ribbons, smoothed her gloves over her wrists, and straightened her shawl. Then she pinched her cheeks and pursed her lips until she had worked up a delicate blush. All attention this afternoon must be on the quest for peace. To that end, she would make herself as lovely as a tuft of wild heather—and every bit as tenacious.

As she descended the carriage, Olivia saw Lord Thorne stepping up to greet her. In a greatcoat of light gray wool, a high collar with a white neckcloth, and straight trousers tucked into tall black boots, he looked very much the distinguished gentleman as he doffed his hat. His gentle smile and warm hand on her arm nearly unraveled her careful composure. When he leaned close and spoke words of welcome and gratitude, it was all she could do to keep from burying her face in his shoulder and pouring out the anguish that boiled up inside her. Instead, she willed herself to remember that this man belonged to Beatrice Bryse, and that he might be Olivia's friend—but nothing more—for the rest of her life.

"My mother is under the care of Dr. Phillips," she said, answering his query after Lady Chatham's health. "She does not fare well, sir. I fear she cannot survive beyond tomorrow."

He fell silent, his head bowed in solemnity at the news. "May I tell you how very sorry I am to learn of this?" he asked in a low voice. "Both my parents were taken from me suddenly. I had no time to contemplate their loss before they were gone. I cannot imagine your grief."

"Thank you. It is . . . it is difficult. Clive suffers greatly. At home, we are all at sixes and sevens, and I fear we shall . . . we shall be so for some time." Before the tears could come again, she took a deep breath. "But I have promised to take him fishing after the tea, and that should cheer him greatly. I hope all is well with your brother, sir. And Miss Bryse."

"William is in high spirits. I believe he means to return to the Naval Academy soon."

"To Portsmouth. Oh, I see." Realizing the assembly had

already gathered for the tea, she started for the church. "Now that your marriage is assured, he must be greatly relieved."

There, Olivia thought, she had done it again. Why could she not keep her thoughts about Miss Bryse to herself? Let Lord Thorne marry whomever he liked! It was not her affair.

"I believe he is relieved, indeed," Thorne said. "William wants nothing more for himself and those he loves than stability and security, though I assure you, he would deny it vehemently. He has behaved in every way the carefree rake, and yet I know very well he would like to see all three of the Sherbourne brothers married and settled—preferably all under the roof of Thorne Lodge."

"You know your brother well."

He gave a mirthless chuckle. "Better than I know myself, I fear," he muttered as they stepped into the narthex.

"But your middle brother has gone away to India," Olivia commented, grateful to follow a conversation that led away from Miss Bryse. "He is not likely to find a wife there, is he?"

"Edmund? No, indeed. I fear he will not meet many eligible ladies where he resides. The few Englishwomen living in India are officers' wives or are married to senior partners in trading companies. Edmund, I believe, is as wise as you have been, Miss Hewes, in electing a life of solitude."

Olivia took his arm as they descended the stone steps to the assembly room beneath the church. How odd that Lord Thorne spoke of marriage as if it were an undesirable option. Unaccustomed to such honesty, she wondered if she might respond in kind.

"I shall have to marry someone eventually," she told him.

"I doubt that Clive will be able to find a suitable wife, and so the task must fall to me."

"You speak of that prospect with little joy in your voice, Miss Hewes."

"No," she said. "I have come to believe that God intends a husband to love his wife, as St. Paul wrote to the Ephesians, and I am hardly likely to make a man love me unless I love him, too. So it seems a hopeless matter."

He halted on the steps, the shadows of the narrow stairwell enclosing them as he turned to her. "You do not believe any man could love you?"

She leaned back, pressing her shoulders against the wall and spreading her fingers across the cool stone for support. "I have not found such a man. Or he has not found me."

"Perhaps he has found you, Miss Hewes, and you are unaware of it."

"Not Mr. Quince . . . he does not love me."

"Someone else, then."

"If so, he has not made himself plain."

"No . . . I think perhaps . . . perhaps he has botched it."

"Botched it," she repeated softly. She gazed at his tall shape in the semidarkness, aware of him standing so near, his eyes on her face. "Is this gentleman rash, do you suppose?"

"I believe he must be. The sort who speaks before he thinks."

"Then perhaps he does not know his own mind." She spoke quickly, unable to make herself stop. Her pulse quivered in her throat, and it was all she could do to breathe.

"You believe he may not know he loves you?"

"I wonder if such a rash man could be certain of anything."

"He is certain of many things, Miss Hewes."

"Is he?"

"And of this, most imperatively."

"Of love?" She trembled as his finger stroked her arm.

"Yes. He is very certain of his love for you."

She closed her eyes as his lips touched her cheek. They were warm, and his breath sent shivers down her neck.

"But perhaps you do not believe yourself capable of loving such a man," he whispered.

"A man so rash . . ." She laid her hand on his shoulder, memorizing the curve of the muscle beneath his greatcoat. "A man so rash that he might ask for one woman's hand . . . yet kiss another in a darkened stairwell?"

At her words, he drew back. "You are right. How could you ever trust such a man?"

"Or love him?"

"Impossible." He turned away. "Forgive me. The assembly awaits us." He took the stairs rapidly now, descending so fast she could barely keep up.

As she followed him into the brightly lit room, she reached out, touching his elbow. "Lord Thorne," she called.

He turned. "Yes, Miss Hewes?"

"I believe I could."

His face registered confusion. "You could?"

"Very much so."

"Dearest lady, we must leave this place at once," he said, stepping to her side and taking her arm. "There is much to be said and—"

"Indeed there is!" Townsman James Bowden of Brooking House approached, clapping his hands in delight. "There is very much to be said, and we all await you, Lord Thorne.

And, my dear Miss Hewes, I am sure you have a great deal to tell us as well. Do come and take your places, for the tea is hot and the scones are ready to be served!"

Randolph covertly studied Olivia as she sipped her tea and chatted pleasantly with the gentlemen who surrounded her. To his relief, John Quince had chosen not to attend the gathering. No doubt the man had been embarrassed at the public refusal of his marriage proposal, and he probably had no desire to participate in discussions aimed at unity—to which he was totally opposed. Randolph felt sure Quince had authored the letter censuring Reverend Berridge and calling for his removal from the church at Otley.

Olivia seemed unaware of Quince's absence as she made polite conversation. She spoke of her mother's poor health, of the new breed of sheep she hoped to introduce to her flock, of her interest in damming a stream on her property, and of her desire to host a harvest ball at Chatham Hall in the autumn. She inquired after Mr. Bowden's family—his wife and four lovely daughters: Ivy, Caroline, Madeline, and Clementine—and expressed a desire to call on them soon. She spoke kindly to Mr. Baine, asked about repairs he was making to Nasmyth Manor, and wondered how his young son, Paul, was getting on in school. The head of the Laird family, as well as the Billingsworths, Kibbles, and Seawards all received her solicitous greetings and polite inquiries.

But each time she tilted her head just so, her gaze slid across to Randolph, and he discovered that he could hardly follow his own conversation. Seated at the far end of the table from her, he made every effort to carry on intelligent discussions with those around him. Yet each time he discovered Olivia's brown eyes fastened on him, he immediately lost his train of thought.

She could love him! She had confessed it—and it must be true. And he loved her. No doubt about that.

How those ill-conceived words had slipped from his tongue, he had no idea. As usual, his rashness had gotten the better of him. All unplanned, he had confessed his love, kissed her on the cheek, and relished the urge to carry her off like some rakish pirate. What had he been thinking? Nothing, of course. He hadn't thought at all. He had merely acted on impulse. As bad as that was, it had produced the most remarkably happy result. She loved him, too! At least, she thought she could. Amazing!

Randolph spied Nigel Berridge halfway down the table, stirring too many lumps of sugar into his tea. What would the minister make of this turn of events? How would he advise his hasty and incautious friend? And how on earth could Randolph find another way to be alone with Olivia Hewes?

He had to kiss her again—that was all there was to it. He could not be satisfied with less. A kiss? How much more he wanted! The sight of her sitting there so prim in her pale blue gown and white gloves filled him with such ardor that he could hardly contain himself. How might it feel to hold her in his arms? to peel away her gloves and press his lips to each delicate finger? to trail his hand down her smooth white neck and know the rapture of her love?

"And Miss Bryse?" Mr. Bowden nodded, smiling at him.

"Pardon?"

"I understand congratulations are in order!" The gentleman beamed. "I believe there is nothing better than a good marriage. Indeed, as the great Martin Luther himself once wrote, 'There is no more lovely, friendly and charming relationship, communion or company than a good marriage.' Mrs. Bowden and I are the happiest of couples, sir, and I pray that your own union will be as blessed."

"Thank you." Randolph stared into his teacup.

"But Miss Bryse is gone away to London, I hear. I am very sorry for you!"

"She is . . . uh . . . yes, gone away." Randolph cleared his throat. "Her family lives there. And she has a great many friends in town."

"Of course she does! A fine lady always moves in good society. And I believe you have chosen a very fine lady for your wife. None finer!"

"Well, I suppose there may be some finer. One, at least, might be finer."

"But the eyes of love view the chosen object of affection as the very finest of creation! Surely, my lord, you cannot deny this."

Randolph glanced at Olivia, who was looking at him with a liquid brown gaze. "The eyes of love . . ." He swallowed and forced himself to focus on Mr. Bowden again. "Sir? You were saying?"

"Why, that in your eyes, Miss Bryse must surely be the finest woman on earth. The most beautiful! The most delicate and feminine! I declare, when I first met my dear Mrs. Bowden—of course, she was not Mrs. Bowden at the time—

I was enraptured! 'James,' I said to myself, 'this is indeed the most charming creature you have ever seen.' And can you imagine what leapt into my thoughts at that very moment!"

Randolph frowned, trying to follow. "No, sir, I cannot."

"Why, it was John Milton himself! Verses of his *L'Allegro* sprang forth from my enraptured breast:

"Haste thee, Nymph, and bring with thee
Jest and youthful jollity,
Quips and cranks and wanton wiles,
Nods and becks and wreathèd smiles.

"And do you know, that is exactly what she has been to me these many years."

"Really?" Randolph asked, trying to envision the stout Mrs. Bowden as a nymph. "All that?"

"That and more. And so it will be for you, sir, when you wed the woman you love."

"Thank you, Mr. Bowden." Randolph could see that Reverend Berridge was rising to call the assembly to order. "Your enthusiasm is much appreciated."

"Very good, sir. And may you have every happiness." James Bowden backed away, bowing as he went.

Though Randolph knew the man's words were kindly meant, he could only contrast this portrait of domestic bliss with the gloomy prospect of the marriage that awaited him. Blast it all! Why had he asked Beatrice Bryse to marry him? And could he ever find a way to free himself from that entanglement? Even if he did, was there really a chance that Miss Hewes would consent to become his wife?

As the woman in question rose to give her speech on behalf

of peace in Otley, he recalled her words to him. She had said only that she thought she could love him. She had not been sure of it. Not absolutely positive.

Yet how could she refuse him? He loved her so deeply. With such passion. Such ardor. On the other hand, how could she ever agree to marry him? How could it all be worked out? Where would they live? A Chatham married to a Thorne? Unthinkable.

"And that is why we must all labor together for peace," she was saying as he stared at her, drinking in the play of candle-light on her glossy brown curls. "Thank you very much, gentlemen." She turned to him. "Lord Thorne?"

"Yes, Miss Hewes?" he asked, lost in her.

"Have you something to say?" Regarding him, she pressed her lips together for a moment. "About the situation within the church?"

"Ah, yes." Collecting himself, Randolph stood and fished in his coat pocket for the speech he had written that morning. "Yes, of course, I have something to say. Thank you very much, Miss Hewes."

Smiling at him, she seated herself and placed her hands in her lap. Randolph unfolded his notes and gazed down at his own handwriting. The words might have been Chinese for all he could comprehend them! Good heavens, he must snap out of this.

"My dear friends and neighbors," he began, focusing on the message he had penned with such careful thought. "God has often used war to further His ends. Battle, war, armed conflict—throughout the ages, these have been permitted by the Almighty. Our excellent minister, Reverend Berridge, has taught us that the Hebrews considered every war as essentially religious, for their God was the God of hosts and their battles were the Lord's battles. They fought against the enemy. Good against evil. God against Satan."

Warming now to his subject, Randolph surveyed the people gathered around him. "We know all too well that war is fought on Earth. England's brave armies are even now nobly engaged in the French and Napoleonic Wars, as they have been these many years. But battle is also undertaken in the spiritual realm. As Christians, we are called upon to engage in such spiritual battles. St. Paul reminds us that 'though we walk in the flesh, we do not war after the flesh. For the weapons of our warfare are not carnal, but mighty through God to the pulling down of strong holds.' In both physical and spiritual warfare, then, we are to fight against the enemy. The enemy, my dear friends, is Satan and those who serve him."

As heads nodded around the table, Randolph felt hope surge through his chest. "You and I are Christian brothers in this battle against evil," he said. " 'We are labourers together with God,' St. Paul told the Corinthians. Our labor is to build up the church as the body of Christ—not to tear it down. Battle will come, certainly. But it will come from the outside. And we must be ready for it. We must join forces, then, and equip ourselves for the coming travails."

He looked each person in the eye before continuing. "My Christian brothers, I beg you let us cease this despicable bickering and rumormongering among ourselves. By this means, we open the door to allow Satan into our midst. Instead, I implore all of us to lay aside all animosity, to shake hands warmly, and to stand side by side against the forces that wish to destroy us. We must stand together, my friends. Stand and reflect the One who has given us life and hope and the promise of heaven. Let us stand in peace!"

As the room erupted in applause, Randolph turned to his chair. But as he did, Mr. Baine stood to his feet. "My lord, I beg your pardon, but Satan is in our midst already. He dwells among us, and his wicked influence must be eradicated! Evil came to us in the form of a man named William Buckland, who twisted the Scripture to his own end, who lectured to us of a heresy he called the Ice Age, who directly defied the Word of God by stating that the book of Genesis was nothing but a fairy tale!"

"He did nothing of the sort!" Mr. Seaward leapt from his chair. "Buckland is a man of God—and a scientist who has studied this situation more carefully than you will ever do."

"He is a liar!" Baine cried.

"How dare you accuse him of such a thing! He has taken Holy Orders!"

"Gentlemen!" Randolph shouted over the rising uproar in the room. "This is my very point. By allowing ourselves to quarrel, we destroy the church. This is not the will of God."

"We are to live as brothers," Reverend Berridge spoke up. " 'We are to be likeminded one toward another according to Christ Jesus.' Above all, we are to be at—"

"Peace!" everyone shouted at him in unison—and then broke into yet another round of quarreling. Mr. Seaward grabbed Mr. Baine by the collar and began screaming into his face. Mr. Baine held up a threatening fist.

"Gentlemen!" Randolph cried out. "Gentlemen, please!" He glanced at Olivia, who had clapped her hands against her cheeks in dismay.

"As humans, we shall always have differences of opinion!" Reverend Berridge shouted. "We must focus on our similarities of belief. In essence, we believe the same things!"

"We must be united!" Olivia said, coming to her feet, her face bright pink. "Please, gentlemen, let us be as one!"

"Peace," Randolph cried, willing himself to be heard over the shouts. "Christ commands His people to live in peace with one another! I urge you to set aside your—"

"Miss Hewes! Miss Hewes!" A footman broke into the room just as someone overturned the table, sending china teapots and cups flying through the air to shatter on the floor. The footman hesitated for a moment, searching the sea of angry men until he spotted Olivia.

Randolph was making his way around the table to her when she saw the footman. "Thomas?" she gasped. "What has happened? Is it my mother?"

Breathing hard, he arrived at her side just as Randolph reached them. "Nay, madam," the footman said. "Your mother's health is unaltered, and Dr. Phillips sits with her yet."

"What then? Tell me at once, Thomas."

"It is your brother, madam. Lady Chatham received a caller while you were away, and Master Clive came into the bedchamber to speak to her as well. The boy collapsed into a fit of passion, rolling on the floor and—"

"Yes, Thomas, what then?"

"And lower your voice, man," Randolph said, aware that

the crowd in the room had begun to calm. The arguments fell apart and the shoving ceased as attention turned to the agitated footman.

"Where is the boy now?" Randolph asked.

"We cannot tell, my lord." Thomas took off his hat and scratched his balding head. "Dr. Phillips called for assistance, and all of us rushed in, and somehow in the midst of it, the lad ran away! We have searched high and low, but he is not in the house. Mr. Tupper ordered me to come to you at once, Miss Hewes, to beg your assistance in finding the boy."

"Mr. Tupper?" she said. "Why should my steward involve himself in this? He is making inspection at this hour. I am surprised to learn that he is in the house at all."

The footman glanced at Randolph, then gave a little cough as he turned back to Olivia. "Mr. Tupper, madam, was in the bedchamber with your mother when the trouble erupted."

"So many? Dr. Phillips, Mr. Tupper, Clive—and another visitor yet?"

"Aye, Miss Hewes."

"Who was the caller?" Randolph demanded. "Who sat with Lady Chatham and her steward?"

Leaning close to Olivia, Thomas spoke in a low voice. "It was the miller . . . Mr. John Quince."

Seventeen

OLIVIA SURVEYED THE ruins of the tea party—the table upended, teacups smashed, crumbs littering the church carpet. She looked at the men, business owners and leaders in the town, who stood breathless and red-faced from their fury.

And then she lifted her head. "I am ashamed of you all," she said quietly. "I am ashamed of myself and my family as well. We Chathams permitted a hedgerow to grow upward like a mighty barrier between us and our neighbors, the Thornes. And now you gentlemen allow a doctrinal dispute to flow like a trickle of water between you—a stream that erodes harmony and gradually will carve out a deep chasm over which no one can cross. Shame on us all."

Sweeping her shawl up from the littered floor where it had fallen, she wrapped it around her shoulders. "Come, Thomas, take me home," she said. "There is nothing more to be done here."

Fighting the fury and frustration that tore through her breast, Olivia started for the door. *Let them go on with their battles,* she thought. *Let the church tear itself to pieces. Let the town come apart at the seams.* Each man was determined to have his own way, and now she understood that nothing could be done to heal the rift. Satan must be clapping his hands in glee.

Lifting her skirts, she turned her thoughts to her own family. Why had so many men gathered at Lady Chatham's bedside—especially when she could speak to none of them? And poor Clive! Someone must have said something to upset him terribly.

As she climbed the narrow staircase, she recalled Lord Thorne and his magical kiss. Did he truly love her? No, it could not be so. If he had cared for her in such a way, he would not have attached himself to Beatrice Bryse. And even if he did feel some affection for Olivia, what hope could there be for them beyond a warm friendship? She was a Chatham and he a Thorne. If nothing else, this continuing dispute in the church had taught her that deep hatreds are not easily healed.

Stepping out into the late-afternoon sunlight, she heard his voice behind her. "Miss Hewes! Please wait."

She continued walking, knowing she must hurry home. All would be in chaos there. Clive had no doubt hidden himself away somewhere, as he often did. And her mother! How Lady Chatham must have suffered—unable to speak as guests and servants clamored around her in an attempt to control her son.

"Please, allow me one moment, I beg you. Please, Olivia . . ."

At the sound of her name, she paused and turned to him. "It is hopeless, sir. There is nothing to be done about the situation. You and I are merely players on the great stage of church history. We can do nothing to change the minds of those men."

"Hang the men—my concern is Clive." He caught her hands. "I believe I know where he is. You told me that you planned to take him fishing after the tea. He must have gone there . . . to the hedgerow."

Relief washed down her back like a waterfall. "Of course! Why did I not think of that? Thomas," she addressed her footman, "return to Chatham at once. Assure my mother that I shall bring Clive to her directly. And tell Tupper to wait for me in the study. I must hear what occurred at Lady Chatham's bedside."

"Yes, madam." The footman bowed.

"And, Thomas," Randolph added, "tell me what has become of Quince. Does he yet remain at the manor house?"

The servant straightened, glancing back and forth between the two, as if uncertain whether to give answer to a Thorne. Finally, his shoulders sagged in surrender. "My lord, the miller departed during the fracas. I do not know where he went."

"Thank you, Thomas." Randolph clapped him on the shoulder. "My horse stands just there. Rather than go on foot again, take him at once, my good man. He is surefooted and will see you quickly to Chatham Hall."

"Yes, my lord. I am much obliged, sir."

As Thomas headed off, Randolph took Olivia's arm. "We shall take your carriage to the boundary of our properties and then walk up to the pond."

"What if Clive has done himself a harm?" she asked as they hurried across the churchyard. "When these fits come over him, he is terribly violent. He throws himself against the furniture and bangs his head on the floor. I fear he may have hurled himself into the water—and he cannot swim!"

"Calm yourself," he said, helping her into the carriage. "We shall know all when we find him."

Her imagination taking wing, Olivia gripped the seat as Randolph gave instructions to the coachman. When he joined her inside the carriage, he wrapped an arm tightly around her shoulders and drew her close.

"What if Mr. Quince followed Clive to the pond!" she cried out. "Oh, why did that horrid man call when I was out?"

"You have answered your own question. It was *because* you were away that Quince felt himself at liberty to go to Chatham."

"But what was his aim?"

"To speak with your mother, I imagine. Can she talk to him?"

"Not a word. The apoplexy has paralyzed half her body. She is very ill—all but insensible, sir."

"Please, you must call me Randolph. We are too intimate now for formalities." He lifted her chin with his fingertip as the carriage picked up speed. "Dear sweet Olivia, please know that I shall do all in my power to bring you happiness. You have suffered long enough."

"What can you do for me? My path is laid out for me, Randolph, as yours lies before you. We can go no other way. I must care for Clive—"

"In this I can help you," he cut in. "I have given the situation much thought. My years at Cambridge left me with many influential friends in London—solicitors, physicians, scientists. With their help, I shall find the very best teachers for Clive. I shall see to it that he is educated and trained."

"But he cannot learn, Randolph. My father had excellent tutors brought in, and I myself have made every effort to teach my brother. He can remember very little. Mathematics escapes him entirely, and he can read only a few words. It is hopeless."

"Hopeless," he repeated. "Has this word now become your favorite?"

She struggled to swallow the lump of sadness in her throat. How right and good this man's strong arm felt around her. How she wished with all her heart that he could bring joy and light into her life, as he seemed so earnestly to desire. But it could not be.

"I shall be all right again once Clive is found," she told him. "After my mother's death, we shall settle ourselves into a pattern."

"And what of us? How shall we be, Olivia?"

She shook her head. "You saw what happened at the tea. Unity is impossible. Once a rift has been carved out, it cannot be mended."

"Do you truly believe this? Can we not be friends, you and I?"

Olivia read the sincerity in his blue eyes, but she knew the truth. "I shall speak plainly," she said. "Your wife will not allow our companionship, nor will the town welcome it."

"And you?"

"And I . . . I cannot imagine mere friendship between us, sir." She lifted her hand to stroke her fingertips across his mouth. "Your kiss has taught me that I would always want more."

"Dearest Olivia—"

As he bent to kiss her again, the carriage came to a halt. She slipped away from him and threw open the door. Before he could react, she had stepped out and was running up the fell toward the hedgerow.

"Stand at the ready," Randolph instructed the coachman as he exited the carriage. "If young Lord Chatham is injured, we shall need your assistance at once."

"Aye, my lord."

The man's veiled eyes regarded him with uncertainty, and Randolph knew it took great effort for Chatham's servants to obey his orders without question. Following their masters' example, the staff and laborers in both families had built generations of animosity between them.

As he sprinted across the moor after Olivia, Randolph wondered how many of the evil deeds he had heard attributed to Chatham shepherds and tenants were actually true. A shepherd who had forgotten to salve the udders of his flock and had ended up with flyblown sheep might easily blame their illness and death on his enemies across the hedgerow. A farmer whose careless hoeing had resulted in a field of weeds could claim that his neighbor had sown tares among his crop. In fact, the hostilities gave a ready excuse to both groups, Randolph realized. Any error, laziness, or unforeseen act of God could be blamed on foes just over the moorland. The worse the enemy, the better one could make oneself appear. How very convenient.

As he caught up with Olivia, Randolph realized she was

weeping. Tears streamed down her cheeks as she stumbled over hummocks, slid through patches of mud, and tugged her skirt loose from the snatching branches of bramble bushes.

"Clive!" she cried out as she ran. "Clive, where are you?"

Randolph considered slowing his pace to match hers, but he decided instead to race ahead in hopes of finding the boy as soon as possible. Following the hedgerow up the fell, he skirted the bank of the stream and searched the horizon for any sign of the thin little fellow. Surely Clive had come this way. Surely they must find him safe and sound. Randolph breathed a prayer as he clambered up the stony scree near the pond.

As his view cleared, he saw that his petition was answered. "Clive!" Randolph swung around and waved at Olivia. "I have found him! He is well."

Not waiting for her answer, he splashed through the stream and climbed to the edge of the pond on the other side.

"Good afternoon, Master Clive," he said, breathing hard and speaking with greater calm than he felt. "How do you get on, sir?"

"I am waiting for Livie to come." He stared glumly at his fishing pole. "She is taking tea in town."

Randolph hunkered down on a flat stone near the young man. "Have you caught any fish today?"

Clive sniffled, and now Randolph saw that he, too, had been crying. "Yes," he whispered. "But I let it go."

"A small one then?"

"Big. But my mother cannot eat fish. She cannot eat at all. And the doctor will not allow me to take her any sherry. She has only water to drink."

"In my opinion, water tastes quite good."

Clive looked up at him. Blinking tears off the ends of his long black lashes, he studied Randolph through the thick lenses of his spectacles. "I know you," he said. "You are the man who taught me how to find the bait. It is green and black."

"Indeed it is. And you are the clever boy who is an excellent fisherman."

"Yes, I am." Clive nodded solemnly. "And you took me riding on your horse. It was raining. We went home."

"We did. And we got very wet."

"I like you."

Randolph smiled. "I like you too, Clive. I believe we are friends."

"Yes, we are. But I do not like—"

"Clive!" Olivia arrived at the pond at last—her bonnet fallen away, her skirt shredded, and her petticoats three inches deep in mud. "Oh, dearest boy. I thought I had lost you!"

"Here I am," Clive said. "I waited for you to come home. Your tea is finished."

"Indeed, it is. Very much so."

Randolph patted the stone beside him.

Olivia picked up her skirts and tiptoed through the water. "Clive, why did you not wait for me to come home? I promised to take you fishing after I returned."

"I forgot about that, Livie," he told her as she settled on the stone beside Randolph. "I like to fish. It is my favorite thing."

"Yes, but you must not go out unless I am with you."

He looked at her. "Why have you been crying, Livie?"

"I was very frightened. I did not know where you had gone."

"I was very frightened too." With a whimper, he buried his head in the crook of his arm. "I was very, very frightened."

Randolph met Olivia's troubled eyes. Laying his hand on the boy's back, he spoke in a low voice. "What frightened you, Clive?"

"The man."

"Which one?"

"Him. The one in Mama's room. I hate him."

"Dr. Phillips?" Randolph asked. "Or Mr. Tupper? Or was it Mr. Quince?"

"The bad man." At this, he flung down his pole and began to sob. "I am bad! I am the bad one!"

"You?" Randolph picked up the pole. "What bad thing have you done, Clive? The only bad thing I can think of is that you dropped your fishing pole and lost your bait. Come along, let us find another caterpillar in the hedge, shall we?"

"No!" Clive knotted both hands into fists and began pounding himself on the head. "Me! Me! Me! I am the bad one! I am bad!"

"For heaven's sake, dearest!" Olivia leaned across Randolph and tried to calm her brother. "What are you talking about? You have done nothing wrong, Clive! Who has upset you? Which man has frightened you so terribly?"

"Him! That bad one!" he screamed.

Concern prickled through Randolph as he watched the boy disintegrate before his eyes. With a shriek, Clive threw himself backward onto the rock and began kicking his heels up and down, beating himself in the temples, turning his head from side to side, and wailing at the top of his lungs.

Olivia clapped her hands over her ears, her face crumpling at the sight.

Randolph observed the scene for a moment and quickly decided he had had quite enough of it. "Come with me, young man," he commanded, standing and quickly doffing his greatcoat.

He reached down and picked the boy up in his arms. All skin and bones, Clive felt like nothing more than a fluttering sparrow as Randolph tossed him over one shoulder.

"Now then," he said, setting off down the bank, "you are frightening your sister and half of Wharfedale with your shouts."

"I did it!" Clive continued screaming as he pounded Randolph's back with his small fists. "I did it! I am the one!"

"Here you go, then," Randolph said, cradling Clive like a sack of potatoes and giving him a heave-ho straight into the pond. Without waiting for the boy to surface, Randolph jumped off the bank himself, landing with a great splash that sloshed water upward in bright arcs across the setting sunlight.

"Ah, there you are!" Randolph pulled the gasping boy out of the water and set him safely on one of his own knees. As Clive coughed up a mouthful of water, Randolph slapped him a couple of times on the back. "Swimming is my favorite thing," he said. "I could swim all day, especially in the summertime. Do you like it, Clive?"

"No!" Bursting into tears again, Clive punched Randolph in the shoulder with his fist. "You threw me into the water! My spectacles are lost! You did it! You lost them!"

"Gone, are they? Well, we had better have a lookout then."

Rubbing his shoulder, he scanned the water. "Do you see them, Clive?"

"No! They are lost! I shall never have my spectacles again!"

"Wait a minute—there they are. Look, just near that stone."

Clive calmed himself enough to peer at the place Randolph indicated. "They are too deep," Clive pronounced.

"Too deep? But this water hardly comes above my chest. Can you reach them?"

"No," he pouted. "I shall fall in again. I shall drown."

"Then I suppose the task is up to me. But I fear I cannot do it without your help, my good man. You must give me a push—a very strong one."

He set Clive down into the water so that the boy's feet touched the bottom of the pond. Indicating his shoulders, he turned away. As he did, he gave Olivia a wink. Standing on the bank, she had watched the proceedings in horror, crying out at the terrible things her brother was suffering.

"Push!" Randolph cried. Clive grasped his shoulders and gave a mighty thrust. After slipping barely under the surface, Randolph bobbed up again and shook his head. "That will never do, my friend. Try harder—a really good shove, eh?" Three more attempts, along with much splashing and blowing of water on Randolph's part, soon had Clive grinning and finally starting to giggle. At last, Randolph dived under the water, snatched the spectacles, and floated to the top of the pond again.

"There you are, my friend," he announced, setting the spectacles onto Clive's nose. "As good as new. We shall have to come swimming again sometime. I think this pond is rather nicer than the one near my house."

"Are you swimming now?"

"Indeed I am. Will you not join me?" Randolph drifted onto his back and paddled about, blowing plumes of mist into the air.

Clive studied Randolph through the droplets on his spectacles, obviously uncertain whether to be angry or not. He glanced at his sister, who was wringing her hands as if she feared the worst. Randolph realized his action had been a bit extreme, but the boy clearly had gotten away with his tantrums for far too long.

"Has your sister never taught you how to swim, Clive?" he asked. "Livie, did you not give your brother swimming lessons?"

She gave a cry of exasperation. "Oh, of course not! And will you both please come out of the water at once? This is ridiculous!"

"Shall we see if Livie wants to come in?" Randolph asked Clive. "Or shall I help her in?"

"Help her in!" Clive clapped his hands and jumped up and down. "Better yet, toss her in!"

"No, indeed!" Olivia gasped as Randolph started out of the water. "Please, I—"

"Come on, then. Get in, Livie, or I shall have to toss you in, as I did young Clive."

"For heaven's sake! I am in my fine tea gown, and I certainly shall not . . ." She looked down at the tattered, muddied hem. With a shake of her head, she kicked off her slippers and waded into the pond. "Now are you happy, sir?"

Randolph laughed. "Happier than I was a few minutes ago."

"Ooh, Livie, you are swimming with us!" Clive splashed his hands in the water. "I love to swim! It is my favorite thing!"

"So do I, dearest," she said, her face softening. Her dark eyes flashed at Randolph. "Now we shall never get him out of the pond, you know."

"Oh, he will want to go home very soon, will you not, Clive? When the sun sets, the water grows cold, and I mean to take myself off to dinner. You will do the same, eh?"

"Yes, I shall." Clive giggled. "Would you like to know a secret? I have my boots on."

"So have I," Randolph said. "It prevents the fish biting our toes."

Alarm flooded Clive's face. "Do they bite?"

"Randolph is only teasing you," Olivia said. "Fish eat bait, and that is all. They are not the least bit interested in your toes."

"Unless your toes are green and black," Randolph said. "Are they?"

"No!" Clive chuckled. "Are yours?"

"I hardly ever look at my toes—except when I wash them. No, indeed, I believe they are neither black nor green."

"You are very silly." Clive drifted over to his sister. "I like him even though he tossed me into the pond."

"I like him too, dearest," she said, slipping a damp arm around her brother. "I like him very much."

"Clive," Randolph ventured, "do you like me well enough to tell me what happened today in your mama's bedchamber? I wish to hear the story very much—but only if you can tell it without shouting. I myself have been known to shout on occasion, but I find that it annoys other people greatly. And shouting rarely succeeds in accomplishing much. So, what do you think?"

Clive's forehead wrinkled, and he gazed at the rippling water for some moments. Finally, he covered his face with his hands and spoke rapidly. "I did it. I am the bad one, but he made me do it, and I did not want to do it, but I did, because he told me to."

Trepidation filled Randolph at this account, but he pressed on. "What did you do, Clive?"

"I shot the gun!" With a great splash of his hands, he burst into tears again. "He told me to do it, and I did it!"

"The gun?"

"On the horse! The gun on the horse, when he took me riding!"

Randolph focused on Olivia. She shook her head. "But you never go riding, dearest," she said softly. "You are not allowed to go—"

"But I did! That day when I went to Otley!"

"Oh, dear—he did go off once," she told Randolph. "After hours of searching, I found him in town."

"He told me to go riding," Clive went on. "And he told me to shoot the gun. He said I should do it, and I did it!"

Chills washed down Randolph's spine. "What did you shoot at, Clive?"

With an anguished cry, the boy turned away and started for the bank. "I shot him! I shot the man!"

"Great Scott," Randolph said under his breath. "Clive, stop at once, and talk to me. Which man did you shoot?"

"*Aaaa!* I shot him! He fell down!"

"Clive!" Randolph placed a hand on the boy's back. Drawing Clive close, he struggled to keep an even tone of voice. "Listen to me. You must tell Livie and me what happened. We love you very much. We shall never hurt you. No one will. Please calm yourself at once and explain what happened."

"He has difficulty recalling events in chronological order," Olivia told Randolph. She ran her hand over her brother's wet head. "You are frightened, Clive; I can see it. But your friend is telling you the truth. We shall not be angry with you. Indeed, we shall help you to feel better. . . . Now, I am going to start the story about the gun, and you must help me to tell it. You were in the house—"

"In the drawing room before tea."

"Yes, and I was talking to Mr. Tupper about the ledgers, as I always do. And Mama was—"

"She was talking to him. The bad man."

"Yes, and then Mama told you to go riding with the man."

"No, Livie! That is not how it was. Mama went out of the drawing room. She went away to the library to speak to you and Mr. Tupper. And the man . . . the bad man . . . he said did I want to go riding."

"And you said, 'yes indeed, riding is my favorite thing.' " Olivia was speaking softly, her words soothing and calm. "So you went outside with the bad man."

"To the stables. And we got two horses. Mine was brown. Or black. Was it brown, Livie?"

"I cannot recall, Clive. But you got onto the horse, and off you went with the man. And you went to Otley—"

"No, we did not go to Otley." He shook his head forlornly. "We went across the moors. We rode and rode a very long time. And he said, 'Where is he? Where is he?' And then he said, 'There he is! Riding along near that wall!' "

"Who was it?"

"A Thorne! And we hate the Thornes," Clive said. "They are wicked people! They are evil, and we despise them! They have caused us no end of trouble, and we hate them—"

"Clive!" Olivia's eyes shot to Randolph's. "What are you saying?"

"The bad man told me to get off my horse. He said we would go hunting now, and that I would like it very much. We sat down behind some large stones on the moor. And he gave me the gun. He pointed it at the wicked Thorne who was riding his horse near a wall. He said to pull the small metal thing. And I did, and there was a loud sound and great black smoke, and I fell onto my back. And when I got up again, I saw that the Thorne had fallen off his horse, and he lay on the ground too, with blood coming out. I had shot the Thorne."

Randolph's body had gone stiff and cold as the tale unfolded. Before its end, he had guessed the outcome. The man Clive killed had been Lord Thorne. His own dear father.

"Dear God, please help me," he prayed aloud. Drawing away from the two in the pond, he tried to swallow the bitter anger that rose in his throat. "Help me. Dear God, help me, I beg You."

As he strode from the water, Randolph could hear Clive starting to cry again.

"He is angry with me!" he said. "He promised he would not be angry, but he is!"

"Clive, who was the bad man?" Olivia demanded. "You must tell me at once! Who was he?"

"That same one in Mama's bedroom today. Him!"

"Mr. Tupper?"

"No, not Mr. Tupper."

Randolph crossed the stream, unable to look behind him.

"Was it Dr. Phillips?" Olivia's voice was desperate now. "Was it the doctor who has come to take care of Mama? The one who looks after you when you are ill?"

"Not him—the other one! The bad one!"

"It was Mr. Quince," she cried. "Oh, heaven help us, John Quince made you murder Lord Thorne!"

Eighteen

"THE CHATHAMS must be held liable!" William slammed his fist down on the table, rattling silverware and making china plates jump across the white damask tablecloth. "That boy murdered our father, and he will pay for it!"

Randolph pushed his chair back and regarded the worried-looking diners assembled in the candlelit hall at Thorne Lodge. Seated across from him, Reverend Berridge had been unable to eat beyond the first course of oxtail soup. He claimed that his appetite had been spoiled by too many currant cakes at the tea earlier that afternoon, but Randolph knew better.

Distressed over the response to the attempted peacemaking, the minister confessed that he had left the church before the meeting's end and hurried home to the vicarage without even seeing the attendees out the door. Hardly had he sat down to discuss the disastrous event with his wife when Randolph arrived at his door with news of Clive Hewes's confession of murder.

Harriet Berridge, who had agreed to accompany her

husband to the manor house for dinner, sat beside him. She wore a soft blue gown that did not conceal evidence of her pregnancy. Her pale face registered shock and disbelief at the unhappy proceedings. Throughout the meal, she had picked at her food, all the while interjecting the kindest possible comments about the Chatham family. It was clear to Randolph that Olivia's friend knew his account of the incident in the pond must be true, but she could not make herself accept it.

And William, of course, had done nothing all evening but rant. "Baron Hewes of Chatham must be brought to justice," he said loudly with another thud of his fist on the table. "He killed our father, and he made it look like an accident—"

"He has not the wit for such a complicated ruse, brother," Randolph declared. "You give him too much credit. He did not plan the murder—"

"But he did pull the trigger!"

"Of course he did. Unless in a tantrum, the boy obeys everything he is told to do. I cannot believe he truly knows right from wrong."

"In that, you may be mistaken," Nigel Berridge put in. "I believe that God has given each creature an innate awareness of good and evil. A dog will not stop to ponder the act before stealing and eating a slice of cheese from the table while his master's back is turned. But if caught and chastised, the dog will slink away in shame, for it knows it has done wrong. Young Lord Chatham has far more sense than a dog, and his tears and wailing during his account of the shooting reveal that he is well aware of his own wrongdoing."

Randolph considered this. "He knows *now* that he did

wrong. But I am not convinced he fully understood the implications of his behavior at the time."

"But you told us how he verbally reviled the Thorne family even while you were standing there beside him in the water," William said. "He spouted all manner of accusations against us. He despises us, and I believe he knew very well what he was doing when he shot our father. John Quince informed him that the man on the horse was a Thorne, and then young Chatham willingly pulled the trigger."

"But his mother had told him repeatedly that our family was evil—just as our parents instructed us that he and all his relations were the wickedest sort of villains. Young Lord Chatham has neither the wisdom nor the maturity to make sound judgments in any realm of his existence. All his young life, he was taught to believe that Thornes were bad. Then along came Quince—"

"You only suppose it was John Quince," Nigel corrected him.

"I have little doubt that man used his influence to convince the boy to pull the trigger."

"But why?" Harriet Berridge asked. "What would Mr. Quince gain by such a wicked deed?"

"A firm alliance with the Chatham family," Randolph explained. "Clearly, that has been his intent all along. Quince hoped to marry Olivia Hewes, and to that end he convinced her mother that he was a worthy suitor—despite all that argued against such an unequal union. But marriage into the Chathams could not be enough for a schemer like Quince. He realized that my father wielded great influence in the region and might thwart his machinations. Doubtless,

Quince saw me as a weaker opponent in his efforts to take the reins of power here."

"Power, then?" Harriet cried. "Is this what drives him?"

"Wealth is the greater motivation, I suspect, for wealth brings power. Mrs. Berridge, your husband has reminded us from Scripture that the love of money is the root of all evil. No one can doubt that Quince cherishes his money above all else."

"We should not be quick to judge our fellowman," Nigel cautioned. "Only God can see the heart. And yet, I confess, I believe Mr. Quince may be the real culprit in this heinous incident."

"It was a diabolical crime," Randolph went on. "I am sure he believes he has gotten away with it entirely."

"I must agree with this deduction," Harriet said. "Mr. Quince hoped that Lord Thorne's death would be taken as a hunting mishap—as it was, until now. He was confident that no one would blame poor Lord Chatham for such a crime, even if the boy did speak of it."

Randolph nodded. "And our clever miller knew that if young Chatham told his story and was believed, Quince could not be held culpable for the murder. He did not actually pull the trigger."

"But Quince was an accessory!" William bellowed. "They should hang! Both of them!"

"What jury will put either of them to death?" Randolph asked. "Brought before a judge, Chatham would be unable to recount the story accurately in any way. Although I believe—I greatly hope—that he may be educated to some degree in the future, he is at this time incompetent to testify."

"Indeed," Nigel concurred, "and anyone who has ever seen the boy would confirm that assessment."

Harriet nodded. "Aye, dearest husband, for Olivia told me that many years ago, the late Lord Chatham took his son to London. It was very important to have the boy examined, you understand, for no peer may take his seat in Parliament unless he is perfectly sane. In town, the finest doctors studied the child and concluded that he was unfit."

"As a baron, he can be tried only in the House of Lords," Randolph said. "His story about John Quince will not be considered credible by any peer who is told of his deficiency, and he is the only witness to the crime. Quince will deny everything, of course."

"Then what recourse do we have?" William glowered at his brother. "Do you know what I think? I think Lady Chatham plotted the entire thing."

"What if she did? She lies even now on her deathbed." Randolph shook his head. "I am sorry, brother, but you cannot string up the old woman on the gallows. Nor will you convince a judge to hang either young Chatham or John Quince."

"Perhaps that steward of theirs—Tupper—could he have been behind the plot?"

"And who would testify to that? No, indeed, I believe Quince has been as clever in this as he is in all his business dealings."

"Yet an attorney may know more than we of the law's intricacies," Nigel said. "Randolph, in two days' time, I go to London to speak with the bishop, and I have reserved a coach for my journey. Shall we travel there together? I believe you would do well to seek the advice of an expert in this unfortunate situation."

"And there is the matter of Miss Bryse," Harriet added. "Only last week, I received a letter from the young lady herself. I understand she is eagerly planning her wedding—though she informs me that you have yet to ask her father for his consent."

Randolph ran a finger around his collar. "Yes, Miss Bryse is . . . most eager. I should speak to her father. Thank you, Nigel, for your invitation. I accept it with gratitude. But I insist that we take my chaise-and-four, for it will make the journey far more comfortable for us than a public coach."

Randolph leaned back in his chair. As he did quite often, he now lifted up a silent prayer of thanks to God for sending Nigel and Harriet Berridge to Otley. A more sensible and Spirit-led couple could not be found anywhere in King George's realm. But he was greatly concerned that they would be driven from the town and from their vital ministry in Wharfedale.

He also feared that John Quince would escape unscathed from his crime. Randolph would find it unbearable to sell his wool to the man who had murdered his father. Yet what choice would he have?

If anything could be worse than these two issues, something even heavier weighed on Randolph's heart. Dread and trepidation coursed through him at the thought of his impending marriage to Beatrice Bryse. Impulse and a misguided understanding of God's will had led him to commit the most grievous error of his life. An error that could not be corrected. Now he must spend the remainder of his years within five miles of the woman he loved most in all the world. Loved and could never have.

"For one who has settled on a course of action, you look very dispirited, brother," William observed.

"I am. Truly, I cannot see a happy ending to any of this."

"Nor can I," Nigel concurred. "But, thankfully, neither of us is God, who can and does know the good He has planned. For we have been promised that all things—even treachery and murder—work together for good to those who love the Lord and are called according to His purposes."

Randolph absorbed his friend's words and tried to believe that God could bring something hopeful out of this, and that one day he might once again feel joy in his heart. Unsuccessful, he stood at last.

"Shall we retire to the drawing room?" he asked the company. "A fire has been laid on the grate—a welcome respite on this cool summer evening. We shall seat ourselves around it and speak of things more cheerful. Good books, perhaps."

"Or cards?" William suggested. "We have not had a game of whist since the Bryses went away."

"And thank heaven for that." Randolph tugged on his lapels to straighten his frock coat as he headed for the drawing room.

Olivia sat at the library window and watched the rain fall across the purple moor. Her black sarcenet petticoat and matching crepe gown with its rows of black chenille roses and black bugle beads itched dreadfully. But she had no energy to climb the stairs to her bedroom, and she was far too tired to change into something more comfortable at this late hour.

Her mother's funeral had gone on forever, it seemed. The night of Clive's confession, Lady Chatham had slipped into a coma. She never knew a whisper of the turmoil that now beset her two children. She died the following morning, and her body was laid out in the parlour. For two days, people filed into Chatham Hall to pay their final respects to the woman whose family provided employment and commerce to half the region.

As Reverend Berridge had been summoned to London by his bishop, he was forced to defer the funeral service to the minister at Ilkley. Lady Chatham would not have liked this turn of events, Olivia knew, but nothing could be done to alter it. As it was, the congregants looked forward to a reprieve from their customary sermon fare of peace, peace, and more peace.

This very afternoon, the pallbearers had carried the casket down to the church. There, the parson from Ilkley gave a somber oration on "ashes to ashes and dust to dust," which succeeded in depressing everybody even further.

Clive had been inconsolable from the moment Randolph had turned his back on them at the pond and walked away. Olivia had managed to coerce her brother out of the water and down to the carriage. Once safely at home, she could not budge him from his room, and finally she gave up trying. Clive missed his mother's funeral service and the graveside ceremony. And even at this late hour, he refused to come out. She would be eating dinner alone, Olivia realized. It had become her custom.

A soft rap at the library door brought a sigh to her lips. She could not bear the thought of speaking to anyone else on this evening. Her head reeled from the sheer volume of issues besetting her. Not only had she spent the past days managing the details of her mother's burial, but she had undertaken the unpleasant task of confronting Mr. Tupper with news of Clive's confession.

At Olivia's questioning, the old steward had blanched so white that she had no doubt he had known the entire plot beforehand. He denied everything, of course. All the same, she released him from his position. With no one hired to replace him, she knew she must tend the details of the manor on her own.

And, of course, there was the matter of how the Thorne family would react to the news that their father had indeed been murdered. If they insisted on bringing charges against the Chathams—and Olivia could not doubt that they would—she must do her best to defend her brother. But how? She could not help fearing the absolute worst.

At a second knock, the library door opened, and the footman entered. "Madam, you have a caller."

"No, Thomas, I—"

"It is Mrs. Harriet Berridge."

She let out a breath. "Very well. Send her in."

A moment later, a weary-looking Harriet slipped into the library and crossed to the window seat. "Dearest Olivia!" she whispered, embracing her friend. "I felt I could not rest until I knew you were well. Please tell me you do not suffer too greatly in your bereavement."

"To tell you such would be a lie, Harriet." Olivia gestured for her friend to join her on the seat. "Despite the many problems my mother caused me, I miss her greatly."

"Of course you do. You have never known life without her. And now you are alone in this great stone house! How you must long for companionship."

"I shall learn to do without it, Harriet, for I have no other choice. You have been my dearest friend these many months, and yet I fear I may lose you as well. What news do you have from your husband?"

"Nothing. I expect he will not write to me but will wait until his return to tell me everything in person."

"You must be very worried."

"I confess I am. I try to keep my focus on Christ, but I have little success."

"Nor do I, Harriet. This world is very much with us, is it not?"

"Indeed it is. And how does your brother fare?"

Olivia hesitated. Should she tell Harriet what Clive had said at the pond? Olivia knew she would feel better just to share the horrific news with her friend, and Harriet was the most trustworthy person she had ever met. But was it wise to reveal so much?

"Clive suffers greatly," she said at last. "He does not understand what has happened to our mother. It was the same when our father died. For months, Clive asked when Papa would be returning home from Portsmouth. Finally, he ceased to inquire and seemed to forget that he had ever had a father. Only rarely now, some small thing will prod his memory, and out will come the account of an event all but forgotten." She paused, recalling that this was exactly how the story of the shooting of Lord Thorne had come to be told.

Harriet took Olivia's hand and pressed it between her own.

"It is as though Clive stores his memories in little drawers which are not easily opened," Harriet said softly. "And now and then, a key turns up to unlock one of the drawers."

"Exactly," Olivia said.

"Just as the sight of John Quince in your mother's bedchamber prompted him to recall Lord Thorne's murder."

"Harriet!"

"Dearest Olivia, I knew I must not keep my knowledge from you. Randolph came down to our house not long after leaving you at the pond. He told Nigel and me the entire story, and we condoled with him to the best of our ability."

Olivia's heart hammered in her chest. "How was he, Harriet? Does he despise us entirely?"

"He made a valiant defense of Clive, though his brother is determined to find fault in everyone."

"Mr. Sherbourne knows!"

"How could Randolph keep such information a secret?"

"But what do they mean to do to us?"

"I do not know. Before Randolph's chaise-and-four arrived to collect Nigel, my husband promised me that he would press for a peaceful resolution."

"Nigel traveled to London in Randolph's carriage?"

"Aye, with Randolph himself. Did you not know they went down together?"

"Oh, heaven!" She leapt to her feet and twisted her fingers together. "He has gone to find an attorney! He will press murder charges against poor Clive! My brother will be hanged."

"Nonsense!" Harriet rose and set her hands on Olivia's shoulders. "Calm yourself at once, I beg you. Randolph has gone to London to ask Miss Bryse's father for permission to marry his daughter. I believe there are many details yet to be resolved. She has insisted that he purchase a house in town, preferably near her family, and they must resolve upon a church, and her wedding clothes are yet to be—"

"Harriet, enough of this," Olivia begged, tears springing to her eyes. "I cannot bear to hear it."

"I am sorry to pain you, but you must face the truth." Harriet gazed into her friend's face. "If Randolph does consult an attorney in London, his purpose is to find some way to hold John Quince culpable for the deed."

"But Mr. Quince cannot be blamed. He will deny everything, and Clive will be labeled a killer. Oh, Harriet, I cannot bear to see my brother suffer any more than he already does."

"Do not cry so, dearest. I assure you that Randolph does not mean to blame Clive."

"He does not mean it, perhaps," Olivia sobbed, searching for her handkerchief, "but when his family can find no other culprit on whom to lay the guilt, where else will they turn but to my brother? Harriet, the frightful truth is that Clive *did* pull the trigger! He *did* shoot Lord Thorne. He knew who rode on that horse, he knew what Quince was telling him to do, and he did it! I am heartsick over it, but I cannot deny the truth."

"You believe that Clive fully intended to shoot Lord Thorne?"

"How can any of us truly know what is inside Clive's head? His brain was malformed by my mother's drinking, and his spirit was poisoned by her words. Perhaps he meant to murder Lord Thorne, or perhaps he was only trying to please the man who had taken him on a lovely horse ride. Harriet, we shall never know the truth. I am sure not even Clive knows why he pulled that trigger." She pressed her handkerchief to the corner of her eye.

Harriet bowed her head. "Dearest Olivia, we must trust God in this. We must turn our sufferings to Him, for only He—"

"I am trying, Harriet!" Olivia cried out. "But where is He? Why does He not make Himself known to me now? I need His assistance, but I feel that I am all alone!"

"He is here with you, Olivia," Harriet said. "He is with you, and His angels cry out to Him on your behalf. You must trust this."

"Must I?" She shook her head. "Why, Harriet? Why does God allow so much suffering? Can you tell me that? He could prevent everything that pains us so deeply on this earth. Why does He not do it?"

Harriet sank down onto the window seat and cupped her hands over her swollen abdomen. "I am not wise enough to know the mind of God," she said softly. "But I do know this: We humans are sinful creatures—far too wicked ever to come into His holy presence. He loves us, Olivia, and He wants us near. However, as payment for sin, He demands sacrifice."

"Why?" Olivia demanded, dropping down beside her friend.

"That is the way of things, of course. If you want a new dress, you must pay the seamstress. If you want to wear the white robes of holiness, you must pay the price. Long ago, God accepted animal sacrifices in payment for sin. But He was not pleased with them. And so He Himself decided to provide the perfect sacrifice. He sent His only Son to earth to die on the cross and pay the price we owed for those lovely white robes." Harriet paused a moment before addressing her friend again. "You have accepted a robe of righteousness, Olivia, and you wear it on your own shoulders. But do you understand its beauty? Do you fully comprehend the enormous price Jesus paid to purchase it for you?"

Olivia sniffled. "No, I suppose not."

"I believe God has given you another little gift to assist you in this comprehension: suffering. In suffering the fear, doubt, and sorrow that beset you now, Olivia, you know a small bit of what Christ suffered for you on the cross. And in understanding the price He paid, you become more like Him."

"I do not feel the least bit like Christ. I feel miserably human."

"He was human, too. Miserably so. He suffered everything we have ever suffered—and much more. So, if we can, dear Olivia, you and I must try to welcome our suffering. St. Paul wrote that if we are Christ's children, we are His heirs. And if we are heirs, we must suffer with Him, that we may also be glorified."

Olivia stared down at her handkerchief through blurred eyes. "You are right, of course. I have been allowed these difficulties, and I must decide how I shall manage them. Harriet, no matter how weak I may seem to you now, I assure you that I have great resolve. I cannot feel God's presence, but I do believe that He is here with me. I mean to keep my eyes upon Him to the best of my ability."

"You are wise."

"I am weak—but I do know that He is strong, and through Him I can do all things." She lifted her chin. "Harriet, I shall go on."

"Of course you will!" She slipped her arm around Olivia and gave her a hug.

"I shall defend Clive against any charges brought upon him. I shall hire a new steward. And do you know what else I mean to do?"

"What, dearest?"

"I mean never again to sell Chatham wool to John Quince."

"Never? But where will you—"

"I shall send it north if I have to. The transportation will be costly, but I understand the northern millers prefer their wool sandy. It will be heavy, and they will pay me more for it. In this way, perhaps I can recoup my losses."

Harriet looked at her friend with sad brown eyes. "You are very brave."

"Or perhaps I shall build my own worsted mill." A smile filtered over her lips. "Yes, I believe that will do nicely. Can you imagine how John Quince will exclaim when he sees a worsted mill rising on Chatham manor?"

"But you haven't the water here to power a worsted mill."

"I shall dig ditches and divert all my streams into one great roaring river. There!"

Harriet giggled. "Now you are talking silliness. But I am relieved to hear you more like yourself again. I shall leave you now and return to the vicarage in hopes that Nigel may have surprised me and come home at last."

As the friends bade farewell, Olivia turned again to the window. Though darkness was settling over the moor, she could hear the rain pattering the windowpane and see its gray pall across the landscape. What she had not fully addressed with Harriet was perhaps her most painful fear. Even now in London, Randolph Sherbourne, Lord Thorne must be speaking to the father of Beatrice Bryse. They would shake hands, clap each other on the back, and the matter would be resolved.

Her future without him was sealed. And somehow in that greatest of all sufferings—the absence of love—she must learn to be happy.

Nineteen

"EIGHT O'CLOCK," CLIVE declared with confidence. Then his dark eyes turned to his sister beseechingly. "Is it eight o'clock?"

Olivia sighed and pointed at the clock face. "Try again, dearest. What number is this?"

He squinted through his spectacles. "Yes, it is an eight! Or is it a six? They look very much alike to me, Livie."

"Do they?" She studied the numbers, trying to see them as her brother must. "I believe they do. But the top of the eight is an entire circle. Do you see?"

"I do see, Livie, but I cannot make it matter."

"It does matter very much. Six o'clock is your bathtime, and eight o'clock is when we eat dinner."

"But Polly will fetch me for both of those, and I need never look at the clock at all."

"Well, that is perfectly true." Olivia leaned back on the settee and took another sip of tea. She swallowed, relishing its warmth. "Put the clock back on the mantel, Clive, and finish your crumpet. It is neither eight nor six anyway. It is four o'clock, which is teatime, and I am exhausted."

Her brother obediently trotted to the fireplace and restored the clock to its former place. "You are tired because you have been talking to those gentlemen all the day long. You should not do that."

"I have no choice. I am trying to employ a new steward. I feel as if I have interviewed half the men in the countryside, and none of them is suitable."

"We ought to go fishing after tea. I love to fish." He sat down and popped half a crumpet into his mouth. Chewing the enormous lump of bread, he said, "Do you know what, Livie? Fishing is my favorite thing."

"Yes, dear, I know."

"I adore it."

"You must take smaller bites, Clive."

"And I know how to find the bait. It is green and black."

"Indeed it is."

"It is caterpillars."

"Well, we are not going fishing today. Our tenants are at haymaking, and after tea I must take Nelly out to have a look."

"I want to go with you, Livie!" Clive leapt up from the settee, nearly overturning the low tea table. "I love to ride! I adore it! It is my favorite thing!"

She groaned inwardly, dreading the tantrum that must follow if she refused her brother this treat. But Clive could not be allowed to ride out on anything but the oldest and most stodgy of mares, so he could hardly keep up with her. Olivia had every intention of making a quick journey through the fields, that she might be back in time to meet with a mill owner who was traveling all the way down from Manchester to discuss her wool situation. Olivia had written to him the day after her mother's funeral, and now, only two weeks later, he would arrive to meet with her about the possibility of purchasing her wool the following spring.

"You must sit down and finish your tea, Clive," Olivia said firmly. "I am not in any humor to—"

"Excuse me, madam." The footman stepped into the drawing room and made a bow. "You have a caller."

"Already? But he said he was not to arrive until after dark." She rose and took the calling card from Thomas's silver tray. "Please keep him in the reception room until I have had time to send Clive upstairs. Tell Mr. . . ." She glanced down at the card and blanched.

Thomas cleared his throat. "It is Lord Thorne," he said in a low voice. "He has brought with him another gentleman, madam. I believe he is an attorney from London."

"An attorney—oh, Thomas!" She glanced over her shoulder at Clive, who was happily slathering honey on another warm crumpet. "I must send my brother up to his room. Can you keep them waiting? No, that will never do. Oh, dear!"

"Shall I see them in, madam?" His face was inscrutable.

"Have I any other choice, Thomas?"

"I believe not."

"Very well. Let the attorney see the poor boy he means to prosecute. Send them in." She hurried back to the settee, hoping to brush the crumbs from her brother's lap.

As she approached Clive, the footman made his announcement. "Baron Sherbourne of Thorne," he said. "And Mr. Rupert Cleveland."

Olivia swung around and made her best curtsy. "Lord Thorne," she said breathlessly. "I was not expecting you."

"Miss Hewes." He bowed. "And Lord Chatham. Good afternoon."

Clive bounced up. "It is him! Randolph! You have come to tea!"

Randolph's face broke into a grin. "Indeed I have. May I introduce my companion to you and your sister? This is Mr. Cleveland. He accompanied me here from London."

Olivia could not deny that Randolph looked as handsome as she had ever seen him. In a lightweight summer suit of gray worsted, he wore a waistcoat of a blue-striped valencia that very nearly matched his eyes. His tall boots told her that he had lately been riding, and she wondered if he had come to Chatham on horseback rather than in a carriage.

Though her heart softened at the sight of him smiling so warmly at Clive, she could not hide the fear that stiffened her entire body. No doubt this attorney had come with him to deliver the direst of news. Mr. Cleveland was as young a man as Randolph, but he stood only to the other's shoulder and was nearly twice as wide.

"Do sit down, gentlemen," she said in as cordial a voice as she could muster. She addressed her footman. "Thomas, send for another pot of tea. And we should be glad of a currant cake."

"Yes, madam. At once."

As he hurried out of the room, she sat, smoothed down the folds of her black gown, and forced herself to lift her teacup to her lips. After an awkward silence that seemed to go on forever, she thought of something to begin their conversation. "I understand from Mrs. Berridge that you accompanied her husband to London."

"Yes, or I should have called much sooner to condole with you on the very sad loss of your excellent mother." He gave a small cough. "Please do accept my warmest sympathies."

"Thank you, sir. My brother and I are as well as may be expected under the circumstances."

"Indeed." He paused as tea was brought in by three maids, who glanced at him—Lord Thorne inside Chatham Hall!—with such nervousness that Olivia marveled they were able to pour out the cups at all. After they had gone, he spoke again. "I wonder if it is too soon to address a matter of business with you, Miss Hewes."

She considered his words as dread coursed through her heart and set her stomach churning. Perhaps she could put off the inevitable, though delay would do none of them any good. On the other hand, she could not risk upsetting Clive, and a repetition of the troubling tale would certainly do that. Finally she answered him. "Does this matter concern my brother, sir?"

"Only as all matters regarding Chatham manor must certainly concern its master."

"Chatham manor? Then you do not mean to . . . to address that other subject? The one that arose before?"

"The subject that arose the last time we spoke together? No, Miss Hewes. I consider that to be closed."

"Closed?" She nearly dropped her cup. "But how can you . . . does your brother . . . how can this be?"

His eyes slid across to Clive, who had managed to smear his cheeks with honey—upon which crumpet crumbs were now liberally plastered from one ear to the other. The boy was kicking his heels against the floor as he chewed, the steady *thump-thump* fraying Olivia's nerves to the breaking point.

"It is true that my brother did not at first agree with me on this matter. But we have discussed it at length, and he has come around to my way of thinking," Randolph said, focusing on Olivia again. "In consulting with Mr. Cleveland, I was advised that the young man in question who . . . who has been afflicted with . . . who bears such a burden . . . sadly this man would not be permitted to take his rightful seat in Parliament."

"Though unable to perform his duties there," Mr. Cleveland spoke up, "he will always be considered a member of the peerage, of course, and if charged with a crime would be subject to trial in the House of Lords. I am confident, however, that no member of that body would consider hearing a case against a fellow peer in such a condition. Even if he were tried, he would most certainly be found faultless."

"A verdict with which I agree completely," Randolph concluded.

"You do? I mean you . . . you do not intend to . . ." She absolutely would *not* cry! But her eyes filled with tears of joy despite her best intentions. "Thank you, sir. I am most grateful."

"This is the only sensible course of action regarding the incident in question. But as for the true culprit, the one we believe conceived the crime and did everything but commit it himself, I think we may have recourse."

"Have we? What can we do?"

Mr. Cleveland straightened and drew a sheaf of papers from the leather satchel he had carried in. "With your permission, Lord Thorne, I should be happy to explain your proposal to Miss Hewes."

"Are we all going to talk a long time?" Clive piped up. "For I should very much like to go fishing instead. Randolph, do you want to go fishing with me?"

"Another day, without doubt. But at this moment, I believe I must stay and continue talking with your sister."

"But that is boring. I much prefer to fish! It is my favorite thing!"

"Thank you, Clive," Olivia said. "Will you be a good boy now and go to your room while we talk? We have much to say, and our conversation here will be deadly dull."

Clive ran his tongue around his lips, licking up crumbs. "No. I shall stay. I like Randolph. He is my friend."

"Very well, dearest, but you must be quiet."

The lawyer smiled at the boy; then he turned to Randolph and spoke in a low voice. "I do see what you mean, sir, and I assure you that my advice was absolutely correct in this matter."

"I am happy to hear it. And what of the other situation? The worsted mill."

"Which worsted mill?" Olivia felt the first flush of hope since Randolph had walked into the room. "Do you refer to the mill in Otley?"

"No, indeed, for I have had an idea which renders that particular worsted mill quite obsolete to both the Chathams and the Thornes." Lord Thorne leaned forward, elbows on his knees. "I say it is my idea, but I must tell you that Nigel Berridge thought of it. While we were in London, he had a letter from his dear wife, who mentioned it . . . or perhaps Mrs. Berridge was the one who thought of it—"

"Thought of what?" she exclaimed.

"Building a worsted mill."

"Here?"

"Between our two properties. If you and I divert the course of several of our healthiest streams into the one that flows down along the hedgerow to the Wharfe, we shall have enough water to power a small worsted mill."

"I consulted with several milling experts," Mr. Cleveland explained. "It does seem entirely feasible. An overseer would be hired, a factory building and millpond constructed, and an engine purchased. I believe an engine of fourteen horsepower could easily spin the wool from both your manors, and in that way, you could deprive Mr.—"

"The other miller," Randolph cut in quickly. "That man would have little business left to him. Though we cannot find any legal way to punish him for his crime, I believe I should be content to deprive him of our trade and drive him out of Otley forever."

"Wonderful!" Olivia cried. "Of course I shall be most happy to participate in this project. But . . . but as to the cost . . . I cannot be certain . . ."

"The worsted mill will pay for itself within three years," Randolph said. "As for the labor of building the factory and digging trenches to divert the streams, I shall put my men to it during the winter when they are too idle for their own good."

"I shall do the same," she said. "I fear, however, that Chatham has not the financial resources to be a full partner—at least not from the beginning—"

"Miss Hewes, I am sorry to interrupt you," Mr. Cleveland said, handing her the stack of papers, "but this is all spelled out in the contract I have worked up. I offer it to you now to read at your leisure. I assure you that Lord Thorne has been more than amenable to you in every area of the agreement—indeed far more than I thought prudent. And yet I have known him as a dear friend since our school days at Cambridge, and I am not at all surprised by his generous nature."

Olivia stared down at the papers on her lap, hardly able to believe what was happening. Charges would not be brought against Clive. And Mr. Quince would be driven out. How could anything be better?

"I am grateful," she said to Randolph. "More than grateful. I do not know how to thank you enough."

"I know how! We ought to all go swimming again," Clive suggested. "That would be great fun. I love to swim! It is my favorite thing!"

"I fear we shall have to find a new pond for our swimming and fishing," Randolph said. "All the dams will have to be torn down in order that your sister and I might have enough rushing water to power our new worsted mill."

"But what will happen to the hedgerow?"

"I fear that sections of it must come down, too. The new stream will choose its own course, and the hedgerow will have to make way."

The ancient feud reared its serpentine head in Olivia's mind once again. "How shall we divide our properties?" she asked. "If the stream is diverted and the hedgerow taken down—"

"Again, madam," Mr. Cleveland inserted, "all that is addressed in the contract. Whatever course the stream takes, Chatham and Thorne will consider the water itself to be the dividing line between their properties. The worsted mill will belong to both families throughout the entirety of its existence."

"But what will happen to the bait?" Clive demanded.

"The what, sir?" The attorney appeared confused. "I beg your pardon?"

"The bait! It is in the hedgerow. It is green and black!"

"The hedgerow will not all come down," Randolph assured him. "Our shepherds will need it to control their flocks. You and I shall have no problem finding plenty of bait for our future fishing expeditions."

"Let us go out today! I love to fish!"

"Not today, for Mr. Cleveland must hurry back to London, and I am called away to dinner with my brother." He stood. "Thank you, Miss Hewes, for your kindness."

"All thanks is due to you, sir." She forced herself to stand, though her knees were still weak from the shock of these developments. "Do you know, I believe the worsted mill was my idea after all. I mentioned it to Harriet as a joke. She must have told her husband, who shared that information with you."

"And I thought it a brilliant solution. A very modern way to defeat our foe." He laughed. "I confess, I should enjoy seeing that man's face when news of our worsted mill arrives at his doorstep."

"Which—in this town—it is sure to do before nightfall." Olivia smiled at the attorney. "We have found, Mr. Cleveland, that rumormongering is a favorite occupation in Otley."

"I believe that pastime transcends rank and setting, Miss Hewes. In London, a sneeze is scarcely heard in Berkeley Square before it becomes pneumonia in Soho."

"So it is," she said with a chuckle as she saw the two men to the door. Before she could stop herself, the words were out. "Speaking of Berkeley Square, I suppose you have purchased a new house in town, Lord Thorne. I understood Miss Bryse was most eager to be settled near her family."

At the look on his face, she clasped her hands together. "Oh, I am so sorry, sir. This is none of my affair, of course. I do wish you and Miss Bryse every happiness."

He studied the marble floor for a moment before speaking. "Thank you, Miss Hewes, but that lady and I have severed our attachment."

"You have!" This news threatened to overwhelm her entirely. "But, oh dear, how very sad for you. I am sure you must suffer greatly—"

"No, indeed." He laughed again. "In fact, it was the house in London that finally ended the prospect of a union. Miss Brysc and her parents were determined that I should purchase such a property, and I was equally determined to do no such thing. Any wife of mine must be content with the country life, for I have had my fill of the city forever. We could not come to terms on the agreement, and now it is at an amicable end."

Olivia grabbed the doorknob to steady herself. "I am sure your period of mourning must last some time," she managed.

"About as long as I would mourn one of my prize ewe's passing, I should imagine." Smiling, he made her a crisp bow. "Good evening, Miss Hewes." With that, he strode from the house.

Olivia shut the door and leaned against it for support.

How could such joy fill her heart? "Clive!" she cried. "Clive, come here at once!"

He raced from the drawing room, a cup sloshing tea as he ran. "What is it, Livie? What has happened?"

"We shall go out riding—both of us. For this is indeed the very happiest of days!"

Randolph made every effort not to look at her. Though they sat shoulder to shoulder in the pew, he attempted to keep his eyes on Reverend Berridge throughout the entire sermon. Olivia was wearing the gown made of fabric Randolph had given her, and he reflected on how much had come to pass since the day he had stepped on her hem and torn her skirt.

Lady Chatham was gone now, and with her passing, he hoped the bitter legacy of the feuding families had come to an end. Thorne and Chatham sat together in church, spoke cordially when their paths crossed in town, and had collaborated on plans for a new worsted mill. The whole town was agog.

The temptation to rejoice was great. But Randolph had made up his mind to perform every duty—indeed, every action in his life—with utter reason and only after careful deliberation. Even though he was now permitted to sit beside the most beautiful and charming woman of his acquaintance, he would behave in the most rational manner imaginable. Her fragrance drifted around him, and the edge of her gown brushed against his thigh, but he gave these distractions not the least notice. Nor did he permit himself to dwell on the way her slender fingers were woven together in a portrait of perfect repose . . . how they lay on her lap just so . . . how her fair skin met the edges of her fine kid gloves . . .

At her sudden jerk, his head jolted up. "Oh my!" she murmured.

"What?" Randolph whispered to his brother. "What has happened?"

"Were you not listening?" William whispered. "Berridge—he is to stay at Otley Church."

Randolph stared at the man he called his closest friend. Stay? Impossible. The meeting with the bishop had not gone at all well. Indeed, their return journey to Yorkshire had been filled with Nigel's reflections on how he might have managed the situation differently, what he ought to have done, how his poor wife would suffer, and on and on. How could it be that the Berridges were to remain at the church?

"And I wish to thank each one of you," he was saying, his voice beginning to quaver, "for the very great kindness you have shown in writing to the bishop on my behalf. That afternoon when I departed our tea in such haste, I was utterly convinced that discord had finally prevailed in Otley. I could not imagine . . . I confess, my faith was far too weak . . . to suppose that upon that very day, you had gathered up the fallen teacups and begun to talk. I left Otley with no idea that you had written out a resolution of . . . of . . ."

Randolph got to his feet. "Of peace," he said.

Olivia rose beside him. "Peace," she echoed.

James Bowden and his wife stood. "Peace," they said in unison.

At this, the Seaworthys, the Kibbles, the Nasmyths, and all the other families joined in one accord, ringing out the word that none had imagined possible. When it was clear the service could no longer proceed in any normal fashion, the organist began to play a closing hymn.

As the final notes drifted away, Randolph gazed on Olivia at last. "I am very happy at this news," he told her. "Never happier."

"I had no idea!" She slipped her arm around her brother, who had sat quietly during the very first church outing of his life. "Harriet told me nothing of this."

"Nor did Nigel mention it to me."

"I believe they must not have learned of it until yesterday. Otherwise, how could I not have known?"

"You do not have to know everything, Livie," Clive said. "Sometimes it is all right not to know."

A tender smile lifted her lips. "Yes, dearest brother, indeed it is all right not to know some things. But this is such glad news."

"I am hungry."

"Then you had better go home to dinner," Randolph said, shaking the young man's hand. "Miss Hewes, it has been a pleasure to see you again. You are looking very well."

Her cheeks blushed a pretty pink. "I believe this is my favorite gown."

He squelched the impulse to catch her up in his arms and proclaim that not only was it his favorite gown, but that she was his favorite creature, that he adored her and—no. He would not do it. Such heedlessness had only caused him trouble in the past. He must make very certain of his feelings for her. Then he would take pains to be sure of her attitude toward him. Perhaps after a year or two of peace and cordiality between them, he might more fully understand God's will in their acquaintance.

"I shall do my best not to step on this gown," he said with a grin.

She laughed, a tinkling sound that caught the edges of his heart. "I am very glad you committed such a grievous sin, sir. If not, we might never have become friends."

Before he blurted something untoward, he gave her a farewell bow and strode quickly down the aisle. William followed, and soon the brothers had climbed into their carriage. As they made for Thorne Lodge, Randolph exhaled deeply.

"You fled like a guilty pup," William exclaimed. "I had just found Miss Bowden and was hoping to make a conversation with her when I saw you sprint out of the church with your coattails flying. What happened?"

"Nothing at all."

William snorted. "Nothing! I should not call Miss Olivia Hewes in her pretty blue gown nothing. Your affection for her is as obvious as the periwig on Mr. Seaworthy's head."

"Affection? Yes, I suppose I do feel a measure of affection for her."

"Come, man, you love her!"

"What if I do? Nothing can come of it. I am determined to be reasonable in this, brother. As Baron Thorne, I have many duties that must take precedence over an attraction that is unwise, to say the least."

"Why is it unwise? You have done all in your power to make peace with that family. Why now such hesitancy to make your passion known?"

"Passion? Good heavens, William. With such phrases, you will be writing novels before we know it." He laughed at this thought. "And speaking of occupations, when do you intend to take yourself back to the Naval Academy? I should think the other officers believe you are quite dead and buried by now."

The carriage pulled into the drive of Thorne Lodge and the brothers descended. "I am thinking not to go back to Portsmouth," William said. When Randolph turned on him in surprise, he spoke again quickly. "You have a manor to oversee and now the new project. The worsted mill. I believe I ought to stay and assist you in that."

"In building the worsted mill?"

"And overseeing it." William stepped into the cool foyer behind his brother. "Do not look at me askance. I have never admired the way John Quince managed his mill. I know you think me wholly self-centered and vain, as indeed I am, but I have a great compassion for children—especially those so unfortunate as to be forced to labor in factories. I should like to run a mill with healthy working conditions, a place where the children would not be beaten and where they might rest on occasion."

"I confess, I am all astonishment at this news."

"You know I like nothing better than to astonish you, Randolph." He laughed. "My tenure here has taught me how much I enjoy the country, and I am not eager to return to military life with all its rules and regulations. With your permission, I should like very much to quit my tenure in the Navy."

"But of course!" Randolph clapped him on the back.

"Nothing could make me happier than to have you here at home."

"You are certain of this?"

"You may make Thorne Lodge your residence forever—so long as you promise not to bring any more gaggles of young ladies here to torment us."

"Actually, I had not noticed how many uncommonly handsome girls live in Otley. Did you see Miss Jane Seaworthy's hair? It is quite as gold as summer wheat. I was entranced."

Randolph laughed aloud. "You, dear brother, have a roving eye, and I doubt that any girl will soon tame you. But as for me . . . no, I did not notice Miss Seaworthy's hair. Nor any lady, for that matter, save the one who sat beside me."

"If I am entranced, you are besotted."

"Perhaps I am," he said. "But nothing shall come of it. Calm reason will prevail in my head at all times. Until I have conquered this flaw of character, this impetuous foolishness that has caused me such trouble, I cannot permit myself any other focus."

With a nod of confidence, he removed his frock coat and set off for the dining room. "Come, William. Let us take our luncheon, for I have much to do this afternoon."

~ Twenty ~

OLIVIA PLUCKED A bouquet of wild heather as she strolled across the moor toward the hedgerow. Only the cry of a curlew broke the silence of the Sunday afternoon, for it seemed that all the world had chosen this moment to doze away in the peaceful warmth. All but Olivia, whose joy so bubbled inside her that she found nothing could keep her indoors. Clive could hardly hold his eyes open through luncheon, and the servants had hurried him off to bed directly. Though it troubled Olivia that such a small outing as this morning's journey down to the church had exhausted him so, she was content to be alone in her wanderings.

She brushed her fingertips along the coarse fronds of bracken and drank in the fresh scent of new-mown hay that drifted from the fields. A strange sense of disbelief made her a little dizzy, and she wondered if she ought to sit down on one of the large gritstone outcroppings that dotted the moor. Could it be true that she was actually so free? Heady at the thought, she gave a little skip and laughed out loud with the sheer wonderment of it.

Chatham Hall belonged to her and Clive now. A weight of responsibility, indeed, but also a magnificent gift! Olivia could open curtains that her mother had kept drawn to ward off the blinding light she blamed for countless headaches. She could open windows, let in breezes, and order carpets carried outside for a long-overdue beating. The land was rich and her tenants loyal. With wisdom, she could introduce new breeds to strengthen her flock and new crops to revitalize her soil.

Clive was not to be charged with murder! How could Randolph have been so noble? Truly, he cared about the boy. He knew Clive had not intended ill but had been led astray by his own mother and by John Quince.

And what of that villain? He had not even shown himself at church that morning. Olivia laughed aloud at the delight she took in his defeat. No one had run him through with a sword or strung him up on a gallows—and she was glad of that. But he would be ruined all the same. His grand scheme had come to nothing and had destroyed his reputation. It could not be long before he quit the town and the worsted mill passed to other hands.

As she neared the hedgerow, Olivia listened for the sound of the brook. Not many weeks from now, her laborers would begin to tear down the dams that had created a series of ponds for her flocks to drink from. As the stream flowed more swiftly, ditches would begin to transfer even more water to the channel. The thought of it delighted her. How majestic the worsted mill must appear, standing on the boundary of the two properties, so new and efficient.

Anticipation skittled through her as she reached Clive's favorite fishing spot at last. The memories of her last visit here tumbled through her—a mixture of fear, joy, and horror. Clive had been lost, but then Randolph found him. Her brother's tears had tormented her, but Randolph had cheered him with a swift dunking in the pond and a silly bit of horseplay that had pleased her no end.

And then Clive had made his confession.

Even now, Olivia thought, as she sat down on the low flat stone beside the water, the recollection of Randolph's expression as he had turned away haunted her. Though he had absolved her brother and partnered with her in the worsted-mill project, did he still hold her family accountable for his father's murder? They were guilty, after all! Olivia held little doubt that her own mother had—at the very least—turned a blind eye to the vile scheme. Certainly Clive had played his part.

No wonder Randolph treated her with cordiality but nothing more. In his heart, he must despise her. She picked up a pebble and tossed it into the pond. Perhaps in time, he would learn to forgive her. But she could expect nothing more of him. Already, he had done more than any other Christian would do to build a peace between them. That ought to be enough. It really should.

With a groan, she flung a larger stone into the water and lay back on the stone.

"I say, good afternoon!"

At the voice, she stiffened and sat up immediately to find the man himself, standing on a stone ledge and peering over the hedge at her. "Lord Thorne! I did not hear you. I did not expect you."

"No, but I have been here for some time. On my side, of course. Reading." He shrugged. "You splashed."

"A stone." She tugged her skirt hem down over her ankles. "I threw it in."

"Ah."

He gazed at her so intently that she felt something must be amiss. She checked her bonnet ribbons, but they were still tied. Tucking her bare hands into her lap, she decided this must be it. He was offended.

"It was a good sermon this morning," he said.

She nodded. "Very nice."

"Clive enjoyed it, I think."

"Yes, but he was tired." She wished he would go away. How silly she must look all spread out on the stone with her bare hands glowing like great white loaves of bread. "He went to bed directly after lunch."

"I believe William is napping as well."

"It is a quiet afternoon." Oh, this was not going well! She moistened her lips and wished mightily that she could come up with a good reason to flee at once.

"May I join you, Miss Hewes?" he asked. "On your side?"

She looked up in surprise. "Oh, but—" Before she could answer him, he was pushing through a gap in the hedge that she had not noticed before.

"I cut through it that day I brought your brother home in the rain," he said, emerging and wading across the stream. "I think we ought to make a gate just here. A way of getting over."

"And a bridge?"

"With the rush of water that is to come, yes indeed. We shall want a bridge." He climbed to where she sat and took a place beside her. "I should think a road might be a good idea as well."

"Between our manor houses."

"Yes." His eyes searched hers. "I believe that would be reasonable."

"Perfectly so. It is silly to go down to the road, for this would cut the journey in half."

"Our mill project will require some consultation."

"Well, yes. You are welcome at Chatham anytime."

"As you are welcome at Thorne."

"I have never seen it."

"Then you must come. Perhaps tomorrow night." He paused, his brow furrowing. "But I ought to think this through first. You must allow me some time to ponder it."

"To ponder dinner?"

He fell silent. "I do not wish to be rash."

"Rash about dinner?"

"Hang dinner—it is you of whom I speak!" He got to his feet and began to pace down toward the pond. "I cannot be impulsive, Olivia. I shall not!"

"Oh, I see," she said, though she didn't really.

"One must think and pray and consult. Rashness leads to erratic behavior. I have been known to shout—"

"Who has not?"

"Yes, but that is not wholesome, and I am determined to correct it." He tore a reed from the edge of the pond. "One must be clearheaded at all times. Reason and good sense are required. One must be rational."

"And never listen to one's heart?" she ventured, her own thudding dangerously.

"The heart . . . the heart is—" he swung around and faced her, his chest heaving—"blast the heart! And blast the head! Olivia Hewes, I love you. I adore you. I believe God brought you to me, and I cannot imagine living one more day without asking you to become my wife."

Her eyes grew wide as he charged back up the bank to where she sat. "Oh my!"

"Say yes, dearest loveliest lady," he cried, kneeling at her feet. "I have loved you from the moment I first saw you, and my love has only grown as I have known you better."

"Randolph!" With a laugh of disbelief, she knelt, threw her arms around his neck, and kissed him on the lips. "Of course I shall marry you, silly man! I have longed to marry you almost since the day we met. When I supposed that could never be, my heart nearly broke in two."

"But that was why I felt so certain I must be more reasonable," he said, drawing her to her feet. "My thoughtless impulse almost took me away from you forever."

"And now it has brought you into my arms." She kissed him again, relishing the sweet pressure of his mouth against hers. He responded, pouring the pent-up emotion of so many months into a crushing embrace. "Please, my darling," she murmured as his lips moved to her cheek and ear, "say you will always bring this fiery passion to me."

"You have my word on it."

He held her as a soft breeze drifted down the fell and caught the bouquet of heather Olivia had gathered. The sweet purple blossoms scattered across the stone as the young couple stood hand in hand, forging bridges and weaving vows and building a future of peace that nothing could destroy.

A Note from the Author

Dear Friend,

I'm always amazed at the things we Christians allow to divide us, aren't you? Whether it's over the choice of hymns, the calling of a pastor, or a point of theological difference, we leap at the opportunity to fuss and fight with each other. I know of people so hurt by these battles that they refuse to set foot in a church ever again. And what a message we send to unbelievers who view our self-righteous hissy fits!

Recently, my husband was caught in the midst of an ongoing denominational battle that is surely making Jesus weep and Satan clap his hands in glee. What great suffering our family faced as Tim struggled to bring journalistic integrity to the forefront. Finally, he chose to walk away from the fight and take another job. As we look back on what we endured during those years, we have learned how important it is to keep our focus centered squarely on Jesus Christ—and on Him alone.

God wants His children to be at peace with each other. I encourage you, like Olivia and Randolph, to do your part to foster harmony instead of dissension. Let's not allow something like a hedgerow or a minor doctrinal dispute to divide us.

And if you've read *Wild Heather* and you're not a believer, please forgive us Christians for our many human flaws. Remember, Christians aren't perfect. Only God, in the person of Jesus Christ and the presence of the Holy Spirit, meets that ideal.

Blessings,
Catherine Palmer

About the Author

Catherine Palmer lives in Missouri with her husband, Tim, and sons, Geoffrey and Andrei. She is a graduate of Southwest Baptist University and holds a master's degree in English from Baylor University. Her first book was published in 1988. Since then she has published more than forty novels, many of them national best sellers. Catherine has won numerous awards for her writing, including the Christy Award—the highest honor in Christian fiction—in 2001 for *A Touch of Betrayal.* In 2004, she was given the Career Achievement Award for Inspirational Romance by *Romantic Times BOOKreviews* magazine. More than 2 million copies of Catherine's novels are currently in print.

TURN THE PAGE FOR AN EXCITING PREVIEW OF

AVAILABLE NOW IN BOOKSTORES AND ONLINE!

English Ivy

"I beg your pardon, sir." The butler stepped into the large drawing room and coughed discreetly. "There is someone to see you. A lady. A very young lady."

Colin Richmond looked up from the ledger he had been perusing for the better part of the morning. "A young lady? And what is her name?"

"'Clemma' is all she can say. Sir, she does seem very troubled. I understand there has been some misfortune near our gate."

Colin raked a hand through his hair and stood. "Very well, then. Send her to me."

He moved to the fire, took up a poker, and stirred the coals. Though it was early May and sunshine filtered through the long windows onto the carpet, the air held a chill he could hardly abide. It was no wonder his father had abandoned Longley for India so many years ago. The house was dank and dreary, a musty scent hung in every room, and the ceilings leaked.

"Miss Clemma, sir," the butler announced.

A small girl with bright blue eyes, pink cheeks, and tumbling waves of golden hair burst into the room and started toward the fire. But at the sight of the man standing before it, she stopped, breathing hard.

"You *are* a pirate," she said in a hushed voice. "Oh, dear me."

"I beg your pardon. I am certainly—"

"Never mind," she cried suddenly. "You must help us! My sisters and I were attacked on the lane. Gypsies took our bags, and knocked my sister down, and hit my eldest sister on the head, and she is bleeding, and she will die unless you come to save her at once!"

"Upon my word."

"Make haste, sir! There is no time to lose!"

Hardly able to reconcile the sight of so small a creature making such imperious demands, Colin motioned the butler for his greatcoat and hat. "Your horse, sir?" the servant asked. "Shall I have it saddled? Or perhaps you would prefer a carriage?"

"Is the scene of this calamity far, child?"

"Near your gate. The gypsies came out of the forest, and there were three of them, very wicked looking indeed! And one had a club, and he hit my sister, and now she is dying. My other sisters have gone for help, one back home and one to the village. I might have stayed in the lane, but I resolved I should come to you even though you might be a ghost!"

"Hmm," Colin said, setting his hat on his head and shrugging into his coat. "A moment ago, I was a pirate, was I not? Well, come along, Miss Clemma."

To his surprise, the little girl took his hand and began to pull him as they left the foyer of the great house. In moments, the two of them were sprinting down the drive toward the gate. It occurred to Colin that despite the urgency of the moment, he was rather enjoying the run.

"And then Caroline refused to give up her bag," the child was gasping out, "because she means to buy a length of cloth to make a new dress for the ball, but you see, that is why the man pushed her down. She should have given it up!"

"And then he hit her in the head?"

"Not her, my other sister. She went to rescue her, and then he hit her, and then Maddie hurried home, but Caroline went to the village!"

There were enough *she*s and *her*s in this tale to confuse any man. As they approached the gate, Colin spotted the figure of a slender woman lying at some distance down the lane. A bright green shawl had slipped away from her shoulders, and her muddied gown outlined the feminine curve of her form. Noting the crimson stain that had spread across the back of her bonnet, he left the little girl and raced on ahead.

"Madam!" Coming to her side, he knelt in the dirt and laid a hand on her arm. Unsheltered by the shawl, the woman's skin was delicate and pale, so velvety he could hardly sense its substance against his callused fingers. But when he touched her, something inside his chest clenched tight in a knot of deepest dismay, and he knew without a doubt he would do anything in his power to protect this fragile creature.

"Fear not," he said, drawing her shawl over her shoulder. "I am here for you."

A pair of large brown eyes flecked with gold fluttered open and gazed at him a moment. "Thank you," she mouthed.

His instinct to scoop her up and rush her away was quelled by the certainty that before him lay a true English lady, a woman so unlike the brazen doxies who plied their trade on the wharves of countless ports. She would never have felt the rough touch of male hands or known the intimacy of a man's close embrace.

"May I . . ." He paused, trying to construct the niceties of speech that had never been his manner. "May I have permission to carry you to my house?"

"Yes." The word was no more than a breath.

Before she could speak again, he slipped his arms around her and lifted her against his chest. She weighed no more than a sparrow, and he knew he must be careful.

"Go back again, Miss Clemma," he ordered the child as she arrived and took her sister's hand. "Run to the house, and tell my man to prepare a room. One with a fire already lit. Take my chamber, if necessary!"

"Yes, sir!"

As he set off up the drive, he could see the little blonde girl darting ahead on her mission. With all the running she had done, she would sleep well this night—if only she could be assured of her sister's health.

He looked down at the woman in his arms. Her lashes, long and black, lay on ashen cheeks, and her lower lip trembled a little with each breath. She was beautiful. And well loved. He sincerely hoped she would live to see the morrow.